THE RUSH

BETH LEWIS

First published in Great Britain in 2025 by
VIPER,
an imprint of Profile Books Ltd
29 Cloth Fair
London
ECIA 7JQ

www.viperbooks.co.uk

Copyright © Beth Lewis, 2025
Designed and typeset by Crow Books

1 3 5 7 9 10 8 6 4 2

Printed and bound in Great Britain by
CPI Group (UK) Ltd, Croydon, CRO 4YY

A CIP catalogue record for this book is available from the British Library.

We make every effort to make sure our products are safe for the purpose for which they are intended. For more information check our website or contact Authorised Rep Compliance Ltd., Ground Floor, 71 Lower Baggot Street, Dublin, D02 P593, Ireland, www.arccompliance.com

Hardback ISBN 978 1 80522 3115
Trade Paperback ISBN 978 1 80522 3122
eISBN 978 1 80522 3139

FSC
www.fsc.org
MIX
Paper | Supporting
responsible forestry
FSC® C013604

For my wife

THE KLONDIKE GOLD FIELD.

KATE

I stepped off the dock and my boots sank to the laces. Skaguay stretched out before me, a flotilla of tents in a sea of mud, stampeders buzzing like flies on dung. I expected such a sight from the reports, but words on newsprint can't prepare a woman for this place. The stink of it. The rush. This edge of the world where civilisation ends and the indifferent wilderness takes over. I loved it immediately.

I was to meet a man here who would take me on the White Pass Trail. It was arranged by Mr George Everett, my financier back in Kansas, yet no man had so far made himself known.

My dog, Yukon, nuzzled my hand, searching for a treat I did not have. A hound of unknown blood, brindle and warm, but with a bite. He was a gift from George Everett's hired man, to keep me company on the journey. Now, just three months on, he was my shadow.

A bustle of men pushed past, knocking my shoulder and almost toppling me. Yukon growled, but the men paid no attention. They hauled canvas-bound bundles, crates of cans

1

and tools, cages full of howling sled dogs. A year's worth of supplies for each man to be carried to the gold fields. It made my back ache to see them, the endless chain of boxes and bags appearing from the hold of the steamer, carried to the waiting sleds and horses.

Gunderson was the man I was to meet. A tall Swede, known to Mr Everett through a riverboat venture some years back. Trustworthy, Mr Everett said, but the muddy water soaking into my boots told another story.

When in doubt, my father said as he kissed me goodbye in Kansas, find a saloon and a woman to help you.

I whistled to Yukon and pulled my feet from the quagmire. I paid deckhands to carry my belongings from the ship to the Pullen Hotel and made for the drier boardwalks that lined the buildings of Skaguay, the gateway to the Klondike.

It was a short walk, but every step I was stared at, laughed at in my muddy skirts, jeered by drunks who all, in their way, said I did not belong. Yukon trotted faithfully beside me as I let those insults slide off me like snow from a pitched roof. I had travelled this far; I would not be put off by words.

'These skirts just will not do,' I muttered to Yukon.

He sniffed at the sodden hems and shook his head so hard his ears slapped against his cheeks.

'How can any woman live up here in petticoats?'

The dog yawned.

The town of Skaguay rushed about me. I wasn't the only woman, I was pleased to see, but there were ten men to every lady at least and most of those ladies were of the working sort, if you catch my meaning.

Men ringed the edges of the muddy roads, smoking, eating, bartering for guides, wares, passage. Horses stalked through the mud, laden to the brink with supplies, pulled by determined souls. A horse was refusing to move, its back almost breaking beneath the weight of its load. A large man in furs yanked on a rope, whipped the horse's flank bloody. Another man – more civilised, cleaner, as if he'd just arrived on the same boat as I – stood beside him.

'Come on, man!' the clean one shouted. 'We must get moving.'

The furred one cursed and spat. 'Your wife will keep. These horses'll break a leg in this mud.'

'I'm paying you to guide, not talk. Hurry it up!'

Something about the clean man was familiar. As if I'd seen his face in a photograph once, slightly out of focus. I could not place him, though I knew him, somehow.

The furred man whipped the horse afresh and the crack of the leather, the scream of the horse, broke my memory. The poor animal finally moved and the clean man was gone in the fray.

I put the thought aside, for it was all but impossible for me to know a man in this place; perhaps I had simply seen him on the boat. Thousands upon thousands had already moved, and were still moving, through Skaguay. Thousands from every corner of the country, even from the world. For me to see someone I knew would be like finding a drop of salt water in a raging river.

A hand grabbed my wrist and pulled me around. 'Good morning, Miss,' said a spritely, small man in a buttoned-up suit.

I wrestled my hand free as Yukon growled. The man put his hands up in surrender, a wide smile under his moustache.

'You mistake me – I am here to help,' he said. 'The name is Picket. Terence Picket. I own the Grand Hotel just at the edge of town, near the head of the trail. I have room and board for only sixty dollars a night. Fifty-eight to you, Miss.'

I knew the type. In Kansas we called them corn-oil sales-men. 'Thank you, but I have lodgings.'

Arranged by Mr Everett, or so I hoped.

'Where might they be? I can assure you, no other estab-lishment in Skaguay has cleaner beds than the world-famous Grand Hotel.'

'I don't need a room. But you may still help me. I'm looking for a man named Gunderson. Lars Gunderson. Do you know him?'

He brightened. 'I do. I surely do.'

And offered no more until I crossed his palm with a five-dollar bill.

'He drinks at the Soak Inn, just a few minutes' walk this way. I believe I saw him enter this morning.'

'Thank you, Mr Picket. You have been most helpful.'

To my surprise, the man tipped his hat to me and went on his way. Yukon relaxed, his tail wagging as he looked up at me expectantly.

'We'll eat when we find Mr Gunderson.'

He lowered his head and walked as if I'd scolded him. A dramatic hound, if ever I knew one.

The Soak Inn was where Mr Picket said it would be. A simple wooden building with a bright white shingle out front, newly painted for the season.

Inside, it was smaller than I expected and pleasantly full. The room was portioned off with an interior wall. Chalk signs offered baths for four dollars or a measure of gold. Two dollars if you didn't mind sharing the water. The smell of the place overwhelmed. A damp mould from a hundred spilled baths, alongside the sour stink of the unwashed waiting their turn.

Yukon and I went to the bar, where a man in a grimy apron was pouring whiskey.

'Help you, Miss? You after a soak?'

'Not today. I'm after a man named Gunderson. He was meant to meet me at the dock.'

The bartender nodded to the far corner of the room, where a man slept on a bench.

'Him?'

'You'll need this,' the bartender said and handed me a glass of water.

I squared my shoulders and moved between the tables to the bench. A guttural snore erupted from Mr Gunderson. Yukon waited behind my legs. I cleared my throat to announce myself.

Mr Gunderson snored on. It was as if the entire room held its breath, watching me.

I kicked the bench, to no avail.

'Fine,' I muttered and poured the water on the sleeping man's head.

He reared up with a cry, rubbing his wet face, hair splayed and flying in all directions. Yukon tensed at my leg as I took a few steps back.

'What in hell? Who's waking me?' he shouted, eyes squinting against the dim light, spinning round, fists clenched, looking for the fight.

'Mr Gunderson?'

His whiskey-filled gaze landed on me. 'Who in hell are you?'

'My name is Kate Kelly. Mr George Everett sent word of my arrival. You were due to meet me at the dock to escort me along the White Pass Trail.'

He blinked, suddenly calm but frowning, staring at me, awaiting the spark of recognition. He was a mess of a man, long blond hair in greasy strings, an almost-white beard stained brown by chewing tobacco, with durable, hardy clothes torn and caked in mud and perhaps blood. His hands shook as he ran them through his hair to tidy it.

'Miss Kelly,' he said with a booming, accented voice. 'I am to take you to Dawson. You going to write stories about the miners?'

The room let out its breath and eyes turned back to their cards and glasses.

'I am a journalist, sir. I will report on the conditions of the camps, the towns and the people for my readers back in Kansas and Missouri. For Mr Everett too, should he wish to start a mining venture here.'

'Oh, oh. You're a long way from Kansas, Miss Kelly.'

'Don't I know it,' I said, as I took in the man before me.

'But don't worry that pretty head. Lars Gunderson keeps his word, and I gave my word to George I would get you to Dawson City.'

Relief came over me, and my shoulders let out an inch of their tension.

'This your dog?' he asked, kneeling, hand out.

'This is Yukon,' I said.

The dog stared up at me, as if awaiting permission, then padded over to the Swede. Mr Gunderson ruffled his fur and nuzzled his face against Yukon's snout. Yukon's tail began to fly. He was smitten, I could tell, and I believed him to be an excellent judge of character.

'A good dog is worth more than gold up here. Bad people will soon as steal a good dog for sledding or fighting. Keep him close.'

I rested my hand on Yukon's head. 'I intend to. When do we leave, Mr Gunderson? I am keen to get on the trail.'

Mr Gunderson stood and looked out of the grimy window

at the sky. He really was tall. Had he been wearing his hat, it would have brushed the beams.

'Tomorrow.'

'Tomorrow? But it's still so early. We could make good time if we left immediately. I must get to Dawson, do you understand?'

He cocked his head and looked at me as if I was a curiosity, a city girl who understood little of this place.

'The day is too far gone,' he said. 'See the clouds? Heavy dark. Rain later. We get too much rain on the White Pass and whoop! Off the trail we go and *crrrk*.' He drew his thumb across his throat.

I would be no good to anyone dead. 'Fine. Tomorrow.'

'Good. You have rooms for tonight?'

'I do.'

'Then let's have us some dinner, courtesy of George. He sent you with dollars, yes?'

I sighed at the delay. 'Yes.'

'Then we will have a meal in the finest place in Skaguay.'

My stomach sank at the thought, given the state of this place. Mr Gunderson took me out into the streets and they were suddenly not so unfriendly, now I stood beside a man. The looks and jeers stopped as if I was off-limits to their thoughts. It exhausted me, sometimes, being a woman in a world of men. Up here in the wild north the men were slowly losing their civility, if they had any to begin with, and it meant danger for a woman alone. As much as I despised the thought, it was good to have a man – a tall, well-known one at that – to escort me.

We ate a meal of meat pie and ale and he procured a bone for Yukon to gnaw. I thought the meat was cow, perhaps horse, but Gunderson corrected me.

'Black bear.'

The chunk of meat in my mouth felt suddenly heavy and too big.

'They come down from the mountains after their big sleep, *pop-pop-pop*, easy to kill. Tasty, right?'

I forced my jaw to work. It was sweet and soft, in some kind of gravy. Good even.

'I never thought I'd eat bear,' I said, pushing the remains around my plate. 'Seems wrong to eat such a fierce predator. Upside down, you know?'

Mr Gunderson laughed and sprayed flakes of pastry over the table. 'You'll see. Upside down is right way up here. Everything goes the other way. You wait until you try beaver tail.'

I smiled and we settled into a companionable silence.

The inn was busy, as was all of Skaguay, with a queue out the door for the pies. Men bought them wrapped in wax paper to take back to their camps, handing over a pouch of gold for the payment to be measured out. A trusting method of doing business; I suspected those scales were weighted in the establishment's favour.

I found my gaze drifting to the window and the shadow of the mountains beyond. I felt them calling to me. I had read stories of wild places like this since I was a child, sitting alongside my sister, beneath the blankets to stay warm.

The winters here, so I read, were harsh, dark times when a man could freeze to death in an hour. Stories spread of bodies found against trees, so peaceful they could be sleeping, or frozen into the river ice after falling through. Even here, now the thaw had come and the sun returned, Mr Gunderson told me of a pair of brothers found near the trail. They'd attempted the journey at the start of winter and were not found until the end.

This was not a land to take risks in, yet each man risked everything just to be here.

We left the inn and Mr Gunderson walked me to my hotel. We passed the wooden buildings, hurried up over days or weeks to accommodate the stampeders, and I caught a glimpse of the canvas city on the flat land to the west. Tents as far as I could see, hemmed in by sharp, rising mountains on either side.

The gateway to the interior, the steamer brochures had said. What struck me, as I moved through Skaguay beside Mr Gunderson, was how I had expected a lawless, frenzied atmosphere. But the place was ordered, loud with its industry and little else, as if each man was looking only to his journey ahead, his supplies and how he would transport them, rather than be distracted by vice and drink. Even the working ladies looked largely unbothered.

Despite the hour, the town was alive with trade: the hardware shop, the outfitters, the wagons jostling each other for space, the men hauling and loading, the tired horses. I thought mostly of the money that must change hands in a place like this. Here was the fortune – not some metal locked in the frozen ground a thousand miles away.

Mr Gunderson left me at the Pullen Hotel, with a tip of his hat and a promise to see me there an hour after sunrise. He had some business to attend to and I realised, as he departed, that I had no idea what that business was. Or anything else about this man I was trusting to take me along hundreds of miles of treacherous trail.

Yukon and I went into the hotel, but found sleep difficult.

I was so eager to get moving. Get on the trail. I re-read Mr Everett's letters of instruction. I filled my first page with notes, and I thought of my sister.

My dearest Charlotte. Up here somewhere.

I opened her letter, received a month ago now, and read the words that had brought me here. Which had me rushing to Mr Everett's door suggesting he finance a trip to the Klondike. Which would carry me through these mountains, to Dawson City.

This may be my last letter. He has finally found me and there is nowhere left to run.

ELLEN

BOULDER CREEK, KLONDIKE, LATE JUNE 1898

There is beauty here. Beyond the tents and sluice boxes. Away from the men and their tools. I like to stand outside and face the mountain. Before the camps wake and the noise begins, in the pre-dawn when the cold bites bare skin and leaves a mark.

Snow clings to the peaks. The ice is breaking on the wide rivers now and the mud thickens with snow-melt. I breathe in the crisp air and it hurts my chest. The mountains here tower and stretch, layering over themselves like a collage. The creek, glacial and milky blue, flows knee-deep over tumbled rocks. I could only love it more if I'd chosen it.

Sometimes I hear wolves in the trees beyond the camps. They search for weakness. There is plenty. A dog was carried off by a wolf last month. I heard the yowling until I didn't.

Standing outside, I remember life before this place. I met Charles as a girl of nineteen and he already twenty-five. My father approved and my mother was dead, so said nothing. The Rhodeses were a good family, if not especially wealthy, with growing interests in shipping and rail. His father owned a horse ranch and bred racehorses on the side. Seattle-born, with cold north-western blood.

His mother supported suffrage and his father enjoyed brandy. They were fine people, in their way. We married a year later. I wore lace from Europe, flowers in my hair and around my wrists. I said my vows in front of God and thought I meant them. It was what a girl did. Court, marry, tend a house, bear children. I didn't know I was meant to be happy about it as well. I accepted my lot with grace and good humour, but in truth, in my midnight thoughts – those that are just for me – I would have been happier alone.

Growing up motherless, with a father more interested in his business than his daughter, my own happiness was not something I nurtured. He was never cruel, never raised a hand to me in anger, but rarely one in kindness, either. He did his best.

They say a girl ends up marrying her father. I look at Charles, snoring in the bed he'd had made in Dawson and paid four men to carry here. My father would never fall so low.

The cold gets too much. My toes and fingers disappear. I've seen men lose them entirely in the chill. They turn black and all but snap off. I stay outside until the tips of my fingers turn blue. Tomorrow I will stay longer.

Inside, I go about the actions of a dutiful wife. Feed the fire, set a kettle to boil, sweep. When the light hits the back window, I am to wake him. Until then, I cherish the time.

We had been married a year when Charles heard rumours of gold in the north. It was the summer of 1894 when his contacts in Seattle and Juneau began whispering of fortune beneath the frost.

We must go, he said. It will be the adventure of a lifetime. I wish to make my own way, Ellen, and not rely on my family's wealth.

He said he refused it when his father offered, but I always suspected his father was the one to refuse. I knew now, too late, that Charlie was not a safe investment. He promised we'd make enough in one summer to live like kings for the rest of our lives. Perhaps too, in mountain air, we would be blessed with a child.

As '94 turned to '95, Charlie – on a tip he'd heard in a bar from Skookum Jim himself – staked two claims on Boulder Creek, never having set foot on the land or washed a pan of its dirt. It was as secure a bet as any man could make, so he said. Our claims, wide strips of land on the bend of a river, were just a few miles upstream from Skookum Jim's own Bonanza claim. We would be rich as soon as the ice cracked.

He wakes, the day begins. He eats and is gone to dig with barely a word. I watch him through the window and remember his promises. He believed them. So did I. More fool me. In our three years here, I've watched every inch of the riverbank be claimed. Tents and cabins put up, men and precious few women fill the gaps, find little and fade away, replaced by more. And still we stay. Still he digs. Still I wash and clean and cook. Beans. Bacon. Pork. Potatoes. Bread. And again and again. The same day over and over. The only bright spots are the trips to Dawson. I go once a month. He goes once a week. Stays the night sometimes. I imagine he has a whore. I imagine my father's money pays for her.

The sun wanes and Charlie appears in the doorway.

'Smelling good, Ellen,' he says of my cooking. Up here, in this wild, untamed place, he's become another one of them. Prospectors. Face more dirt than skin, beard grown long, hair stringy beneath a scuffed hat. They are all just Man now. He was Charlie once. With thick, clean hair, brown as chestnuts. I married him too young.

'Salt pork and potatoes. Same as always,' I say.

'Always good, though.'

'It's been waiting. You were meant to be back by five. You break your watch?'

'Don't be sore, Elly, I got into the gravel by the creek. Gravel hides gold. I had to keep digging.'

'And did you strike?'

'Tomorrow. I can feel it.'

Always tomorrow.

He eats with his boots on. Sleeps with his coat on. Shotgun by the bed.

'Claim-jumpers ain't no joke, Ellen,' he says, 'I got to protect what's mine.'

He never talked like that in Seattle. *Ain't. Got.* His gentleman's tongue is turning foul inside his mouth. Dirt under his nails. Cuts on his hands. Back and neck bent from working a shovel. I didn't marry a common man. A workman with rough hands and rougher manners. I married Charles Rhodes. A man with prospects. Now look where we are.

We were one of the first up here. Trekking through the winter. Choice land. A large claim. But so far, only flakes. Not enough to survive. It's my father's money that keeps us in pork.

I decided long ago to make the best of this place, this life, the fortune it is sure to bring, but my husband, his failures and vices, makes it difficult.

As the day ends, I watch him sleep, his animal snores fill the cabin.

I lie down beside him, but sleep does not come for me. It rarely does.

I feel something. A change on the wind. Perhaps the end

of all this. Perhaps the beginning of the life I should have had. The shotgun shines in the moonlight. Winter is over, the snow is melting and the rush is coming.

MARTHA

'I'm a common woman turned uncommon lady,' I said to the gent leaning on my bar, 'but you can call me Martha.'

He's got eyes for me. Been in Dawson a day, already half-emptied his pocket in here. I gave up trying to warn them to keep some back, he'll need it for the passage home to whatever prairie state he came from, but there's no telling a man with gold on his mind.

'Have a drink with me – I'll be rich in a month and I'll marry you,' the prospector drawls. That's my whiskey working. Heard it all before. Believed it only once.

'You come back when you're rich and I'll sell you a bath and a private dance from one of my girls.'

'How about with you, Martha?'

Being polite, I smiled, but I didn't have patience this morning. 'You can't afford me. Now I recommend you head over to the Aurora Café for a hot meal. Tell Tom that Ma sent you and he'll knock a penny off.'

The man lingered, those soft, drunk eyes on my corset and

waist.

I lifted my chin to Harry, standing watch by the door. The big man, in his clean shirt and buttoned-up collar, came right over, hauled the prospector up.

'Time to go, fella,' said Harry and the man's eyes went wide as a fish.

'I'm goin', I'm goin'.' He pulled away and stumbled to the door. Laughing like these idiots do, he shouted, 'A month! I'll be back in a month and then you're gonna marry me.'

I cleared his glass and Harry went back to his post.

A drunk slept on the card table, but I left him there; otherwise the Dawson Hotel, *my* hotel, which I'd built timber by timber with my own hands, was empty.

'Keep an eye,' I said to Harry.

I balled up my apron and climbed the stairs. Twenty rooms. Two dormitories. Six bathtubs. A dollar for a cold soak, five for hot. A dollar to sleep on a blanket on the floor. Thirty dollars a night for a bed in the dorm. Hundred for a room. Two hundred for a private with one of my girls. Two thousand for a month, and I had three gents already booked up through to winter. I had a claim up at Forty Mile that helped pay the bills, but only a fool looks for riches in gold up here.

I knocked at room three and went in without an answer.

Molly was still sleeping in the gent's bed. He'd been up at dawn to hunt down a claim. I'd made him breakfast and sent him off with a tip to check Goose Neck Creek near the Yukon River. He'll be gone three days and come back poorer. They always do.

I pulled the blanket off Molly and slapped her bare backside. 'Up.'

'Is he gone?' she said, looking to the door.

'First light. It's past nine. You got chores, my girl.'

She groaned and righted herself. Weren't no modesty in this place. I seen it all before. Except those bruises.

'He do that?' I brushed my hand over her shoulder, over the red-purple welts.

She winced. 'No. Not him.'

'Who then?'

'It doesn't matter.'

'I won't have men hurting my girls – you tell me who.'

She looked down at her knees. 'I was clumsy. You know what I'm like after a gin.'

'I know you don't get soused enough to lie to me. I got rules in my house, you know that. No lying and no moonlighting or you're out on your ear. Talk.'

Molly huffed, like a child, but she weren't a child. She was in her twenties. Married once even, widowed now. But she had a clean white face, not ravaged by pox or scars like so many, was small enough to be dainty and knew how to play the lady. Made her popular with men looking for a taste of high society. Made her valuable to me. Made her a target for Bill Mathers, who wanted her for his own place, though he was convinced he loved her, tried to charm her over to him more than once, but she knew his like and was happier here, with me. Though, of course, this weren't a brothel – not like those shacks in Klondike City. My girls were dancers and entertainers, finest in the Yukon. Just so happened they some-times gave private shows to wealthy miners, and the Mounties looked the other way.

'Tell me, Molly.'

'Leave it, Ma. It's only a bruise, I'll put some powder on it.'

I watched her get up, pull on her dress and pin up her hair.

'I got rules,' I called, but she was out the door.

I pulled and balled the sheets with an anger building in

18

my chest. I righted the pillows and opened the window. Did the same in the next room. Went about my duties quick and quiet, seething at Molly's disregard. After everything I'd done for her.

In the next room, Giselle was getting dressed. She hushed me as her man was still snoring, buck-naked, sprawled in the middle of the bed.

'You gave him a good time, I see,' I said as we stepped out to the landing.

'Old bastard passed out after one pump. Had to roll him off me. Got his arm over me though, didn't he, so I had to stay there.'

I laughed. 'Easy night.'

Giselle clicked her teeth. 'You hear that snoring? I'm half-deaf!'

I bent to pick up the sheets and a pain shot through my gut.

'Ma?' Giselle was at my arm. 'You all right?'

The pain went as fast as it came. Always did. Nothing but trapped air, I guessed. I waved away Giselle's worry. 'Fine, fine, just my old bones. There's bacon in the pan. Get yourself fed.'

Giselle moved past me, but I took her by the arm. 'You keep an eye on Molly for me, you understand?'

The girl, who weren't a girl either, frowned. 'This about the bruises?'

I cocked an eyebrow. So it wasn't a secret. 'What do you know?'

'I don't know who done it,' she said, realising she was caught.

'Tell me, Giselle.'

She looked around, lowered her voice. 'She's been seeing a man. Off the books. Least, off your books. Might be love, you never know. She came home, night before last, moving a bit slow, you know? Like she was hurting. She said she was tired, but she wasn't using her left arm much. Told me she took a fall. Had too much to drink. You know what she's like.'

I knew. 'Thank you, Giselle.' I gave her a few coins for her trouble. 'If you hear anything else about this man . . .'

She took the coins and kissed my cheek. 'My lips to your ears, Ma.'

'Go on now,' I said, and she trotted off down the stairs.

I watched her from the landing. Molly appeared from the kitchen with two plates. The pair of them were full of talk of their evenings. Molly laughed between mouthfuls and I could only think Giselle was telling her about her sleeping cockstand.

I watched them with a darkness growing in my heart. I'd built this place from the ground up. Knew every board and nail, could read the history of fights and fires in the wood grain. Helped dozens of girls get on their feet and get out richer. This was my home and, like any, I had rules.

No lying, snooping or moonlighting. I offered my girls a safe place to work, room and board, gents vetted by me, money up front, protection from ending up in Klondike City: the mud and louse-filled shacks full of desperate women hanging out their doors. These girls came up here for the same reason as all of us – to find their fortune. And women only got a few options open; one of them is the oldest profession in the world. If they're going to do it, I'd have them do it somewhere safe. And I only took half the fee for my troubles. A better deal than they'd get anywhere else in the Klondike. Hell, better than anywhere in the country, I reckon. But I wasn't to be taken for a fool. If they broke that rule, they would be out. Molly knew that, same as the rest.

My hands gripped the railing, nails digging crescents into the wood.

Relationships are like ice out here. They form quick and strong, but can break just as easy. Molly had been here close to a year, survived a winter, but now at the dawn of summer she was still a mystery to me, had secrets in her as deep as the Yukon River. A good worker, but choosy with her men and careful about finding herself in the family way, which I appreciated. Kept an eye on the others too, especially the new girls; gave them pennyroyals and made sure they were using their sponges. But now she was lying and seeing a gent on the side, two things I couldn't forgive.

I felt a wave wanting to crash over me. Holding itself back, frozen in mid-air, awaiting the thaw. Something dark was cresting over the mountains. The rush of change coming again.

KATE

Dawn came and, with it, an excitement and trepidation I'd not felt since leaving Topeka. Yukon snuffled on the bed beside me. Today we would embark on a journey that had killed dozens, if not hundreds, and forced hundreds more to turn back. These were men, strong and prepared, and what was I to that? A woman with muddy skirts, already tired from the journey.

Yukon woke and jumped around the bed, tongue lolling, tail pumping. He licked my face and whined for food.

I opened a can of meat and let him make a mess of it. I looked at my dress, my shoes, my bonnet. The tideline of mud, the water soaked up to the knee. I lifted the dress and the weight of it astounded me. I would be carrying enough up that trail. I could not carry half of Skaguay's mud with me too.

'These won't do, will they, Yuke?'

The dog paid no attention.

I had an hour before meeting Mr Gunderson and would make the most of it. I dressed quickly, ensured my bags and trunk were packed and labelled, then whistled to Yukon.

Skaguay was quieter than it had been yesterday, but still the town was alive with people. Lines of laden horses and donkeys were being checked and packed. Men were tying down loads and hollering to their partners to move quicker. Always quicker.

I went to the outfitters across the street. One of the bigger buildings, doing a brisk trade even at this hour. A high counter dominated the room and a woman stood behind it. It instantly put me at ease. Snowshoes hung on a wall. Another wall was all hats. In the centre of the room, a stack of crates with a fully built rocker box for washing dirt. Hessian sacks, gold pans, hand-tools. Behind the counter, neat piles of clothes went to the ceiling. There were picks, shovels, axes, signs declaring 'dynamite sold here'. I was somewhat in awe of it all. Here was everything a man – or a woman – would need to pull riches from the earth.

'Help you, Miss?' asked the lady behind the counter. She looked at me with a wary eye and I didn't blame her.

'I need pants. Sturdy boots. A coat, a hat. Skirts have no place on the trail.'

The woman raised her eyebrows and a smile broke over her face. 'Right you are.'

In twenty minutes I was kitted for the trip. I threw in a gold pan for good measure, as I was sure Mr Everett would be keen for a first-hand account of the conditions and methods of mining.

I changed into the corduroy pants and suspenders in the back room and the woman whistled when I appeared. Yukon yawned from his place in the corner. The leather boots were second-hand, worn in but not worn out, and I chose a wide-brimmed felt hat to keep the sun off.

Beneath a glass case on the counter were knives. One in particular caught my eye. A long, slender blade with a wooden handle carved with roses. A woman must have protection, my mother always said. She meant a husband, but I would rather have a blade.

'That too.'

I paid and strapped the knife around my waist. I felt like a Klondiker, prepared and eager to be on my way. The equal of any man in this place. I hefted on the coat – a green woollen frockcoat – and bid farewell to the woman.

'Good luck, darlin',' she called.

I was away, into the streets of Skaguay, suddenly invisible against the tide of similarly dressed men. I still had time before meeting Mr Gunderson, so I strolled about the town, taking it all in, wondering what Charlotte had thought of it when she came through this way. It shocked me still that my sister – the more proper of us – had made this journey. I longed to hear of it. Had she taken the Skaguay road or the Chilkoot Pass from Dyea? Had she travelled alone or within a group? When I found her, I would question her on every detail.

I passed by a dozen more outfitters and general stores, a circulating library, a doctor, a saloon, a gin parlour, a barber, all calling out their trade. I passed smaller stands: a man with a single table selling shoes for a dollar. Another selling lucky gold pans. Another selling hammers and picks.

'Penny for your future,' came a strangely quiet voice. I turned to see a woman standing in the doorway to a tent, which was painted with all manner of symbols and colours. She was old, with kohl eyes and red lips, and wore gold coins on a purple shawl around her head.

'Penny a reading,' she said and opened her arm as if to usher me inside.

The thick smell of incense wafted out as she moved. Sandalwood and cedar and something else. Inside, I could see red patterned carpets, with a table and two chairs in the centre. Not a hint of mud.

'Thank you, but I am due to meet someone,' I said.

The woman smiled and nodded. 'Come back, should that change. I see death in your future.'

I let out a small laugh. 'Aren't you meant to tell people you see riches and love?'

The smile was gone. She held my gaze with those black-rimmed eyes. 'I tell men what they want to hear. But I tell women what they need to know.'

Her tone unsettled me more than I liked to admit. Something about this woman didn't seem to fit with this place. As if she'd appeared with the dawn and would disappear with the dusk. Yukon whined beside me, pushing himself into my legs. I listened to my dog and walked away. I felt her eyes on me every step until I rounded a corner and made my way back to the Pullen.

Mr Gunderson was waiting outside and I got to within an arm of him before he knew me. He pulled off his hat, as I did mine, and laughed.

'Good Lord, Miss Kelly! You are fit for the Klondike and no mistaking.'

'Good to see you, Mr Gunderson. I trust you slept well.'

'Well enough. I had your bags taken to the horses.'

'How long until we reach Dawson?'

Mr Gunderson rocked his head from side to side. 'If Lake Bennett and the Klondike are thawed, less than two months, I'd say. If the ice is still there ... only God can say.'

My insides shrivelled. 'Two months?'

Did Charlotte have two months?

'Yah. It's a long road. Perhaps we can be quicker if Mother Nature stays on our side.'

'Then let's not waste a moment.'

We had seven horses. Two for riding, four for carrying our things and a seventh carrying bales of hay. Yukon ran alongside them. As I wasn't coming here to prospect or to mine, I wasn't obliged to bring the requisite year's worth of supplies and nor, as he was technically a packer, was Mr Gunderson. He had minimal belongings upon his second horse. We would be swift and, I hoped, would reach Dawson City in half the time. The mounted police who weighed each man's provisions and granted passage saw my papers and nodded us through.

My hope kept me going as we rode along the streets of Skaguay, following the same path as thousands of others. The line of horses stretched from the town into the mountains – I saw no end of it. Ahead would be the White Pass Trail, forty-five miles through a treacherous canyon not built for horses, up to a freezing summit and down a muddy, loose slope, then across a boggy valley floor to Lake Bennett. But at least it was not the Chilkoot. Just looking upon the Scales and the hellish snow-covered mountain pass was enough to turn back the hardiest of prospectors.

I believe Mr Gunderson saw the worry writ on my face as we began our journey, for he took my hand and offered a warm smile.

'I will look after you,' he said. 'So will that hound of yours.'

Yukon bounded ahead, tongue hanging out of his mouth, happy to run after so long stuck in a ship and a hotel. He ran back and forth to us and did not snap at the horses.

I let myself smile. 'Thank you, Mr Gunderson.'

But the fortune-teller's warning rang in my ears. She saw death ahead.

I tell women what they need to know.

I looked at Mr Gunderson, at the long road before me, and I thought of my sister waiting in Dawson City for me, fearing for her life. Did the death the woman spoke of lie there? Or on the trail before me? Or in the man beside me?

I felt for the knife on my hip and steeled myself for the wildness to come.

ELLEN

The day wears on and while Charlie digs, the man comes. He is the same man we've seen in Dawson. The same one who has come here before.

Checking in on old friends, he calls it.

His name is Croaker and he doesn't knock. He calls from outside and I am to come running. I don't run to my husband and shall never run to this man.

Croaker is large. Built for intimidation. His hair is black and barely a scrap of skin shows between beard and hat.

'Ahoy there to the cabin,' he calls and I close my eyes and breathe.

I open the door. 'Hello, Mr Croaker. My husband is working the claim right now. Can I offer you a drink?'

He takes off his hat as a gentleman might and comes closer. I see the sores on his cheeks beneath the hair. See the black tooth that won't fall out.

'Oh, mighty kind of you, Mrs Rhodes. I'll take a whiskey.'

I already had it on the table when I heard his horse. I pour

28

and hand over the glass and don't invite him inside. I stand at the door like I'm enjoying the view, looking anywhere but at him. He sips and strolls, glancing at the cabin, our two horses in their pen, sniffing and spitting as he goes.

'You've made yourself a nice home,' he says.

'Thank you, we try our best.'

'Got some missing shingles. Broken window. Your outhouse there could do with some new boards.'

'It's been a tough winter for us all.'

He sucks his teeth, makes a sound that turns my stomach.

Down the valley I hear picks and shovels, the sound of a wagon bumping over rails and of water washing rocks. Men sing their work.

'Quiet up here, huh? Struck yet?'

I don't answer. He doesn't expect me to.

'Seems all those folks down there are having better luck than Charlie. Why is that, you think?'

'I couldn't say.'

'Uh-huh.' He shakes the pole holding up the porch, checks its strength. 'Your Charlie staked these two claims a time ago, ain't that right? One in your name, one in his, as is the law. Way he tells it, he was pointed up here by Skookum Jim.'

'That's right.'

'Fine story. Makes for good talk over a drink.'

But . . . I feel he wants to say. But it's not true? Cold doubt creeps over me and I suddenly want this man gone.

'Is there something else I can do for you, Mr Croaker?'

He leans against the porch pole, sipping his whiskey and looking at me in a way I don't care for, but have got used to in this place.

'Charlie is a lucky man. Fine woman such as yourself don't belong up here with us rough types.'

I set my teeth. 'I am content. Now, if you'll excuse me, I ha—'

'Frank?'

Charlie has his shovel over his shoulder. His face is grim and tired and he looks from Croaker to me and back.

Croaker smiles at me, holding it for a moment too long, then pushes himself away and turns to my husband.

'Good to see you, Charlie.'

The men shake hands. 'Frank. What can I do for you?'

'Let's not talk business in front of the lady.'

Charlie shoots me a look over the man's shoulder. Croaker towers over him, makes him look small, weak, where I used to think he was otherwise. Croaker claps his hand on Charlie's back and they walk a few feet away, lean close. Whisper.

Charlie's face turns ashen, his jaw flexing as he listens. A shake of his head.

I sense the air change. The smell of their conversation turn. Croaker pats Charlie's back, then his open hand turns fist, grabbing Charlie's shirt. Croaker leans closer, says something I cannot hear. Charlie nods. They part.

Croaker thrusts the empty glass into Charlie's hands, pushing him back a step.

Charlie takes it.

Croaker turns to me, puts his hat back on. 'Thank you kindly for your hospitality, Mrs Rhodes. I'll see you next time.'

Then he is on his horse, yanking the reins. The animal cries. Down the trail, prospectors stop and watch him go. Then look back at us as if we have a pox. Everyone knows Croaker. And who he works for.

Charlie stands silent, idle, shovel in the dirt.

'What business do we have with that man?'

He looks up as if just remembering I'm there. 'Nothing of consequence.'

I step down from the porch, into the mud. The sun has been with us and the ground is soft but manageable. It will dry to dust as the summer burns on.

'Tell me, Charlie.'

'A wager. I bet too much at cards and lost to Mr Croaker. That's all.'

I sigh. 'Do you need me to write to my father?'

Charlie frowns, then smiles weakly. 'Perhaps it would be wise. A small stipend – enough for the wager and for some new equipment. Dynamite. There are boulders too big for a pry bar. They are selling a new rocker box at the hardware store. They say it can catch the tiniest of gold flakes.'

'We need nuggets, not flakes.'

'And we'll have them. We'll catch more gold than any man in the Klondike with that box. It's not cheap, but it's an investment in our future. You'll see to it? With your father?'

His eagerness repulses me. Even more so than Croaker's eyes on my body. Who is this man I've married?

'I will,' I say, my teeth clenching against the words. 'He will be happy to help, I'm sure.'

Charlie's face lights up and he kisses my cheek. 'We'll head to Dawson first thing in the morning.'

I watch him go back to his digging. Down the valley I can still see Croaker, stopped to talk with a prospector I know as Early. Some call him Bird. Early hands over a cotton bag the size of my fist. Croaker inspects it, weighs it in his hand, then moves on. Early pulls off his hat and wrings it. It is hard to see at such a distance, but I believe I see anger, or fear, in his face.

I catch his eye. I'm the woman on the hill to them. Known, but untouchable. Early blinks, nods and lifts his pick once again.

I see the ripple Croaker leaves. The men no longer sing. The picks hit harder.

Charlie digs until past dark and comes back sore and quiet. We eat and he sleeps, and I stand outside in the cold.

The last of the snow clings to the mountainside, bright in the moonlight. The wind whispers, bringing murmurs from the camps below. Men sleep deep and early here and I watch them all.

My horses are hushed in their pen. The wagon waits for the morning trip. The cold doesn't sting as much tonight. Summer has come and it has brought something new with the melt.

MARTHA

DAWSON CITY, KLONDIKE, LATE JUNE 1898

'Twenty pounds of apples, five of butter,' I said to Sutter, owner of Sutter's General Store. They say these prospectors can eat, but it's my girls who empty the cupboards early.

'Yes, ma'am. You makin' your pies again?'

I smiled. 'I might be.'

'Put me down for two.'

'Sure will, John. You'll deliver this afternoon?'

'Freddy will be round with the cart.'

I nodded and took up my shawl. Despite the sun, it was still cold. Still snow on the mountains, and at night the mud still froze in the streets. Time for Ma's hot apple pies and a mite of comfort as these men started their toil after a winter waiting. I felt for them, the hope they were clinging to. It only took a few months of empty dirt for them to turn tail and haul ass back to the world.

Dawson had changed again. New businesses sprang out of the mud overnight. I walked the boards and felt the bustle of it. I'd always loved the noise and life of this place. Two years ago, when I'd bought my land, Dawson was a few shacks on the bend of a river. Some three hundred people. Now it's a hundred times that. It's never quiet, never boring.

A couple of gents were building a hardware store at the end of the street. Prime land. Not theirs, but rented. Tents and carts filled the spaces in between, selling second-hand goods that miners had abandoned. The claim office had a queue out the door and hawkers bothered every man, promising claims worth millions and virgin land not far away.

It weren't honest work, but it was work and, up here, we all have to make a living somehow.

I dropped in on the post office, which, along with my hotel, was one of the oldest buildings in Dawson.

'Ready for the summer, Ma?' asked Harriet, behind the counter. A round woman, built mostly of stone, it always seemed.

'Can we ever be?'

Harriet laughed. 'That's the God's honest truth of it. You seen they're paving Front Street?'

'I've seen.' Trying to turn Dawson into a well-to-do southern city was like trying to get an ox to pull by asking nice.

'They can put pretty stones on it, but Dawson will always be a mudhole, and they know it. They try to get me back in a corset and they'll have a riot on their hands.'

'Never a truer word, Harriet. You got anything for me today?'

'You got a letter.'

She handed over the envelope and I knew at once who'd sent it. I tried to keep the smile away, but Harriet was quick.

'Good news?' she asked, leaning on the counter as if we were gossiping at a tea dance. 'A man perhaps?'

I put the letter in my dress pocket and gave Harriet a

quarter. 'I'd say it's none of your business, but we all know you steam the letters.'

A wide grin spread over her wide face. 'I don't know what you mean, Ma.'

I went to leave, but stopped short. 'You hear anything about my Molly?'

'Might have.'

I put another quarter on the counter with a weary hand.

'She's been in. Collected two letters already; both arrived after the first thaw, sent a few weeks apart.'

Nothing bad in that. Everyone got letters sometimes, and they get held at Lake Lindeman or Bennett if they hit the weather at the wrong time.

'You steam them?' I asked.

She shook her head. 'I didn't recognise the name, so I didn't care for their news.'

'What do you mean?'

Harriet rested her chin on her hands and smiled. Over a barrel. I threw down two quarters and the woman quickly snatched them up.

'Thank you for your generous donation to the post office.'

'Harriet. Why didn't you recognise the name?'

'It weren't hers. She said she was picking up for someone else, but I wasn't sure.'

'What was the name? And if you make me put my hand in my purse again, I'll slap that grin off.'

'I don't remember. That's the God's honest truth of it. It was a busy day, had people in and out from sun-up and still knocking for their packages at midnight. I only recall because I don't often see your girls in here and you're like family to me, so I keep an eye out for them like I would my daughters. If I had any.'

'I appreciate it.'

Harriet nodded. 'You and my baby brother had any trouble with the new stampeders coming in?'

'Couple of drunks, couple of gents got rowdy after losing a claim at cards – you know the story. Harry can handle anything this place can throw at him. Same as you.'

Harry and Harriet. Both named for their father. When their mother pushed out a girl first, he named her after himself anyway. When she had a boy a few years after, he figured why not double up? Men and their legacies.

In the ten minutes I was in the post office, Dawson had woken up. Hundreds of people thronged the streets. It was post day, delivery day, supply day. Most folk came to town once a week and Friday was as good a day as any.

Trappers came to trade their furs, miners queued outside the assayer's office, women carried bags of food and cans, or stared through the windows of the two dress shops, hoping their men would find gold soon, so they could get out of their worn-down smocks.

There was music to the place. Shouts of traders and costers, snatches of piano from the dance halls, cafés doing a lively trade in breakfast, the buzz of conversation and excitement at striking: what they would do, where they would go, what lives they would have. You couldn't walk two steps in Dawson without being bothered by it; had to thin yourself down to get between the carts and stands and new buildings put up on every scrap of land, no matter how big.

The air changed, the excitement dimmed and I saw why. Coming up Front Street was a small group of Indians led by Chief Isaac. I waved, and he raised his hand in return. Had a smile on him that would light up even a miner's worst day. His people were dragging a cart of moose meat. Easy to know a moose carcass by the size; there weren't no animal bigger up here, and these folk could hunt them better than any sourdough with a rifle.

Chief and his men moved into Princess Street and I could hear the whispers that followed, see the looks and sneers. Some in town didn't pay the Indians no mind, but others didn't hide their unkindness. Wish I could tell every one of them to show some respect; without the Chief, the people of Dawson City wouldn't have made it past the winter of '96. We all would have starved to death without that man feeding us.

When they were gone, the town regained itself. The buzz came back.

I breathed in the energy of it. The smell of it. Dung and mud and man, and the hot smell of sawn wood. Nothing like it.

My hotel stood proudly on the corner of Front Street and Queen, on land I'd bought with my own money, first woman to hold land in Dawson, before Bill Mathers and his like had bought up the rest of the riverbank and turned this frontier town into his own private empire. He'd rent out tiny patches of land for a price that'd make your eyes bleed. Gouging every man for every penny. Bill was the worst kind of man. Built everything on blood and the backs of others. He weren't a stranger to killing to get what he wanted, and he'd had old Doc Hoffmann in his pocket. When one of Bill's girls got sick, or he got too angry and broke an arm, Doc would patch them up and send them away. Bill even shot a man once, and the doc said the man did it to himself. All kinds of accidents happened at Bill's place, and the Mounties cried bad luck.

I'd built a life here – one I loved, one that was mine – but I knew how quick a life could change. Throw of a coin. Strike of a pick. Turn of a card. Whim of a man like Bill.

I took to my office at the hotel. A room on the balcony

where, through an open door, I could see the front door and Harry standing watch. I had Jerry on the bar and, while it was still quiet, I took out the letter.

I held it in my hands, felt the ink scratches under my fingers. He had a heavy hand when it came to his writing, like he was making sure the words stuck, so I wouldn't miss one. His letters were always short, to the point and over in a second. I wanted to savour it long as I could. This letter had been a thousand miles in the travelling. From his hands to mine. He would've kissed it. He told me he always did.

I brought my lips to the paper and—

'Ma!'

Molly's voice was like a punch to the chest. A second later she appeared in the doorway. I put the letter in my drawer with a shaking hand.

'This better be good.'

Molly's face said she knew she'd pissed me off, but whatever it was, it was more important. She took a step inside my office.

'Bill's here.'

'He alone?'

She shook her head.

My lip flinched. 'He asking for me?'

'Not yet. Jerry's given him top shelf.'

That was good. Gave me time.

Molly stayed at the door, looking down at her shoes like she wanted to tell me something else. I didn't have the patience. All I could think of was Sam's letter sitting in that drawer, unread and waiting.

'What was that – a letter?' Molly asked, and I shot her a look so fierce she backed out a step.

'That's private, and I don't take kindly to prying eyes.' I said it harder than I should've, but I still couldn't get her lies out of my head. What else was she hiding from me? Maybe nothing. Maybe everything.

Bill's laugh carried up the stairs.

'You stay out of sight of Bill, you understand me?'

'Yes, Ma.'

Molly nodded and left. She was the only one I wouldn't let that man have. She weren't strong enough and she knew it. He'd charmed away a few of my girls in the past and I weren't about to let it happen again, especially not with a girl like Molly. Despite Bill having more money than God – most he'd stole from those who earned it – and promising to make her a queen, take her away from this life, Molly never argued, never went behind my back to him, so far as I knew, but that made him all the keener, and Bill was a man used to getting what he wanted. But she was no fool. She knew he was full of horseshit and she'd end up on her back and on his payroll.

I took the key from around my neck, locked the drawer and tucked the key back under my dress. I pressed the metal against my skin, made sure it was there. Safe. Like my letter.

I checked my hair in the glass, tidied a strand or two, squared my shoulders.

Out on the landing, I made sure not to look Bill's way. He was there, holding court at the bar with his man, Frank Croaker. Harry shifted when he saw me, but I shook my head. I weren't in any rush. Bill could wait. This was my hotel and I weren't to be summoned. He knew it, but still, that man could push my buttons.

He leaned with his back on the bar, laughing with the prospectors who had gathered close to hear his stories of striking at Bonanza Creek. To see his two gold teeth and his dozen gold rings. To ask to work for him. To beg. Everyone knew

Dollar Bill Mathers. He could find gold by sniffing for it. Could make money by smiling at the ground. He owned almost every scrap of land in town and he wanted it all. Especially my hotel. The crown jewel of Dawson.

He could go hang.

'There she is,' came his voice. Not loud. Never loud. But it cut through the noise all the same. No one quite knew where he was from; his story changed in the telling. Some said he was Irish, others English. Some said he was Texan-born and others said he was born right here in Canada – that's why he knew so much about finding gold. It was in his blood.

I didn't give a hot shit where Bill was from, all I cared for was him getting the hell out of my hotel.

'Bill. Frank,' I said and started down the stairs. 'How's business?'

Bill's gold grin always unsettled me. Like he weren't quite human any more.

'I'm a blessed man, Martha, what can I say? You see Chief Isaac in town? He's trading a moose.'

'I saw. You buying it, hooves and all, or you going to leave some for the rest of us?'

He laughed. 'I'll save a haunch for you, Ma. Will you make me a moose pie like you used to on the trail? You hear that, folks,' he raised his voice to the rafters, 'Martha here made her fortune in pie crusts and water bottles.'

His flirting weren't for fun, it was to show all those round us that he knew me before. He had a piece of my past and he'd poke at it whenever he cared to.

'You don't usually come drinking here,' I said.

I reached the far end of the bar. The prospectors had gone quiet, drifted back to their card tables. Frank Croaker stood quiet at his master's side like a good dog.

'I do enjoy a change of scene every now and then, and this

40

place has such a . . . gentle feel. It's always so quiet.'

He was baiting me already. Quicker than usual. 'Must be I attract a more refined clientele.'

'Must be.'

Giselle came out of the back room and headed upstairs. She cast a look over her shoulder at Bill, smiling like I'd taught her.

'You sure do have the prettiest ladies, though. Where's your Molly? She owes me a dance,' he said, watching every step.

'She's unavailable.'

'She's wasted here, Martha. I'll treat her like a queen, you know I will.'

'I know exactly what you'll do. What do you want, Bill? As much as I enjoy your visits, I've got business to attend.'

He sidled close to me. I could smell the lavender soap his laundress used. Bill didn't dig any more, didn't need to; the only time this man broke a sweat was in a bed or in a brawl.

He tapped his hand on the bar, showed off his rings. Some were plain, some inlaid with jewels, some with medallions. He'd taken them as payments or stolen them off the dead. One had blood crusted on the stone.

'Ten thousand,' he said quietly.

'What are you talking about?' But I knew.

'That's a fair offer, Martha. Ten for this hotel and its land.'

I leaned close enough to see the grey wisps in his black hair. I met his eyes. 'No.'

He sucked his teeth, eyes turned a mite harder. 'Twelve. Final offer. You won't get better.'

'This is my home, Bill. Home for my girls too – a safe one. How many of your girls end the night with a bloody face? How many of them keep half their take? You even feeding them? I seen them on the streets, skin and bone. I won't have that happen to mine.'

'Dancers, ain't they? *Entertainers?*'

I felt a prickle on my neck. 'That's right.'

He tutted. 'You know Officer Deever don't like vices on display. One word from me and he'll have you shipped down to Lousetown before the week's out, to scratch around with the other whorehouses.'

An old threat that didn't scare me any more. 'You speak that word and you'll be joining me at the weekend. You're never getting your hands on my hotel, Bill. Stop wasting your time.'

He lowered his head, tapped his rings on the bar. 'You ... you're a real ten-minute egg, Martha Malone. One day. One day you'll have no choice and that offer will be for two thousand, if you're lucky.'

I glanced at Harry, my bear, ready to strike at my word.

'Is that a threat, Bill?'

Bill broke into a smile and straightened up. 'A threat? Why, a gentleman doesn't make threats. Does he, Frank?'

The dog shook his head and put his empty glass on the bar.

I smiled. 'You forgetting? I've known you since this city was two shacks and an empty river. We both know you're no gentleman, Bill.'

He barked a laugh. 'You got me there, Martha.' He downed his whiskey and took up his hat. 'Well, I'd best be on my way. I've got my own business to attend to now. Plenty of fine men just arrived on the boats are looking for work and company and it's in my good nature to provide. Always a pleasure, Martha, I'll be seeing you.'

Bill and Croaker strolled to the door, nodding goodbyes and shaking hands with the desperate prospectors. At the door, Bill stopped.

'Say,' he said, 'you hear about the fire down by the dock?

A whole storehouse and everything in it turned to cinders in one afternoon.'

'Course I did,' I said, and a drop of cold water ran down my spine.

'A lot of good folk lost everything in that fire. All they had, wrapped up in one wooden building.' He patted the door frame. 'Still, we can always rebuild, can't we? If we got the gold, of course.'

He gave me a wink and finally left. The air rushed out of me and I held on to the bar to stop myself falling. Molly was at my side, appeared from some hidden place. She held me by the arm.

'Ignore him, Ma. He's all talk.'

I held on to her hand. 'No, child. He ain't.'

Molly nodded to Jerry and he put a glass down, filled it to the brim. I thanked him and took a sip. First drink of the day couldn't come too soon.

'I want this place jumping tonight,' I said loud, so the girls watching from the landing could hear. 'Every seat and bed filled. I can't afford breaks, and I can't afford to lose trade to that man. That piano and gramophone don't stop, you all hear?'

Murmurs and calls of 'Yes, Ma! You got it, Ma!'

Like an army on orders, they set about preparing for the night.

I finished my drink and took another. Upstairs, Sam's letter burned a hole in my desk drawer, but I wouldn't read it until the stink of Bill Mathers had been scrubbed off every inch of this place.

I'd made a promise to myself a long time ago, when I'd first seen who Bill Mathers truly was. The kind of man who would take what you love and snap its neck, just to watch you scream. I didn't love much in this world – just one man and this hotel. The man at least was out of Bill's reach for now, though I imagined his letter told of a visit, but my hotel, that taunted Bill every day he had to walk by it. I'd see my home burn before I let that man take it from me. I'd light the fire myself if I had to.

KATE

The trail out of Skaguay wound up and into the mountains. They were the Saint Elias Mountains, I learned from my reading. A wall of rock and ice and scree, so daunting and yet so beautiful I wished to be among them as quickly as I could. I thanked God and Mr Gunderson I had a horse to carry me.

'You all right there, Miss?' asked Mr Gunderson. I looked at him and he indicated my face. My smile. Then made a face himself.

I laughed. 'Indeed. There is something about this place that speaks to me. There are no rules here, just a destination and a dream. Every man or woman may make of themselves what they want here, should they have the will.'

'A claim full of gold helps too.'

'But it's not all there is. Look at these mountains. We don't have mountains like this in Kansas. We have precious little of anything in Kansas. It's beautiful here, is it not?'

'Oh, yah. She's a beauty all right. But she'll kill you soon as kiss you, if you're not paying attention.'

I smiled again. 'My kind of woman.'

Now Mr Gunderson laughed. A hearty sound that reminded me of my father.

'How does a woman like you end up a journalist, of all things, eh?'

'My father is a newspaperman. Owns three regional presses and is planning a Senate run. When I turned sixteen he gave me a job at the paper. Knew I wanted to write.'

'That how you came by Mr Everett?'

'Yes. He was a local businessman, acquainted with my father. I met him several times.'

And convinced him to finance my search for my sister, though he did not know it.

'And now you are here,' Mr Gunderson said with a kind smile. 'What does your husband say about your travels?'

I shook my head. 'I'd sooner take a prison than a marriage. My father encouraged in us girls a desire for independence. I believe he wanted boys, so treated me and my sister as he would a pair of sons. Much to my mother's annoyance.'

Mr Gunderson laughed again. 'She want you in dresses?'

'And he wanted us climbing trees. He taught me to fish, to tie knots. I loved it all. My sister, however, decided to rebel by following her heart to unsuitable pastures. They've not yet forgiven her, won't even talk about her; it's as if she doesn't exist to them any longer. One day, I hope, they'll see sense.' I did not want to dwell or explain further, so swiftly changed the subject. 'What of your family, Mr Gunderson? Do you have children?'

'A mother across the ocean and a father in the ground. I have a wife somewhere, though when I last saw her she said to come back rich and clean, and I don't yet have enough gold for a bath.' He let out another booming laugh that I couldn't help but join.

Up ahead, a horse reared with a terrible scream and my laugh was cut short.

Yukon's ears pricked. The stampeders rushed to the horse, grabbed its reins and tried to keep it under control.

'Wait here,' said Mr Gunderson. He kicked his horse and joined the fray. The poor beast held up the line, and people behind were starting to curse.

The horse had a full load on its back and it reared again. I heard a sickening crack and the horse collapsed.

The men around it watched it flail on the ground for a moment. One man nearby stayed on his horse, an angry, impatient look about him. I recognised him in a moment as the clean man I'd seen the day before, shouting at his packer. All that hurry and he was only a few dozen feet ahead. His familiarity still nagged at me, but I could not place it.

Mr Gunderson shook his head and another man took out his pistol and shot the beast in the head.

I jumped at the sound, so sharp and sudden, so loud in the clear air.

The men unloaded the dead horse's supplies and strapped them to their other horses. The trail moved on and Mr Gunderson returned.

'Broke its back, rearing like that. Damn shame.'

I couldn't speak. We rode past the animal, prone and lifeless, discarded by the trail, all because of this rush. Yukon sniffed at it, then went to bite.

'Yuke!' I snapped and the dog came to heel.

I rode in silence for an age. The cruelty these men showed their animals. Their desire to move, move, move, quick and relentless. Every man here was coming to this place a year after the rush. Every man had invested their fortune, such as it was, in this endeavour; and every man feared the man beside him would stake the richest claim before him. The desperation scared me.

We rode higher and the plains and foothills of Skaguay changed to hemlock and white spruce forests. Trees towered around us and the trail forced itself between them. It was slow, a few dozen feet an hour if we were lucky.

We'd been riding since dawn, and night was but an hour away. My back ached from the saddle.

'I'm getting down,' I said to Mr Gunderson, who was all but sleeping.

'Stay close,' he murmured and his head lolled.

I climbed down and checked the horses, fed them each a few handfuls of hay. They had been good. No trouble and no accidents. Perhaps because their loads were so much lighter than those around them. Every other horse I'd seen looked tired, head low, each step a painful chore. I could not help them, though I wished I could convince the men to treat them kinder.

I gave Yukon a rough stroke and fed him another can of meat.

The forest was a deep moss green not found in Kansas. The woods a mix of pine and cedar, dead standing trees – widow-makers I heard them called – spiked through the canopy like burnt matches. I stared at the darkness between them. The ground was churned to a mess of rock and mud and each step was a threat. I feared the night here. A chill came over me and I tightened the collar of my coat.

The stampeders moved a few steps and stopped again.

This muddy strip of men and horses was the only hint of

civilisation here. Along this route some trees had been cut down, but the forest was not diminished. It seemed alike to a mosquito on the hide of a buffalo. It could sip all it wanted, but the animal remained. Alaska, Canada, they were that animal and they remained, despite man's best efforts to drink them dry. The gold would be mined and the last of it found eventually, perhaps a year from now, perhaps a hundred. The men would go and the land would return to itself and its quiet.

I breathed in the clear air, but it was tainted by horse and dung and a thousand stampeders.

Yukon finished his food and bounded towards me. There was no respite. No place to camp and no chance of clearing this forest before night.

Behind, I heard a saw working at bark and, a few moments later, a call of 'Timber' and the crash of a dead tree felled. Axes went at the trunk and I imagined a fire would soon be lit.

'Miss Kelly,' said Mr Gunderson, alert now after the crash. 'Stay close. There are wolves in these woods. They'll call for Yukon, draw him out into the dark. You're best putting a rope on him.'

As much as I hated the idea of lashing my dog, I could not bear the thought of him running into those trees. Hearing his barks and those of the wolves chasing him. I took a rope from one of the horses and looped it over Yukon's neck. He did not protest.

'How far have we travelled?' I asked.

Mr Gunderson rocked his head, as he always seemed to do when asked a question. 'Maybe ten miles.'

My heart sank. 'Ten miles? Is that all?'

'That is quick for us. In the summer, some men are stuck in Skaguay for a week before moving. Then they take another month to reach Lake Bennett. Slowest stampede in history.'

He laughed, but I found no humour in it. I had expected progress, forward momentum at least, not being stuck in a queue for days on end. A rush indeed!

'What do we do if night comes and we're still here?'

Mr Gunderson frowned as if my question was pointless. 'We sleep on our horses. The horses follow those in front as we rest.'

'Do the horses not need to sleep?'

'Not tonight.'

We moved at a crawl for the next few hours. When night came, so did the cold. Fires were lit along the trail and men huddled for warmth. I pulled Yukon up on my horse with me and wrapped him in my coat. His warmth was enough to keep the chill at bay for a while.

As much as I yearned for adventure, I yearned more for a bed.

I pulled my hat down firmly on my head, tucked my scarf into my coat and huddled with Yukon.

Sometime in the night I woke to snow falling. Every time the horse moved, I woke again. Mr Gunderson slept as if the saddle was a feather bed.

When dawn finally came, we had emerged from the trees and were greeted by a whole new horror.

The trail changed from forest path to a narrow strip of gravel skirting the side of the mountain. It squeezed the line to one or two horses abreast. This was it. The place I'd feared the most upon reading other stampeders' accounts. The White Pass itself.

To my right, the mountain rose to impossible heights, still heavily sheeted with snow, a wall of indifferent rock. To my left, the ground dropped to a valley floor hundreds of feet below. And the path itself was barely six feet wide, cut into the rock by animals and man. The sheerness of it made my stomach flip and shrink. One wrong step . . .

I see death in your future.

The fortune-teller's warning blared like a ship's siren in my mind. Here? Now?

Rivulets of meltwater cut through the path, turning sections to slick mud. Huge leg-breaking rocks littered the way, too big to move.

Mr Gunderson rode up alongside me.

'Don't look down,' he said, 'or you'll see the bodies.'

My mouth went dry. 'Bodies?'

'Horses. Men. Horses break a leg, fall off, take a rider with them. Others die of exhaustion and the stampeders push them off. Some horses jump rather than take another step. There are thousands down there.'

I dared not look, yet my curiosity burned.

Mr Gunderson was more solemn than I'd seen him. 'Welcome to the Dead Horse Trail, Miss Kelly. If we are cursed to die anywhere, it will be here.'

ELLEN

I whisper to them. The horses calm. They are skittish at night, wary of wolves. The dawn is relief but not safety. In the night come the wolves, in the day come the bears, but always there are the men.

I dress to ride and, while Charlie sleeps and the light is not yet full, I go to Bluebell. My blue-roan quarter horse. A quiet, reserved animal with no temper. Goldie, a palomino quarter, is Charlie's and holds an opposite demeanour. Hot and quick, she urges Bluebell on, while Bluebell keeps the younger in check. A portrait of a marriage, perhaps.

I hush and harness Bluebell.

The trail I have worn around the cabin is still and cold. The forest is not yet awake, but the light is enough to ride by. I feel Bluebell's warmth beneath me. A tug on the rein and the horse turns. A touch of my heel and she speeds. For once, I am in control. I make the decisions and my horse abides.

'I fear Charlie is lying to me,' I say to the horse and the forest.

Neither answers.

Down in the valley, steam rises in great plumes. The miners are melting the ground frost. There is a steam boiler, brought in from Canyon City before winter closed the river. A miner will pay fifty dollars to use one of a dozen hoses for half a day to melt his ice. The man who owns the boiler need never mine, though of course he does. Gold fever takes us all.

Somewhere in the spruces, the birds wake. I don't know their names or types. I think to buy a book to tell me, but money doesn't go far here. I go half a mile into the forest. The ground turns rocky this far up the valley. The soft bank becomes granite gorge. Un-mineable and so forgotten. There are no men here. No sea of tents or fires belching black smoke. No noise but that of nature and the wilderness – what little of it still exists.

There are grouse and rabbits. Squirrels dance through the branches. Bluebell's breath comes in puffs. We stand at the edge of the gorge. The water rushes, breaks over jagged rocks too hard to soften. The sound is music.

I think I see glints of yellow stuck in the cracks. I think I see nuggets resting below the water, held firm by the boulders.

Gold fever takes us all.

I pull Bluebell away and we return to the cabin as the day heats and the men wake.

'All ready?' Charlie asks. He pulls on his jacket and slings a bag over his shoulder.

'The wagon is sound. Horses hitched.'

He goes to the corner where a floorboard has been cut and loosed. He lifts it and takes out two jars. One is full of gold and the other barely half. Small flakes and chips, not the nuggets we were promised.

He then pulls out a leather wallet. Inside, my father's money. A few notes, a few coins. So little after being given so much. And yet I am to ask for more.

The road to Dawson City is two hours by wagon and it is mid-afternoon when we finally start our journey. It used to be pleasant. When we first came here, the land was virgin. The valley thick with trees and shrubs, blueberry bushes, thorns. We fought our way through inch by inch, axes and saws. Now the trees are gone. Replaced with tents, chimneys, smoke and men. The valley below our cabin is bald. Stripped. The wood used for fires and sluices. The land is transformed. Cut with shovels, overturned and rinsed for its value.

There will be a mudslide soon. Now the melt has begun, the land will loose itself and wipe the miners away. Last year three men died, buried in the dirt they loved.

Charlie plays a harmonica. The sound travels in the empty valley and miners look up from their work. Some call out requests, others tell him to hush. I don't mind it. For all Charlie's faults, he plays well and the sound is pleasant enough to pass the time.

The Klondike River is still frozen and will be for another few weeks. When the ice cracks, the ferryman and his wife will return and charge every miner for passage. There is no place in the Klondike where money does not replace kindness. It is a place where even a woman alone can make her fortune. I think about that often.

The ice trail is marked brown with dirt and dung. Either side is pristine white. A man in furs, perhaps a native, sits far off with a fishing line. He tugs it, then lets it rest. We pass and the man drifts from view.

We approach Dawson along the riverbank. A sprawl of tents stretches a mile out of the city. It is somewhat in order, thanks to Robert Steele and his Mounties, but those men are few and the miners are many. They live atop each other in rows, muddy and starving. Most will leave soon. Some will die. Groups gather around stoves, metal cups in hand, steam pouring off them. The cold is cruel here. Only the promise of gold keeps them warm.

Charlie chivvies the horses and we pass into the city.

It is so loud I want to shrink. The saloon pianos are playing as the afternoon gives way to evening. Stampeders and those here to make money from them spill out of gambling dens, sour with drink. A quarrel near an eating house ends with fists and a drawn gun. Conmen sitting by the roadside try to entice us to play the pea-and-shell game or Find the Lady. The morning traders stand at their doors and call out their wares.

Charlie draws the wagon close to Sutter's.

'Elly,' he says and turns in his seat to me, 'I have some business. Will you get the supplies and send the letter to your father? I'll see you at the hotel.'

What use is there in arguing? Telling him I don't wish to ask my father, yet again, for money? But Charlie will give me a speech about how hard he works for us, our future, our children when they come. I am tired of hearing it.

So I nod. I always do.

He kisses my cheek and jumps from the wagon. A wave and he is away in the growing throng.

In Sutter's General Store, empty but for me, I am greeted as if by an old friend.

'Mrs Rhodes,' John says with a wide smile. 'What a treat. Don't often see you down here and, may I say, it's good to see you well.'

'Thank you, John.'

'Mr Rhodes with you?'

'He is about some business.'

'Fine, fine,' John rests his palms on his counter. 'What can I get you?'

I give him my list.

He inspects it and says, 'We don't have the sugar in yet – I hear it's coming on the next steamer, but I got a couple cans of molasses. Ten cents less too.'

'That'll be fine.'

'Your wagon outside? I'll have Freddy load it up.'

'Much obliged.'

While he gathers my items, I browse the shelves. The usual fare, cans of meat, boxes of biscuits, tobacco, coffee. But there, on a shelf beside jars of bright candies, is a bar of Runkel's Vienna Sweet Chocolate. I haven't had chocolate since Seattle. There, this would be ten cents. Here, four dollars for the bar, marked up so high it is almost flying, like everything in the Klondike.

Then I see the rocker box Charlie asked me to put on his list, but I refused. Two hundred and seventy-five dollars for a wooden box with holes in it. It sickens me, the cost of it all. Even if you strike gold, the leeches will suck it out of you the moment you set foot in the mud.

I turn back to Sutter. He isn't rushing to pack my order. He stands behind his counter, tapping his fingers on the wood.

'Everything all right, John?'

'Mrs Rhodes, there is the matter of your account.'

My skin prickles. 'Account?'

'It's owing – some three hundred and seventeen dollars.'

I feel the world begin to spin. 'Charlie handles all that. He's got the ... he's got all the gold. He's going to come by after his business.'

Sutter smiles. He's a gentle man and I can see the pity in his eyes. 'I know you're good for it, Mrs Rhodes. Hell, you two have been here since before the rush, you're not like these stampeders. I want to do right by you. How about I put this order on the account and, when Charlie comes by, he can settle up and we'll talk no more about it.'

'I appreciate it,' I say. 'It's been a hard winter, you understand.'

'One of the worst,' he says. 'Say, do you sew? A lot of miners come in here, and the outfitters, with holes in their clothes. Easy fixes mostly, but they don't have the skills. A seamstress could make some good money off those.'

'A kind suggestion, I'll think on it.'

But I won't. To become a maid to those men, mend their ripped shirts and darn their socks, have them around me, have their things in my home. I have not fallen so far. Not yet.

'I must be going,' I say. 'I'll have Charlie come by.'

Sutter smiles, but it isn't warm any more. 'Please do. Good day, Mrs Rhodes. A pleasure to see you, as always.'

I force my smile and leave.

I step outside and my anger bubbles up my throat. Hundreds of dollars of debt to Sutter. Thousands to my father. And Charlie looking to get into more.

All for the gold he can't even find.

I walk to the post office. The letter to my father burns in my pocket. I wrote it while Charlie was packing the wagon. He read it. Made sure I asked what he wanted. Made sure I didn't speak ill of him, though I wished to.

The post office is busy, miners and the occasional wife come and go. Packages change hands, letters are opened before they even leave the building. News from home. A warm scarf knitted by a distant mother. Trinkets. Money hidden in a new pair of shoes.

I stand in line.

Outside the window, people swarm. Wives – for they are almost always wives – walk slow, tired. One woman for every ten men. I wonder if they think as I do. How can they not?

'Morning, Mrs Rhodes,' Harriet says. 'It's good to see you, and that's the God's honest truth of it. How are you doing up there?'

Harriet speaks directly, with no airs about her. She is not like any woman I knew in Seattle, more's the better.

'Morning, Harriet. Good to see you too. Oh, we're fine. Any letters?'

'Yes, ma'am. One for you and one for your husband.'

She collects them and slides them across the counter. I put down two pennies and they're gone before I pick up the mail.

My letter is from my father, as expected, addressed to Dawson City, as all letters here are. I turn over Charlie's and see the same hand. I don't believe my father has ever written to Charlie. I have never seen it, at least. The letter is slim, a single sheet. Mine is heavier, bringing news of home. Why would he be writing to Charlie?

I feel the letter I am to send in my pocket. I close my hand around it. But Charlie's name in my father's hand screams at me. The debt screams at me. The empty gold pans. The whispered exchange with Frank Croaker. The nights Charlie spends away. It all screams.

'Anything to send?' Harriet asks.

'No.' I let go of the letter. 'Not today.'

MARTHA

'There ain't no place like the Dawson Hotel of an evening,' said one prospector to another.

'You not wrong,' said the other. 'Only place in town with a woman's touch. Them pies too, just like my wife makes.'

The two stood at the bar because every stool, seat and ledge was taken. Good customers; money to them too. I watched every man in the place for the one who was beating on Molly. She'd powdered the bruises, but I could still see the shadow.

Old Man Carmack played the piano. The girls flirted. The men gambled and drank and ate plates of pork and beans and wedges of Ma's Apple Pie, a taste of home they paid through the nose for. I watched from the end of the bar, feeling none of the joy and ruckus.

Giselle snared a gent with a gold pocket watch and a tidy moustache. Louise was being fought over by two, making a game of it, like I taught her. My two other girls, Tess and Laura-Lynn, were both hanging off the shoulders of a gent I didn't know, but who'd been lucky at cards all night.

Molly weren't nowhere.

'You seen Molly?' I asked Jerry, tending bar.

'I seen her in the back when I went to get another crate. 'Bout a quarter-hour ago.'

'Thanks, Jerry.'

In the kitchen, my cook Jessamine, a big ole gal from Texas way, served up plates like she had four arms.

'Get you somethin', Ma?'

'Molly come through here?'

She clicked her teeth and snorted. 'Ain't seen her since morning. You tell her she needs to eat, she's gettin' skinny. Fellas want some meat on their women. You tell her that.'

I put my hand on Jessamine's shoulder and kissed her cheek. 'Your beans are burning.'

She snatched up a spoon. 'Ah, horseshit!'

I went on, through the kitchen to the store. It was full, after Sutter's delivery, and had a door to the street on the far side. I kept that locked, but it weren't locked now. I went to it quietly. Heard voices.

Molly and a man. I put my back against the wall.

'You have to go,' Molly was saying.

'Not without you.' He didn't sound dangerous, just desperate.

'I can't go with you. I've got a life here.'

'I can give you a real life. We'll travel the world. I'll make you a queen.'

She sighed. I heard hands brushing cotton, footsteps in the mud. Their voices turned soft.

'Molly, please. I love you. You know I do,' he said and something in the gent's tone made me believe him. He weren't drunk at least.

'I ...' she began and I heard heartbreak in her voice. I chanced a look out the door. The gent had his back to me,

60

but I could see Molly. See tears on her, even in the dark. They were forehead to forehead, hands entwined. Lovers and no mistaking.

'I want to marry you,' he said.

She pulled away from him. 'I have to go, Ma will be worrying after me.'

He took her arm. 'Why do you care about her? She's using you. Keeping you on your back for her profits.'

I flinched. He weren't wrong, but he weren't all the way right, either. Took all I had in me not to burst out the door and grab that fucker by the throat.

'It isn't like that,' said Molly, sudden grit in her. 'She cares about me. She's like a mother to us. You don't understand – you never will. That's your problem. I can't marry you. I won't.'

She wrenched her arm free and moved past him to the door.

The man grabbed her. 'You can't do this to me. Wait. I'm sorry. Molly, please. I'll take you away from here. Give you the life you deserve.'

She got up close to him, eyes like fire; I seen that look before. 'Give it to your wife.'

His fight left him as she did. I pressed my back against the wall.

Molly slammed the door behind her. Turned to lock it and saw me. She near screamed, but kept her tongue. 'Damn, Ma, you scared the life out of me.'

I stepped out of the shadow. 'You all right?'

She nodded once, then shook her head. 'You hear all that?'

'Yes, child.'

Molly crossed her arms. Her anger made her shake.

'You love him?' I asked.

'It's none of your business,' she said, her tongue sharp as a pick.

I folded my arms across my chest. 'It's all my business, girl. All of this is *my business.*'

'I'm not allowed a personal life? Not allowed friends?'

'He didn't sound much like a friend. My rules is no moon-lighting and no lying and, far as I can see, you're breaking both. Careful what you say next, girl.'

Molly didn't move for a moment, didn't speak. I figured she was thinking of a lie. 'I'm not charging him, if that's what you're worried about.'

'I'm worried about you! He the one give you them bruises?'

She looked down at her feet, all the venom gone out of her. 'No. He'd never.'

'I saw him grab you.'

Her eyes met mine. 'He'd never.'

I didn't push it, but I still weren't sure. The way he'd grabbed her, the change in his voice. He was sure capable of it. Any man was.

'Then who did?'

'No one.'

I'd had about as much as I could take of her lying in my face. I balled up my fist and wanting to take a swing, but I never would. I calmed myself enough to speak.

'Take the night off. I don't want to see you in the bar this evening.'

Molly nodded, wiped her face and went to say something, but changed her mind. She walked away.

Soon as she was gone, all the anger rushed out of me and sadness rushed in to fill the space. Molly was a smart one; smarter than me, I'd wager, and for a spell I'd tipped her to take over from me when I finally let go of this place, but now? I'd sooner see it in the hands of a stranger than a liar.

I wish I'd seen the man clearer. Just his back, his build.

Same coat as every man up here. Same hair gone long, without money for a barber. He looked like every miner, but she must have seen something in him. As riled as I was, I envied it too, to tell the truth. That touch, that lover's whisper, the promise of more. Sam's letter was still unopened in my drawer. Unread. Those whispers put to paper were good enough for now, until the time was right, if it ever would be. It had been months since his last visit. Months of no man coming close to me, and thank God for it, but when I saw those two together, I felt every hour of those months. Every step of that distance between us.

I see men falling for my girls all night, declaring themselves and being taken to heaven for a reasonable price. But love? Love is rarer than gold up here, and God knows you can't have both.

I heard a crash from the saloon. A breaking glass or the start of a fight. I felt heavy for it. The weight of this place bearing down, when sometimes I wanted to run north, to him. A dream and a notion only. A trapper's life was no life for me and, when Sam was done, caught enough, traded enough, he'd come to me. This was my home, for better or worse, and I needed to tend it. Molly would keep till the morning.

The hotel was full, the customers getting louder. Whiskey flowed and the piano hopped. The cards were flying and gold dust was spilling on the floor. Men flaunted their wealth, held in canvas bags and glass jars. One slammed his jar down, shouting drinks on him, and the cheer went up. We had one of them a night, at least.

I took his gold and drank with them. Drank more than I should have.

Harriet stopped by and we gossiped like hens. She found herself a man and took him home, despite Harry's glaring.

The night went on and I laughed and I danced and I played a tune on the banjo. Ain't no place like the Dawson, that's the truth.

When the music stopped, and the men left, the quiet buzzed in my ears.

'To bed, Jerry,' I said and the barkeep threw his cloth over his shoulder.

'Let me help you, Ma.'

He guided me upstairs to my room, the whiskey working on my legs, turning them soft. At my door, I patted Jerry on the shoulder and he went back down to clean up.

I went to Molly's door, opened it. She was asleep in her bed, so sound, some of that anger toward her softened.

I went to my office. Sam's letter called to me from the drawer and I went to it.

I took the key from around my neck and unlocked it, found the letter. His handwriting as familiar as my own. I brought it to my face, breathed it in. Smell of ink and wood and something else. Him.

I turned it over, ready to break the seal and hear his voice.

But it was already broken.

Had I . . . ? The whiskey turned my memory to mud. Had I opened it before Molly interrupted me? Before I'd got a chance to read it?

I knew I hadn't. But I must have. It had been in a locked drawer all day, and the key had been around my neck.

Even drunk, I knew my mind and myself. I hadn't read this letter. I hadn't opened it. My office was unlocked through the day, which meant anyone could come and go. I'd sent Jerry up for some small change. Sent Harry to get the receipt books. Sent Giselle for a bottle of gin. Even a gent could wander in, should he be minded. Could be anyone. But someone had been in my office and found a way into my drawer and tried to make it look like they hadn't.

I had a snake in my house, and a snake who knows your secrets is gearing up to strike.

KATE

The Dead Horse Trail was silent and deafening at the same
time. The wind whispered through the valley and the wildlife
was sparse. The only sounds came from those who did not
belong here. The crack of whips and the animal screams, the
shouts and dull thudding punches of the men forcing their
beasts to their deaths.

We moved at no pace at all. A step every few minutes, stopping often for an hour or two at a time while a group wran-
gled their horses or a load slipped and had to be re-secured.

Mr Gunderson showed no frustration, yet I was hot with it:
one more delay from shouting and forcing through the pack.
Yukon whined and nipped, angry at being tied on to the back
of the nag behind me .

My horse stopped, sniffing the ground. I looked at what he
was nosing and saw a bone to the right of the trail, nearest
the mountain. A horse skull, still attached to a few bumps of
spine. Scraps of skin and hair clung to the bone. With a sick

66

feeling, I looked to the left, where the trail dropped to the valley floor, and saw the animal's pelvis and legs. There was nothing in between. The dirt was darker here. Specks of white in the mud. Bone, crushed under foot and hoof. This animal had died here and they had walked over it, ground it down to nothing.

I held bile in my mouth. Humanity, it seemed, was the first sacrifice on the trail for gold. I dreaded what I might find at the end. What kind of men would be at the gold fields? What kind of men did my sister live among? If they were still men at all.

A cry went up behind us. A huge black horse reared and threw his rider. The man disappeared over the edge and the shock hit me. His screams echoed through the gulch until they were abruptly cut short. The black horse did not calm. His load came loose and crashed onto the trail.

The horses close by panicked, began to buck and spin. One slipped, toppled over. A God-awful crack silenced the poor animal.

Men shouted, grabbed reins and whipped flanks until they bled.

The black horse bucked and kicked a man in the chest. He flew backwards, hitting the wall with a deadening thud.

A man pulled a revolver and aimed it at the black horse.

Mr Gunderson and a dozen others roared, 'Don't!'

But the man pulled the trigger. The gunshot cracked the air.

The black horse fell into the gulch and a sound – one I'd never heard before or since, nor cared to – stunned the stampeders to silence.

Thunder.

But not from the sky.

I looked up at the mountainside, the heavy sheets of snow.

Mr Gunderson yanked on my horse's reins. 'Ride!'

He slapped the horse and it took off. Panic gripped the trail and every horse and man surged forward.

Cries went up. 'Avalanche! Avalanche!'

The thunder grew to a roar. Ice and snow tumbling over each other.

But there was nowhere to go. The trail was packed, horses clambered hoof over head. Men abandoned their loads and ran between them. Some slipped and went over the edge. Horses and their loads tumbled into the gulch, dozens at a time.

'Yukon!' I shouted and heard his bark somewhere behind. 'Mr Gunderson!'

'Keep going!'

The roar of the ice grew and grew. I dared a look up and saw it, a great cloud of snow rushing down the mountainside. The power and fury of nature bearing down upon arrogant men, screaming, *You're not meant to be here.*

The avalanche hit the trail behind us and swept a hundred prospectors, horses, packers off the edge and into the abyss. Screams were cut mid-throat. Panic reached its peak as the ice chased us along the trail.

I pushed my horse, steering it close to the mountainside, racing it past more heavily laden beasts, less experienced riders, jumping it over boulders and bodies. Yukon's horse followed. The packhorses behind that, and Mr Gunderson at the rear.

The ice crashed a few dozen feet behind us and the stampeders who were caught disappeared, churned within the white and carried into the valley. Dead with their horses.

'Go!' came Mr Gunderson's shout.

The trail was turning, widening, away from the path of the avalanche.

I dug my heels into the horse's side and snapped the reins. 'Faster!'

The horse obeyed.

The trail was clogged with people running, riding, screaming. One grabbed me, tried to climb on my horse. I kicked him hard in the face and cracked his nose. He fell, bleeding, and was trampled.

The ice was catching us: ten feet away, eight, five.

'Yah!' I screamed.

I kicked at anyone near, led the horse over squirming, churning bodies. All I could think of was to survive. It didn't matter the cost. I had to survive this.

I pulled my horse around a man trapped beneath his animal, crying and begging for help. I didn't stop. Nobody stopped.

There was the turn. I heard Yukon barking close behind. Heard horses and men and roaring ice, a sound so dense and primal it turned my very marrow cold.

I was there – the turn! I yanked my horse around the rocky corner and barely a second later the avalanche crashed behind me, funnelled by the mountainside.

The roar gradually quietened, replaced by terrible sounds of pain. The injured screamed. Broken legs. Crushed arms. Supplies lost. Horses gone. Friends, family, washed away in a tide of ice.

My head swam, ears rang and buzzed. Everything was muffled.

'Yukon?' I called, my voice weak and hoarse. I had been screaming, but I had not heard myself. 'Mr Gunderson?'

A weak bark from somewhere near the snow.

I picked my way back towards the turn, now blocked by ten, twelve feet of ice.

'Yukon?'

He yelped and I finally saw him. He was on the ground, the horse he was on half-buried in the snow.

I dropped off my horse, my legs trembling, and stumbled to him. People moved around me, collapsed and dazed; some wept, others dug frantically at the snow.

Yukon was still tied to the saddle, but the rope was twisted around his neck. His tongue lolled, barely able to breathe. He yelped and pawed at me.

'It's okay, Yuke. Hush now.' I tried to untie the rope, then remembered. I pulled the rose-handled knife from my belt and cut him free.

He fell onto my lap like a child and let me hold him. He was shaking, cold and terrified, nuzzling and licking me. The relief was overwhelming. And yet short-lived.

'Mr Gunderson?' I said weakly.

He had been behind Yukon. Behind the other horses.

I stared at the wall of snow, the broken things sticking out from it. Supplies turned to splinters. Horses turned to meat. Men turned to memories.

I sat on my heels, Yukon panting in my lap. What was worth standing for now? My guide was gone. Ripped off the mountainside and thrown to the gulch. His supplies. Most of mine. Lost. Destroyed.

My carpet bag and canvas sack were still tied to the back of my horse, but my trunk had been on Yukon's horse. The brass-studded side stuck out from the snow, crushed like an egg under the weight of it.

Letters lay like dead leaves in the scree. Letters from my sister, Mr Everett.

I pulled myself up, with Yukon stuck close to my side, and collected them. Each one a promise of news, help, fortune, change. As I reached for them, I saw blood on my sleeve. I ignored it. There was no pain and I could not yet face the idea that the blood was not mine.

I don't know how long I sat there. A few moments, a few hours, it did not matter.

'Are you hurt?' A voice cut through my daze. 'Miss, are you hurt?'

I looked up and saw a woman. Older. Strong. She had a bloody cut on her cheek, but all her concern was for me. She shook my shoulder.

'Are you hurt?'

I lifted my arm and saw the ragged strips of cloth hanging from it, each tainted with blood.

The woman cradled my arm, examined it. I felt nothing.

'It doesn't hurt. But . . . he's . . . it's all . . .'

She knelt beside me, put an arm around me. 'I know, love. It took half our supplies.' The woman produced a long rag from somewhere and tied it around my arm. 'Nasty scrape. Looks like you got it off the wall.'

A faint memory of riding too close to the mountainside. The horse whinnying and something snagging my arm.

I looked at the woman, at the blood pouring down her cheek. 'Are you . . . ?'

'I've had worse. You by yourself?'

I put a hand on Yukon and she understood.

'Come on. You're riding with us.'

I let the woman pull me up and guide me back to my horse. I leaned against the animal. Felt the power of his heart. He was panting, eyes wild, but he soon calmed. I patted his cheek and pressed my head to his.

The woman and, I supposed, her husband were gathering their supplies, repacking what they could, finding orphan horses to carry it.

All around me was madness and chaos, but I was still within it. I let it pass around me and did not allow their fear into me. For if I did – if I felt the true terror of the moment, of how close I came to death, what that might mean for Charlotte – I would throw myself from the edge to escape it. Charlotte needed me and I would not go back, after coming this far. The way was blocked to me, as much by ice and snow and nature's rage as by my own mind.

The fortune-teller had been right. If I ever saw that woman again, I'd wring her neck and take joy from it.

I took what I could from my trunk and packed it on the horse, then I gave it a candy from my carpet bag. I found a tin of dog food for Yukon, but he was not interested. I mounted the horse and Yukon jumped up with me. I doubted he would want to be apart from me the rest of this journey and, truth be told, I would not be without him.

I left quietly; the woman and her husband did not notice. They would take days to organise themselves and pick their way through this mess. I did not have those days to spare. I needed to move, to be away from this mountain, this mass grave.

I rode past broken stampeders. Many were horseless and without provisions. Others had survived with a little and were trying to take stock. Some had injuries so severe they would not last the day. Others would be in pain for months, wishing the avalanche had claimed them.

I rode on, following the trail. Trying not to think of Mr Gunderson and how I wished he was here with me. How sick I felt at his loss, despite knowing him only a week. My arm began to ache and sting, but I did not have the water spare to wash it, or the bandages to bind it.

My horse climbed to the summit of the White Pass, the

border into Canada where the Mounties waited with guns for any man not paying his duties. Beyond that, we descended to the valley floor. I guided the horse over the cracks and crevasses that could snap his leg, the swamps and mires that could swallow him whole, the bogs full of corduroy logs turned end up, which could disembowel him.

But the most dangerous – what I feared most – were the scores of desperate men who had just lost everything.

I hid from them, kept my hat and scarf over my face. Camped away from them and rode through White Pass City at the base of the mountain, stopping only to feed the horse and myself. I pressed onwards, my head down, pausing when the valley finally opened to stunning vistas. Where the white-topped mountains were endless and all that had happened on the trail so far felt as distant as they were.

ELLEN

DAWSON CITY, KLONDIKE, LATE JUNE 1898

We spend the night in the Arcadia Hotel at the edge of town. Barely a room, but clean enough and cheap. Charlie doesn't come back until far past midnight and he stinks of drink. I'd spent the day wandering through Dawson, staring in shop windows and at the playbills at the Tivoli Theatre, wishing I had the money to spare. Wishing I'd chosen better for a husband.

I wake in the morning and Charlie is already gone. A note where his head should be: *Business to attend. I'll be back this afternoon. Take care, my love.*

My love. Am I really, Charlie? Or are they just words now? Simply what you say to your wife? Perhaps he does mean them, and it is me who doesn't. Our love was so quiet, I barely noticed it slip away.

I take out the letters from my father. I read mine last night while waiting for Charlie and now I take it up again, reading it over as I still can't believe his words. The bulk of the pages come from a parish newsletter. My father's own letter is a single page. Inside are a hundred dollars in small bills. The letter is brief:

Dearest Ellen,
I have been patient and supportive of your union from the
start, yet I can support it no longer. I have been paying your
husband monthly to ensure you are at least fed and clothed.
This ends now. I am sorry, Daughter, but you are a wife and
it is your husband's duty to care for you, not mine. I hope you
will return from the foolish quest you have set yourself with a
full purse and I look forward to the return on my investment. I
will write with news now and then, but of money, I wash my
hands of you both and wish you well.
Yours,
Frederick Calloway

Last night, reading his words, I had felt shot through the chest. Forsaken at last. Cast adrift in this sea of dirt. And this morning the hurt is no better. I had always thought, in the back of my mind, that Charlie would give up this claim and return to the warm embrace of society and family. Though as the years went on, I feared the life I left was nothing but a memory and I would not fit it again, should I return. I tried to keep my graces and decorum here, my hospitality and my sense, but they wash away, like dirt off the mountain, bit by bit until nobody recognises what's left.

My father's missive is heavy in my hands. Without his money, and without a strike, we won't last the year. This empty land is all we have, along with spiralling debt and winter just a few short months away.

I wish to walk into the wilderness and let the wolves have me.

I wish to wring Charlie's neck and tell him to do better, work harder, stop spending what little we have on frivolities and whores.

I look at the money – the last I imagine I will see in my lifetime.

I tuck it in my pocket and pick up the other letter. They are dated the same day, and I believe Charlie's note will say the same as mine.

I leave it unopened.

I put my letter in the fire. Watch the flames take my father's words.

In the throng of Dawson, I am invisible. My dress is plain, my shawl patterned but demure. My hair pinned neatly. I forsook fashion and beauty the moment I stepped onto the steamer. It has been years since I powdered my face or painted my eyes. Yet I still draw the occasional glance, even a smile and a word. More because women outside the brothels are rare, rather than because of my own appeal. I turn away from it, pretend I don't hear.

I walk with a heavy step. The town has changed in an instant. Before, it had been a place we were passing through, waiting for our turn of fortune until we returned to the world. But there is no return. There is no fortune. For those without gold, the Klondike is a prison and a tomb.

My prison.

My tomb.

The last hundred dollars are so light in my pocket they may as well not exist. I walk without aim and pass a window. Bright wrappers catch my eye. A stack of Runkel's Vienna Sweet Chocolate. Four dollars. I buy one without caring. I step outside and am about to take a bite when I hear raised voices. A commotion across the street.

I know the building. It is something of a bank, a money-lender owned by Dollar Bill Mathers. Outside, three men push a fourth. He falls in the mud and they laugh.

The man picks himself up. With a jolt, I see it is Charlie. Spat on and pushed. Hat in hand, like a beggar. I press myself between post and wall and remain invisible.

'Pay what you owe,' shouts one of the men.

'Now, now, boys,' comes a voice.

From the doorway steps Frank Croaker, Mather's red right hand. There is barely a man in Dawson who doesn't work for him.

Frank holds his hand out to Charlie, claps him on the shoulder. 'You know how to rid yourself of every penny of debt you owe?'

Charlie hangs his head. So weak. Simpering. I pity him afresh.

'I can't do that. I'm close, Frank. Another week and I swear it, I swear. We'll be rich.'

'How much will another week cost?'

Their voices drop and I don't hear the figure, but I can guess. More than we have. More than we can pay back. More than that land will ever give up.

Croaker hears what he needs and pulls Charlie back into the bank.

The debt spirals. The dirt yields nothing. Still Charlie toils. It would be admirable, were it not so misguided. I want to leave him to his fate but, despite myself, I do not wish to see him hurt. A new feeling sinks in my gut. I *cannot* see him hurt. He is all I have now and he must work the claim. He must strike gold or we are both doomed. Yet he has bedded himself with devils. Bill Mathers, Frank Croaker, they would think nothing of killing him for what little he has. Charlie does not even know how little he has.

'Penny for your future.'

I turn. In the alley between the store and another hotel is a tent. A woman stands outside. She is a spot of colour in a mud-brown city. Red-and-gold shawl, purple dress studded with crystals. Eyes black with kohl and lips ruby.

'My future?' I ask.

'Or your fate.' Her voice is quiet, yet carries. It unnerves me, but I don't know why.

The tent is painted with symbols and suns. Inside, I see carpets and chairs. A table with a glass ball.

'A penny to know.'

What harm is there?

'All right. A penny.'

I step down into the mud and she ushers me inside the tent. It is warm, yet has no fire. The smell of spice and cedar rises from smouldering sticks. The inside of the tent is red, the ceiling painted with a night sky. The stars and moon gold instead of silver. The carpets are soft, the pile full. I have not walked on carpet since leaving Seattle. It is like stepping into another world.

She gestures to a chair and takes the other.

A lark is all it is and, today of all days, I need the distraction. I had been to a fortune-teller at a county fair once. She'd gazed into glass, shuffled some cards and said I would marry a good man and have three children. To most, such a future is all they want, but I wanted none of it and so none of it came to pass. I did not marry a good man.

I expect similar of this woman. Find gold. Strike it rich. A life of luxury with my husband. I imagine she makes her own riches telling the miners the same.

The fortune-teller places her hands flat on the table, then turns one palm up to me. Waits. I place the penny on it and she closes her hand in a fist. She then opens her hand and the penny is gone.

'How ... ?' I begin to ask, but the woman shakes her head.

She lights a candle and her eyes flare.

A pack of cards appears, but they are not the gambling kind. I did not even see her reach for them, but they are in her hands.

She shuffles them slowly and we enter an awkward silence that I feel I must break.

'I've not seen you in Dawson before,' I say and she does not respond. 'Did you just arrive?'

She tilts her head as if that will answer.

'Which trail did you take?'

She looks up at me. 'I come and go as I please.'

'But the river is still frozen. Did you use dogs? That must have taken weeks.'

'None of that matters. Ask the cards your questions, not me.'

I open my mouth to ask of gold, but realise I do not care.

'What will happen to my husband?'

The fortune-teller smiles and shakes her head. 'That is not your question.'

My mouth goes dry. She is right.

'What ... will happen to me?'

She nods and places the cards on the table. She fans them into a crescent in one smooth motion.

'Pick five,' she says. 'Hold them in your hands. Do not look at them.'

I slide five cards out of the fan. My hands shake and I realise I am fearful of what this woman might tell me.

I hold them. The paper is worn, soft. The pattern on the back is red and gold, a faded flower like one would find on perfume bottles from France.

'*Giglio bottonato*,' she says and I look up from the cards.

'I'm sorry?'

'The Florentine lily,' she says, smiling. Her face is kind, the skin around her eyes crinkling with years of such smiling. 'My grandmother's grandmother painted these cards in her home in Italy. Now I have brought them here to show the future to this new world.'

'What future is there here?'

She shrugs. 'For men, they think they will be rich. They believe their future is in their own hands, but it never is. I tell them what they want to hear. Women,' she meets my eyes, 'I tell them what they need to know. Whether they want to hear it or not. Do you want to hear it?'

My head says no. This is a foolish thing for a woman to do. A waste of a penny. But with a few lines on paper, my father has undone the future I expected.

'Yes, I do.'

She nods and sweeps away the rest of the cards in one clean movement. 'Lay your cards face-down in the centre of the table.'

I do as she says.

She turns the first one face-up. It is a crude handmade drawing of three swords, each piercing a heart. The image is uncoloured, but I feel I can see the red of the blood.

'Three of Swords,' she says and lays the card gently on the table.

'What does it mean?'

'Many things. The swords pierce the heart of a person. They speak of challenges, but that can come in many forms.' She taps the card with a long nail. 'The three can mean the end of something, perhaps a business interest, but no . . . I don't see that for you. The end of something else. A marriage.'

'My husband is—'

But she holds up her hand. 'This is for you. Not for me. I will speak what the cards tell me, and you will understand it as you need to.'

She turns over the next card. A knight in armour holding a chalice. Drawn in black ink.

'An uncommon card in this place, for it is not one that men want to see drawn,' says the woman. 'The Knight of Cups. He is an adventurer grown weary, wishing only to return home, but unable to. Battles hold no more excitement for him and he wishes to ride away from it all. But for you, this is a welcome card. You have a change looming, but I do not know if it is the one you wish for or the one you merely think you wish for.'

Despite the warmth in the tent, I feel cold. How could she know of my desire and inability to leave? How could she know my marriage may be ending? But then I see. My story is the story of all Klondike women dragged up here on promises. Men wish for gold, women for freedom. I see the wheels, know the mechanisms to be false, and yet I dread the next card.

She turns it. Her eyebrows rise. 'Intriguing . . .' she murmurs.

'What is it?'

'This card . . . it is not for you.'

I look at it closer. A young man holds a staff over his shoulder. He walks across a field, eyes to the sky.

'Who is that?' I ask.

'The Page of Wands. A person of independent mind who does not follow rules set forth by man. I believe this is a person you will meet. They will change your perspective. Your mind. Perhaps your heart.'

I look at the card's face. Handsome. Beautiful even. Fear grows in my stomach.

'How?' I ask.

She shakes her head. 'I cannot say.'

She turns the next card. Four figures. One flying on bird wings aiming an arrow at the three below. They stand in a line. They reach for one another, but do not touch.

'The Lovers,' she says.

'They don't look like they are in love.'

She smiles. 'Some take romance from this card. Others do not. The Lovers represent choice. A crossroads where you must take one path and forsake the other.' Her finger hovers over the Knight card, 'Maybe a choice to leave,' then over the Page, 'or a choice to stay.'

She turns the last card and a demon stares up at me. Fangs. Wings. A gaping maw in its stomach. Imps dancing beside it, chained and screaming. I feel I can see it move. See the many mouths open.

'*Il Diavolo*,' she says and I need no translation. 'This is a special card.'

'It is horrible.'

'No, no. The Devil has many meanings, but none of them are to be feared.' She looks over the other cards, as if seeing them all anew. A smile grows on her lips. 'The Devil is the forbidden. The taboo. The desire we cannot speak aloud and yet that consumes us. It is passion that goes against what the world wishes of us. Some interpret it as freedom itself.'

'What does that mean?'

She taps the Page. 'A lover, maybe. A man you will meet who will ignite that passion. But you are married, are you not? This is a love that cannot come to pass under the eyes of God. You will have to make a choice. To stay or to go.'

'What do I do?'

'I cannot say. But the truth of these cards is clear to me. You will be forced to make a decision that will change the direction of your life. It will seem impossible, but the choice must be made. It will be a choice of passion. For a person, or for yourself.'

I sit back on the chair. My face flushes hot.

'How do I know I'll choose the right path?'

She picks up the Devil card. 'Because of this.'

I frown. 'What do you mean?'

She smiles, but I cannot read it. It isn't the enticing smile to lure me in here. It is something darker.

'I'm sorry, I can say no more.'

'But you must! I have money – can you do another reading? Shuffle the cards again.'

She places her hand on mine. Their warmth calms me. 'I can say no more.'

She ushers me to the door.

I follow on trembling legs. I should say thank you, but I can't bring myself to speak. She opens the tent. Light and chaos flood in. I squint against them.

'Good luck, Ellen,' she says and the tent door closes. She is gone. As if she never was.

I walk away in a daze. Had I told her my name?

I look back. The tent is just a tent. The paint dull, muddy. Nothing mystical about it.

My senses return. I curse myself for going in there. Wasting a penny on that. And what was I told? I will have to make a choice. Who does not?

I shake my head. 'Stupid woman,' I call myself.

I walk to the Arcadia Hotel, where my husband waits on the wagon. He is bright and smiling and is lying to me.

'Elly! Look, I got it.'

He points to the back of the wagon, laden with Sutter's produce. And there, lashed down, is the rocker box. Two hundred and seventy-five dollars.

'Wonderful,' I say and climb onto the wagon. He kisses my cheek and squeezes my hand.

'We'll be rich before the week is out,' he says and I know he believes it. 'Did you send the letter to your father?'

I lie and nod. 'Did you see the letter I left from him in the room?'

The tiniest flicker in his cheek. 'I did. It was talk of a business opportunity. He wants my investment once the gold comes in. I will think on it.'

Lies upon lies. I knew my father's letter to Charlie would have cut him off as sharply as his letter to me. I let him have it. He believes he is clever. Believes his lies will not catch up to him, but they give chase.

I think on the cards. The Page. The Lovers. The Devil. Wild passion and freedom await with another man. A forbidden man. Heat grows inside me.

'Are you all right, darling?' Charlie asks and the heat wanes at the sound of his voice.

'Yes,' I say. 'Eager to be home, is all.'

He believes this too.

MARTHA

'Line up, girls. And you, Jerry,' I said. 'Doc Pohl is coming for the check-ups.'

My girls, Jessamine and my two fellas, Jerry and Harry, lined up outside my office. Molly stood at the end, next to Giselle, eyes on her feet, arms wrapped over her stomach. Wouldn't lift her head to look at me and, truth be told, I could barely look at her. The rest of them sighed and leaned, bored of waiting already and it had barely been a minute. The girls clucked and the boys talked of gold.

Jessamine was first in line, always was. She stood straight, none of that lollygagging, and looked nervous.

'Who's Pohl? He new? Where's Doc Hoffmann?' asked Tess. 'I don't want nobody down in my cunny who I don't know.'

'What you talking about, Tess?' said Giselle. 'You got gents down there all night that you don't know from your own pa.'

'I don't got to pay *them*!' she said and the girls laughed.

'Neither do you,' I said, cutting all that off. 'I pay the doctor.

You do what he says. Hoffmann retired, thank God, and was out of here soon as Pohl arrived. He's young and handsome, by all accounts. Came up the river by dog-sled this winter.'

Tess crossed her arms and slumped against the wall. 'Young handsome doctor, you say? Maybe he'll do my check-up free when he sees my goods.'

'Quit that talk,' I snapped and they went quiet.

I was in no mood. One of these people here went in my office, picked the lock on my drawer and read my private letter. One person here knew about Sam. Knew what I loved, where I'd be weak. I'd find that snake today and break its damn neck.

My office door opened and Pohl leaned out. 'Ready for the first, Mrs Malone?'

'There ain't no "Mrs" about it. I'm not married, Doctor,' I said. 'You call me Martha, like everyone else.'

'My apologies,' he said; he weren't flustered, kept the same expression on his face, then looked at the first in line. Jessamine. 'Miss?'

Jessamine glanced at me, I gave the nod and she went in.

Ten minutes and she was out, rolling down her sleeve.

'He said I got a hard pulse and to stop eating salt,' she said, unimpressed.

'He knows what he's saying. You'd best listen.'

She clicked her teeth and went away muttering.

The next girl went in and I joined them. Figured I'd watch my girls, see if I could spot the nerves. I often sat in on the exams anyway, just to make sure old Doc Hoffmann weren't swindling me.

Doc Pohl was cut out a different cloth than that man. Hoff was all rough hands and quick checks, in Bill's pocket, and more than once talked of lice when there weren't none, and I'd lost trade for a week. The girls had hated it. I always thought

86

he might have got some kink out of their more intimate exams. Took too long over it, if you asked me. But he'd been the only doc in town and I needed my girls healthy.

Pohl was kind, talked to them, heard their ailments. He checked them all downstairs, same as Hoff did, but Pohl did it quick, gentle. Had them keep their skirts on and made a modest affair of the whole thing. The girls looked at me, eyes wide, thinking this was some kind of miracle man. Good-looking and he cared? Every one of them was in love by the end of their exam.

He treated Harry for a cut on his arm that was starting to turn, and Jerry for an itch in his eye. Those that needed it, he gave them pills and ointments, told them to wash inside after each client, talked about rubbers, but they were too expensive to get up here, and gave them directions to eat an orange or take a draught of lemon juice a day to keep scurvy away.

'You have remarkably healthy girls here, Mrs ... Martha,' he said, washing his hands in a basin by the window. 'I have seen a lot worse in other houses in Dawson. You must care for them a great deal.'

He really was handsome and couldn't have been more than twenty-five. 'They're family. This is my home. I like to keep a tidy house.'

'And you, are you well?'

I crossed my arms, was dreading him asking. 'Can't say I've got time to be sick, but I have been feeling some pains, here, for a couple months now.' I put my hand low on my stomach.

'I see,' he smiled. 'Please, if you don't mind.'

He gestured to his table. A foldable thing that I thought would snap closed during every exam. I loosed my dress and let it fall to the floor. I stood in my bloomers and vest, then climbed up and lay down.

'Any chance you could be pregnant?' he asked as he put a band around my arm and put his stethoscope on the inside of my elbow.

I laughed and it hurt. 'Only if God's looking for another.'

He smiled and took the band off. Then he put his hands on my stomach, started pressing down in places. 'Any pain?'

'No.'

He moved lower. 'Here?'

I winced. 'That's the spot.'

He nodded, felt around a bit more, then gave a tight smile. 'All right. You can get up now.'

I did and he checked my eyes, ears, looked in my mouth, at my teeth. He was quiet, though, and I didn't like that one bit.

'You find something, Doc?'

'There's a small – and I mean small – lump in your abdomen. Could be gas or a cyst or something entirely innocent.'

'That's what giving me the pain?'

'Most likely.'

'What's it mean?'

He went to the basin and washed his hands again. 'Nothing right now. You're healthy as an ox. We'll keep an eye on it, though. Come see me in a couple of weeks and I'll check again.'

'All right,' I said.

I got my dress back on and tried not to think on what he was saying. Or not saying.

Pohl packed up his kit and his table. 'I'll send a boy round with the bill this afternoon.'

I nodded. As he was leaving, I said, 'Doc. Should I be worried?'

He smiled again. 'No, ma'am. No sense in worrying. It'll be nothing, I'm sure.'

He left then. I watched from the balcony as he made his way past four of my girls, all cooing and flirting, but he was a gentleman in and out of the exam.

I sat on my couch. Felt around in my stomach where he'd been pushing, but I couldn't feel anything. I felt well enough, except now I was pissed off. Every person in that room had looked me in the eye and one of them was lying.

I went to the balcony and clapped my hands. The talking stopped. 'Get everyone here, now.'

Jerry ducked his head into the kitchen, and Jessamine and Molly came out a moment later. Harry whistled at the door and Giselle skipped back in. The rest of the girls were lounging, but they sat up when they heard my tone.

'Last night someone went into my office. Someone picked the lock on my drawer and read a private letter of mine.'

I watched them. Giselle grinned, eyes darting from girl to girl, from Harry to Jerry, looking for the crack. She was a hound for gossip and this was red meat.

'There weren't no money or whiskey taken, and the drawer was locked when I came back to it. It weren't no miner or gent snooping. Whoever it was knew what they were after.'

Tess looked bored. Harry, with his bandaged arm, kept his eyes on me like a good soldier. Molly stared at her shoes, scuffing them along the boards like a scolded child. Either she knew what I was talking about or she figured she was beyond my ire. Either way, that scuffing added a brace of logs to my fire.

I raised my voice and she finally paid attention. 'I want to know who it was. You come see me if you did it. We'll talk. We'll work it out. You got until the morning or, I swear to God, I'll find you myself, and I ain't a forgiving woman.'

I caught a last look at Molly; her foot was quiet.

I slammed my office door behind me and it took a while before I started hearing talk again. Each one of them downstairs was shook, and rightly so. I had a feeling the first up the stairs would be Giselle, pointing the finger at one of the others. But that wouldn't be until later. Until night, when she could slip away without the others seeing. I had time.

I took out Sam's letter. I still hadn't read it. Almost couldn't bear it, knowing someone else had read his words before I did, but the doctor had put a fear in me and I felt I didn't have any time to waste being sore about it.

Martha,
It's been a harsh winter up here. The snow has been coming
every day, laying powder on top of ice. The rivers look like
they'll never melt. A blizzard destroyed my roof a week past,
bent up my stove pipe. The trapping has been good. Martens.
Beaver. Lynx and wolves. Four big bear hides and a silver fox.
A silver fox, my love!
    I wish I could come to Dawson to sell them myself, see you,
get me some of your apple pie. It's beans and beaver up here
and I sure miss your sweetness. But I ain't going to be running
the dogs any time soon. I busted my leg. Got my foot caught
in a bear trap. I'll be sending Davis to town for the sale. You
remember him? Give him a bath, will you? The fella stinks of
dog.
    I won't lie to you, Martha, I know you hate that. I ain't in
the best shape, but I'll be right again and I'll be on my way to
you soon as I'm walking.
All my love,
Sam

I read it again. I read it a dozen times before I could bear to put it down. He was so far away and hurt. A bear trap could cut a man's leg clean off. Snap the bone, shatter it to splinters. This letter was sent a week ago at least. Sam could be dead already. His leg could get the rot and he could be dying, shivering and sweating. But what could I do? I pressed the letter to my chest and felt my eyes sting.

I was nothing if not a practical woman. Davis would be here soon – a week maybe, if that – and he'd tell me the truth of how Sam was. If he was bad, I'd take Doc Pohl north with me and help him. I'd pay men to carry him back to Dawson.

And leave the hotel? Leave Bill to sniff around, for weeks. I'd come back and he'd have stolen it right out from under me.

I wanted to scream. To cry and scream out all that anger and fear, but that was weakness. This hotel had eyes what were looking for weakness, ears what were listening out for the weeping. I weren't about to give Bill Mathers and his damn spies any rope.

I composed myself, checked my face for signs of sorrow or illness in the glass and readied myself for the evening and the revelry it would bring.

It was past midnight and I was taking a rest in my room when there came a knock at the door. I expected Giselle, but it was Laura-Lynn. She was a quiet girl, pretty in her way and had a simple, wifely aspect, which a lot of the gents took to.

I patted the bed and she sat down.

She looked at her hands and wouldn't speak for a time.

'You know who it was?' I asked.

She nodded.

'You'd best tell me.'

'What you gonna do?'

'That's not your concern.'

Laura-Lynn went quiet again. Getting up the courage to tell on her friend. I knew the agony of it. But hers didn't last long. These girls were sisters when they felt like it, but they'd quick as stab each other in the back if they thought it'd get them what they wanted.

'It was Molly,' she said and my heart dropped.

'Why you think that?'

'I seen her going into your office last night. I've seen her go into your office a lot, Ma. She said something about a secret you had. She wanted to know it. Said she'd seen you holding a letter when Bill Mathers stopped by yesterday.'

I didn't want to be believe it, but I had been holding Sam's letter and it had been Molly who saw me, and she saw where I'd locked it away. Laura-Lynn weren't there, unless she was hiding in a doorway down the hall, so Molly had to be gabbing. That made it worse. Taking a secret and keeping it was one thing, but whispering it to every Sally and Samuel like it was hers put an anger in my chest so deep it cut my bones.

I struggled to keep from running down the hall to that girl, pulling off whatever gent was with her and tossing her out on her ear, naked as Jesus.

'Ma, I think . . . I think she's seeing Bill Mathers.'

My eyes widened. Shock weren't the same as surprise, and I weren't surprised. Bill had had a cockstand for Molly from the moment she'd stepped off the boat. I knew he'd find a way. Damn him. He must have given her the bruises, made her fearful. Made Molly lie to me. For what? Is that why she couldn't run away with that gent she said she loved? Because of Bill?

'I seen her with him in town a couple of times,' Laura-Lynn went on. 'Cosying up at the Tivoli Theatre and Bill's saloon.

Laughing, kissing, you know. I figure they're sweethearts, but he ain't paying as far as I know.'

I took a breath and forced down the rage into a neat box. 'Thank you, Laura-Lynn. You did right coming to see me.'

She got up to leave, but stopped by the door.

'There's something else. She was asking me for my rich gents. The ones in the gold and who had nothing but dust. Asking their names, where they were mining. She asked Giselle too. I figure she's been nagging all the girls.'

'You tell her?'

Laura-Lynn shook her head. 'She's got no trouble finding gents. She can't have mine too.'

'All right. You can go. Not a word of this to no one, you hear?'

She let out a small laugh. 'As if. I don't want "snitch" on my tombstone.'

She left and closed the door quietly behind her.

I lay back in my bed, but I knew there would be no sleep for me that night. My heart ached for Sam, for Molly and what she'd done. She knew about him. About my love, and his love and his hurt. God, I was angry; that girl took all my fondness of her and spat on it. Seeing Bill Mathers. Of all the people she could be bedding, why him? But I knew the answer. When Bill wanted, he could be the most charming fella this side of the Mason–Dixon. And he had money. Up here, on the edge of things, where the law was only words on paper no one could read, a man like Bill Mathers was a king, and every girl up here wanted to be his queen.

I had hoped keeping Molly away from him would have saved her from that. But she'd made her bed and she'd made it with that soulless piece of shit. Now she could damn well lie in it.

I flung my door open so hard it banged against the dresser,

smashing a glass.

Downstairs the piano didn't miss a key, but some folks cast their eyes up. On the balcony, doors opened to see what the commotion was; gents and their girls watched me stride across the boards, thunder in my eyes.

'What's the trouble, Ma?' asked one gent, but he didn't get an answer.

I went to Molly's room and threw open the door. She was unlacing, gent on the bed pulling off his breeches.

'Get out,' I said to the man.

'Now hang on,' he tried, standing up, outrage starting, but I shot him a look so fierce he backed away.

'Out.'

He grabbed his coat and hurried past me, muttering some nonsense about a refund. Molly had a fear on her. She was in the corner, a trapped mouse, and I had my claws out.

'Ma . . .'

'Don't you *dare*,' I said, spitting every word out like it was a burning coal.

'Please, Ma. It isn't what you think.'

'You read my letter?'

'What? Of course I didn't.'

'You saw me with it. The only one who did. And you would dare lie to my face. I want you gone.'

Molly grabbed my hands. 'Please don't! You know me, I would never lie to you.'

My chin quivered and I bit my lip. Could barely get words out without letting tears out with them. The anger in me was hot, my temper right up to my hair and I couldn't hear that begging. Couldn't hear nothing beyond the rushing blood in my ears.

'You ain't lying? Who gave you those bruises, huh?'

She looked to the door, where Laura-Lynn and Giselle were standing. Molly's eyes went hard. 'It doesn't matter. They're nothing.'

The red flared in me. '"Nothing." Must be a mighty big nothing that's worth lying to me over. You're out,' I said, my voice shaking. 'Get your stuff. Take what you can carry, I'll have the rest sent to you.'

'Ma! Please, let's talk about this. I don't know what's happened!'

I met her eyes. Those big doe-eyes I could charge extra for now full of tears. 'So you ain't giving Bill Mathers a free ride? Along with that other fella, huh? There any man in Dawson you're not bedding for free?'

She opened her mouth, but couldn't lie quick enough. When she spoke, her voice was paper-thin. 'I'm not . . . who said . . . ?'

'Get out.'

Her breeding was gone, those high manners and society charms. The real Molly finally on show, now she'd been caught. She dropped to her knees and grabbed my skirts. 'I've got no one. You're all I have, Ma.'

'You got that boy you love. Go to him.'

She sat back on her heels, the fight leaving her, the tears falling free. 'He's married. Besides, I ended it – you heard me. You can't do this, Ma. I didn't do anything wrong. You can't do this to me.'

I bent down to her, lifted her chin and brought my face right close, so she couldn't mistake me.

'This is my house. I can do what I want.'

Molly's chin trembled, those big eyes were shot through with red. Her voice weren't the clear ringing bell it used to be, it was cracked now. Broken, like her. 'I don't have anywhere else to go.'

'Then you go to Bill. You tell him I'm done with you. I had two rules, Molly. You broke 'em both.'

Her eyes widened and I'd never seen such fear so close. 'Ma ...'

'*Get out of my house.*'

She sat back on her ankles and put her face in her hands. I felt the quiet from the hotel, like every person in here held their breath, listening. Let them; they'd hear I weren't no one to be crossed.

I turned my back on her and walked away. Giselle and Laura-Lynn rushed from the door. The rest of the girls were looking out their doors or up from the bar. All the miners were staring. Jerry, Harry. Even Jessamine had stepped out from the kitchen.

'What you lot gawking at?' I shouted, the rage in me ebbing away to despair. 'Jerry, get everyone in here a shot of bourbon. Play that damn piano!'

A cheer went up. The music resumed and I went into my room and leaned my back against the door. Tears threatened my eyes. Full and fierce. But I stopped them. Sucked it up like my mother taught me. Don't let 'em see you cry, she'd say, and if you do, make 'em pay for it.

I had half a mind to go running back to Molly and wrap my arms around her, forgive her. But she was in bed with Bill, and God only knew who else. She knew why my hatred of that man ran so deep. They all did. They knew why I'd burn this place before seeing it in his hands. But she took that blade and cut me with it.

I heard crying on the balcony. Mutterings from the other girls. Slow steps that stopped outside my door.

'Ma, please,' came Molly's voice. I closed my eyes against it. Tried not to hear her. 'I didn't do anything.'

A few minutes passed and I heard her footsteps move away. I went to the window, looked out over the slanted and mismatched rooftops of Dawson, tried to put my mind somewhere else. But I couldn't. Down in the street, Molly stood in the mud, bag under her arm, shawl thrown around her shoulders. The lights from my hotel and a dozen saloons and stores lit up the streets, but behind them, out of their glare, was the real darkness. The place of thieves who'd cut your throat for the gold flake stuck on your sleeve.

Molly was staring at that darkness. She looked like she did when she first came here, skittish, lost. A pretty lamb in a den of wolves. She looked down the street, toward Bill's saloon, then up at my window.

Her eyes found mine. Even this far away I could see tears, glistening in the lights. Her face broke and, with it, my heart.

I could still change my mind, couldn't I? Call down to her. Dawson was dangerous, cut-throats in every corner. She weren't safe. She kept denying it, didn't she? But she'd read my letter, stuck her fingers in a part of my life I kept mine, and she'd let that monster into her bed. There weren't a sorry big enough for that.

But still . . .

I ran from my room, down the stairs and pushed past the drunks, past Harry.

'Ma?' he called, but I didn't stop.

I burst out the doors, expecting to see her standing there, expecting to see her waiting. I'd let her apologise again and I'd forgive and get the truth out of her.

But Molly was gone. Her footsteps lost in the mud with a thousand others.

KATE

I arrived at the southern tip of Lake Bennett, worn to the bone, feet bloody from walking alongside the horse, back stiff from riding it, my grazed arm sore and itching. Yukon limped and panted each step. We had travelled alone for weeks. I was not quick, despite travelling light, and I watched those I recognised from the avalanche pass me again and again. One day on the trail was much like any other. Beauty hiding brutal truth. Towering mountains and black spruce forests stood beside paths beaten into the landscape by desperate men and the bleached, crow-picked bones of their horses.

At Lake Bennett I found a city of white canvas tents sprung up on the banks, reaching miles down the valley in either direction. The place swarmed with people, thousands upon thousands camped and waiting. The sound of it! The smell! It overwhelmed and I could find nowhere to escape it.

I'd never been as tired. Never as cold or hungry. Half my food had been lost in the avalanche and the other half rationed to mouthfuls. But I'd made it. Survived an ordeal that would have made any man turn back without judgement. All I had to do now was find a boat, sail it north and I would be in Dawson in a matter of weeks.

I pushed through the throngs of people, their tents, their supplies, the piles of timber and frames made for boat-building, the rows and rows of flat-bottomed vessels and the men selling them. I tied my horse to a post and, Yukon at my heels, followed the buzz of conversation towards the shore. I would buy a boat, or buy passage on one. I would leave that night if I could.

I reached the water and all those thoughts fled my mind. I dropped to my knees in the mud.

The lake was still clogged with ice. The river beyond it impassable.

I felt the futility of my task in every inch of me. Felt Charlotte being pulled further and further from me. My legs were lead, and even the stones cutting into my knees and the churned slush of mud and ice numbing them could not make me move.

Why did I ever think I could do this?

I thought of poor Mr Gunderson, what he had said: if the river was frozen, only God could say when the journey would resume. It could be weeks before the ice melted. Months even. Charlotte might not have that long.

I looked about me. Thousands of people were camped around the lake, pushing for what little land remained. They waded through the mud, checking and rechecking great mounds of crates and bales, their boats upturned and useless. The temporary city was endless and I was one woman alone within it.

I had no tent. No supplies. No companion. All had been lost in the avalanche. But I still had Mr Everett's money and, in this lawless place, there was nothing it could not buy.

I stood, every inch of me aching, and set about my first task. To find a place to sleep.

'Excuse me,' I said, grabbing a passing man.

He looked shocked at the intrusion, but soon found his manners. 'Miss?'

'Do you know where I can get dogs? A sled to take me over the ice?'

He laughed. 'Ain't been dogs here for weeks.'

My heart sank further into the mud. No way out. Too far and too dangerous to walk. I wasn't any good to Charlotte dead.

'A hotel then?' I asked.

He pointed along the shore. 'Better be quick.'

I let him go and he blended into the masses until I could no longer pick him out.

I led my horse through the ramshackle town, Yukon trotting beside us. The trail spewed more and more people into this tiny strip of land, though thankfully the stream was weak and the rush was slowed by the avalanche blocking the way. It would take weeks to dig it out, I was sure.

I found what they were calling Bennett City, where a few wooden buildings had replaced the tents. Skaguay had been a hasty town, put together in a matter of months, yet there was at least some organisation about it. A central street, a sense of momentum, of passing through, but here all that was gone and chaos reigned. A saloon fit to burst with rowdy custom. A building calling itself a hotel, with a full sign in the window and drunkards on the doorstep.

The two streets of Bennett, if one could call them that, were barely passable. Mud up to the knees, horses and gear sinking, men struggling against it. One such man I had seen before on the trail. I had thought of him as the clean man, but he was that no more. He was caked in mud and his face, once shaven, now sported a beard. He pulled on the horse himself, over-loaded with supplies and knee-deep in the mire.

'There she is,' came a voice from behind me. I turned and saw the kind woman from the trail, the one whose scarf was still wrapped around my arm. The one I didn't want to wait for, though we ended up in the same place anyway.

I smiled. I didn't realise how good it would feel to see a familiar face.

The woman and her husband stood in a line of others and beckoned me over. They were queuing for the outfitters. The stall – not even a building, but a lean-to with two men at a table – sold abandoned supplies. The line stretched halfway to the lake with those recently arrived.

'You made it,' she said.

'Just about.'

The woman knelt to Yukon. 'And so did you, pup.'

She reached into her pocket and offered him a piece of jerky. His tail went and I believe he fell in love right there.

'I'm sorry I left like that after the avalanche. I wasn't think-ing clearly.'

'None of us were. Where are you pitching? We have our tent half a mile up the east bank.'

'I don't know. I don't have a tent; that was with . . . on the other horses.'

She nodded. The line shuffled on and I kept pace.

'You're staying with us then.'

Her husband looked up then, as if just realising his wife was speaking. 'Oh?'

'We can't let this young lady sleep in the mud, now can we?'

He looked at me. 'I suppose not. We got space.'

He had a soft, round face and a voice to match. She wore the pants between them, that much was obvious.

'I'm Kate Kelly,' I said and held out my injured arm.

'Elizabeth Jones,' said the woman, 'but I only answer to Biddy. This chunk of cheese is Walter. We're heading back to our claim after a winter down south, getting fat.'

She patted Walter's barrel-like belly and he rolled his eyes.

'I'm too old for this,' he muttered in a not unpleasant way.

I felt myself relax around them in a way I hadn't so far on this trip, not even with Mr Gunderson.

A gunshot bit the air.

Everyone jumped, covered their heads, searched for the source.

It was him. The not-so-clean man. He sat in the mud, panting, pistol in his hand, dead horse in front of him. He shouted something I couldn't hear and pounded the muck with his fists like an irate child.

'Who is that man?' I asked, more to myself than anyone else.

'I heard about him,' said Biddy. 'Back in Skaguay he was buying up everything, just to get to the weight limit. Didn't even seem to care if his gear was quality or not or if he had the right stuff. He's got money, you can tell, but he's not spending wisely.'

'Wisdom'll save your life out here,' said Walter. 'That and a good coat.'

Biddy smiled and nudged him.

'I feel I know him,' I said.

'I never heard his name, but I like to know who I'm riding with, so I asked about.'

A true gossip is worth more than gold to a reporter. 'Oh?'

'All I know is he's heading to Dawson and making quick time about it. Been trying to find dogs to take him, so watch out for that pup you got.'

'He must have the fever worse than most.'

The man pulled himself out of the mud and shouted to a group of men nearby. Packers. He pulled money from somewhere and threw it toward them. It landed on the ground and the men swarmed.

I shook my head. Realised Biddy was doing the same.

'Behaviour like that will get you killed up here,' she said quietly, then turned her attention back to me. Smile wide on her face. 'Now, what about you? There are no right-minded women in the Klondike, that's the truth of it. I asked after you too, Miss Reporter.'

'I'm surprised anyone took notice of me.'

Biddy waved her hand. 'A pretty girl like you, out here by herself? You're the talk of the trail, my dear. Now, let's us gals leave Walter to this line and you and me will start on supper.'

Biddy and Walter's tent was warm and tidy and did indeed have plenty of room. A pipe ran up from the stove and out of a hole in the canvas, a black iron kettle sat bubbling on the blacktop. Soft yellow light from oil lamps pushed away the cold grey light of the outdoors. There were two sets of bunks, a table and chairs and a stack of crates, which I assumed were their remaining supplies.

'Take a load off,' said Biddy and pulled out a chair.

I had not sat in a chair since Skaguay. My back protested, refused to relax. Yukon was in his element, lolling on the wooden boards by the stove, showing his belly to all-comers. Biddy made the tea and sat with me.

'I thought you'd turn back,' she said.

I cradled the hot cup and let the steam rise over me. 'Sometimes I wish I had.'

'You must have something big calling you to Dawson.'

A gossip has a wonderful way of nudging just the right

buttons to get their titbits. I didn't begrudge it; if nothing else, it was a small joy even to speak to someone. To have someone show an interest. I had left many things back in Kansas, but a concerned friend was not one.

'I was commissioned by a man named George Everett to write about the experience of those in the Klondike, for various newspapers in Kansas and Missouri. The road here, the mining, the living conditions. He is interested in a venture. And there are newspapers back home that will pay for my reports.'

How far away that seemed. Another world, another life. For weeks now all there had been was the trail, one step at a time, in a line of others doing the same. In a beautiful place that would kill you without knowing or caring. The expectations of a man so removed seemed petty in the face of these mountains, this ice, the horrors of the White Pass.

Biddy gave a wry smile. 'He must be paying you a king's ransom to go through all this.'

'Only when I return.'

She laughed. 'I ain't after your money, sweetheart. I got enough of my own. But really, you doing all this so you can tell a rich man where to mine and what to bring with him?'

What use were secrets here?

'No, not really. My sister is in Dawson. She sent me a letter.'

Biddy sat back. 'I thought as much.'

'I believe she's in danger. I have to get there, help her.'

'Nobody is going anywhere for a while. The ice is thick in the Klondike and every sled dog from here to Seattle is spoken for. You can't fight nature, much as these folk try. I'm sure your sister has people up there looking out for her.'

I smiled, weakly, at Biddy and she took that as a steer to a new conversation.

'You don't have a tent, you don't have any supplies. I take it you don't have a boat?'

I shook my head. 'My guide was to arrange it all.'

A moment of solemnity settled between us. The sound of the avalanche rang in my ears and, I believe, in Biddy's too. It was not something easily forgotten by those who were there when the mountain fell.

Biddy reached out for my arm and unwrapped her scarf from it. The wound was dry, healed to thick scabs of red and black.

'That's going to scar.'

I looked at the ridges of the cuts. 'What's another scar?'

She watched me as I ran my fingers over the scabs. It was a graze that ran the length of my forearm, small scratches mixed with wide cuts. I pulled down my sleeve and took a sip of tea from the steaming cup.

'You got grit in you,' said Biddy. 'That's good. You'll need it.'

She set about cooking a meal and refused my help. Walter returned an hour or so later, pulling a sled laden with gear and supplies: a storm lantern, snowshoes, fishing poles, crates of tinned meat and more.

He smiled when he saw me. 'I got your friend here something.'

He knelt to Yukon, who was still dozing by the fire. Walter rubbed his belly, then opened a tin of corned beef and dumped the contents in a bowl. Yukon twisted and rolled in an ungainly fashion, trying to right himself, and I could only laugh.

'Thank you,' I said, and Yukon's guzzling spoke his gratitude clear enough.

Walter put a crate of tins on the table. 'For you both.'

I frowned. 'You didn't have to do that. I can pay you.'

He held out his hand, shook his head.

'We won't take your money, darling,' said Biddy from the stove. 'So stop offering.'

I looked in the crate. Tins of various meats, potatoes, fruit, carrots, peas, beans. So many beans.

'This is so kind, thank you.'

'She's coming on the boat with us,' Biddy said to Walter and he nodded.

'No, it's all right, I'll find passage.'

'Biddy's made up her mind,' said Walter, smiling. 'Ain't no changing it now, trust me – I've tried.'

He took off his boots, kissed his wife and lay down in one of the bunks.

Biddy looked at me. 'All right?'

I felt a rush of emotion. All this kindness, it almost hurt, as if I could not believe it was real, because this world wasn't kind, this world wasn't generous, and yet somehow these people were. And they'd found me. I could only nod, for if I spoke I would burst into tears. Were they more than they seemed? Was this some ruse or con to steal from me? Yet what did I have to steal? Some money they clearly didn't need, a dog who could do little for them. Perhaps they were just good people. The idea seemed at once absurd and wonderful.

'Good,' said Biddy. 'Now get yourself comfortable, we've got a long wait for that ice to break. Then it's a month on the water, at least.'

I did as she said and, that night, slept as soundly as if I was in my own bed back in Kansas. Yukon slept with me, and even Walter's snores couldn't disturb me.

It was in that tent, warm, secure, after a good sleep, that my excitement began to return. The horror of the days before dulled to a bad memory and the spirit of adventure returned.

I, the younger daughter of a well-to-do family, was not meant to be here. I should have been married, knee-deep in children and misery, when all I wanted was to be a writer. I would have been if my mother had had her way, but I thanked the Lord every day that my father didn't share her view.

I was a child of the outdoors, a wild thing, made more of mud and scrapes than manners and poise. My father did not try to change that. He knew, because he was the same, that trying to make me something I was not would be like trying to alter the flow of a river by standing in the water and shouting. My sister was not so lucky. My mother's words meant more to her, cut deeper than my father's reassurances. I wondered sometimes if that was why she ran away with that boy, why she married so rashly, to escape a mother who expected so much, and yet so little, of her first child.

I thought of Charlotte constantly in those days at Lake Bennett. Spoke of her to Biddy: of our youth in Topeka, how I would sneak candies from the store while she distracted the owner, how I ripped my Sunday dress (on purpose) and Charlotte hid it from my mother, spun a tale of it being stolen by raccoons. How I would spend nights out in the woods camping under one of mother's best sheets, making a fire and fishing for my own dinner. Biddy listened and told her own tales of their gold-mining success and obsession, of how they now owned a fine, sprawling home in Portland, where once they were on the verge of starvation.

'Gold can solve all your problems if you let it,' she said.

'Or cause them,' I replied, and she barked out a laugh.

'What will you do when you get home?' Walter asked me.

I shrugged. 'I am not at all sure I will go home. I believe my life is just beginning.'

We settled into a routine of sorts. Waking, cooking, reading, playing cards, exploring the camp, drinking a little too much in the evening, and repeating it all the following day and the days after. My frustration at the delay often boiled over into snapped comments and thrown cards, but they were always patient with me.

The days were warming and Biddy suspected it wouldn't be too much longer. The stream of people joining the tent city had slowed to a dribble. The avalanche would have blocked the way for weeks, if not months, so there was a welcome respite from the constant shuffle for space.

It had been a week of waiting when I saw the clean man again. I had taken to wandering the shore, watching the boat-builders work their whipsaws. I was sitting upon a crate, sketching a lone man braving the ice to fish, when a shout came from behind me.

'Get off that!'

I started, dropped my pencil in the mud. I retrieved it and, when I stood up, there he was. Directing all his ire right at me.

'Excuse me?' I said.

He strode over. Gun bouncing on his hip. 'I said get off. That's not a seat.'

'I'm sorry. It is a crate, though, and I don't think I'd do it any damage.'

His face behind the beard was red, his eyes hard. 'I don't care. You're trying to steal from me, aren't you?'

'No. I'm not. I'm sitting.'

He sneered. 'Don't give me that back-talk, woman. You get gone. I don't want to see you anywhere near.'

I squinted at him. 'I know you.'

That surprised him. 'What? You don't know me.'

'I do. But I don't know why. Who are you?'

'None of your goddamn business. Get the hell out of here!'

He was a taut string. Not an especially big man, didn't seem built for this place, and his troubles on the trail said as much. I walked away, more annoyed than anything else. How infuriating to know someone and yet not. It was like having a seed stuck in my tooth and no pick to loosen it. But one thing I did know: it was not only horses this man treated with disdain and disregard. I avoided him from then on, watching him from afar, sketching his likeness in my book. Yukon growled when he saw him, as if the dog knew exactly who the man was and wanted me to stay as far away as the trail would allow.

ELLEN

BOULDER CREEK, KLONDIKE, LATE JUNE 1898

Dawson seems like months ago, yet only two days have passed.
Quiet ones. Fruitless ones. I clean, he digs, I clean, he digs.
The fortune-teller's words won't leave me. A lover. A choice.
The end of a marriage. Freedom.

The river flows, the ice melted. Perhaps he will come on the
next wave of boats. Perhaps he is already here.

I go to the river. Charlie shovels dirt into the new rocker
box. A line of sluice boxes snakes the bank. Trenches, pits,
piles of dirt and felled trees blight the landscape. Boards mark
a path. This is a mine for three men and yet Charlie digs alone.

'Elly,' he says and smiles to see me. 'Is it lunch already?'

The sun is barely halfway to its zenith.

'I came to see you. How is the new box?'

He grins like a child. 'See for yourself.'

The rocker box is already sodden and covered in dirt.
Something new turned old in just a few days.

He puts aside his shovel, then takes the top off the box and
lifts the wooden lattice, which catches the biggest nuggets.

Hessian sacking lines the box beneath to catch the finest gold. Charlie runs a finger through the dirt caught in the sacking. Something glints.

'You see it?'

I lean closer. A nugget. About the size of a bean. And another. And a third. And all around, grains of gold. I feel a chill come over me.

'You struck?'

His smile falters. 'I am close. This is just a taste. A few hours of washing a new section of the river. Up there, you see?'

I see a ragged hole cut in the land where a stand of alder had grown.

'I see.'

'This is rich land, Elly, I know it.'

'Is that why Bill Mathers wants it?'

Charlie looks like I have struck him. He tries to laugh away the question. My expression tells him he cannot.

'Well,' he says, 'Bill has expressed an interest in the land.'

'How much is he offering?'

'A trifling sum.'

'How much, Charlie?'

'Ten thousand dollars.'

My breath leaves me. 'And why have you not shaken his hand? That money would do so much for us.'

In truth, as the shock leaves me, I see it would buy us passage back to Seattle on a steamer and the rest would go to my father.

'This land is worth a hundred times that, and Bill knows it. Ellen, you have to trust me. I am your husband – I know best in these matters.'

I laugh. I cannot help it, but I do. Charlie's hopeful eyes turn hard.

'You'd best get back and make lunch. I'll be hungry,' he says. He holds my eyes and I his. It is an old game we play. Who will look away first.

I almost tell him I know of our debts. That my father has forsaken us because of Charlie's failures.

Not yet. My powder remains dry. But I hold his eyes.

Charlie blinks.

He always does.

He does not return to the cabin for lunch or dinner. I put a plate outside and collect it empty a few hours later.

The days are longer now. The light stays until past eleven and rises at four. Charlie works each minute and I wait for the cry of 'Gold! Gold!' that never comes.

Soon the sun will barely set, the light will stretch into darkness and the madness will begin.

I have slept but the light has not changed. Charlie is not in bed, but I hear his pick at the rocks. He has not spoken to me in a day and I am glad of it. Perhaps I must find my own way to leave. To make money apart from my husband. Yet should he find out, I would lose it, for what is mine is his, as is the way of marriage. The freeze comes in a few short months. I must leave or find an income before then, or be stuck here through a deadly winter we cannot afford.

I perform the morning chores. Collecting water. Boiling it. Preparing a breakfast. Cleaning. Cleaning. Cleaning.

I sing as I scrub the floors and do not hear the horse approach.

The pick stops its beat and my song falters. Then I hear them. Voices. Hurried and unwelcome.

I go to the back door, wipe my hands and press my ear to it.

A woman's voice. Charlie speaking in whispers. Silence, then soft murmurings. Then a raised voice, the simmering of an argument.

I open the door and see my husband push apart from another woman.

'Ellen,' he says. 'This is ... um ...'

I enjoy his discomfort and let it linger. She, however, shows only shame.

'Mrs Rhodes,' she says, 'I beg your pardon for the intrusion.'

'Who are you?'

She shakes her head as if shaking loose her manners. 'My name is Molly. I'm a ... friend ... of Mr Rhodes.'

'I see. And what are you doing here?'

Charlie steps forward to me. 'She was returning my pocket watch. I must have dropped it when we were in Dawson.'

He holds it up and I know full well that it has been with him. I allow him the lie, drawing on my last reserves of social grace.

The poor woman is desperate, looks like she hasn't eaten in days. I have seen her before, in Dawson, outside a hotel, but she always looked well kept. Hair in the latest styles, lips rouged, but never too much. An air of class about her, though her business was clear. Suddenly my suspicions of Charlie's whore are no longer the bitter thoughts of a gold widow.

I look at them both. They know they are caught. I can leave them their fiction or I can explode it.

'How kind,' I say. 'Would you like to come in? Supper is about ready.'

Charlie's eyes bulge. He begins to protest. I find I am not angry, but curious who this woman is who can hold my husband's affection.

'Oh no, I couldn't, I just came to speak to Charlie,' Molly replies, then looks at him. 'To return his watch.'

'I insist,' I say. 'It will be nice to get to know one of my husband's friends. Isn't that right, Charlie?'

He is a caught fish. Mouth agape. 'Yes. Yes, of course.'

Molly looks at him a moment longer. 'Then yes, I would be happy to.'

I step aside for my husband's mistress and do not hold the door for him.

She takes off her shawl and I hang it. She smells of dirt and sweat. There is a shadow on her skin, unwashed and allowed to linger. For a moment she looks embarrassed, and I feel a pin-sharp sadness for her. But it quickly fades. 'What a lovely home you have,' she says.

'It does us well enough,' I say.

Charlie sits at the table, for he doesn't know what else to do. His hands tap and scratch and do not still; his gaze bounces from wife to whore, whore to wife. Molly sits straight-backed, poised as if at high tea.

'It is a dream, a home like this and on such rich land,' she says, and I laugh.

That surprises them both.

'Isn't it? Rich, I mean?' she asks and looks at Charlie.

'It is. Richest land in the Klondike,' he says. 'I just have to dig a bit deeper for it than the boys down in Bonanza. We're higher up the valley here, there is more soil to remove.'

An excuse I keep hearing.

Molly smiles. It is polite and practised, and I wonder what of her is her and what of her is the brothel. As I watch her, I see sadness. I see an ache in her, as if she has not slept a full night in years. She is a handsome woman brought low by this place, these men, this love of gold. A sadness I know well.

I begin to prepare coffee and a meal. I turn my back and feel their eyes connect. Feel a silent longing pass between them. I envy it, though not in the way I expect.

'May I help?' she asks.

'No, no, you're a guest. Ellen doesn't need any help,' he says and I share a look with her. A knowing one. A man has spoken and we must abide.

I find I do not hate her, though I enjoy Charlie's discomfort at her presence. His squirming and averted eyes.

I serve the meal – thick slices of ham, boiled potatoes, cabbage greens, bread – and sit across from her.

We eat and I watch.

'Molly here is a talented artist,' Charlie says.

'Oh no, I'm not at all,' she replies, but I see the smile. The beginnings of a blush.

'She's modest too. She drew the Dawson Hotel once, didn't you? You wouldn't know the picture from the real thing. It hangs there now. In the bar.'

'Really? I didn't know you were so acquainted with that place,' I say and Charlie's pride dims.

'I'm not, but I have stayed there a time or two on my visits to town. It is as respectable a place as any.'

We all know different, but the Klondike is built as much on the false claims as the real ones.

'Where is your husband, Molly?' I ask.

'I have none. He died a time back and left me with debt. I heard there was a fortune here.'

'And you came to mine?'

She looks at Charlie. His smile is gone, his eyes sombre. 'Yes, I suppose I did.'

'By yourself?'

She looks back to me. 'The women in my family have always had an adventurous streak, you could say.'

'Something needed up here. Do you own a claim?' I ask.

'No, but I wish to. I fear if I wait much longer, it will be too late, though, and without the capital . . .' She lets the sentence fade.

'That is why you're here, then? For money?'

She looks up at me with wide eyes. I can see why Charlie fell for her. Innocence. Deference. Dreams. All things this place has beaten from me.

'No, Mrs Rhodes. Not at all. I . . .'

'Good, because there isn't any. Right, Charlie?'

'That's enough, Ellen,' he says and I abide.

I could ask more questions, hear more lies, uncover the whole truth of their acquaintance, but I don't want to. I am not angry at her. I don't wish to hurt her. She is as much a prisoner in this place as I am. As much a victim of unkept promises as I.

Charlie, however, I cannot look at.

Finally the plates are empty, the coffee drunk.

'Thank you, Mrs Rhodes,' she says. 'That's the best meal I've had in years.'

Another lie, but I'll take it.

'You're kind, Molly. You'd best be on your way now.'

Charlie stands. 'I'll see you out.'

He steps outside, puts on his boots and I am alone with her. There is a feeling between us. An understanding.

'Mrs Rhodes—'

'There really is no money,' I say. 'If you wish to see my husband, do it elsewhere. I won't have gossip. A woman has little here but her reputation, and I won't see mine tarnished.'

'Truly, Mrs Rhodes, I did not come here for money.'

'Then why?'

Her chin trembles as she opens her mouth to speak.

'Ready?' Charlie appears at the doorway. Molly gives a tense smile and the moment has passed.

I watch her go with him. Down the steps, across the beaten earth of the yard to the horses. Her brown mare tied beside Bluebell. That look on her face stays in my mind. If not for money, then what does she want from my husband?

They look back at me. They want privacy. A moment together. I linger, wonder if I should grant it. I think again of the fortune-teller and her prophecy. Of what might await me.

I close the door and leave them to themselves.

The woman said I was at a crossroads, that my marriage would end; but inside me, it has already, in every way but the law. Charlie brought his mistress to my home. She came here, knowing who she was and who I was. I should have been blistering with rage. I should have thrown her out, and Charlie with her. But I felt none of it. I feel none of it.

My marriage is over. Yet the play goes on.

I hear muffled words. Feet scuffing on dirt. I go to the window. He has Molly by the arm, his face close to hers. I see the set of his brow and the anger there. She tries to pull free, but he holds. In her other hand, the reins.

He is speaking, but her face is turned away. Turned towards me. She sees me.

I see her pain. I see something break in her. She is afraid of him and, in that moment, so am I.

She tries to pull away again, but his grip tightens. She winces.

I open the door.

'Charlie,' I shout.

A spell broken. He lets her go, steps away, puts the smile back on the Devil's face.

'Yes, dear? I was just—'

'I need you to chop some wood. We're low.'

He frowns. 'There is half a cord out back.'

'It is gone. I need more before the fire dies.'

I lock eyes with Molly. She rubs her arm, breathes away the fear. There passes between us an understanding. Women, in this place, with these beasts of men, must protect one another.

She mounts her horse and Charlie flinches, lifts a hand to grab the rein.

'Charlie. The wood,' I call and his hand drops.

She moves beyond his reach. 'Thank you, Mrs Rhodes, for the hospitality.'

'Molly . . .' he says, quiet but full of longing.

'Goodbye, Mr Rhodes.'

She pulls away and we both watch her ride down the trail.

Charlie strides to the back of the cabin, to the axe and block. He sees the woodpile. The neat stack that will last us for another two weeks at least. He says nothing, only takes up the axe and begins.

I watch Molly go. Watch the miners down the valley tip their hat to her. I wonder about her life. What kind of a woman comes here alone? What kind of a woman has that freedom? What woman can make a life here through wits and her own steam? Make her own decisions. Control her own fate. Live as she wishes.

That evening, as I lie in bed by myself, with Charlie still out washing rocks, I ask myself a question: would I stay here if Charlie was gone?

To my surprise, the answer is not an immediate and deafening 'No'.

It is not this land I wish to be free of, but the man I am forced to share it with.

Or perhaps – and the realisation comes like a drench of

iced water – that I am forced to share it at all.

Freedom. Wasn't that what the fortune-teller's card had shown? There is freedom to be had here. A new kind, unknown in the old world.

Perhaps here, on the edge of the new, that freedom may also belong to a woman.

MARTHA

'Ma?'

I didn't want to hear. I stared at the wall, at the drawing of the hotel Molly had done over winter. She drew it how she imagined it would look in summer. I'd framed it, hung it above the piano.

'*Ma?*'

I pulled myself away. 'What?'

Jerry, behind the bar, nodded to the door. A woman stood there. Something familiar about her, but on a second look I couldn't place her. Couldn't tell her age, but she wore a heavy shawl over a dark-red dress. Embroidered with patterns, small coins sewn on, a red scarf over her head and her eyes black with kohl.

'Help you?' I asked.

She smiled, lips thick with paint. Something jingled as she walked across the floor.

'You're Martha Malone?' she asked.

I stood up from the piano stool. 'I am. And you are?'

'Here to help.'

'I don't need help.'

'Not yet. But you will.'

Jerry, drying glasses behind the bar, watched us both with a smirk. It was early, none of the girls or Jessamine were up and Harry was still at home. The place was empty but for us three.

'You have a beautiful home,' she said. She seemed always to be smiling, you could even hear it in her voice, but it weren't smug.

'Thank you. What do you want?'

The woman was so still. I'd never known such calm. People in Dawson are all jitters and shouting, rushing around after gold and women, but her? None of that touched her.

'Do you know what I do?'

I looked her head to toe. 'I can guess.'

Another smile. 'Give me a table. I'll tell the fortunes of every man who walks in here.'

I folded my arms across my chest. 'What's in it for me?'

'A third of my fee.'

I weighed it up. Men up here were dumb and desperate; they'd pay good money after bad to hear they would strike it rich and go home a king. Especially from a woman who looked the part as much as she did.

'Half.'

She sucked her teeth. 'Forty per cent.'

'Half.'

Her smile grew. 'You have a deal, Ma.'

I stretched out my hand to shake on it.

'On one condition,' she said.

'Condition?' I repeated. 'You're asking of me – I'm the one should be making conditions.'

'This one costs you nothing but time.'

'What you want?'

'A reading with you.'

I let out a small laugh, shook my head. 'I don't go in for all that mumbo-jumbo.'

'It's just a conversation. There are things you need to hear.'

'What kind of things?'

Her eyes flicked to Jerry and back. 'A reading is all I ask. Then you can decide for yourself if I'm good enough for the table.'

What the hell; for half her take, I could give her ten minutes. I lifted my chin to Jerry and he put down the glass he'd been cleaning and disappeared out the back. I offered the woman a chair and we sat together.

'You got a crystal ball or some such?' I asked.

'Yes. But it's not for you. Tools like that are for them,' she nodded toward the door, to the people going about their day. 'I tell them what they want to hear. But I will tell you what you need to know.'

'What do I need to know?'

'Let's find out.'

The chair was suddenly uncomfortable, one leg too short, it rocked, made a sickness rise in me. I'd fix it. Or have Harry fix it. He was good with all manner of trade. Or maybe I'd trade Tom at the Aurora for some new ones, he always had—

'Ma?'

My attention snapped back to her.

The fortune-teller's hands were waiting, palm up, on the table. 'Your hands, please.'

I shifted, tried to get comfy. I gave her my hands, rested them in her palms. Her skin was so warm, like she'd had her hands by a fire all morning.

Her thumbs brushed against my palms, over all the lines

and scars. She looked like she was reading a book, not skin, eyes roaming back and forth.

'What do you see?' I asked.

She stretched out the skin on my left hand. The line curving around the base of my thumb was broken.

'You are a good person, beneath the show you put on for these people,' she said.

A show? Was she calling me a liar? 'Hang on now.'

'Just as the sun does not mean to burn you, what I say is not meant to hurt. It is merely the truth as I see it.'

She held my gaze and I hers long as I could, but there was something about this woman – her own show – that made me wary. Like she weren't quite real and soon as she walked out my door, she'd disappear.

'What truth is that?'

'You have a great deal of love within you. For your home. The women who live here. And,' she stroked one of the lines on my palm, 'for a man. You don't see him often because your lives are not on the same path. You weave about each other like dancers, touching, then parting. But that will not last much longer.'

My throat went dry. 'How . . . how do you know that? Who told you?'

Her smile turned sad. 'You did. Your fate is etched in your skin. A book of you. I have merely learned to read the language.'

I swallowed, felt my teeth grind. 'What else does it say?'

She looked again. The smile faltered. 'He is stuck, hurt. But there is more.'

I felt the horror return. The letter, the fear when I'd read those words.

'More?'

She turned her attention to my right hand. 'There is darkness ahead. A death you cannot prevent.'

'Whose death?'

Not his, I prayed, please not him.

She shook her head, frowned. 'I cannot see. But you will blame yourself for it.' She gripped my hands and pulled me closer. 'You will face a choice between what you think you want and what you truly want. Listen to your soul. This place, it is not real. It is but a blink in the eye of the world. Do not give your life to it.'

'My life?'

I gasped as her nails dug into my palms. I tried to pull away, but she held me. Drew me closer until our foreheads all but touched.

Her voice turned urgent whisper. 'I see fire.'

I heard Bill Mathers's veiled threat all over again. *You hear about the fire . . . ?*

I yanked my hands free.

'That's enough,' I said. My heart was going, breath trembling in my throat. 'You need to leave. Deal's off.'

She sat back, put her hands flat on the table. She weren't smiling any more. 'You are balanced on a knife's edge, Martha.'

'Did Bill send you to scare me? That it?'

'No.'

The word, said with no anger or fear, just a cold fact, made me believe her. What a skill she had.

'Out – I want you out,' I said.

She looked down to my belly. 'Your time is no longer your own. Use what is left wisely.'

I stood up, bent down to her so she couldn't mistake me. '*Get. Out.*'

She held my eyes for a second too long and I felt myself

falter. Like I wasn't looking at a woman, but at someone else. Something else. A demon made skin and hair.

The woman blinked and that feeling snapped away.

The smile returned and she stood. 'Take care, Martha.'

Soon as she was gone, I came over queer, dizzy with bright spots in my eyes.

Jerry came back in then, saw me alone, head in hand, and was at my side in a heartbeat.

'All right there, Ma?'

I weren't. In so many ways. But she'd said Sam was hurt, stuck. That, at least, I could do something about. 'Jerry, can you send word to my claim – get two of the miners there, strong ones, to come see me. Today.'

'Yes, Ma,' he replied and threw the towel on the bar, grabbed his jacket from underneath and rushed out.

I closed my eyes and tried to breathe. Tiredness hit me like a landslide and I made my way upstairs. The fortune-teller's words sang in my head. The warning. The threat. Whatever it was. Choices and death and fire. It was all bullshit. Crazy prophecies meant to make you part with coin, get a charm or a bag of dirt to fend it away and go off feeling protected against the world. A scam, nothing more. Hell, I'd make a killing from her if I could bear to look at her.

No matter how much I reasoned it, the strangeness of her didn't go away. The look in her eyes that weren't quite right, the stillness that didn't seem human at all.

I waited at the bar until the two miners came in. Jerry had done well. They were the strong ones. I didn't know their names, but they had eyes not dull with drink and still had all their teeth, which weren't a given up here.

'You wanted to see us, Ma?' the first one said, taller, red beard.

'I got a job for you. Ain't easy, but I'll pay you half a year's wage once you get back.'

Their eyes turned to gold coins.

'I want you to hike up to Beaver Lake. To the trapping station there. You know it?'

The other one nodded; he had a scar across his eye and a voice like gravel down a sluice. 'I know it. Used to hunt moose up there.'

'Good. I want you to go there, ask after Sam Bridger. He's a friend, been hurt, help him out best you can, then come back.'

The pair exchanged a look, like they were weighing it up. 'Half a year's wage?' red beard said.

'On my life. I ever not paid you?'

Another look and that decided it. They both shook my hand and off they went.

It was like a bubble burst in my heart and I could finally relax. It'd take them maybe a week to hike up there, and Sam's friend Davis should be here by then.

'Ma!' Harry called from the door, a second before it swung open.

Bill Mathers strode in, swaying drunk. In his hand was a bottle of whiskey.

'Martha Malone!' he roared, half-cheerful, half-vicious.

The rest of my clientele were pin-drop silent. My girls were out their rooms, gents and all.

'What the hell are you doing here, Bill?'

He showed his teeth. Gold and rotten together. 'What you do with her?'

'Who you hollering about?'

'*Molly*. Where is she?'

Bill came to the bar. Frank Croaker walked in behind him, gun pointed right at Harry's chest.

'She ain't here, and you're too drunk to do anything about it if she was. Get home, sleep it off.'

He took a long drink from the bottle. Brown liquor ran down his chin. 'I know you threw her out. What kind of person does that? Puts a girl on the street.'

'She's a woman, Bill. Not a child. And it ain't your concern what went on between us.'

He took a step toward me. 'She got a man? Huh? That it?'

I tried to keep my trembling inside, but Bill was two arms away from me and there weren't nobody between us. 'I said it ain't your concern.'

He raised his arm and smashed the bottle on the floor.

I jumped. Harry tried to move, but the gun kept him down. Bill picked up an empty glass from the bar and threw it hard on the wood. Glass scattered over the bar, right to my hands. The rest of the miners, damn cowards, just watched.

'Bill,' I said, keeping my voice low, 'time to go.'

'I'll find her,' he snarled. 'Then I'll be coming for you.'

He ground the glass under his boot and spat on the floor. Then he broke into a smile and knocked on the bar like he was tapping out a thought. He took out a tobacco pouch from his pocket, and my heart turned to ice in my chest.

'Listen up,' he shouted and pulled out a rolled smoke, put it to his lips. 'Any man here brings me that girl, I'll give him a hundred dollars.'

Murmurs and shifting feet, looking all around as if she'd be hiding in the damn corner.

'That all she's worth to you?' I said.

Bill laughed. His fingers went to his waistcoat pocket and he took out a matchbox.

'The lady is right. Let's make it two hundred.'

Talk about a red rag to a bull. Half a dozen men ran outside to look. Others started whispering.

'What's the matter with you, Bill?' I said.

He laughed, but it quickly turned sour. Bill didn't answer; it'd take too long to list everything, so instead he struck the match. Lit his cigarette, then he dropped it, still burning, into the pool of whiskey at his feet.

I see fire.

The flame turned blue and spread.

He stared right at me. Wanted me to scream and run and beg him. But I would never beg. He should've learned that by now.

I held my nerve. Held on to the railing. Watched as the flames licked my bar, his boots, caught on his pants. He smiled so wide it near touched his ears.

'She's mine, Martha. You hear me? Molly is mine.'

He stepped out of the flames and nodded to Frank. Frank let Harry go and met Bill at the door. This time Bill didn't turn back, just walked out, fire clinging to his boots.

'Jerry!' I shouted.

He had a pail of water ready and hurled it over the bar. The fire died with a hiss.

I swept away the broken glass on the bar and a piece caught my hand, cutting my palm straight across. I made a fist to stop the bleeding and scraped my foot across the blackened boards – barely touched by the heat, nothing but a smudge that'd scrub out with salt and a hard brush. Didn't realise until then the fear that fortune-teller had put in my head. She'd talked about fire, but in a town like this, fire was common as rain. I took a breath, cursed myself for thinking her words meant anything, then put my face back on.

I looked around at all the miners and workers gathered, waiting. Harry was back at the door, Jerry looked flustered behind the bar and the girls were still.

'What is this?' I cried out. 'A damn funeral? Play some music! Clean this up and let's have us a good time.'

They were slow to move, but they did. One of the porter boys ran for a brush and mop. The piano struck up, the drinks started flowing and hot meals came out the kitchen.

I stayed in the middle of it, bloody cloth wrapped around my hand. Played poker and faro, took their money, lit their cigars. It was all a distraction. If I stopped, if I went upstairs to be alone, I'd think about it all. The fortune-teller's warning, Bill's violence and rage, Sam over and over, but mostly Molly. Her face in the dark, staring up at me from the street. I'd hear her voice again, pleading, saying she didn't do anything. I'd called her a liar, but what if I was wrong?

I went to Harry, pulled him close to speak in his ear. 'Find Molly, before Bill does.'

KATE

The cry went up at dawn on the last day of May. The ice had melted. The river was open. The rush was on again.

Chaos filled the camp on the shore of Lake Bennett. Boats crowded the water as their owners filled them with their outfits and themselves. Mounties numbered each boat and took the names of those aboard, so they would have a record if the boats were lost, as so many were.

Walter and Biddy were the most animated I'd seen them, but had none of the manic urgency of the other stampeders.

'Ain't no sense in hurrying. The river is long and the way treacherous – we take our time and reach Dawson whole,' Biddy said as she cooked a breakfast of bacon and beans.

I was itching to leave. Two weeks stuck in this place was enough and I couldn't bear another day.

I packed all I could, with Yukon bouncing beside me, eager to be on his way.

When I could do no more, I went about the town and watched the action. Boats, which had been wintered upside down, were flipped and dragged down muddy channels by half a dozen men at a time. A group of twenty or so men had made a chain to load their three boats, each man with eight hundred pounds of food and gear. They sang a work song and I dashed between them to continue my walk.

There was the clean man, angrily barking his orders, yet barely helping his packers. He saw me and put his hand on his gun. I changed course to avoid another confrontation.

My blood was hot with the excitement of it all. The sudden explosion of movement, like a race had begun while we were all sleeping.

The noise of it all! Every man was shouting, roaring laughter, singing. Every part of the quiet lakeside was a tumult of packing and pushing and vying to be the first boat to leave.

At nine, the first did. By the end of the day, eight hundred more had joined it. The lake was covered in unwieldy wooden craft with inexperienced pilots and, despite it being thirty miles across, it seemed like I could have walked from one shore to the other without getting wet.

Walter and Biddy still held an infuriating lack of urgency. I packed their belongings with them and helped load them onto the boat, my own already there, tucked neatly under the bench.

'We must depart,' I said as we stood on the shore.

'And we will,' said Biddy with a tone of impatience I had not heard before. 'Do you see, out there, the boats are in a panic. Look.'

She pointed to a craft already sinking, its passengers frantically trying to bail out the water. Nearby, three boats crashed into one another.

'We'll go tomorrow. Noon,' Walter said and the decision was made.

One more night in Lake Bennett, then onwards to Dawson.

*

It was after one when we finally set off on the lake. The morning had been leisurely; all that was left to do was dismantle the tent and set up the small stove in the boat, so we would not have to stop so much to eat or get warm. Perhaps a hundred boats left with us. From the water the shore looked messy, bristling with vessels and the broken skeletons of wood used to build them.

The weather those last few weeks had been largely fair. A few spots of rain, a little snow at the beginning, but nothing that could be deemed noteworthy. Until now.

A storm of sleet and driving wind made progress slow and miserable. Walter rowed against the wind, but we barely moved; all he could do was stop us from going backwards.

The storm lasted until past sundown, which in these summer months was close to midnight. Biddy and I lit lanterns and tried to keep the stove hot while shielding our faces from the needle-like ice. Yukon was curled on a folded canvas bed by my feet, shivering despite his fur.

By the time the storm eased, we had gone only a few miles in nearly twelve hours. It would take us months, instead of weeks, to reach Dawson at this rate. I could still see the spot on the shore from where we'd set off and my heart filled with despair.

'Don't look back,' said Biddy, as she scooped water from the lake and put a kettle on to boil.

I looked ahead. Walter was still rowing. A machine of a man. Now the wind was soft, we began to move.

There was an island in the middle of Lake Bennett and we decided to stop there for a rest. As much as I wanted to keep moving, my back and neck were aching terribly from bracing against the wind and I could barely feel my legs. The thought of sleeping in that position was unbearable.

We arrived on the shore of the island at perhaps two in the morning. I was dizzy with tiredness and it took all my will-power to collect wood for a fire. We set out our bedrolls close to the heat and I pulled my blanket up to my eyes. Yukon tucked himself against my stomach and I managed a few hours of uncomfortable sleep.

Dawn came and I took the time, while Walter and Biddy still slept, to walk around the small island with Yukon.

'Look where we are, Yuke,' I said and stroked his head. 'An island in a lake in the middle of the wilderness. Have you ever seen the like?'

He looked up at me and gave a short whine that said he wanted to play.

I found a stick and threw it for him again and again as we walked. The island was not big, maybe a mile around, with a few trees in the centre. It looked untouched by the stamped-ers until I came within eyeshot of our little camp and saw, up the slope from the water, a grave.

A cross was driven into the ground at the head of a mound lined with white stones. On the cross, the name J. Mathews and the age, just twenty-six. A year older than I. A terrible sadness hit me then. What happened to this man that he would end up here? Then I thought of poor Mr Gunderson, taken by the avalanche. He would have no grave. Nor would the hundred others caught in that disaster. I had known this road was dangerous, that people died, but to face it, see it, was a different matter. This wild place was unforgiving and did not take kindly to those who would cut down her trees and dynamite her rivers. How many graves littered this trail? How many were unmarked and unknown? Their families waiting for news of riches, when all that would come would be silence and sorrow.

The weather was kinder that morning and we made good progress along Lake Bennett and into Tagish Lake. Hundreds more boats had launched and were dotted along the water. Some were moving fast and organised, the men rowing in unison to a coxswain's call. Others were rickety skiffs and scows, and if they didn't sink in the chain of lakes that led to the Yukon River, they would surely be torn apart on the rapids. I felt for those men, could see the hope and desperation in them, but I feared they would never make it to the gold fields.

Our boat, however, was an ox by comparison. Slow and well made, it felt like traveling aboard a much bigger vessel, yet without any space to move.

Yukon was always restless, so many days cramped in a small boat, doing his business at the stern for me to shovel into the water. He sulked and whined and ate more than he should have, but I could not blame him; for an animal to be caged like this must have been torture.

Walter and Biddy were fine companions and, over the days of our travel and the weeks of our confinement in Bennett City, I felt I'd come to know them well.

From Ireland originally, after marrying they'd decided, like so many others of their country, to board a steamship to New York City. She found a job in a textile factory and he worked on the docks. They had been there a year when the Draft Riots began and they were swept up in the violence with their countrymen. They left afterwards, rode the rails to Chicago and settled. I asked after children but Biddy changed the subject and Walter was silent, their grief palpable and barely a scratch beneath the surface.

When the great fire burned through Chicago, they lost their home and moved on again, this time to California.

'The sun turned me red as a beetroot for weeks,' Biddy said. 'I couldn't stand it.'

And so north again to Seattle, which is where they were when news of Klondike gold reached them.

'We didn't hesitate,' said Walter. 'We like to think we're citizens of the world and we're just seeing as much of it as we can.'

'Nomads,' I smiled. 'I envy you, truly. A free life is not something everyone may have.'

Biddy put her hand on mine. 'But it is something everyone deserves.'

We sailed through the lakes, and distance grew between us and the other boats. Sometimes I could not see another and felt so wonderfully alone on the water. Like I was truly part of the world, treading lightly upon it and leaving no mark. When the weather was calm we rowed through the night, all taking turns at the oars. The work was hard and uncomfortable but, as each day passed, I felt my body grow stronger. My stamina increase. I felt myself growing into the person I needed to be to survive in this place. And I enjoyed it. Every muscle-tearing pull on the oars.

When we camped on the shores, a dozen lights would flare up along the waterline, on either side of the lake, signalling other groups on their journeys.

In those short nights, when the sun dipped for only a few hours at a time, I thought of Charlotte.

She was older than me by two years, but treated me as her equal, growing up. She was taller, prettier, with a shock of dark hair to rival my brown. She was Mother's daughter, where I was my father's. I remember her laugh, so infectious and raucous, not at all proper for a lady, but she never bridled it. We lived just outside Topeka, on a sprawling piece of land bordered by cornfields. Charlotte was in love with a boy named Stephen, a sweet, doting lad from one of the farms nearby. My parents weren't fond of the match – he was not good enough, they said – and a feud grew between Charlotte and our parents that split apart our family. When she and Stephen ran away together to St Louis to 'live in sin', as my mother called it, the rift widened beyond repair. I believe their flight was at Charlotte's bidding rather than Stephen's. She wanted the city life, the excitement of it all, and believed she was in love. I visited once, though I did not tell my parents where I was going.

'Katie,' she said, as I met her from the train, 'you will love it here. The city is never still!'

She was right. I did love it. The movement and jostle and rush of it. It had been a year since she and Stephen had gone off together, but she was alone now.

'He moved back to Topeka a few weeks ago,' she said. 'He has soil for blood and corn for bones.'

'And what do you have?' I asked.

'Steel.'

We sat up that evening, talking of love and ambition. 'I wish to write,' I said. 'For newspapers, to see the world and speak of it to the masses. Mother doesn't approve, of course, thinks I should be married off, and Father would like me to stay close, sell ads in his *Gazette*.'

Charlotte took my hands, her mood shifting at the mention of them. 'Do you remember those stories you wrote of the three girls who had a boat? They would go on adventures, solving mysteries. You used to scribble on scraps of paper when we were children.'

'I remember.'

'Mother tried to burn them, but I kept them. They are under a floorboard in my bedroom at their house.'

'Why would you do that?'

She smiled. 'Because you were born to write. Father approves of you, though he doesn't say it aloud, so ignore our mother. Do not let your choices be made by someone who regrets their own.'

I heard the true meaning beneath her words. 'Do you miss them, Mother and Father? They miss you, though they won't admit it.'

'Sometimes, but I won't let them decide for me. We have one life, Katie.'

'What will you do with yours?'

The smile grew. 'I shall marry a rich man, paint every day and live without worry.'

We laughed and talked into the night and woke beside each other in her bed. I left the next day, intent on moving to Chicago to make my way as a reporter.

That was the last time I saw her. Five years ago. There had been letters for a while, then came news of a marriage to a man I'd never met – how furious that made Mother and Father when they received the letter. I saw only a grainy photograph of them together in the paper, and then silence for two years until this last letter. The one full of despair: *This may be my last letter. He has finally found me and there is nowhere left to run.*

'Kate?' came Walter's voice. 'Get the rope there, love, we're pulling in.'

I was back on that windswept lake, suddenly shaking, and not from the chill.

'Where are we?' I asked, gathering the rope, as second

nature as breathing now.

'Top of the Marsh. About to head into the narrows.'

This was the head of Marsh Lake, the last of the major lakes before entering the winding straits of the Yukon River and the notorious White Horse Rapids. We pulled to the shore alongside a few other boats and the dog bounded onto land, jumping and howling. The men at their own camps laughed at the ridiculous hound and waved to us. We joined a group of four strong-looking men at their fire and spent a pleasant evening exchanging stories of the water and what was to come.

The group of stampeders told of Miles Canyon, a stretch of river leading into the rapids.

'It's a narrow pass where all the water of the Yukon is funnelled into a space two men wide. Rocks sharp as kitchen knives hide an inch below the surface and, if that weren't enough, right in the centre of the canyon is a whirlpool. A great heaving vortex that'll rip your boat to splinters and drag you under.'

'And then you get the rapids themselves,' said another. 'Mounties made it so you got to have a pilot. None of us have run it before, but we hear there's men at the rapids taking a hundred dollars a trip.'

'Do we have a pilot?' I asked Biddy and she nodded to Walter. I felt a touch reassured, but Walter was old and these rapids didn't sound like an easy ride.

'We'll be walking anyhow,' said Biddy.

'What? Walking?'

'Women ain't allowed on the rapids.'

'Says who?'

'Says God and Man, my girl,' Biddy replied, a little sore at being questioned. 'Walter can handle it.'

'No, I must go. I want to. I have no time to waste walking. Besides, it sounds exhilarating, and I am here for adventure and to report on everything a man will go through to get here. I won't walk.'

Biddy squared her shoulders to me. 'Walter won't take you. Ain't no man yet taken a woman through those rapids. The walk is only a day and then we'll rest up and be out, not three days later.'

Walter shrugged. 'It is dangerous. Best walk the bank with Biddy, keep her safe.'

My anger rose. Just because I was a woman, I was barred from the experience. This so-called danger. I must read about it and watch, while men lived it. If I was man enough to survive the Dead Horse Trail, then what was a little river to that?

'If you shan't take me, I'll find someone who will,' I said finally.

'Good luck,' said Biddy.

But I didn't need luck, I had money. In the morning I went to the friendly group of men on the shore and asked them to take me. They were all reluctant at first. Spouting the same reasons – women weren't allowed – but I noticed they seemed light on gear, as if some had been lost.

'I'll pay you, handsomely,' I said. 'A hundred dollars. Same as you'd pay a pilot. It looks like you need it. Another hundred if you take me all the way to Dawson.'

The one in charge, a man named Benjamin Fallon, looked at me, in my pants and stout coat. I was not a woman like they had seen on this trail before.

'One hundred and twenty-five – two-fifty in all,' I said. 'You won't know I'm there.'

Fallon looked to his friends, who all between them either shrugged or nodded. A smile grew on my face.

'All right, Miss Kelly. You get through the canyon with your folks and we'll meet you at the banks before the rapids.'

I went back to our camp with a spring in my step, but it seemed I had put Biddy's nose quite out of joint by securing passage elsewhere for the remainder of the trip. She was in a sulk with me all down the next stretch of river and only warmed back up when Yukon started licking her boot.

Miles Canyon was a narrow corridor, bordered by sheer cliffs of rock. The water was forced into a space far too small for it. The river was unsettled as we approached, the current moving in ways I'd not seen before. Swirling and shifting, almost appearing to run backwards. Walter readied himself with the oars. I tucked Yukon under my legs and the dog did not protest; he smelled the danger on the air and kept himself quiet. Biddy tied two ropes to the central post below Walter's seat and we each held one.

Then the boat jerked forward, caught by the current. The water swelled beneath us, the boat creaked and yawned. We sped on. Walter powered the oars, steered us away from the walls and, just as I was beginning to enjoy myself, we were spat out onto a slow stretch.

'That was not so bad,' I called above the sound of the water.

Biddy barked a laugh. 'That was not the White Horse!'

Walter guided the boat to the shore, where six or seven more were lined up, including the men I had arranged passage with.

They waved when they saw us. 'You made it,' Fallon called. 'Come, we're going to scout the river.'

Yukon and I jumped out of the boat as we came to the bank. The excitement carried me up the canyon side to the lookout, past the few women and several men who had decided to walk around. But my excitement dwindled when I saw what awaited.

Miles Canyon had been ripples. This was a torrent. We watched a boat crash into the waves, spin out of control. Supplies fell out like confetti, and a man went in trying to grab them. He was swept down the river, screaming.

'There is the trouble,' Fallon said, pointing to a bend where a cluster of rocks made the way narrow. 'Like threading a needle, getting through there, so I hear. You still want to ride it?'

He was looking at me. At my slack jaw and wide eyes. The shock wore down to nothing and my determination returned.

'Yes,' I said.

'Ben, Ben!' came a voice from the trail. One of Fallon's companions was waving, hurrying up the path. 'Got ourselves a pilot.'

'We'll leave within the hour,' Fallon said.

I went cold inside. Within the hour. So little time to prepare and, I supposed, so little time to fret. I unpacked my gear from our boat and hauled it into the other. The time slipped away and it seemed like only minutes passed when Fallon called for me to join them.

Biddy took my hand. 'Be careful, you hear? People die in that water. Don't be one of them.'

'I won't. Thank you, Biddy, Walter, for everything.'

Walter clapped his hand on my arm and nodded. He scratched Yukon's head as a fond goodbye and I hugged them both. That was enough. No sense lingering.

Then I was away, into Fallon's boat. The pilot, a man named Jack, sat in the middle, oar in each hand. Once out of the quiet stretch of water, we entered the treacherous White Horse Rapids. The river grabbed us and hurled us down the canyon. It roared, drowning out all other sound and thought but this.

We were shot forward so fast my neck whipped backwards. I felt I was lifting, the boat rushing from under me. I held on tighter to the rail and tighter still to Yukon. The prow of the boat rose and dropped, smacking into the water with great slaps and explosions of icy spray. My head hit the side of the boat and stars filled my eyes, but I was too exhilarated to feel pain.

We slowed, the pilot puffing, red-faced, with the effort of steering through this carnage. I thought we were past it, but he cried out, 'Brace yourselves!'

And we plunged into the fray again. The waters foamed, seething, boiling, crashing against the canyon walls, against us, threatening to flip the boat. I never enjoyed anything as much in my life!

The pilot held course and spun us around a jagged rock, turned us into a crushing wave as tall as me, and out again. Water lashed against the prow, filling the boat, soaking us. Then we were shot out into calm water and the ride was over, leaving only the all-consuming desire to do it all again.

Yukon, however, did not feel the same. The poor animal jumped off the boat, shook the water from his brindle coat and ran up the shore to hide behind a rock.

That's when I felt the blood on my face. The warm flow of it.

'You all right there, Miss Kelly?' said Fallon, helping me off the boat, such concern in his eyes. His hair was wet and plastered to his head; he had lost his hat in the churn.

I was in a similar state. I touched my hand to my head and felt the beginnings of a bruise. 'I'm fine, just a . . .'

I swayed. Fallon caught me and eased me onto a rock. He handed me a canteen of water and I drank it slowly.

'It's the shock of it all,' I said. I'd had a wound like this before, fallen out of a tree when I was a child. Charlotte had been horrified at the amount of blood pouring down my face and onto my church dress, but it had looked so much worse than it was. I pulled a handkerchief from my pocket and pressed it to the cut.

'I reckon you're the first woman to run those rapids,' Fallon said and I believe I saw in his eyes a new-found respect. 'We must press on, while we have the light. Can you manage it?'

He reached out his hand for me to take and pulled me to my feet. He clapped me on the shoulder.

'Let's be away.'

I washed the blood from my hands and climbed into the boat. Head sore and sick to my stomach, with Yukon whining under my feet for food, we set off again. I gave him some jerky and as we pulled away from the shore, another boat came down the rapids, upended. The men crawled onto the bank, sodden and sorry for themselves, everything lost in less than a moment. Then we were gone, looking only forward, to Dawson and my sister.

Should all go well, we would arrive at the city in six or seven days, more than a month after embarking from Lake Bennett. The group of men were kind and didn't mind a woman with them. They teased and spoiled Yukon and were set on their task of making it to the gold fields as quickly and safely as possible.

As the nights grew longer, I made notes of my journey, as I would have to send word back to Mr Everett upon my arrival in Dawson. That seemed so distant. My existence had become the endless forests and mountains, the stretch of river. What lay behind and ahead did not matter, just the moment I was in. What a place to be: the end of all things and the beginning.

The river was wide and calm and we had gentle, easy sailing.

As we pushed further north we had to dodge ice floes and fallen trees, pull hard on the oars to beat the current. We camped at night and sailed early, making steady progress north. One of the men had a guitar and we sang in the dark, something that had calmed me since I was a child; and despite all the perils and tragedy that had befallen me on the trail so far, the days in that cramped little boat with a half-dozen strangers were among my happiest.

ELLEN

BOULDER CREEK, KLONDIKE, JULY 1898

Charlie leaves in the middle of the night. I hear him and do not stop him. He'll be back in a day, poorer, tail between his legs. It's been a week since that woman was here. A week of near-silence. He expects me to question him, be a wife and act hysterically. I won't. That annoys him.

'Why don't you shout?' he'd asked me the previous night.

'What would that accomplish?'

'You'd show you care at least,' he'd said.

I'd raised my eyebrows and kept my tongue. Now he was gone.

I wait a day, busy myself as best I can, but he does not return. I ride up the creek on Bluebell. This time the light is full and I see glittering in the water. I go to it. Kneel on the mossy bank.

I reach my hand into the freezing water and grab a handful of gravel. I let the sand wash away and I hold the rocks. There in my palm, a nugget of gold. Rough on the edges, not worn smooth yet. The size of my thumb. Five times the size of any

Charlie has pulled from the ground. I look at the water and see the rest. Sparking as the sun hits them.

I remember a winter conversation with Charlie: 'You should mine up at the top of the claim. I've seen gold in the water.'

He looked at me as if I was a fool. Such condescension in his eyes I wanted to claw them out. 'It's just the sun playing tricks. The gold is here.'

'But, Charlie, I've seen it.'

'You don't know what you're saying, Ellen. That land is empty, I have checked. Don't you think I went up there when I took these claims?'

Another lie to save face. To cast me as the idiot wife. I did not argue. I hadn't the will for it any longer.

He'd put his hand on my shoulder. 'Leave the mining to me; all you need to worry about is keeping me fed and the house warm. Can you do that?'

I had dug my nails into my palm so hard they drew blood.

I sit back on my heels now and turn the nugget over in my hands. I can't stop staring at it. There is a magic to gold. The way it catches and keeps the light. The way it appears to glow. It is metal straight out a frigid river, but feels warm. As I look at it, I understand the fever better than I ever have before.

The boundary line of Charlie's claim is halfway down the hill. The land I stand on is mine. A quirk of Klondike law means a man can only stake one piece of land at a time, but a married man can put land in his wife's name. These five hundred feet of riverbank, as it stretches up a steep gorge, were deemed too difficult to dig, so Charlie named them for me. It means the gold in my hand is mine, and mine alone.

Somewhere behind me, a sound. Like a heavy step on twigs. I turn.

I think I can hear breathing. Animal, not man. Bears make

a home in these woods. They come down from their mountain dens to feast.

I clutch the gold in my fist and stand slowly.

The brush here is dense. Tall. It can hide a bear, a moose. Another huffing breath and a step.

My heart leaps to my throat. I ready myself to run, though I doubt I would get far.

Bluebell steps from the thicket. Shakes her head.

My breath blasts out of me. 'Damn you.'

She had loosed herself from my knot and wandered. I take her reins, pull her head down to mine.

'You beast,' I say and press my forehead to hers.

She whinnies and stamps. There are nerves in her. A worry in her eyes. I look to the forest. Listen. I feel eyes on us. I put the nugget in my pocket.

I mount Bluebell and ride back to the cabin. A horse is tied up outside, where Goldie should be. A black stallion. Frank Croaker's horse. He calls it Quick, and it lives up to its name.

I do not see the man himself.

I lead Bluebell to her pen and let her eat hay. As I turn, I see him, sitting on my porch, watching me.

'Good afternoon, Mrs Rhodes,' he says, with a smile I don't trust.

'Mr Croaker.' I dust off my hands. I feel the nugget in my pocket. Wonder if he can see its shape. 'Can I help you?'

His lip hooks. 'I hope so. You seen a woman here? Young enough, pretty.'

I feel my gut seize. 'No.'

'You sure? Charlie knows her, if you get my meaning. Name of Molly. I heard from some miners downriver she was out this way.'

'I haven't seen her. You're the only visitor we've had. Besides, if my husband brought home a mistress, do you think I'd let her in my house?'

He rocks his head side to side. 'I suppose not. A good woman like you deserves better. He here? I'd like to ask him.'

'Charlie's on a trip to town. You'll find him at the Arcadia.'

'Seems like every time I come here, you tell me Charlie is away.'

'You have bad timing,' I say and he laughs.

He stands up and strolls to me like he already owns this land. He looks at me like I come with it as a prize.

'Or maybe my timing is just right,' he says, standing only a few feet away.

My back presses against the horse's pen.

'Charlie isn't selling the claim,' I say, an effort to distract him from his course. 'He should. This land is useless.'

He looks at me from head to toe. I feel his eyes as if they are hands running all over me.

'I reckon the land is fine, but it's your husband that's useless.' He takes a step closer. 'He useless everywhere?'

'I don't know what you're talking about. I'd like you to leave now, Mr Croaker.'

Closer still. I can smell his breath. His sweat.

'Leave? While we're just getting to know each other?'

He grabs me by the throat. The shock of it drives all the air from my lungs. He pushes his body against mine. It is like a mountain has fallen on me. The wooden fence bites into my back.

I hammer my fists against his chest, but I might as well be hitting rock. Behind me, Bluebell brays and rears.

He releases my throat and I finally breathe. His hands are all over me, rough and grasping. His mouth is on my neck.

'Stop! Mr Croaker! Stop!' I scream and scream, but he ignores me.

Won't someone hear? Won't someone help?

'Come now, Mrs Rhodes, where is your sense of hospitality?'

He forces a hand between my legs. I claw at him, dig my nails into his neck and scratch. Blood beads. I don't stop.

He growls and where I saw carnal desire before, I now see rage. A fear grips me so deep that I cannot move. I know I am about to die.

Croaker heaves himself off me and I hope, for a moment, this ordeal is done. But I am wrong. He grabs my wrist. Pulls me towards the cabin.

'No!' I shout and pray. 'Let me go!'

I dig my heels into the dirt, but it does nothing to slow him. I must not let him get me inside that cabin. I must not. I *will* not.

I shift my weight, rush towards him. It overbalances him and he stumbles. I twist my wrist, but he keeps hold. Desperate, I grab a handful of dirt and sharp gravel and push it into his eyes.

He roars, blinded, and finally his grip loosens.

I pull free and run. To the horses. To Bluebell.

But he is on me in a second. He grabs my hair and I am yanked backwards. Fire sears through my scalp.

'Hey! Stop!' comes a call. A saviour's voice.

I see Early, the miner from downriver, rushing towards us. He tackles Croaker and I am free once again.

'Run, Mrs Rhodes,' he shouts.

I do not stop. I throw open the horse pen and leap onto Bluebell. In a second we are away. But a second later I hear a gunshot.

I look back. Frank Croaker stands over Early. The miner reaches up a hand, the other clutched to his chest. Croaker shoots him again. Then he turns to me. Lifts the gun.

I snap the reins and Bluebell hastens.

No bullets chase me. No more shots echo in the valley. I pass the miners, their work stopped. They look up at Croaker, at the body of their friend. Some take off their hats.

Then I am round a bend and away. I think Croaker will chase me. Use that well-named stallion to run me down. But I don't hear hooves. I don't hear the shout of *yah!*

I ride without stopping until I get to the river. The ice has melted and the ferry is running. I have nothing on me but the gold in my pocket and I hand it over without care. It is far more than the cost of passage, and the ferryman looks at me, the state of me, and hands it back. Tells me to pay him on the return. His kindness suddenly overwhelms me and I cannot speak. I cling to Bluebell as we cross the river.

It hits me then, in that moment of stillness. I see Early's hand reaching, seeking mercy where there is none. I hear the gunshot and see the hand drop. That poor man. That kind man.

Tears come hot and fast and I bury my face against Bluebell's flank, stifle the sound with a cough. The others on the ferry don't look, don't care. When the ferry bumps against the far bank I wipe my face on my sleeve and think only of the next step. The next thing I must do to survive.

I ride to the Arcadia, to find Charlie has taken no room there, but I don't care. I wish for only a door and a lock. I am given a room and inside, safe, I collapse to my knees.

I breathe but it hurts. My neck is tender from Croaker's hand. I feel the film of his spit on my skin. My head throbs and smarts and I worry what state my back will be in, for I can feel an itch.

I call for a bath. The girl brings the tin tub, then a bucket of cold water and three kettles of hot. She looks at me. There is pity in her eyes and I think she knows. I think every woman would know, with a look. She fetches me a towel and bobs on her heel.

The water is pleasant, but the soap is hard and the block used by many. I scrape away the remains of others and undress.

In the glass, I see the bruises. Purple and red on my arms, my hip, my neck, my thigh, growing and darkening before my eyes. I turn, look over my shoulder and bite back my breath.

A vivid red line runs across my back. The thin material of my dress and shift did little against the sharp bar of the horse pen and the weight of Frank Croaker. My skin is torn in places, blood smeared inside my clothes. My dress is ripped and I have no other.

I wash standing, for the tub is small. The water turns milky. I hold my tongue as I run water over the wound. The milk turns red.

Women do not often travel alone here and I am soon confronted. A gentle knock at the door. 'Mrs Rhodes?'

'I am bathing,' I snap, perhaps a little angrier than I should have.

'My apologies. It's Barnum, the manager. I was wondering, uh – what I mean to say is, well . . .'

I step out of the tub and wrap myself in the towel. 'What is it?'

'May I come in?'

'No, sir, you may not. What do you want?'

'Well, how is it that you mean to pay for the room?'

I dry quickly and step into my dress. I wince, silently, as the cloth brushes my back and I feel the blood run.

'Mrs Rhodes?'

I button up and fix my hair. He knocks gently, as if I could have fallen asleep. He tries the handle.

I open the door and the weaselly man jumps back. I hold up the nugget and his eyes shine.

'This is worth three nights,' I say.

He reaches for it. 'Where did you pull that? Your husband never paid with gold so big.'

'That is not your concern.' I draw back my hand and his own pauses. 'Three nights.'

He nods. 'Three nights, that's a deal.' And he plucks the gold from my fingers. I hate to let it go, especially to such a man as this. He scurries away. A rat of a man, only ever after profit. His rooms are cheap and pleasant, yet I do not trust him. I suspect the three nights will turn to two, maybe one, before I am asked to leave.

My only hope is to find Charlie, tell him what has happened. Perhaps the Mounties can arrest Frank. As soon as the idea comes, I laugh at the absurdity. There is no punishment for a man like that. Yet I must live the punishment, feel its mark on my skin. The shame growing in my chest. How will Charlie react? Will he call me a whore? Believe I invited it? I have seen before his lack of compassion for those he deems less moral than himself. He has no power over Frank. No recourse against him that Frank could not counter, tenfold. Charlie would have little option but to lay the blame at my feet. I won't have that.

I have had a taste of what might befall a woman alone in this place and I realise how helpless I am. That shames me more than any man's unwanted touch. I will not allow that shame to swallow me and yet, right now, I am dangling, clinging to the teeth of it.

I now have no money, and a husband lost somewhere in this warren of a town. It is not even late. All that has happened to me has happened in the full light of the sun.

I stay in the room a while longer. Until the remains of the shock have worn away and the light is more forgiving. I have no hat, no shawl, no money, and I must go about Dawson alone. I ready myself.

I step out onto the boardwalk. Wind whips past me and I cross my arms against the chill. I feel exposed. A cracked tooth stinging with every breath. I walk slowly, feel the material of my dress snagging on the ripped skin of my back. In town it is as busy as ever. More so, as the first boats after the thaw have arrived. New stampeders fill the stores and saloons. Wagons and sleds fill the streets, loaded with new gear and fresh faces. There are more women this time. A group of them carry their own bags, and I suspect they're headed for the dance halls. A woman, her hat low, obscuring her face, unloads her possessions from a boat full of men. A dog bounds around, barking at anyone who comes close. I watch them for a moment. One man shakes the woman's hand as she leaves. She passes me, dog trotting faithfully behind. A woman alone, and wearing pants. I watch her, striding out confident of her own purpose. What must that be like?

I watch her until she is gone between buildings. Then, as if the world resumes, the sound returns. I look after the woman, but she is gone among the crowds. Every charlatan is out, offering worthless or imaginary claims. Every coster and barrow boy is shouting their wares to hungry mouths.

I despair at finding Charlie in all this. I spend hours watching Bill Mather's office, the saloons, the Dawson Hotel, yet he doesn't show himself. The light wanes and the smell of meat pies drifts on the breeze. I have not eaten since breakfast and my stomach aches for it. Yet I have no money and I won't be brought so low as to beg.

The sun dips, but does not set. The light turns from gold to pale grey and the streets empty in favour of the warm bars and bedrooms. I stay. I walk. I look. I dare not ask if anyone has seen him. What kind of woman loses her husband?

It is never quiet or still in Dawson but, in the late hours, it is the closest it can be. I walk through some of the smaller streets where the buildings are not so fine, nor the people who live in them. I walk along the river where the boats are unloading. I am ignored. Invisible.

I am taking a rest in one of the bigger streets off the main one when I see him.

After hours of searching, for Charlie to just *be there* seems unreal. He does not look like himself. Dishevelled, his collar open. No jacket. He wrings his hands and shakes his head. His back is to me.

I am about to call out to him when he turns. On his hands is something black. On his chest are great smears of it. His face is wretched. He takes a few steps back towards an alley, rakes his hands through his hair. He changes his mind and turns again, away from me.

He walks, then he runs.

When he is gone, I go to the alley.

At first I see nothing. The light is poor and the place is filled with piles of garbage, broken crates, leftover boards.

My foot hits something firm and I see it.

I see it and I cannot believe it. My hand goes to my mouth.

A woman's body lies on the ground. She is dark with blood or mud, and I know the same covers my husband's hands and shirt. I know I will have to wash it from his clothes and never ask how he came to have it on him.

I must see who it is. I must know. I must know what I am living with. I brush hair from her face and the horror of it stills my heart. I do know her. My husband knows her. She sat

154

in my home a week ago. I saw his anger towards her, his hand gripping her arm.

I touch her face. Feel the warmth fade.

'Molly,' I whisper as if it will rouse her. But it does not. She is dead and, it seems, my husband is her killer.

MARTHA

DAWSON CITY, KLONDIKE, JULY 1898

'Anything?' I asked Harry.

The big man shook his head.

'Keep looking,' I said and he nodded, went back to his post at the door.

How can a woman just disappear like that? Unless Molly weren't lost. Unless she was with Bill or that gent of hers. Bill would never tell me if he had her, and I didn't know that gent from Adam. She could have been down at Lousetown. Plenty of places to hide in Dawson; plenty more for a good-looking woman.

Days passed and no other word from Sam. No sign of Davis, neither. I had men on their way looking for him. I couldn't do more. I kept telling myself he was fine. He was living and breathing and healing enough to come down the trail on a dozen fast huskies and wrap his arms around me.

I held on to that hope like it was an ember in a snowstorm.

'Are you Martha Malone?'

I turned round and saw a woman. On her own and not at all dressed for it.

'Who's asking?'

She had mud up her skirts – what girl out here didn't? – but no shawl or coat, not even a hat. Looked like she'd rushed out her house after eating dinner and ran all the way here.

'I need to speak with you, it's important.'

Her voice was low and urgent and I got a sense off her that she weren't the kind for girlish gossip.

'All right.'

I led her to my office and, when the door was closed, she dropped onto the couch and broke into tears.

'Jesus, love, what's eating at you?' I asked and poured her a dram of the good stuff.

She drank it and it seemed to calm her down. 'You own this place?'

'I do.'

She was a skittish horse. Push too much, speak too loud, and she'd bolt. But it was like she couldn't get the words out. They were too hard, coated in pain like a bad pill. Then I saw her wedding ring and I understood.

'Your husband come here? See my girls?'

She met my look and a flicker of something else passed over her eyes. Then she nodded.

'Thought as much.' I sat on the couch beside her, put my hand on her knee. 'It don't mean nothing, you know. For these gents it's the same as having a boxing match or gambling. A way to blow off steam. It don't mean he don't love you.'

I'd given the speech before, and I'd give it again before my time was done.

'It's not that. I don't care about that. It's . . . you had a girl here, Molly?'

'That's right. You know her?'

She nodded. Tears welled up in her eyes. 'I . . . you need to send someone.'

A terrible knowing came over me. 'Where?'

'The alley next to the barber's. Molly is there.'

'What are you saying?'

'I can't—' she shook her head, then gripped my hand. 'Please. Send someone.'

'You mean . . . ?'

She nodded and my blood turned ice.

'Stay here,' I said and was away out the office in a blink.

I swept down the stairs, hostess-smile plastered on my face, nodding to customers but not hearing their questions or having any thought to them but getting past.

Harry saw my intent and met me at the door.

'The alley by the barber's. You know it?'

He nodded.

'Let's go.'

The midnight sun was grey that night, and deep shadows clung to the corners. I couldn't walk fast enough, but never wanted to get there. I knew what I'd find. From that woman's look, the sorrow twisted up in her, I knew. But until I was there, until I saw it with my own eyes, she was still Molly.

We reached the alley. Harry went first, lit a match.

There she was. On her side, like she was sleeping, but her eyes were open.

'Fetch the doc and the Mounties,' I said to Harry. 'I'll stay.'

Harry went at a run.

The city of Dawson was always moving, shouting, roaring, drinking, fighting. Not in this alley. Not this girl.

The silence hurt.

The stillness hurt.

I knelt beside Molly in the mud. It was light enough I could see her face, her shape, but dark enough that I couldn't see the details. I brushed my fingers across her forehead. She was warm, but strange to touch, and all I wanted was to wrap her up and take her home. A place she should never have left.

It was a moment and Harry was back, Doc Pohl with him, a young Mountie running to keep up. The doc took me by the shoulders and lifted me away. I let him. I was empty now, hollowed out. I didn't feel anything, just numb through and through and tired, like I could sleep on my feet. Felt like I was freezing to death, like them stampeders who tried the trails in winter.

I let the men work. The Mountie asked me questions and I answered them: a woman told me to come here. I found her like this. Didn't move anything. The woman's in my office.

'Thank you, Mrs Malone,' he said.

I didn't have the energy to correct him.

'Harry,' said Doc Pohl, 'would you carry her to my office?'

The big man was holding in his own tears. He lifted her so gentle, held her to him like she was a babe in arms, carried her out that godforsaken alley.

The Mountie went to the hotel. Doc and I followed Harry.

People in the streets, what few of them there were, stopped what they were doing and watched us. Some took off their hats or made the sign of the cross on their chests. Most were quiet and, soon as we passed, they went about their evenings. Death was common enough here. He stalked the place. They said he lived on the Dome, the high hill where all the creeks started. So it goes, Death made the gold to lure men here so he could pick 'em off. But in my experience, it was always the women who went to the Reaper hardest.

Harry laid Molly on the doctor's table while Doc Pohl lit his lamps.

I saw her in the light for the first time since I cast her out.

In that week and a half, she'd changed. She was thinner about the face, new lines crinkled around her forehead, dark circles round her eyes.

'Head back to the hotel,' I said to Harry. 'Clean up and make sure that woman don't leave.'

Then Doc and I were alone. Doc closed her eyes and the shining horror of it all dimmed to a candle flame.

'I have to undress her,' he said with a note of sorry in his voice. 'Would you like to step out?'

'I'm not leaving her,' I said.

I helped him, made sure he weren't too rough, like the other doc always was. But he was a lamb, treated her how she deserved, after all life had thrown at her.

Molly's dress was caked in mud, soaked through, and it wouldn't come off easy. I picked up the doc's scissors.

'Wait,' he said, putting out his hand to stop me. 'You could clean it, sell it?'

I shook my head. 'I don't want to see anyone wearing this that ain't her.'

He dropped his arm.

I cut her out of her dress. Doc helped ease her arms out and we laid her back gently. He got her a sheet, for her modesty. Then he started his examination.

I watched without really seeing, like I was sleeping with my eyes open. I saw him touch her, and clean her and lift her arms, legs, check her fingers. I weren't really there. This weren't really happening.

Except it was. And I'd known it would. That damn fortune-teller had laid it out for me. There would be a death I couldn't prevent and I'd blame myself for it. Well, sure as ice is water, here it was. Why'd it have to be her?

'She fought them.'

I looked at the doc. 'What?'

He had hold of her hand. Was pointing to her fingertips. 'Skin, under her nails. She scratched her attacker. It'd leave marks – deep ones, by the amount of skin.'

I looked down at Molly. 'Well done, girl.'

'She has bruises on her neck. And here, she was stabbed.'

There was a mark on her belly. Small, barely an inch long. Hurt to look at it.

'At a guess,' Doc began, 'she was strangled, fought back, got a good hit on the man, then he finished it with a knife. She'd have bled a lot. The mud hid it.'

My eyes filled with stars. I gripped the table to stop myself from falling and, just like that, a stool was behind me and the doc was guiding me down. I heard him pour water and then it was in my hand.

'Take a few deep breaths, Martha,' he said. 'We'll find who did this.'

I shook my head. 'I already know.'

'You think it was Bill Mathers?'

'Who else?'

'Don't go down that road. He's dangerous, and you go charging in there with accusations, it'll end badly. Let the Mounties do their work.'

'Bill and I built this town. He ain't the only dangerous one.'

Doc didn't argue or back-talk me any more. He went to Molly, got a basin and a couple of cloths and handed me one without a word. We washed her together in silence. Mud and blood sluiced off her, showed her skin and her story. The bruises all over, on her arms, her neck, a fist-shaped one on her belly. The place the knife went in. They all spoke of the pain she endured the last few days of her life. The last few moments.

I should've kept her safe. Kept her inside. The guilt broke my back. The girl broke my heart.

I sat with her a while, brushed her hair, while the doc cleaned up.

'First day I met Molly, she walked into my hotel and asked for a job,' I said. 'I looked her head to toe and told her to try someplace else. She weren't strong enough for it. Would last a week at most. But she wouldn't leave. She said it had to be here because all the other hotels were run by men. I said, there's only one job here, oldest job in the world. She said it wouldn't be the first time she'd lain with a man she didn't love. She had a tongue on her. Had a heart. She was running – from what I don't know, but I knew the look, half the girls here have it. Molly never told me where she was from. All she'd say was it weren't here, so it didn't matter.' I stroked her cheek. 'I didn't know her past, what family she had, where she grew up; all I knew was she'd come to the ends of the earth and found me. It was my job to look after her, and I failed.'

Doc put his hand on my shoulder. There weren't nothing to say that wouldn't sound like a sermon, so he kept his tongue.

'I'm going to find the Mounties,' he said.

'I ain't leaving her.'

'I didn't think you would.'

He got his jacket and left.

Dawson was never silent, but the quiet in that room was the closest I'd come. I didn't talk to her, didn't sing a lullaby. She weren't sleeping, though she looked it. She weren't in there. All I felt was heat, simmering inside me. A woman can hold her rage for a lifetime. Men fight theirs out. Spend it nightly, a few punches here and there. But I'd hold mine until I got the truth out of Bill Mathers. Until I saw the cuts she made in his skin, marking him as a murderer. Then I'd let it out.

The door burst open.

I jumped up, and the stool crashed to the floor. I put myself between them and Molly. But my worry was short. A woman stood in the doorway. Dressed like a man, but still a woman. Young, pretty. Familiar, but a stranger.

She was panting, wild. She looked beyond me to the table. She choked a cry, covered her mouth and all but fell inside.

'Charlotte' was the only word I could make out.

'Who?'

The woman pushed me away and went to the table. She dropped to her knees, elbows on the table, head right beside Molly's. She wept loud and open.

'How did you know Molly?' I asked, gentle as I could.

She looked at me then with a wretched face, tears full in her eyes. 'Molly? Her name is Charlotte Kelly. She's my sister.'

KATE

My eyes must have been lying. Seeing her there on the table, it had to have been a fever dream. A death dream. I'd fallen in the river. I'd slipped down a mountain. The cut on my head was worse than it appeared and sleep had taken me.

But I was awake. And my sister wasn't.

I was on a chair, a glass in my hand. A woman poured whiskey and I drank it before she sat down. She poured another.

'What happened to my sister?'

I heard the words the woman spoke, but I didn't understand them. Strangled. Stabbed. Murdered.

'Who ...?'

The words came into focus, and so did the woman. Her outline sharpened. 'We don't know. She was found this evening.'

I looked at my sister on that table. Still and cold. A sheet covered her body, but her head, her face, her hair was free.

'I came here for her. She ... oh God.'

I couldn't breathe. The tears burned before they fell.

'What's that?' the woman said and I heard it. A whining, scratching at the door.

I was numb, spoke as if a machine. 'My dog.'

She went to the door and let Yukon in. He came to me, rested his head on my lap. His presence roused me.

'I'm sorry,' I said to the woman, 'but who are you?'

She straightened her back. A proud person in a world of fools, no doubt. 'My name is Martha. I own the Dawson Hotel. Molly . . . Charlotte . . . worked for me. She—' Martha bit back her emotion. 'She was a good girl. Good worker.'

It was more than that, I could see, but I had no energy to press. 'I went to the hotel looking for her . . . A man at the door said you were here.'

I hadn't seen my sister for years and now, the first I laid eyes on her, she could not look back at me. She could not smile, or laugh like we used to.

I went to the table, touched her hair. It was soft, gritty with mud, but brushed. Martha?

She joined me as the door opened and a young man bustled in. He saw me and stopped. Then he saw Yukon and started to complain, but Martha stepped between us.

'This is Molly's sister,' she said. 'This is Doc Pohl. I didn't catch your name, love.'

'Kate. And she isn't Molly. She's Charlotte.'

The doctor's bedside manner returned. 'I'm sorry for your loss, Miss. Did Martha tell you what happened?'

'Most of it,' she said.

Most? I rounded on her. 'What else do you know?'

She sighed. 'There will be a man in this town with scratches on him someplace – face or neck maybe. That is who killed her. There is a woman in my hotel who found her, told me to go looking.'

'Then let's go. I must speak with her.'

I whistled for Yukon and the dog pulled his nose from a bin and came. I paused, turned back to the body on the table. The best I could do for Charlotte now was find who did this and see them hang. I kissed her forehead and tried not to notice the strangeness of her skin, the cool heaviness, the death within her.

In a moment I was out the door and into the dark, muddy streets of Dawson. I had been here only a few hours when I'd first found my way to the Dawson Hotel, which Charlotte had spoken of in her letters. I saw the Mounties there, two of them, in bright-red serge jackets. They were like bloodstains among the muddy attire of the miners.

I had come a thousand miles, travelled for months, escaped death on a mountainside, bled and screamed, to save my sister, and I was too late. All for naught. All for the sake of an hour or more. An hour! Had I managed to get on one of the first boats out of Lake Bennett I would have been here in time. Damn Biddy and Walter for their slowness! Damn the ice for stopping me! Damn me! Damn it all!

'Kate.' Martha's soft voice and soft hand on my arm calmed me enough to breathe again.

We had stopped on a boardwalk on a street I didn't know, in a wooden city built on gambling and gold. It was brimming with stories and people and opportunity and yet, to me, it was empty.

'You were muttering. And your hand,' she said and opened my fist.

In my palm, four crescents of blood from my fingernails. I stared at the blood as if it was not mine.

'Let's clean you up.'

Martha nodded to the large, handsome building across the street. She led me inside and the noise assaulted me. After weeks on the trail, with the sounds of nature and quiet conversation, this was an explosion. Music, chatter, shouts from the gambling tables and from the kitchens; women on the balcony cooed, though I saw their eyes were down, their entreaties lacklustre.

A Mountie stood awkwardly by the bar, hat in hand, clearly awaiting Martha's return. I wasn't sure if he had been here earlier. Every moment before entering the doctor's office had become a blur.

'Officer Deever,' Martha said, approaching him.

'Ma,' the Mountie said with a nod, and his awkwardness disappeared. 'Can we speak in private?'

Martha nodded. She moved to leave me, to signal to her barman to ply me with whiskey until my pain was deadened, but I would not have it.

'I'm going with you,' I said.

'This may not be something you want to hear.'

'She's my sister,' I said, with all the venom I felt.

They knew Charlotte, thought they did, but no one knew about me. No one even knew her name. She was hiding so deep in this place I didn't know if I could dig her out.

'Molly had a sister?' the Mountie asked.

I shot him a hard look. 'Charlotte did.'

'The woman who found Molly – Charlotte – is waiting in my office.'

Yukon had found himself a bone and a friend in the barman. He curled himself up in a corner and gnawed.

Martha led me and the Mountie upstairs to an office. It was empty. I saw her grip the doorhandle.

'They often run off, think they'll get in some kind of trouble just being near a murder,' said the Mountie. He fiddled with his hat. 'Any idea who the woman was?'

'I've seen her in town before. I'd guess a miner's wife. I'll see if she's hanging about outside.' Martha closed the door and through the glass I saw her sweep down the stairs.

The Mountie turned to me. 'What can you tell me about your sister?'

I met his eyes with steel in mine. 'She's dead.'

He lowered his head, cheeks reddened. 'I don't mean to be insensitive, you understand. I need the facts is all, to find whoever did this.'

'The facts?' I said. 'What facts can you hope to learn when you don't even know her name?'

The Mountie kept his patience, barely. 'Listen, Miss Kelly, we all want to figure out who did this, so if you know anything – know of anyone who might have wanted to hurt her – you'd best tell me.'

'I do.' I thought of Charlotte's letter: *He has finally found me and there is nowhere left to run.* I took the letter from my pocket, offered it to the Mountie. 'Her husband.'

The Mountie seemed confused. 'I thought her widowed?'

'A wish. She ran away from him a year or two ago. He was a violent man who took a hand to her more than once. She feared for her life. She wrote me that letter at the turn of the year. I didn't know before that; I had no idea where she was. She said she'd gone city to city to escape him, but he'd always found her. She came to the ends of the earth and still he found her.'

'Can you describe him? Give us an idea what to look for?' he asked.

I shook my head. 'I never met him. They married in secret and he would not allow her to see me after. I saw only a grainy picture of him in a newspaper announcing their union. Charlotte sent me the clipping. He was about so high, average frame and brown hair and beard.'

'That's every man in the Klondike,' he said unhelpfully. 'His name?'

'Henry Gable.'

He took a small notebook and pencil stub from his breast pocket and wrote it down. 'We'll put up notices, ask the locals. I'll let you know if I hear anything.'

The man left and I felt a terrible sense of falling. That was it. A few words and these men in red would ask some questions, as if that would find a scoundrel in a place like this.

I don't know how long I was standing there, numb and tired, when Martha returned.

'That woman's long gone, damn it,' she said. Then she seemed to notice me. 'You all right?'

A picture on the wall had caught my eye. A mountain and a cabin, drawn in thin black ink. I went to it. Knew it.

'Charlotte drew this,' I said.

Martha joined me. 'She had an eye. Real talent, that one.'

The scene showed a creek bed, sluice boxes.

'Will they find who did this?' I asked.

Martha looked at me with a sharp eye that quickly softened. 'I don't know, truth be told. Mounties think they're the law here, but we know they aren't. They're a stamp on a paper and are more concerned with getting *a* man than getting *the* man.'

'Who wanted to hurt my sister?'

Martha sighed. 'She was mixed up in some bad business.'

'What business?'

'She was seeing a gent. They had a break-up and it weren't too friendly.'

A fire lit within me. 'Who is he?'

She shook her head. 'I don't know. I never saw him, never knew his name.'

I looked again at the drawing. My sister only ever drew what she'd seen.

'Can I see her things? Her room?'

Martha had the good sense to wait at the door. The room was small and dark, the curtains drawn. I lit a lamp and took it in. It was a mess. The bed unmade, clothes flung over a chair. The nightstand open.

'She took a bag with her when she left, but it weren't big. She didn't leave her room like this. Someone must have been in here,' Martha said behind me. 'And it weren't me.'

There was a trunk in the corner forced open, its contents – mostly dresses and linens – pulled out over the floor. I went to it, lifted the broken lid and brought the lamp close.

I moved the linens aside and found a thin bundle of letters. I recognised them immediately as ones I'd sent. Beside them, a book tied with ribbon; smudges of ink and charcoal on the outside said this was where she would draw. Below that, a ring box with a gold band inside – I assumed it was Charlotte's own. And last, a knitted square of red wool she'd had since childhood. A comfort and charm she carried with her always.

There she was, my Charlotte, her life as I knew it inside one box. She'd brought so little of herself to this wilderness, even left her name at the dock, but she had these things. I picked up the square and tucked it into my shirt, close to my heart. Then took up the sketchbook.

I stood and turned back to Martha. 'Whoever ransacked her room was not a thief, else they would have taken her ring. They were looking for something in particular. Is there anything missing?'

Martha stepped inside and looked around. Really looked. Every surface, every scrap of floor.

'I don't know. I don't think so.'

I picked up the sketchbook, but couldn't bring myself to open it. These pages were a window into my sister's life, into her soul. It was all that was left.

Martha put her hand gently on my shoulder. 'Kate, it's been a day. I'll fix you a room.'

The weight of the last few hours came down on my shoulders the instant she said it. 'I'll stay in here, if it's all the same.'

Martha, I'm sure, felt it macabre. 'Are you sure?'

'I am.'

She did not try to change my mind. I could see the hurt in her, the love she had for Charlotte – her Molly. But Martha was her madam, her keeper, and I found it hard to feel sympathy when, in a few days, this room would be cleaned out and another girl, fresh off a boat, would take up residence, entertaining the miners and paying this woman for the privilege.

At the door Martha stopped and, as if she heard my thoughts, said, 'She was family to me, you understand. That means you are too, whether you want it or not. I'll have Jessamine send up some food. We'll look after your dog, too.'

A crushing guilt came over me. I clenched my jaw to stop myself falling apart and managed to nod.

She closed the door gently behind her and I was alone.

I felt Charlotte all around me. A whisper in the air I couldn't quite hear. I lay on her bed and breathed in what was left of her. The faint scent of the woman I knew still clung to her sheets. I fell asleep quickly, bitten to the bone with tiredness and heavy with anger. I tossed and turned to terrible dreams, of screaming, blood and fire, of the fragile strength of men and the iron rage of women and, within it all, the flashing picture of my sister lying dead on that table. And those awful words echoing through every moment: *I see death in your future.*

I woke with a terrible conviction in my soul. I would find the man who did this, whether it was Henry Gable or some other. I would find him and, with my own hands, I would kill him.

ELLEN

I stare at my cabin in the dawn light. Goldie is back in her pen with Bluebell. Charlie is inside. The ride back was a blur. The ferry ride another debt. Bluebell knew the way, and the half-light of the small hours, when the sun doesn't shine but never sets, turned the ride into a strange, grey trespass.

I see a shadow in the dirt before me. A dark stain where Early died. My heart gives a painful lurch as if it is being pulled from my body, down to that dirt. His body is gone, but I doubt to the cemetery. I wonder when he will turn up, or if. Where he will be and what story will join him. Will I speak up when he does? Then I'd have to admit what Croaker did. What he tried to do.

The thought turns my stomach. I shan't be pitied. I shan't have gossip. And I am not ready to live it again in the telling.

Charlie is not sleeping, as I expect. A light burns in the window and his shadow paces. I step up onto the porch and listen.

He is weeping, but I feel no pull to comfort him.

I see him again, covered in something dark, running from the alley. From the body. From his mistress, whom I saw him grab and scare on this land.

I breathe again the warm air of summer and wish I had a blade.

I open the door. Charlie, sitting on a chair, his elbows on his knees, head in hands, looks up. What a wretched face. Tear-streaked, muddy. He is in an undershirt and his briefs, a kerchief round his neck. The laundry tub is half-full of water.

What I had hoped would be mud is not.

His clothes are in the water. Stained red with a woman's blood.

'Elly,' he says and breaks into a fresh wave of tears.

He drops off the chair onto his knees. I am stuck between pity and disgust. He grabs my dress and buries his face in my stomach. Holds me like he hasn't since we were married. I let him. I do not coo or hush him. I do not stroke his head or bring him to his feet.

Do I tell him I know? Do I risk it? A man could do a terrible thing to stop himself going to the rope. Anything to cover up a crime. Kill his wife perhaps, if she knows his truth.

'What happened?' I ask.

I will lie until I can't any longer.

'I'm sorry. I'm sorry.' He says it over and over.

'Charlie, tell me what's going on,' I say, with no fear in my voice, but I know he would want to hear it. 'You're scaring me.'

He looks up at me at that. 'Don't say that, Elly, never say that. I would never do anything to hurt you.'

'Your lies are hurting me,' I say, and I mean more than what happened last night. 'Tell me what's going on.'

'I have failed you. As a husband. As a man. I have failed.'

He weeps again. I kneel on the floor, so I may look at him

directly. 'Get a hold of yourself, Charlie, and tell me why there are bloody clothes in my washtub and why my husband is mewling like a child.'

He quietens. Chided enough to still, but not to anger.

He tells me of Molly. The truth of it, this time. He was a weak man, drawn to pleasures of the flesh. But she became more. A friend. A shoulder. She knew his secrets.

That hurt more than I expected. He told her things he could not tell me.

'What secrets, Charlie?'

He gripped his head. 'Please don't ask me that.'

But I knew. Debts. Bill Mathers. My husband's poor business brought Frank Croaker to my door. His weakness made Frank think he could do what he did. I imagine my hands around Charlie's neck.

'Why is my washtub full of blood?' I ask.

He looks at it and his tears well up again. It makes me sick to see it. I wonder what my father would think. He would kick the dog while it whined.

'Molly ... I found her in an alley in Dawson. She was bleeding, insensible.'

She was alive?

'I tried to carry her, but she was in too much pain. I called out and nobody heard. I would not leave her, so I stayed until she left herself. Someone killed her, Elly. That poor woman.'

Not you? Something in his voice makes me almost believe him. But lies stack. One turns out to be true and falls away, but I still balance atop the tower made by my husband. He stands beside me on firm footing while, beneath me, the land shifts with the wind.

'Say something, my love. I beg of you,' he says.

I look at him again. He cares for her more than he ever

did for me. My husband is broken. In this place, the lame are picked off by wolves.

'What am I to say? Your mistress is dead and your clothes are bloody. Did anyone see you?'

He shakes his head. But I know he is wrong. If I saw him, who else might have?

'What are we to do, Elly?' he pleads. As if I hold the answer to our future. I have my own, and he is not a part of it.

'I do not know. But, Charlie, are there any other lies?'

I give him his chance at honesty.

He frowns at me and does not take it.

'Nothing. There is nothing. Is my infidelity not enough?'

I sit back on my heels. 'Frank Croaker came here.' I watch his face change. 'He spoke of money owed to Bill Mathers. We are all but cut off at Sutter's. I'll ask again, Charlie. Is there anything else I should know?'

He turns into a caught animal, the weeping gone. He is husband again. In one lift of a lip, twitch of a cheek, I am put back in my place.

'Every man here borrows to get started and, when the gold comes in, those amounts will be paid back in full. I know my business and I'll thank you not to question me.'

He stands and I am below him, still on my knees.

As is right.

I laugh. It catches him strangely. I am expected to nod and defer, but I look at the man, trembling and unsure, then to the tub of red water, then I realise, for the first time, that I have power in this marriage.

I stand. I look him in the eye and his defiance wilts.

'I'll thank you not to speak to me like that again,' I say and he cannot meet my gaze. 'I loved you once, Charlie. I trusted you. But that is not what we are any longer. If you do not start treating me with the respect I deserve, I will leave you. Do you hear me? I will walk away and you will be alone with your secrets and your dirt.'

His expression breaks once more. 'Please, Elly, I'm sorry. You're right. There are debts. I am trying. I work every hour God sends, and yet this land – this cursed land! It yields so little, and it kills me to see men a few hundred feet away picking nuggets from the riverbed. It's as if this claim was rinsed before we took it. I wished for such a life for us. Please, Elly, don't forsake me now. Not when I need you most.'

'You must strike, Charlie, for both our sakes,' I say. 'Go now and dig. I will clean this up. That shirt, however, is for the fire.'

He nods. 'Yes. Thank you, my love.'

He kisses me on the cheek, but lingers. Kisses me again on the lips. I taste death and turn away. He understands, in his way, and I see the confirmation in his eyes that we are no longer man and wife. He has killed that.

He dresses quickly and goes. As the door closes, I sway. Grab a chair back to stop myself falling. I scream without sound and clutch a fist to my gut.

Is my husband capable of murder?

It is a question I've asked myself since seeing that poor woman in the alley, and one I still have no answer for. I do not trust him. I do not believe him. I heard no shouting for help in Dawson that night. I saw his aggression towards Molly upon her visit. I see her blood in my home.

I pull myself together. Damp down the fear.

I push up my sleeves and wring out the shirt. Blood covers the front, from collar to waist. I see the shape of fingers. A handprint on the right breast. Hers?

I ball it up. I turn to the fire, open the stove door and I am about to throw it in.

But I do not.

Something keeps me from hiding my husband's crime. If he will not let me go, perhaps this will be my insurance.

I hang the shirt to dry, else it will fester. I sit and watch it. Unable to think on anything else. The sun rises and blazes beautiful and unknowing through my window. It is wrong, I think, to have such beauty in the day after so foul a night. I find – now I think of my independence, my future, my possible life – that I grow to love this land. The freedom of it. But I do not love him. And one may not exist without the other. At least, not yet.

I hear Charlie's pick at the rock outside. It is rhythmless. Uneven. But it is the music of this place. When the shirt is dry, I ball it up, hide it and throw a rag in the fire in case Charlie checks the ashes.

It is done. The die cast and the players about their turns. Where this will end up, I do not know, but now at least I have my own secrets and, with them, the power they bring.

MARTHA

'Everyone come down here. Someone get Jessamine,' I said and one of the girls went into the kitchen.

It was morning, sun out blazing, making a mockery of the night before. It hurt to see that blue sky and feel that warmth. It was a normal morning far as they all were concerned. A few of the girls were down already, nursing a coffee. Jerry was watering down the whiskey and, upstairs, three girls were hurrying gents out their rooms.

Weren't long before everyone was around the bar. They all knew of course; if you're living and breathing in Dawson City there ain't no such thing as a secret. But still, they needed to be told.

'Pour us all a drink, Jerry,' I said, but the man was already lining up the glasses.

The girls, fellas, kitchen boys and Jessamine all took one. The saloon went the same quiet as deep winter, when the world seems to take all the noise and put it behind glass.

'You've all heard by now,' I said.

Eyes went to the floor and the girls took each other's hands.

'Well, it's true. Our Molly is dead. Though I don't know what kind of rumours are going round yet, I'll remind you she was family, and we don't speak ill of family.'

Harry sniffed back his tears. What a burden he had, being the one to carry her. Such a soul to him, a quiet giant who'd snap a neck as soon as coo at a puppy. I put my hand on his arm, all the comfort I could muster. A few girls started crying, like it had all just been gossip, but now it was real. A woman – a friend – was dead and the weight of it hit them.

Upstairs, I heard a creak on the board by Molly's room and looked up. For a terrible moment I thought I saw her. Thought she was back and last night was nothing but a nightmare. But it weren't Molly. Her sister stood at the rail. All eyes went to her and back to me.

'Who's that?' asked Giselle.

'That is Molly's sister,' I said and the murmuring began. Worse than hens, these girls. 'She'll be staying awhile and I'll thank you to show her kindness.'

I raised a glass to Kate, inviting her to join us, but she shook her head.

'What happened to Molly?' Laura-Lynn asked in her soft voice. There weren't no love lost between them two, but she at least had the sense to pretend.

'Far as we can tell, she was . . .' I felt Kate looking at me and my heart broke for her. 'She was murdered.'

'Lord!' said Laura-Lynn.

'Who would . . . ?' asked Jerry.

I shook my head. 'Wish I knew. A gent, no doubt. Someone she was seeing, maybe. The Mounties are looking.'

'Where is she?' asked Jessamine. 'She gonna be laid to rest?'

'She's at the doc's office. I don't know about a burial yet.' I looked up at Kate again, but her face was carved out of stone. 'But we'll give her a good send-off, I can promise that. If the Mounties come asking, I want you to tell the truth, you hear? We want this bastard caught, and caught quick. I hope to heaven above this man only had his eye on Molly, but just in case, I don't want any of you going about town alone. It ain't safe.'

Giselle scoffed. 'This is Dawson City, Ma. It's never been safe. We all know that.'

'Molly knew it too, and look what happened to her,' I said, harder than I should've, but it quietened them down.

I raised my glass and, slowly, everyone joined me. 'To Molly. May God bless her and keep her.'

'To Molly,' they echoed and we drank.

In that most solemn moment, the door swung open and a devil stood on the threshold. Frank Croaker strode in and settled himself at the corner of the bar, grinning at us.

'What's a man to do to get a drink in this place?' he said.

I put my hand on Harry's arm. The fella was a keg of black powder and Frank was striking a match.

'Not today,' I whispered and Harry calmed.

I nodded to my girls to get gone and looked up at Kate on the balcony. She frowned and made to come down, but I shook my head. The look in my eye was enough to still her.

I took a breath, damped down the flames in my chest and turned to Frank.

'What do you want?'

'A drink, of course. What else?'

'I don't have a mind for your games today, Frank. Speak your piece or I'll have Harry speak it for you.'

'Testy, testy,' he said.

He turned and rested his back against the bar, so I could

see the left side of him. Scratches. Three lines of red across his neck, not even scabbed yet. A day old at most. I couldn't believe it. I couldn't take my eyes off it. My ears filled with ringing bells and I near fainted. Then near ripped his throat out. But I didn't let a moment of that show.

'I got a message for you,' Frank said, like today was any other day. 'Bill wants to see you.'

'If he wants to see me, he can come here.'

'Says it's important. About your girl.'

'Then he can come here,' I said again.

Frank picked at his nails. 'Bill says if you don't come happy, I'm to sling you over my shoulder and carry you through town to his door.'

Harry stepped toward him. 'You can try it.'

Bless that boy. Frank squared up to him. Harry was a head taller and a foot broader, but Frank was dangerous in his own way.

'Fine,' I said and the men moved apart. 'I'll go.'

I got a shawl from the coat rack by the stairs and followed him to the door. I paused by Harry.

'I want you to look after Molly's sister,' I said, quiet, so Frank didn't hear. 'She's kin.'

'Yes, ma'am.'

Harry locked eyes on Kate and I knew he wouldn't let her out of sight for as long as I was gone.

I knew the way to Bill's place, but I let Frank think he was leading me all the same. I kept seeing those scratches. Course it was him. Doing Bill's dirty work, as always. Bill must have found out about Molly's other fella and got angry. Bill ain't one to share, or take kindly to coming second.

Bill had his office in a saloon at the other end of town. Called it the Nugget, after the first chunk of gold he pulled out a river someplace. Story went it was as big as his fist. Biggest nugget ever found in the Klondike, bigger than any found in California in the fifties. I didn't believe it. No one ever saw it, and I figure if it'd ever existed, it weren't Bill who found it, but some poor miner who Bill bought out. That man never lifted a pick and shovel in his life.

The Nug was smaller than the Dawson, and Bill hated that.

Frank showed me inside. A few miners and some of his girls were sleeping at tables and on benches. The floor was covered in spilled hooch and broken glass and the place had a smell of rot about it. It weren't my first time in here, but I could count on one hand how many.

Bill was sat at a table in the back corner of the room, where he could see everything going on. He was in a tall leather chair he called his throne and had his feet up on the table and a sharp-faced girl beside him, rolling his cigarettes.

'Martha Malone,' he said and sat up, putting his feet on the floor.

'Bill Mathers,' I said.

The girl looked up at me. She was thin, young, new this year and already close to breaking. I knew the look.

Bill turned to her. 'Thank you, Annie, you run along now.'

The girl dutifully kissed his cheek and got up to go, but she dropped a cigarette and spilled the tobacco on the floor. She flinched, expecting a hit no doubt, but Bill didn't move. Not with company. But later. I sighed without showing it.

Annie tidied up best she could, then hurried past me.

'Can I get you a drink, Martha?' he asked, the smiling devil.

'Not today, Bill. What do you want?'

Bill's smile dropped. 'What happened to Molly?'

I glanced at Frank, who stood at the bar watching me. 'She was killed last night. I found her.'

'In an alley by Fred's barber shop,' he said. 'How'd you come to be there?'

I didn't know the woman who'd found her, but there was no telling if Bill did. 'We needed some bacon, and by Fred's is the quickest route to Sutter's.'

That part weren't a lie, at least. That alley cut ten minutes off the walk.

'Why didn't you send a boy?'

'They were busy. What is this, Bill? You bring me here to question me? The Mounties already did that.'

'I know,' he said. 'Deever was in here last night. He's a good man. Got a nice wife. I hear you got a new girl too, just arrived – pretty by all accounts, even if she wears pants. I'm sure you'll change that in no time.'

He meant Kate. But all in my house knew, as of this morning, who she was to Molly, and Bill clearly didn't. That meant someone told Bill about Kate last night. My stomach turned over, but I wouldn't take his bait. 'What's the idea, marching me over here?'

Bill stood up. His face took on a serious mask. 'A girl I cared for is dead, Martha. I'll turn over this whole town to find who did it, if I have to. I got men looking, you see. Mounties are all well and good, but they're stuck in the law and sometimes the law favours the man breaking it.'

I caught Frank's eye. 'I reckon he'll be found pretty quick, all things considered.'

Bill rounded the table. There was nothing between us now and I felt suddenly exposed.

'What do you know?' he asked.

'Nothing. Except that I got a lot to do and you're keeping me from it.'

'I wouldn't want to do that. So tell me quick.'

'I don't know anything about it. Look closer to home, Bill. You surround yourself with cut-throats and you're surprised when someone ends up dead?'

His face twitched. His eyes darted to Frank, then back to me. Was that an idea forming? Suspicion growing? God, I hoped so.

'My men are loyal and do as I say. They knew not to touch her.'

Frank shifted, tugged his collar, showed the scratches.

'You're a goddamn fool, Bill.'

I was the one person in all the Klondike who could say to his face what others were afraid to say behind his back.

'That ain't friendly,' he said, then he cocked his head to the side and a smile came over him. 'I'll chalk that up to your condition. I got to say, you are looking a little pale. Sick perhaps. You best rest. Maybe head down south this winter where the air's kinder to a woman. Take that fella of yours too – what's his name, Sam? I'll take care of your hotel for you.'

I kept my face clear of all I was feeling best I could. Bill knew too much. All my private moments taken and cast onto the mud for all to see. Someone was passing secrets. Only Doc knew about what he found in my stomach, and he weren't the type to break his oath. Someone'd been eavesdropping. I thought of Giselle hanging on the doors, gossiping, ears like saucers catching all the milk. I thought of the dozen people who could've gone into my office and read Sam's letter, told Bill there was a man who loved me and a way to hurt me. A way to make me sell.

'I don't know what you're talking about,' I said, but I knew I weren't convincing nobody.

'I think you do, Martha Malone.'

I'd accused Molly of it all. Of reading my letter, of passing news to Bill, but she couldn't have known Kate was here. I'd cast out the wrong girl. The rat was still in my house.

My chest tightened to a fist. 'I have to go.'

'Twenty thousand,' Bill said.

I met his eyes. Unreadable as always. 'What?'

'For your land and your hotel. You got property along Main and the river. I want it all. Twenty thousand is reasonable. If you want to sell your claim up at Forty Mile, I'll take that too.'

I barked out a laugh and the fist in my chest eased for a breath. 'I ain't looking to sell.'

'Everyone is looking to sell. How about thirty?'

'How many times we going to do this dance, huh? That land is mine. I'll see it go to the dogs before it goes to you.'

Bill's patience was wearing out. His smile had turned sneer. 'I want to do right by you, but you're making it hard. You and me, we go back a long way. You remember when we first got here?'

'I've done all I can to forget.'

'I haven't. You were making pies in Skaguay when I met you. I never loved a woman like I loved you, Martha Malone. Ain't never had a woman like you in my bed since, neither.'

Disgust welled up from some place I'd tried to hide. An overflowing well of shit and darkness. 'That woman is dead.'

'Naw,' he said, and the Devil returned. 'Not yet she ain't. Thirty thousand, Martha. Last and final offer. I won't ask nice next time.'

'No.'

His anger flared and he stepped closer. 'I didn't want to do this, but you left me no choice. You got a month to accept my offer – that's more than enough time to get your affairs in order. One way or another, that land will be mine by end of summer. A month, you understand me?'

'Go to hell.' I spat on the floor and walked out.

No one stopped me, though I half-expected to feel a bullet hit my back. My head spun as I tried to make sense of all he'd said. Molly weren't the rat. Molly might still be alive if I'd listened. God damn me for not listening. Bill had men looking for the killer, but how close to home was he going to look? Clear he didn't know about the scratches or Frank would be in irons already. That meant Doc Pohl weren't the one to tell him about my illness, whatever it might be. I hated puzzles and I was stuck in the middle of one, half the pieces missing, the other half chewed up. Nothing fit together.

I walked without seeing. Without hearing. All I wanted was to get back to my hotel, to my family, my home. Find that rat and toss it to the wolves.

KATE

What do you do when your purpose is robbed from you? When your family is ripped from you? I'd never known anger like it. Anger was too weak a word even, for what I felt. I had barely slept, for whenever I closed my eyes I felt Charlotte's arms circle around me, as they did when we shared a bed as children. I woke every hour that first night, the sky always horribly light, and lost her all over again. Watching Martha conduct her orchestra in the bar, telling them all about my sister as if they knew her – surrounded by all those girls she profited from, by the giant who stared at me, unblinking, as if a prison guard to a rowdy inmate – only fanned the flames of that anger.

I didn't know what I was going to do, but I knew I could do nothing in this hotel. I took Charlotte's sketchbook, as perhaps this had been what the person was looking for when they went through her room.

Downstairs I found Yukon cosying up to a larger, older woman who didn't seem to be one of the working girls. The rest of them had gone about their day, but this woman sat quietly, as if the weight of the news just laid upon her was too heavy for her to stand.

'Come on, Yukon,' I said, and the dog reluctantly pulled himself away.

'I'm Jessamine,' she said. She held out her hand, covered in old cuts and burns, her apron, I now noticed, splattered with flour and sauce.

I shook her hand and she returned hers carefully to her lap.

'You look like her,' she said.

'I know.'

'She'd come into my kitchen, nagging at my heels for cornbread or an extra slice of bacon. I gave in, sent her on her way with a tap on the backside, like I did my boys when they'd get underfoot.'

It both hurt and soothed to hear of Charlotte's life. 'Was she treated well here?'

'Oh, there's no place better in all of Dawson. Ma cares, more than she should.'

I felt a snag of guilt at thinking so ill of Martha, but it passed quickly. 'Perhaps not enough.'

Jessamine just smiled. 'Molly was happy here.'

'Until she was killed,' I snapped and clicked my fingers to Yukon. 'And her name was Charlotte.'

I walked away, couldn't bear to look back at Jessamine, at the sadness in her face I knew was there. I had been cruel in my tone and I was sorry for it immediately, but the anger inside me didn't know social graces, or polite conversation. It knew only fire and hate, and it swirled around a picture of her, dead on the doctor's table.

I went to the Mounties' barracks at the edge of town. Surely, by now, they would have found Gable or at least have some clue as to where he might be.

The man on duty locked eyes on Yukon as we approached, wondering, I supposed, whether to draw his weapon against a violent beast. It was not until I was within ten feet that he finally looked at me. He stared curiously at me in my pants and jacket. 'Help you ... Miss?'

'There was a murder last night. I need to speak with who-ever is in charge.'

He paled. 'Molly. I heard. Damn shame. I liked her.'

I saw him in his breeches, handing my sister money for her time, and it made me sick. How many of the men in this town, in the mining camps, would say the same?

'Can I see the officer in charge, please?'

'Second tent on the right. One with the flag.'

The barracks were all but empty. Two rows of four tents, each surrounded by a stake fence, spoke of a larger force due to occupy it, but I saw only one other man, a cook by the looks of him, standing over a steaming pot. I had seen no Mounties in town, either.

I came to the tent and thought to knock or announce myself, but the canvas was flung open and a grim-faced man stood in the entry.

'Miss Kelly,' Deever said and I wasn't sure if he was sur-prised or angered that I'd bothered him.

He didn't invite me in; instead he came outside. This would be brief.

'Have you found him? The man who killed my sister?'

Deever sighed. 'No, Miss, but it's not even been a day. I'll be asking questions, you can count on that. We'll find 'em.'

'Please. She was all I had.'

'I understand. But, Miss, you got to make peace with the idea that he won't get found. Men up here close ranks against the law.'

Yukon let out a low growl, which I knew to be wind but the Mountie took as a cause to step away.

'Sir, this is not some petty thievery or customs swindle. This is murder. A woman is dead and someone here is responsible. You must find them.'

'We'll do our best.'

'Have you found her husband yet? Henry Gable?'

'Not yet, but we're looking, I promise you.'

His tone did not fill me with confidence. He put his hand on my shoulder as if to show me out. I flinched away from the touch and made my own way.

Once outside, I looked behind and saw Deever speaking with the guard. Issuing an order to not let me back inside, perhaps.

I knelt down to my dog, rubbed his jowls and chest. 'We may have to search for the man ourselves, Yuke.'

He licked my face, which I took as agreement.

We passed through the city of tents where most stampeders ended up, after arriving and discovering there was little land remaining to claim. Some left within a few days, but many stayed, hoping to buy a claim, although most ended up working for others, digging for a wage instead of for themselves. Thousands of tents struggled for space along this stretch of riverbank, circling around a wooden city, pressing in on her edges.

The tents had little thought behind their arrangement. Closer to town they had roads between them, but further out the order descended, as thousands came and had nowhere to stay.

It was early still, but the miners were awake, stoking fires, washing in shared tubs, cooking the three Bs: bread, bacon and beans. The men here were thinner, wiry, the work and the environment whittling them down to sticks. Many were hunched or had teeth missing, and what few women I could see were ash-faced and similarly afflicted.

Nobody paid me any attention, but I felt watched.

'That's a good dog,' came a reedy voice from behind me. I pulled Yukon close and found the speaker. A young man with sunken eyes and a crooked neck. Blond hair almost grey, and half an ear. 'I'll buy him. How much?'

'He's not for sale.'

He came closer. I kept one hand on Yukon and the other felt for the blade in my pocket. 'This is the Klondike – everything's for sale.'

'Not my dog.'

The man knelt and reached for Yukon. I saw his ear closer and it looked as if something had bitten it off. Yuke bared his teeth and let out a low warning.

'Move away, sir,' I said.

He twitched and licked his teeth. Then stood. 'Fine animal. Good money in dogs. You want to sell him?'

I backed away, wary suddenly that this man had little memory for what was just spoken. 'No. I do not.'

'Well, all right. Good day to you then. And you, pup.'

He walked off down the muddy street, hand knocking at the side of his head.

Nobody had noticed the exchange and really it had been nothing, but it left me shaken. I hurried through the tents, the mud sucking at my boots, the stink of waste and the unwashed turning my stomach.

I heard a shout and it sounded for all the world like Charlotte. I did not hear the words, but it stopped me dead.

There she was, a woman alone, staring at me, but it was not my sister. For a second it was; for a second her face was

Charlotte's, but then it was gone. The reality was no less disturbing, though, for the woman smiling at me from across the boards was one I had seen in Skaguay.

'Penny for your future,' she said and her voice carried across the distance and settled as a whisper in my ear.

Yukon bounded towards her before I could stop him. She greeted him as if they were old friends, scratching his ears and cheeks. I went after him and tried to pull Yukon away, but he was in love. The fickle mutt.

'Hello again,' the fortune-teller said. She was the same: kohl eyes, red lips, a purple shawl around her shoulders, fringed with gold coins. She was a splash of colour in a drab, cold world.

'I saw you in Skaguay,' I said. 'How are you here?'

'I've always been here,' she said, standing straight and leaving Yukon at her feet in a state of bliss.

'You told me there would be death in my future.'

She smiled. 'There is death in all our futures.'

'Come on, Yukon,' I said and dragged the dog a step. He whined and pulled against me.

'It seems your friend wants to hear his fortune.'

'He is a wilful beast who goes where the food is.' I pulled harder. Yukon finally relented and we moved away.

'Your sister was with child when she died,' the fortune-teller said and the air went out of me.

'What?'

The woman held open the door to her tent. The same tent, covered with swirls and symbols, but brighter somehow, as if newly painted.

'What do you know of my sister? How can you ... ?' But she didn't answer, just ducked inside and waited.

Yukon twisted away from me and darted in. This dog!

'Yukon, come!'

But he did not.

People like this woman preyed on grief, on the dreams of the unfortunate and on the yearning of the lonely. I would not be one of them. Yet she knew something of my sister and, despite every inch of me screaming otherwise, that was enough for me to step over the threshold.

'Your dog has a kind soul,' she said as the canvas closed behind me. 'He will protect you.'

'What do you know of my sister?'

She gestured to a chair. 'Please.' She sat in one opposite, rested her hands on the clothed table.

Everything was quiet, despite the hundreds of people outside and the thousands beyond. I could hear them still, but it was as if we were separated by thick glass, not the thin fabric of a tent.

I took the seat. 'Please tell me.'

She held out her hands for mine. With a frustrated sigh, I gave them. She rested her thumbs in the very centre of my palms. A strangely intimate hold. It shook me a little from my anger. She continued to hold me and the anger continued to fade.

'Your sister was with child,' she said slowly.

Every word sounded like a whisper in this place, even my own voice. 'How do you know?'

'She told me. You are a reporter, correct?' I nodded. 'Then I shall tell you what you need to hear in the way you need to hear it.'

'What does that mean?'

She wore a permanent smile, but it was no longer unnerving. The discomfort I'd felt upon seeing her in Skaguay was gone, though I did not understand why.

'Charlotte found me when she needed to. She was alone and fearful and, despite being in love with a man and him loving her too, she was in despair.'

'Why?' Then it dawned on me. 'He is married?'

She nodded. 'She told me she carried a child and did not know what to do.'

'What did you tell her?'

'What she needed to hear. That she would not have to worry about the child, for it would not survive her.'

I felt sorrow crawl up my throat and still my words. 'Did she ... did you tell her she would die?'

The smile faded and she pressed harder on my palms. 'Yes.'

I closed my eyes and tried to breathe. My dear Charlotte. She had to live in this place, knowing.

'Do you know who?'

'No. I saw only a shadow with a blade cut a thread. It is frayed into three strands and you must bring these together again.'

'What do you mean?'

'Three women. Each a part of her life and death. Her past, her present, her future.'

'What future? She is dead.'

'Death is not the end. Merely a door.'

'I don't understand you. Threads and doors! Tell me who killed her.'

She pressed her thumbs again and the anger faded. A great sense of relief came over me, as if I'd set down a heavy pack at the end of the trail.

'I do not know who killed her. I do not know if you will ever find that answer or if it will ever be enough to calm your storm. But there is light in your future. There is love. You will be Charlotte's future, should you choose to live it. You will need those women for what is to come.'

'Who are they?'

The smile returned. 'You will see. Charlotte's life is woven through them all.'

'And what is to come?'

'A great reckoning between the god of this town and its devil. Fire and gold. This place is built on the curve of an eggshell. The weight of this city will soon be too much for the land to bear. Three men will end this folly, and three women will keep it alive.'

'I don't understand.'

'I know. But you will.'

She finally let go of my hands and I sat back. 'Who are you?'

She dismissed the question with a shake of her head. 'Just another woman trying to make her way alone. Same as you.'

'I imagine the miners pay you well to hear they will leave here rich men.'

'They do, but most will leave here penniless, and some will stay for ever.'

Like Charlotte. The anger returned, but not as fierce; now it was mellowed with sadness.

'Do not worry, Miss Kelly,' she said. 'The truth has a way of unearthing itself.'

She said the last in such a way that it made me look at her again. Another cryptic prediction designed to match any number of circumstances? Or something else?

I had had enough. The tent was stifling and close, and I suddenly longed for the noise and clamour and crisp air of Dawson. I reached into my pocket for some coins, but she held up her hand.

'No charge,' she said. 'I only ask that you remember what I have said.'

'I will.' How could I forget?

As I went to leave, she stood. 'And, Miss Kelly, watch your step. There are more wolves on the streets of Dawson than in the forests beyond. But you do have friends here, do not forget that.'

I clicked my fingers to Yukon, who obeyed at once, and pushed aside the canvas. The world returned, the light and noise flowing back into me, breathing life to my bones. I did not look back at the woman; something told me to look back would undo her work. Instead I looked up at the sky, at the darkening clouds, and welcomed the rain.

ELLEN

BOULDER CREEK, KLONDIKE, JULY 1898

I have been back from Dawson two days. Two days since I found Charlie bloody and weeping. Charlie works until he falls, as if trying to atone. He doesn't speak of going to Dawson. I suppose now he has no woman to visit. I find I do not hate him for it, but there is another feeling there. Envy perhaps, that he found someone to love and I have not.

These days have been held in a dull pattern. Charlie will not let me help him. Mining is man's work and I am too delicate. I am to tend the home, but the home is bare and small. Two rooms and, with Charlie barely in them, they remain neat.

Most mornings I ride Bluebell to the upper claim. She knows the paths well, but today I have walked.

The path to the upper claim is steep, rocky, almost impossible to traverse with equipment. Charlie blindly laid claim to a cliff face – un-mineable, he said after he saw it.

Except it is not. Further up, the land evens to a plateau before ascending again. It is an oasis. A wide, flat bed of meadow grass and sparse trees. Blueberries grow in their thousands and now, past midsummer, the berries are fat and sweet.

I go to the river and see it there. Glittering beneath the shallow water. The plateau is a natural sluice box. The shale is nature's miner's moss. I reach in and pick out a small nugget, the size of my thumbnail. Then another and another until I have a handful.

The land rent is due at the close of summer. The Mounties will come demanding their hundred dollars and I will pay them from my own pocket, because Charlie's are empty. I put the gold into a silk pouch, a memento from my life in civilisation, and hide it in my bodice. Where Charlie will never look again.

Once I have enough, I will leave him. This place. How could I have thought a woman alone could make it here? I would be at the mercy of any man like Frank Croaker, who wished to harm me. I will empty this claim of its gold and buy passage away. Back home? To my father? Or somewhere new? I miss the land already, just at the thought of leaving it. But, on this day, I do not feel brave enough to stay.

I turn to leave my sanctuary and stop.

A bear sits in the meadow, eating blueberries. Black with a pale snout. I lower myself back down. It sits between me and the path.

A year in the Klondike and I have only seen bears as dark spots on the mountainside. Never so close. I cannot run, for there is nowhere to run to. It does not seem to notice me. It pulls plants towards it and strips the berries with its lips, almost gently.

It is a giant. Fear freezes my blood. I am only thankful Bluebell is not here, for she would be a fine meal for a bear.

Should I scream? Startle it? I open my mouth, but no sound comes.

The wilderness has found me; it encroaches on us, as we have on it. Pushing back against our forced occupancy.

The bear stands and huffs, looks towards me. A moment passes where I believe I am dead already and looking into the eyes of the wild Reaper himself. But the bear does not charge. It does not growl. It sniffs the ground and wanders away. Calm as a lamb. As if I was not even there. Invisible.

My heart beats again. I do not move until I hear nothing but the water. When I stand, my legs are weak. I force them on, down the trail. Suddenly the forest is full of threat. The trees hide bears. The brush hides wolves.

I am not as afraid as perhaps I should be.

Not as afraid as when I return to the cabin and see a red-coated Mountie riding up the trail.

'Ma'am.' He takes off his wide-brimmed hat. 'I am Staff Sergeant William Deever of the North-West Mounted Police. Are you Mrs Charles Rhodes?'

I flinch. Do I not even have my own name any more?

'I am. My husband is working the claim.'

'Could you fetch him for me?'

I nod. My neck is tight and my blood still cold.

I wonder if I should tell Charlie to run. I think of the bloody shirt, balled up under the floorboard. Does the Mountie know? Can he smell it?

I find Charlie in a far corner of the claim he hasn't worked before. He is clearing brush and alders. He starts when he sees me.

'There is a Mountie here,' I say and he drops his pick.

He runs his hand over his mouth. 'What did he say?'

'Just that I was to fetch you.'

'All right,' he retrieves the pick, then thinks again and puts it down. He brushes twigs and leaves from his shirt, tucks it into his pants, flattens his hair.

The Mountie is waiting by the horse pen, stroking Bluebell, feeding her grass. Goldie paces in the corner, unwelcoming to strangers.

'Sir,' Charlie calls and the Mountie turns with a smile.

'A fine pair of animals you have here. Might be the best-kept horses in the Klondike.'

Charlie squints against the sun and it gives him a look of suspicion. 'Thank you. We grew up as horse people in Seattle. I worked as a ranch hand on my father's farm soon as I learned to walk.'

A story he likes to share, for it shows he knows how to work hard. A value in the north. The truth of it, from his father's lips, is that Charlie worked a summer at thirteen and was so slow he had to be replaced by a hired man. He does not know how he disappoints his father. And mine.

'That will do you right up here,' says the officer. 'You might know why I've come to see you today, Mr Rhodes.'

'Oh?'

'A woman was killed in town two nights past. A doxy at Ma's hotel.'

Charlie looks at his boots. 'I heard.'

The Mountie looks at me. Then back to Charlie. 'May we speak in private – this is delicate.'

Charlie catches my eye. 'My wife isn't fragile and she knows my habits.'

The Mountie raises his eyebrows, but accepts this. 'You knew her, is that right? She came here about a week before she was killed.'

'That's right,' Charlie says. 'How did you know that?'

The Mountie nods towards the lower mines. 'Men like to talk. What did she want?'

Charlie opens his mouth, but I answer.

'She was looking for money,' I say. 'But we don't have two flakes to spare and we sent her on.'

The men stare at me. How dare a woman speak! I tire of that look.

'It's true,' Charlie says. 'She'd been cast out of the Dawson.'

The Mountie nods. We're telling him something he already knows.

'Do you know a man by the name of Yannick Early?'

That catches me side-on. I look at the ground, the spot where he died. Where Frank Croaker killed him. I never knew his first name.

'He worked down the river at the mining camp,' Charlie says, as confused as I. 'What's he got to do with this?'

'Seems no one has seen Mr Early since the day the girl died. He left all his belongings: good pair of boots, even a pouch of dust.'

The world spins around me. The colours blur and streak.

'What does that mean?' Charlie asks because I cannot.

'Nothing by itself.'

'You can't think . . .' I say, 'that Early killed her?'

The Mountie makes a patient face, as if he speaks to a child. 'Nothing is certain yet, ma'am. Did you ever meet him? What was he like?'

Charlie shakes his head. 'Only to wave to on passing. We keep to ourselves up here and the miners do the same.'

'And you, ma'am?'

I see Early rushing towards Croaker. I see him pulling the man away. Saving me. Shouting at me to run, even as he is beaten. I see a good man die. And now, in the eyes of this

Mountie, I see a good man's name about to be blackened.

But in order to tell the truth, I must speak of Croaker. Of his hands on me and his intent. Of the debts and empty ground and, when one thread of truth is pulled, the rest unravels. I see the bloody shirt being discovered. My husband blamed. Jailed. Hanged. And me alone here, with nothing and nobody.

'No. I didn't know him.'

'You know,' Charlie says and I recognise the tone, confident yet transparent to any who are familiar with him, 'now I think about it, the day Molly came here, after she left she rode past the miners down the river. A few called out to her. Early was one of them. He shouted loudest – that's what made me look. I think he might have chased her a few paces.'

I wish I could speak against it, but I am trapped yet again.

'You sure it was him?'

'Yes, sir.'

'Thank you, you've both been most helpful.'

The Mountie puts his hat back on. He shakes Charlie's hand and nods to me. He mounts his own horse, a noble chestnut stallion, and rides away. We watch in silence. I can almost hear Charlie's thoughts. Almost see the glee in his eyes. He turns to me and I know what he will say.

'Can you believe Early did that?'

'No. I can't.'

'He always seemed such a gentle fella. But I suppose it goes to show one can never truly know a person.'

'You're right, Charlie. One never can.'

He hears what I intended and tries to correct himself, but I have turned from him. I go to the cabin and close the door and he goes back to the dirt, where he belongs.

MARTHA

'What's in that head of yours?' Sam asked, his voice still soft from sleep.

'Thinking this is a dream,' I said. 'And I don't want to wake up.'

'You not bored of me yet?'

I smiled. 'If I ain't after more than a decade, I don't think I'm going to be.'

The sun came through the window and lit up his face. His beard was short and well-kept, like it had to be in the city. He was working the dock and hated it, but it wouldn't last much longer.

Seattle woke up around us. We heard the clattering of folk getting ready in rooms above and on either side, slamming cupboards and drawers, cursing their lateness, rushing out to the landing and barrelling down the stairs. But in this room we were protected from it all. We had the light and warmth and breath of devotion.

'When are you leaving?' he asked.

'I take the ferry to Skaguay on Friday.'

'Wish I was going with you.'

'You should. You can make pies and darn my socks.'

He laughed and pulled me close.

'Or you could mine, look for gold,' I said, only half-joking.

'That ain't the life for me.'

I rested my head on his chest. 'What you going to do?'

'I heard a fella down the docks was looking for trappers. He's starting up a company in Alaska.'

'There ain't no money in fur. No one wants it no more.'

'There's less in mining.'

I sighed. 'Why we always got to do this? Spend a few weeks together, then part for months. Only together when we're together.'

He wrapped them strong arms around me and kissed my head. 'You got your life and I got mine. When the time comes, we'll bring them lives together and stay put. But right now you want to be in the Klondike taking all the money those fools got, just like you did in Arizona when they found gold down there.'

'My boarding house in Tombstone was where we met.'

'Maybe your hotel in Dawson will be where we grow old.'

I huffed. 'You should come with me. Run it with me.'

'I can't. I ain't ready for settling. I want to be away from those gold-crazy fools. I want to be in the wild, with the mountains and pines, doing what I love, where I love.'

'What about our love?'

I felt him sigh. Felt him get impatient at my questions. 'It ain't going nowhere. You got my heart in your hands, Martha Malone, and soon as I have two coins to rub together, I'm going to marry you. I sure would like to be Mr Malone.'

I laughed. 'I'd like that.'

*

It weren't our time then. Nor on the next visit, when I was making pies for stampeders in Skaguay before they took on the White Pass or the Chilkoot. Nor the time after, when I was in Dawson, building the hotel. Nor the time after that, or after that. But it would be, one day. In the meantime we both found comfort where we could and never asked questions. It was our agreement, for living separate lives.

At least that's what I thought until I got his letter. Read he was hurt. Bad enough he couldn't make the trip. What if there was no time after? What if that last time had been the last?

I stared into my mirror at the old woman staring back. I'd waited a lifetime for the love of that man.

'And I'd wait another,' I said to myself. 'I ain't built to be a wife, least not yet.'

Then I looked up at the ceiling, past the boards, past the shingles, up into the sky and right into the face of God Himself. 'Don't you dare take him from me.'

I wiped away a tear, straightened my sleeves, my collar, and pinned my hair. Then I went out into my hotel to collect.

'Morning, Ma.' Giselle kissed my cheek and I held out my hand. She dropped a pouch of gold into it and I felt its weight.

'He going to be a regular?'

'A girl can dream.' She smiled, but it weren't the full, happy smile I was used to.

'What is it, Giselle?'

She didn't speak right away, which weren't like her. 'It's about Molly.'

I stepped closer and dropped my voice. 'Tell me.'

'I didn't think about it, but now she's gone . . . I don't know if it might have been important.'

'Spit it out, sweetheart.'

'You know anything about Molly's husband?'

That weren't what I was expecting. 'He's dead, by her telling.'

Giselle shook her head. 'She lied. She told me he used to beat her. She ran away from him and came here, changed her name to disappear. Before she ... you know ... she told me she was scared. She'd got a letter in the winter from some lady she boarded with in Seattle. He'd tracked Molly down, the lady told him where she'd gone. I guess she felt bad for it, that's why she wrote Molly, to warn her.'

My head spun and I didn't know what to say. 'Why didn't you tell me before?'

'I didn't think it was true. Thought she was telling tales. But when Kate came, calling her Charlotte, I knew she weren't lying.'

'Damn, Giselle. You think her husband came here? Found her?'

She shrugged. 'Maybe. I don't know. I'm only saying what I heard.'

'She tell you his name? What he looks like?'

Giselle shook her head.

'What about the bruises she had on her arm?'

'I truly don't know where they came from.'

'There anything else you ain't told me?'

'No, Ma. I swear it,' she said and drew a cross over her chest with her finger.

I let it all sink into me. 'Don't tell another soul about this, you understand?'

She nodded and made the cross again.

I went on and spoke to the other girls, got their fees. End of the week I'd do the tally, give them their shares. I put the take in the safe and went to Molly's door – what used to be. I couldn't hear no one inside, but I knocked anyway.

The bed creaked, but no one called out and I didn't bother further. Least I knew where Kate was. I'd barely seen her these past few days. She'd know about Molly's husband surely, but it would keep until she was ready to talk.

Downstairs, the dog had found himself a place near Jessamine's feet. She griped about it for the first day, another mouth to feed, but now she'd take a bullet for that mutt. I found them playing on the kitchen floor, rolling around like children, her laughing, him licking her all up the face. Didn't have the heart to stop it.

'I'm heading out,' I said to Jerry.

I went to Sutter's first. Fresh food goes bad quick in the summer, and the monthly order turned weekly.

Dawson was quiet, the mud on the boardwalks dried to dust. The sun weren't high, but it was already too warm for comfort. That's the trouble living up here all year – you get used to the cold. It gets in your bones and your blood runs fast as the rivers, stuck under ice, but still rushing. The summer swells us. Makes us slow and forgetful. The sun don't help. These few weeks it stays out are the worst of the year.

I knocked on Doc Pohl's door. He answered after a minute and looked harried. Had his sleeves rolled up, his hair a mess, looked like he hadn't slept in days.

'Martha. Are you sick?'

'I came about Molly's burial. We need to get her in the ground.'

He nodded, but didn't look like he'd even heard me.

'What's happening? You look like you've done ten rounds with the Devil.'

Doc's brave face all but crumbled away. 'Come in.'

He stepped aside and I saw the mess of the place. I followed him through to a door at the far end of his room, trying

208

not to look at the table opposite. At the ice blocks melting quicker than the sleds could bring them in, surrounding the body wrapped in canvas. The ache in my chest grew sharp and I wondered if it would ever leave me again.

The door led out back to the square of land they used to store bodies in winter until the ground thawed enough to dig graves.

In the summer the flies found it, turned the muddy yard into a swamp. Today, though, it was filled corner to corner with tents.

'Here,' Doc handed me a clean rag. He put one to his face, covering his mouth and nose. I did the same.

He lifted the flap on the closest tent and a smell came out so bad I had to turn away.

Inside were a dozen or more cots, each holding a patient. They groaned or were silent. Even in the dim light I could see some were covered in a red rash, and all were shivering, some holding their stomachs. All of them looked two steps from death.

'What is it?' I asked, through the cloth.

'Typhoid fever,' Doc said and closed the tent. 'Twelve cases in the last two days. One dead so far. I'm getting more men in every day. I don't have the space to house them, treat them. I've put in an order with Sutter's for more quinine as that seems to ease it, but it isn't a cure.'

My insides ached just seeing what was in that tent. What it meant for the town. 'How's it spread?'

'Water. Faeces. Don't drink any water you haven't boiled first. Tell everyone you know the same, Martha. The miners need to move their latrines away from the rivers. They need to stop shitting in the water.'

He ran his hands through his hair. I'd never seen the doc

shook up. And truth be told, it scared me.

I put my hand on his shoulder to guide him back into his office. 'I'll spread the word.'

'This place!' he cried. 'It's a perfect storm of disease. The miners are worked to the bone, they only eat beans and bread. All are malnourished, half have scurvy. I pull more rotten teeth than I have jars to put them in. A healthy man gets typhoid, he is sick for a time but then recovers. Here, one man in five will die of the same. The Reaper is coming to Dawson, Martha.'

I didn't take well to hysterics. 'This is the Klondike, Doc. Death is part of the deal.'

My bluntness stopped his fever head-on. It weren't right for a doctor to think like that and that's one point the old doc had over Pohl. He'd known the truth of this land and he didn't let it get in his head or his heart.

'I need you to pull yourself together,' I said, 'because I need you to check on me. I ain't feeling spry today.'

Doc Pohl nodded and went to wash his hands. When he came back, he was the calm man I liked.

'Sit up on the table for me,' he said.

I lay down and he started to feel around my stomach. 'You been feeling any pain?'

'Nothing worse than usual.' But truth was, it *was* worse. Like bad gas, but sharper. I don't know why I didn't tell him, but somehow it felt like if I did, it would mean more than it was. I'd have to tell people. Tell Sam. Bill would think I was weak and he would use it to take all I had.

He pressed above my hip bone and a shot of pain went through me. I bit my breath. 'Damn.'

He stopped and let me sit up. 'Well. Good news and bad news. Bad, the mass I felt has got a bit bigger. Not by much.

Good news is you're not feeling any pain from it. Soon as that changes, you let me know.'

'I will.' The lie felt heavy in my mouth. I could hear the constant drip from the melting ice surrounding Molly, like it was a clock counting down my days.

'I'm going to give you some tea to help move your bowel along. It may be a build-up, you understand, rather than anything sinister.'

I was far too old to get shy about shitting, but bless the doc for trying.

He went to his cupboards and found a folded paper envelope. Then he took a couple of jars off his shelf, measured in some of the dried leaves from each, handed it to me. I gave it a sniff. Ginger and something else. Weren't nasty, at least.

'Senna,' he said. 'It's a herb, gentle enough for children, but effective. A spoon of that in a cup of boiling water. Once a day for now. Come back next week and I'll check again.'

I stood up from the table and straightened my dress, put the tea in my pocket.

'Thanks, Doc.'

I walked past him to the door, where I heard him sigh. 'Have they found who killed her yet?'

'No. But it ain't for lack of trying.'

'You mentioned the burial?'

I put my hand on his arm. 'I'll make the arrangements.'

I heard moaning from outside, and the doc's calm manner disappeared. He raked his hand through his hair.

'Doc,' I said and he looked at me, 'you ain't God. You can't help everyone. This place ain't for the weak. They knew death was punching their ticket the moment they set foot on the trails. You'd best start understanding that. Not everyone is worth saving, neither.'

'Do you truly believe that?'

'After a few years up here,' I said, thinking of Bill and his threats, of Molly and who hurt her, 'I do.'

He lowered his head and the moaning came again, louder and more pained. 'Thank you, Martha, but I'm a doctor and I have to try.'

He went to the back door, put on his mask and left me. I worried for a moment I'd offended him, but I stuck by what I said. If I'd learned anything during my time in the Klondike it was to be ruthless. To cut off the frostbitten fingers before gangrene took the hand.

KATE

DAWSON CITY, KLONDIKE, JULY 1898

I watched from the corner, the ghost in the room. The women looked at me occasionally but most ignored me. Only Giselle said a kind word here and there. She was a sweet one; loyal, it seemed.

'Boil water before drinking or cooking with it,' Martha told her staff, assembled in the bar.

I sat at a small table with Charlotte's sketchbook, flicking through pages of her life I didn't witness. A miner posing with a smile. A line of sluice boxes. A cabin by the river. Street scenes, observed, I imagined, through her window. There were rough sketches of the hotel itself, of men and women, a few of Martha, one of her laughing. I couldn't bring myself to turn the final pages, see the last drawings my sister had made. Then there would be nothing new of her, she would truly be gone.

'One of my gents had it,' said one of the women – Laura-Lynn, I think, 'I sent him on his way.'

'Good,' Martha said, 'it ain't no joke. You keep clear of anyone with it and you wash your hands.'

The group agreed and dispersed. I stayed as I was, turning pages of sketches, but not really seeing them any longer. Yukon was bothering the cook for scraps and I did not know what to do. My purpose had shifted from helping Charlotte to seeking justice for her, and I didn't know where to start.

'Penny for your thoughts.'

I looked up at Martha standing beside me. The fortune-teller's words came back to me again and again: *You do have friends here.* I did not yet believe her, though I was beginning to.

Martha smiled down at the sketchbook, at the drawing of her laughing. I handed it to her.

'Good Lord,' she said in a whisper. 'Would you look at that!'

'She had a gift for seeing what others didn't.'

Martha's smile faltered and she took a seat at my small table, tucked away beneath the staircase.

'We got to talk,' she said. 'It's Mol—' she caught herself, 'Charlotte. She needs to be buried.'

My heart twisted. There was a small part of me that had hoped I'd be able to take her home. Lay her to rest in Kansas soil. But she'd hated it there, left as soon as she could. Married out. Then ran from that to the end of the world. In the letter that called me here, she spoke of the mountains, the air, the colour of the river water in summer, the life coursing through this place. She loved it here. She thought she was free.

'I know,' I said. 'Will you . . .' I could not bear it, the thought of finding a cemetery, a pastor, a casket, having strangers speak over her, talk of a life and a woman of which I knew so little.

'I can make the arrangements,' Martha said and I was immediately grateful.

I met her eyes and saw the sadness within them. The sadness of someone who had lost a friend. At least Charlotte had not been alone here. Except at the end.

'Thank you.'

'There's something else,' she said, her voice changed, turned serious. 'Molly told me she was a widow. That her husband died in an accident; she was vague on the details. But turns out it weren't true. He's alive.'

'He is. But he isn't a good man.'

Martha nodded. 'The word is he was coming to find her. Coming here.'

I looked down at my hands. Martha knew, then. What use were secrets here, now? I met her eyes and told her the truth: Molly's letter, my reason for coming here, their whirlwind marriage and subsequent collapse.

'She was scared he would kill her if he found her.'

Martha closed her eyes and sighed. 'Maybe he did. What does he look like?'

'I don't know. I never met him.'

It was as if I had knocked the air from her with those few words.

'I'm sorry. I saw a blurry photograph of him for their wedding announcement in the paper. He is about yea high,' I held up my hand, 'dark hair and slim build.'

'Shit! You could throw a grain of rice up here and hit twenty men matching that.'

'We'll find him,' I said. 'I'll question every miner if I have to.'

'You may have to, sweetheart.'

She patted my hand as she left and I went back to the sketches. Holding this book was the closest I'd felt to my sister in years. Charlotte sketched everything and everyone. But one face appeared more than any other. A man in all manner of poses. Standing by the window, lying shirtless in bed, rough shapes in various degrees of detail. One was more complete than the rest. A portrait so clear it could have been a tintype.

Giselle walked past to the stairs, and I jumped up. 'Giselle.'

She stopped, one foot on the step.

I pulled out the picture and showed it to her. 'Do you know him?'

She chewed on something and looked down at the page. 'That's Charlie Rhodes. He's got a claim on Boulder Creek, off the Bonanza. Don't know which claim, before you ask.'

'What was he to my sister?' I asked.

She shrugged, wiped brown spit from her lip. 'Ma told me to keep an ear out on any gents she was seeing.'

'Was he the only one?'

Giselle sighed, bored suddenly of the questions. 'Only one I saw, but every man in town had his eye on Molly. They weren't all friendly like Charlie, neither.'

'What do you mean?'

'Means a place like this ain't safe for a pretty girl by herself.' She stepped close and took in every detail of my face. 'You'd best muddy up before you draw attention.'

'Would he hurt her, this Charlie Rhodes?'

Giselle's hardness softened for a moment. 'Who can tell what a man will do. Especially up here.'

She left then and I stared at the picture of another man my sister had become involved with whom I knew nothing about. First the farm boy she'd gone to the city with, then her husband, from whom she fled fearing for her life, and now this man. It broke my heart to think she had escaped one dangerous man and ran headlong into another.

A Klondike funeral happens quick.

The next day, three days since Charlotte's death, Martha closed the hotel and every girl and man in the place wore whatever black they had. We walked together through the streets of Dawson, to the cemetery just outside town. A dozen holes were already dug. We weren't the only mourners. A few people stood at gravesides, watching a pair of men put bodies in the ground one by one. Each sewn up in canvas.

We stood around my sister's empty grave, waiting. Yukon at my feet, noble in his silence.

The doctor, Pohl, stood beside me. 'How are you?'

'I don't know. How is one supposed to feel in these situations?'

'However you like.'

I looked at him and he smiled sadly. 'You sound like a man with first-hand experience.'

'In another life. Up here, we have a chance to start over. It's the only reason anyone is here after all.'

'It's not why I'm here,' I said. 'I came for my sister. Do you know which . . .'

'There,' he said and pointed to a canvas bundle set aside from the others.

Beside the dead men, Charlotte was so small. Almost nothing. But she had been everything.

Finally the gravediggers came to her. I flinched as they lifted her. It seemed so rough and thoughtless and yet there was no other way. They carried her to the grave and set her down beside it. I wished I could see her face one last time, but I was grateful not to. She was not my sister any more. Just a body.

I looked at the open graves, the pile of bodies and, beyond it, the sprawling town, lines of smoke from fires and, beyond that, the mountains, the forests, singing with the wind.

At the edge of the cemetery was a man standing alone. An eerie feeling of familiarity came over me. His face was shadowed by his hat and I couldn't make out his features, yet the feeling remained. Could this be Charlie Rhodes – a man I had only seen on paper – or someone else?

Both of the gravediggers climbed into the hole, only three or four feet deep – the lowest they could dig before hitting the permafrost – and slid Charlotte's body towards them. Together, they laid her to rest in the black ground.

The pastor, a rake of a man with a pinched look, opened his Bible and read a verse. 'Jesus said unto her, "I am the resurrection, and the life: he that believeth in me, though he were dead, yet shall he live." We therefore commit this woman's body to the ground, earth to earth, ashes to ashes. May she rest in peace.'

'She had a name,' I said to the pastor. 'Do you know it?'

His face twitched. 'I don't.'

The mourners beside me looked around uncomfortably. Martha put her hand on my arm to calm me.

'You would bury a woman and send her on her way to heaven without knowing her name?'

The man sucked his teeth and looked at the cross lying beside the grave. 'We therefore commit Charlotte Kelly's body to the ground and hope her soul finds peace beside Almighty God.'

Martha's hand relaxed, and I along with it. The anger did not burn as bright as it had, but it was not extinguished.

'Hear! Hear!' said a man on the outskirts of the party.

Heads turned and we saw who spoke. Martha's grip returned, sharper than ever.

'That's Bill Mathers,' she whispered to me. 'Stay quiet. I mean it.'

The group held their breath, waiting for Mathers to continue, but he said nothing else. He walked to the edge of the grave and picked up a handful of dirt. He brought his hand to his lips, held it there as if in prayer, then threw the dirt into the grave.

I felt Martha's nails dig deeper into my arm. Yukon pressed against my leg as if he knew of the man's reputation and was fearful for it.

As Mathers turned he saw us both. To me he nodded, respectful, at least seemingly so; word travels and he must have known who I was. But to Martha he sneered and leaned close.

'Tick-tock, Ma.'

Then he was away, through the girls. He smiled at them and they back to him, flirting even at a funeral, even when one of their own was cold in the ground. It sickened me. He didn't go far. Just stood at the fence with two men I hadn't seen before and watched.

I stepped to the edge of the grave and picked up a handful of dirt. I stared down at my sister's body, wrapped and still, in that shallow hole. The heat of the sun prickled my brow and, behind me, a few of the girls grew restless, fanning themselves. I dropped in the dirt.

'Goodbye, Charlotte,' I said only to myself.

As if a dam broke, others now stepped forward and did the same, until each had taken a turn. Some crossed themselves as they did it, others kissed a crucifix or medallion. Each had their own way.

Martha was last. She spoke a few words under her breath as she threw in the dirt. She dusted off her hands and we all moved to leave. Then Yukon let out a low growl and I immediately saw its cause.

The Mountie, William Deever, walked towards us, hat in hand. Out of respect or the heat, I couldn't tell.

'Ma, ladies,' he said and nodded to the big man, Harry.

'What are you doing here?' Martha asked.

At the fence, Bill Mathers stood straighter.

'I have news. I wanted you to hear it before anyone else. All of you.' Deever looked at me, then his eyes went to the grave and he looked away.

'Spit it out, man,' came Mather's voice from the back of the group.

The Mountie squeezed his hat between his hands. 'We believe we have identified the man who killed Molly.'

The group suddenly came alive with mutterings and whispers.

Martha turned and raised her hand. 'Hush! Let the man speak. Go on.'

'Thank you, Ma. We are charging Yannick Early with the crime of murder. He ain't been seen since the night of, and we know he and Molly had dealings.'

The silence hurt. Even the gravediggers had stopped to listen. It seemed the whole town just down the hill was straining to hear.

'Are you sure?' Martha asked. Her voice was cracked at the edges.

He nodded. 'By all accounts, he was one of her regulars. He killed her, then he fled. Left all his belongings and hightailed it out of here.'

'I knew him – quiet one, always paid and never roughed up my girls. It don't seem like him to do that,' Martha said.

Deever shrugged. 'Fit of passion, fit of rage; man is capable of anything.'

A man and a dog share that trait; they can be kind and soft up to a point and then out come the teeth.

'Where did Early go?' Martha asked.

'We don't know, but there weren't any ships leaving that night or the morning after, so we're guessing he went overground.'

I stepped forward. 'You're guessing?'

Deever lowered his head. 'Based on all my questionings, yes. But I'm not guessing with nothing. Early was seen with Molly the day before she died.'

'Why aren't you out searching for him?'

He all but laughed, then remembered his manners. 'Miss, I barely have enough officers to patrol this town. You think I have the men to launch a search party? Yannick Early is as good as dead. If the wolves don't get him, the winter will. Either way, Molly will have her justice.'

I looked at Martha and couldn't read her. The girls gossiped behind me, speaking of this Early as if he was friend and neighbour turned bad.

'He always seemed like one of the good ones,' Martha said, joining up all their thoughts into one.

'They usually do,' said the Mountie.

A moment hung between us where there was little left to say, yet so many questions that yearned to be asked. Something about this was too neat. Too easy. What of Gable? And this man Rhodes? Both knew her well and at least one wanted to hurt her.

'Where did he live?' I asked.

'A mining camp at a creek off the Bonanza,' he replied.

'Which creek?'

He looked to Martha as if for permission to tell me. 'Boulder.'

The same as Charlie Rhodes. That could not be a coincidence. A fire lit inside me.

How convenient the man they accused could not answer

for himself. How troubling a poor miner may take the blame for a richer man's sins. Even here, on the outskirts of civilisation, the problems inherent in the world cannot be left behind. Gold is king everywhere, after all.

'Thank you, Deever,' said Martha. 'Come by the hotel. We're having a drink in Molly's honour. Be good to have you.'

'That's kind,' he said, without committing either way.

Martha walked past him, a silent signal to us all to follow. Bill Mathers came to speak with Deever as we left. I found myself looking for the other man: the one who had been standing at the edge of the cemetery, the familiar one I could not place. But he was gone into the faceless crowds.

I wasted no time. While Martha and her girls drank to my sister's memory, I packed. The only thing I took of her was the sketchbook. This was Charlotte; everything else in this room was the girl they called Molly.

I slipped out the back of the hotel. I needed to be sure who killed my sister, and the Mountie's 'guessing' and 'as good as' did not fill me with the certainty I needed.

I found a wagon heading towards Bonanza Creek and agreed the passage if I would pay the ferry. Yukon jumped up into the back, settled across my lap, and we were away.

ELLEN

A stranger walks through the mining camp. The miners tip their hats, then they stare and mutter. He does not look like them. Clean-shaven. Slight. He speaks to one man, then another, then is gone from my sight. A dog trots after him.

I turn back to my chores with a strange feeling in my chest. As if the air before a storm, charged and restless, fills my lungs.

I busy myself. Prepare a meal. Sweep again. I feel the stranger. A new presence close by, and I cannot concentrate.

I must walk.

I go up the trail, past Charlie, who does not see me. He digs at the alder patch again, clearing the topsoil. Cutting down to where he believes the river once flowed.

The bears have moved on to fish at the lower, quieter creeks. The river gleams with meltwater from the Dome. I scoop a handful of gravel and let the rocks fall between my fingers, leaving the gold in my palm. This is all Charlie dreams of. The strike. The soft weight of the gold in his hands. Four nuggets the size of cherries. One even bigger. I collect as much as I can hide without Charlie noticing. I stare at the pieces. So much panic and death for something so plain. It feels as if half the world has come here, chasing this metal, scarring the land beyond healing. If a desperate man – one of the miners down the creek – sees what I have, I will be robbed. Perhaps killed. Was that what happened to Molly? Did she have gold someone wanted? I know it was not as the Mountie said, that Early had killed her, so why?

I sit for a while, the gold warming in my palm. The air is thicker now, as if boiled down to stew by the summer sun. I think of the stranger I saw. The way he moved, unlike any other miner. The dog faithful by his side.

It is passion that goes against what the world wishes of us.

She'd said that. The fortune-teller. I think of the handsome, beautiful figure painted on the card.

You will have to make a choice. To stay or to go.

Is this the man she spoke of?

'No, Ellen,' I say aloud as if it will make my words truer. 'That man is another hopeless miner. My choice is not between men, but between shackles and freedom.'

I look down at the gold in my hand. At the river full of it. My freedom waits in the water.

The weight of the gold in my pocket, though not much, brings a welcome comfort. I will hide it when I return, in the silk pouch where I hid the rest, until I have enough to leave.

The walk down the hill is easy, but when I come in sight of the claim, I slow.

Charlie is not at the alder patch. A panic rises in my chest. Did he follow me? Does he know? But then I see him. Walking towards the cabin, pushing his hat up his forehead to better see the person waiting by the horses. And the dog at the stranger's side.

Charlie greets the stranger with a handshake. Then he laughs, but I don't hear why.

I cross the claim, along the path of boards over the mud and gravel. Charlie has his back to me, doesn't hear my steps. But the stranger does. Over my husband's shoulder he looks and I see the truth. Eyes meet mine. Time seems to slow.

I almost trip and the world rushes back.

'Hello,' says the stranger and Charlie turns. His smile falters when he sees me.

'Ellen, this is Miss Kelly,' he says and steps aside to introduce us. 'She is a journalist, can you believe it? Here to write about life in the gold fields.'

'Kate, please,' the woman says, her eyes on my husband. Then her gaze falls on me and she reaches out a hand.

Soft, light, as if made of bird bones and kid leather. After so long with only the touch of roughened men – calloused, scratched, heavy – it is odd to feel anything else.

'Pleased to meet you,' I say. She has a half-healed cut on her forehead and I wonder how she came to have it. I wonder, suddenly, a lot of things about this woman.

Inside the cabin I make coffee she drinks and put out bread she politely refuses.

Another woman in my home. The last who sat in that chair is dead. She even looks like her, about the edges.

Charlie acts as if he sits in a mansion, not a two-room shack at the end of the world.

'Have we met before, Miss Kelly? You look familiar,' he asks.

'I'm afraid that's impossible. I only arrived a few days ago,' she says. His frown lifts and talk turns to the mines, but I linger on the thought. She *is* familiar, but I can't think why.

I listen to them. Her eyes are firmly on Charlie, occasionally flitting to me, then back to him. She is a woman in a man's profession, so must act like one. I am invisible once again. She holds a notebook, but does not write in it. Her dog rests his head on my foot. Charlie speaks of sluice boxes and riffles as if explaining to a child. He speaks of quartz and gravel, of how the gold settles in the rocks, how to work a pan. It is the better part of an hour before the conversation lulls and she looks to me.

'Do you work the mine too?'

'No, no,' Charlie speaks for me. 'Ellen's far too busy keeping the house. She needn't bother herself with rough work.'

I believe she sees my expression sour. I believe a woman at a hundred paces could see it, but a man – even beside me, even my husband – is blind.

'And you have no hired men here?'

'Just myself and my own two hands,' he says and holds them up.

I sip my cold coffee and scratch the dog's head. Kate notices.

'I confess,' she begins, 'I came here with an agenda of sorts. I had hoped to find work in the gold fields.'

Charlie sits back in his chair.

She continues. 'My financier, Mr Everett of Topeka, Kansas, he's more money than a Rockefeller and likes to know all the details of an opportunity before committing his quite considerable resources.'

I see Charlie's eyes burn. He leans forward to her. Towards talk of money.

The dog yawns and rolls himself across both my feet. I try to wriggle free, but he is heavy and I haven't the heart to wake him. Again she notices.

'Go on, Miss Kelly.'

'Kate, please,' she says and drags her attention back to my husband. 'I would like to work for you – Mr Rhodes, Mrs Rhodes – for a few days. To gain first-hand experience to better inform my employer. I would work the mine, for free of course, for I am not the worth of one of those men down the river, but I am strong and capable and not afraid of mud. I would ask for board only. Perhaps you have a tent?'

My breath holds in my chest. That is not what I expected. I had thought perhaps she would ask questions, write them down and maybe take a photograph, if she had one of those new Kodaks, but this?

'Miss – Kate – this is no work for a woman,' Charlie says, but he does not sound so convinced as when he says the same to me.

Kate looks at me as if for an ally, but I know my voice would not help.

'I assure you, Mr Rhodes, I am up to the task and, if you find I am not, then you have lost nothing in wages.'

He strokes his chin and says nothing. I see her jaw tense. She grows impatient with him. I let myself smile.

'I'm sure Mr Everett would be grateful for the assistance and will compensate you accordingly when he takes up his claim.'

Charlie's hand stills. I see the calculations in his eyes. Debt piled on debt and a wealthy man owing him a favour. She sees it too. She glances at me, notices how I watch her.

'I believe we can come to an arrangement, if that's the case. Who I am to stand in the way of a journalist and her story?'

He spreads his arms as if a welcoming king, and I wonder if he knows how like glass he is.

'We have a tent,' I say, 'from when we first came. It may not

227

be the cleanest, but I'll help you put it right.'

'Good thinking, Elly,' says Charlie, 'We have no spare stove, but you're welcome to set a fire out the front for warmth. Ellen will do your cooking.'

Kate looks at me with mild panic. 'Oh no, I'd never impress that on you, Ellen, I'll tend to myself. I won't be a bother.'

'It's no bother.' Charlie speaks for me again and if there was not a dog on my feet, I would kick him. 'Is it, Elly?'

I clench my teeth. 'None at all.'

'Thank you. Both of you. You don't know how grateful I am,' she says and looks at Charlie with a strange light in her eye. Is that hunger? Or rage? There is a concealed truth in this woman that we have let into our home. Is she looking to steal my husband from me? If so, she can dispense with the charade and have him. But there is something more. I can feel it.

I fear she is the person the fortune-teller spoke of. The adventurer who shuns the rules of society. The choice. The forbidden. I see the Devil card again as I watch her and my husband by the door, as he takes her outside to tour the claim. I see her look back at me and smile and then not, and seem sad for a moment before the straightness in her back returns. She whistles to her dog and he leaps to her.

'Now you're free,' she says with a smile. I know she means my feet of the dog, but those words lodge in my chest.

I am free.

MARTHA

DAWSON CITY, KLONDIKE, JULY 1898

'Three more dead in as many days.'

Doc Pohl paced my office, wearing a hole in the boards with his fretting.

'Another thirty cases this morning. I'm out of room at the clinic. I'm turning people away, Martha. Dying people.'

'They can die just as easy in their own beds as in yours,' I said and he stopped. Stared at me like I'd said I wanted to sell his mother.

'How can you say that? These are people.'

'And there's a few hundred more stepping onto that dock every other day.'

He shook his head, started pacing again. 'If I had a bigger space to house them . . .'

'Then all you'd have is more bodies at your front door.' I stood up from the couch, put my hand on his shoulder and he finally stilled. We'd had this talk before in harder words, but the poor man was on the edge of panic and I softened up a mite.

'You're one man. Give them the medicine they need and the advice with it and let them go with God. He'll choose who is staying and who is going, you understand?'

I saw the grit grow in him then, the law of this land and the pact we all make to live in it. Death comes a-calling and God ain't home.

A knock came at the door and I stepped back.

'Yeah?' I said and Tess appeared.

'It's Giselle,' she said in that quiet voice of hers, what made a gent think she was innocent and demure, though that girl was anything but.

'What about her?'

Tess looked at the doc. 'She's burning with fever. Says it feels like she's got rocks in her belly.'

Doc's face fell. 'Show me.'

I followed them both to Giselle's room, where the girl was curled up in her bed, blanket up tight to her chin, but shaking all over. I could hear her teeth chattering from the door.

'Lord,' I said.

Tess made to go close, but the doc grabbed her hand. 'Don't touch her. Don't touch anything in here. Go wash your hands right now. Twice, with scalding water and soap. Tell every girl in here to do the same. Now. You understand?'

Tess's eyes were saucers. She rushed out the room with her hands up, afraid to touch anything.

'Giselle,' Doc said and knelt down, so the poor girl could see him.

'Doc . . . I ain't right.'

'I can see that. Don't worry, though, I'm going to help you. Martha, will you fetch my bag? I left it in your office.'

I did as he asked, a terrible fear coming over me with every step. Giselle. Not Giselle. She was strong as a carthorse and

230

sharp with it. She couldn't go the same way as those flea-bitten miners. When I came back to the room, Doc was drying his hands, sleeves pushed to his elbows. He'd poured a glass of water and, when he saw me, he held out his hand for the bag. He went through it and found a stoppered bottle. He poured a measure of whatever it was into the glass and swirled it around.

'I need you to sit up, Giselle,' he said and, to her credit, my girl tried to move, but let out a cry that hit my bones. She clutched her gut and moaned, slumped back down.

'I can't.'

'You can and you will,' Doc said, all that uncertainty gone out of him. All that panic replaced with his duty and his oath.

He slid his arm under her and lifted. She groaned and cried, but he didn't stop. I went to help, but he shook his head. Finally Giselle was upright, propped up with an extra pillow.

Doc handed her the glass. 'Drink this. All of it.'

She didn't argue, but her hands shook so bad she couldn't hold it. He did it for her, tipping it, taking breaks, until it was all gone. Giselle sank back down and Doc sat beside her, stroking her hair, cooing like a mother over her baby. I wondered then if there was something more between them. Something like love.

Doc looked to me and the sorrow in his eyes said I was right. 'Give her bone broth – as much as she can take, but at least two bowls. Quinine twice a day. If she throws it back up, give it to her again. Make sure nobody comes in unless they have to, and make sure she doesn't leave. And wash your hands. Dear God, wash your hands.'

'I will. Is she . . . will she be all right?'

Doc looked back to Giselle, still now, sleeping, and didn't give me an answer. 'I'll stay with her for a while.'

I stood outside the door trembling. I went back to my office and washed my hands. Scrubbed till they were red raw and tingling. Then I did it again.

Doc left sometime in the afternoon and I told all the girls to leave Giselle be. I'd tend her. They were ashen with the news. Afraid for themselves as much for her. Asked if they'd get sick, if they'd die. Laura-Lynn said Giselle should be out in the sick tents with everyone else and I put it down to fear, but that girl could be cold and I was seeing it more and more.

'Whatever you do,' I said to them, 'don't tell a damn soul. There ain't no danger to anyone 'less they go in that room, so if you value your place here, you'll bite your tongues. Understand?'

The agreement came, but it was a murmur, not a shout.

The evening rush started around eight when the miners clocked off. The spread of fever across town didn't do anything to stop them enjoying themselves. If anything, they drank more, gambled longer, like they was trying to spend all their gold before the sickness came for them too. It wouldn't last; soon as they saw it up close, they'd hunker down.

I came down from giving Giselle her bone broth to a welcome face at the door.

Harriet was talking with her brother, but it weren't the usual joking and pushing and playful sniping of siblings. Harry's face was stern, brow knitted up like a sweater. His eyes found me and he nudged his sister.

I got a dark feeling in my gut.

'Evening, Ma,' she said.

'You look like you got the world on your shoulders,' I said.

She sighed and shook her head. 'Ah, shit. I got some news.'

I glanced at Harry. His eyes were burning a hole in his sister's back. I chewed on my cheek and nodded. 'Come on then.'

We took a table in the corner. Harriet, usually bubbling over with news and gossip, wind-blown cheeks and rough hair, looked like she'd had all the air driven out of her with a gut punch.

'Spill it, Harriet.'

She wouldn't look at me, only at her hands making fists on the table. 'It's Tom.'

That weren't what I was expecting. 'At the Aurora?'

She nodded.

'Goddamn, Harriet, spit it out. What could be so awful? He dead?'

She looked at me then and a bit of life came back to her. 'He ain't dead, for crying out loud. He sold up.'

'To who?'

She made a face. 'Who you think? That old weasel caved and sold up to Bill for half of what that plot is worth.'

I sat back in the chair. 'Shit! Who's left? Sutter?'

'He bought out Sutter too, yesterday. Bill's keeping him on, though, for the summer at least. Just me and you now, Ma. Then Bill will own Dawson.'

'Not while I'm breathing, he won't.'

Harriet leaned close and took my hand. 'That's what I'm afraid of.'

I patted her arm. 'Don't you worry about me. I'm stronger than I look.'

'So is he. And he has the Mounties in his pocket.'

'We ain't without friends, either. Remember that.'

She nodded, but I could tell she weren't convinced. Our friends were being bought out. She got up to leave, but stopped halfway. 'Almost forgot.' She dug into her pocket and brought out a letter, crumpled at the edges. The ink ran from rain somewhere on its journey, but I knew the hand.

Sam.

'Thank you.'

Harriet squeezed my shoulder, then took a seat at one of the poker tables. She'd take those miners for every nugget, and I'd be glad of it. Rather she have it than them.

I went straight upstairs, into my office and closed the door.

I opened the letter and my heart hurt for fear of what Sam's words might say. His hand was weak. His letters shook in the reading. The lines veered:

Dear Martha

My damn leg. The rot got in and I'm burning. Could lie me on the Yukon on Christmas Day and I'd thaw it down to Whitehorse. I got enough food for a few weeks, but the wood's running low. Heaney from the next valley split some logs for me, but it won't last past two weeks. He said he'd take this letter to the riders, but he'll be gone for a month. There ain't no one else knows where I am but you.

I ain't too big a man to say I'm scared, Martha. If I don't write again, know I love you. My heart to yours. Our time will come.

Sam

His name spilled off the paper. A tear fell from my cheek and split the ink on the S. I let the letter fall to my lap and pressed my palms to my eyes.

Don't you cry, Martha Malone; if you do, you won't stop. Go to him. Pack up and go. It might be your last chance. The voice screamed inside me to get on a wagon, a horse, a damn dog-sled – whatever it would take.

234

But Giselle. And the hotel. And my girls. Soon as I set foot out of Dawson, Bill would move in. Take it out from under me and I'd come back to nothing. No one. My men were on their way, they'd help. I had to trust in that. It'd been a few days. They'd be halfway to him; a few more and they'd be at Beaver Lake. But what would they find? I couldn't think on it.

I balled my fists on my knees and swallowed a scream.

A sharp pain shot through my stomach and into my spine and blasted the air out of me. I felt my belly and there it was, the mass. I'd barely thought on it, with everything else, but it was there, silent and deadly, strangling my insides. I knew it weren't a blockage or gas. It was death, growing quiet and unseen until it was big enough to act on its nature.

The fortune-teller's words came back to me: *There is darkness ahead. A death you cannot prevent . . . you will blame yourself for it.*

I thought she'd meant Molly, but now I weren't sure. Not with Giselle dying down the hall, and Sam dying in some far-away forest, and me dying slow in my own bed. That woman had said something else too.

You will face a choice between what you think you want and what you truly want.

But how would I ever know which was which?

KATE

I quickly got the measure of Charlie Rhodes. A man with little talent and too much self-confidence. A frustrating combination, something I could sense in Ellen from the moment I met her.

A strange couple, barely speaking or sharing time. He ignored her indifference, if he even noticed it, for he didn't seem to talk to her unless he was hungry or spotted a scrap of mud on the cabin floor. And she . . . well, I could not quite get a grasp of her yet. Yukon, however, had taken a liking immediately. He would follow at Ellen's heel as she fed the horses and drew water from the river. She seemed glad of the company and I could often hear her, while I was being given lectures on the different types of gravel, playing with and sweet-talking Yukon while he jumped for sticks and thrown rocks.

In the day and night since coming to Boulder Creek the weather had taken on an unpleasant warmth. The air was thick and heavy in my lungs, and my head ached at the end of the day. I could work only in a vest, for anything more would bathe me in sweat. Charlie worked in pants and boots alone, save for a kerchief around his neck that he never took off. To his credit, he never looked at me or made a comment he would not make to his wife or mother. I sensed he had no interest in me romantically and my relief could not have been greater, for the thought put a sickness in my stomach that would not dislodge.

Charlie was a detailed, if impatient, teacher and showed me the ropes of gold mining.

In the summer, in a poor man's mine, a man digs into the riverbank and bed in a spot determined only by his own intuition. He piles dirt and gravel into great mounds. This he feeds into a sluice. There is a short run of troughs, a few feet perhaps, ten at the most, with flowing water, which another man is supposed to keep moving by pouring buckets down from the top. Another man is to feed these troughs with shovelfuls of dirt. The sluice washes the gold from the clay and soil, freeing it to be found. The gold is heavy, you see, and once free of the clay and rock, sinks to the bottom of a pan or a rocker. At the end of the sluice is another mound, at least on the Rhodes claim. On others I have seen, this slurry of muddy water and gold goes into a huge basin to be panned by the weaker or newer hires or, on occasion, by wives looking for extra income.

In the richer mines there are dozens of workers, hydraulic lifts, twenty-foot-long sluice boxes and jet-washes to loosen the hillsides. Some have huge shafts dug down to the bedrock in the winter months, to be panned and sluiced in the summer when the frozen dirt holding the gold has melted.

Charlie insisted his gold was finer than that of his fellows down the hill, so his slurry then went through his rocker box. This had a carpet, called miner's moss, within it to catch the smallest pieces – something often missed, he said, by those on other creeks.

'The fortune is in the dust, not the nuggets, you see,' he said, but he was convincing himself alone.

I carried buckets of water from the river to the end of the sluice. It was further away than it should have been, but when I suggested moving it closer to the water, he said I was wrong. My arms and shoulders ached, but I felt them strengthen. It was a brutal exercise, sapping even the strongest man of his energy in a few hours. It strips the land of its trees, leaves scars on the river and changes its course. It is an angry business and I felt the land rebelling against it.

But when I saw my first gold, I understood.

The glint of it in the pan. The way it appeared and disappeared with every wash until it was all finally revealed. A thick line of metal men value more than their lives. I picked out a nugget the size of a corn kernel, rubbed it between my fingers. Felt how dense it was. Unlike any other metal. Barely a metal at all, it held its own warmth and felt soft to touch. Looking at it was like looking into a fire – one can barely seem to look away.

Charlie saw my face and plucked the nugget from my fingers. 'Careful, Kate, or the fever will take you too.'

I let it go with a wrench and went back to my work.

I had thought only the weak-minded gave in to the pull of gold, but I saw the truth of it. We are drawn to what is precious, what can grant us our desires, what can be found in dirt by any with a right and a pan: rich or poor, immigrant or citizen, man or woman, everyone is equal in the race for gold. That is the great lie of this place. The lie of gold itself.

I was not here for that. I was here for my sister. And the pull of gold was nothing to the pull of revenge.

I watched Charlie Rhodes as we worked together. Looked

for scratches on his skin from Molly's nails, but he was always caked in mud or his neck obscured by the kerchief.

I watched Ellen too, in the evenings or when we took lunch, when I caught her staring out at me or caught myself staring at her. It was not beyond possibility that a woman, upon finding out her husband had a mistress, could wield the knife herself.

Yet Ellen didn't seem to care what her husband did. She didn't care he was spending his days with a stranger, a woman no less. She cared only for her horse and, now, my dog. Yukon would still come when I called and sleep beside me in my tent, but not without a belly rub from Ellen to say goodnight first.

It was on the second day of hard labour and sleeping on the uneven floor of a tent that I got up the nerve.

'Mr Rhodes,' I began and he laughed. We were taking a break from the sun and the work, sitting by the creek.

'How much dirt must we shift before you call me Charlie?'

I smiled. 'Charlie, then. I'm not one to gossip, but I heard some rumours when I was in Dawson about a miner from this river who might have killed a girl, then ran off.'

He sniffed and the levity in his voice disappeared. 'Yannick Early. He worked two claims down. One of Bill Mathers's men.'

'I heard about Mathers. They say he's a Klondike King. Owns the mines, but doesn't work them.'

'That's right. But he doesn't own this one.'

I sensed the pride in him right away, mixed perhaps with something else. A thread to pull later. 'Did Mr Early seem the type to do something like that? The word in Dawson was he was a quiet man.'

Charlie shrugged. 'One can never tell, right? Men are capable of anything up here if the mood strikes.'

'Even murder?'

He scratched his neck beneath his kerchief. 'Especially murder.'

Charlie and I worked until midnight, making the most of the late sun, for Charlie said it would only last another month or so, then the chill of September would set in and, soon after, winter would lock the land and its people in ice.

I found sleep hard to come by, the light never quite dimming enough to drift off, then brightening again seemingly immediately. At least in Dawson I had been able to shut the curtains and hide beneath a pillow, but the tent was white and let in a constant pale light.

I was lying in my makeshift bed – a few blankets and sacking laid over each other as a mattress, my own coat balled into a pillow – when I heard the front door of the cabin open and close.

I was already dressed, for I never undressed except to bathe, and that was not regular. I went to the door and peered through the canvas. My tent sat off to the south, between the cabin and the horse pen, and I could see them both clearly.

Ellen, shawl over her shoulders, walked towards the horses. This was not the first time I'd seen her. She often took her horse and rode it up the claim and out of sight. She would return more than an hour later, before Charlie rose, and for a time after each ride she smiled as if rejuvenated.

I don't know what prompted me, perhaps Yukon nuzzling my leg, tail thumping, or perhaps my own curiosity about this woman and her habits, but I followed. I watched her lead Bluebell out of the pen, feed her a treat from her palm and seat herself on the horse's back. With a gentle click of her tongue, Bluebell walked.

Yukon moved to dash after her, but I grabbed his collar. 'Hush, Yukc. You must be quiet and stay close, do you understand?'

He cocked his head and gave a short whine.

I took that as his agreement. I gave him a scratch under his chin and rubbed his head the way he liked. 'Good boy.'

Yukon stayed at my heel, silent as a wolf on the hunt, as we crossed the claim and followed Ellen's path into the trees.

The way was easy for a time, then took a sharp turn up the side of the valley. A switchback path had been cut through the undergrowth, by Ellen or by nature, I couldn't tell. I couldn't see her, but sometimes caught the sound of Bluebell's hooves.

Soon the path levelled onto a vast, open plateau, a hidden oasis of meadow grass and blueberry bushes. The smell of the place was intoxicating after so long around mud and stone and an unwashed man. Rich forest mulch, both dank and sweet, flowers in bloom and alive with insects. An untouched paradise in the middle of a wasteland. I could see why Ellen came here of a morning and returned smiling.

Bluebell was tied on the far side of the meadow, but I could not see her rider. Yukon sniffed at the flowers, caught scents he'd never known and was too excited to follow quietly.

I went to the horse and saw, a dozen or so feet away, Ellen kneeling by the river, her hands dipping in and out of the water. Loose hair caught the dappled sunlight, lifted in an invisible breeze. I found I wanted to know her. What turns her life had taken to deposit her here. What kind of life she wished for herself.

I crept closer.

She whipped round. Gold fell from her fingers into the grass. In her other hand she held a gun.

ELLEN

I lower the gun, but only halfway. I brought it for the bears, but it does as well with people.

'It's just me,' Kate says. This stranger who has inserted herself into our lives.

'Just you,' I repeat and my earlier intrigue is replaced with irritation. She followed me. To my land. 'And who is that?'

She tries to smile. 'Could you put the gun down?'

'You followed me.'

'I was curious is all. I've noticed you in the early mornings take a ride and come back glowing.' She smiles as if at the memory of seeing me so.

My grip begins to tremble. I put down the revolver and see what Kate sees. Gold in the grass. I pick it up as she kneels beside me.

I watch her find a nugget. Then look to the water, where more wait.

'This is . . .' she begins.

'Mine. This claim is in my name. Charlie does not know it

is rich.'

She looks at me with astonishment. 'Why not?'

I dry the gold on my dress, offer my hand for the piece she holds. She gives it, without question or attempt to conceal. An honest streak, it seems, amid a cloud of deceit.

'Charlie has no head for money.'

'But surely you must—'

'Must?' I turn to her. 'Must what? Who are you, Kate Kelly? Why are you here? I do not believe for a moment your interest lies in mining. Especially with my husband, who, it should be clear by now, knows little of his occupation.'

She does not meet my eyes. She is quiet, appears to look for the right words. The right lie. I watch her as she stares at the water. There is a brightness in her, a fervour I used to have, but not for so long now. I feel it sometimes, here, where the wilderness has not been stripped to rock. The old blood heats. Thins. Life returns.

She looks at me and the heat grows.

'I am here to learn, that's all,' she says.

'I do not believe you. Do you have intentions towards Charlie?'

Her laugh is explosive. Such shock in her eyes, as if I have said the most ridiculous thing.

'No. God, no. I have no desire to steal your husband. If you trust nothing else about me, you may trust that.'

I believe that is the first honest thing she has said since coming here.

I feel myself warming to her, despite my worries. I smile at her laugh and she way she bulges her eyes and shakes her head at the idea of Charlie as husband. She has a familiar look about her, but I know I have not met her before. I would remember.

'Are you sure?' I say. 'Because you may have him. He is of little use to me.'

She laughs again. The sound fits this place. I do not remember the last time I laughed. God, how dire is that? Charlie used to make me laugh. When we first met, he was a clown. Used humour to sidle himself close to others where his skills in business would not allow him. I wonder if he made Molly laugh. If she saw in him all I did and more. If she finally saw through it and that's why . . .

'Ellen?'

Kate's hand is on my shoulder. She looks at me with concern. 'What is it?' she asks.

I shake my head. 'Nothing. I am tired is all. We should be getting back.'

'What were you thinking of then? Your expression turned grave so suddenly.'

A subtle shift in my person that Charlie would never notice. I feel the weight of secrets on my back. I fear it will break my spine. Kate watches. Sees. She is a stranger here. To my claim. To the Klondike. What harm can there be to speak a little and ease the burden?

'There was a girl murdered in Dawson City a week ago. I met her once. She was my husband's whore.'

I see her flinch at the word. 'I stayed at the Dawson Hotel when I arrived and it was the talk of the place.'

'She came here a few days before she died. She and Charlie had a quarrel. A lovers' tiff.'

'What happened?'

'Not much. A few heated words. Nothing of consequence.'

Kate leans closer, her voice quicker. Urgent. 'But she was murdered. Could those words have been a threat?'

'They weren't,' I say. 'She left soon after. I do not know

where she went or who she saw.'

'The Mounties say it was a man named Yannick Early.'

'Early did not kill her.'

She leans back. 'You sound so sure.'

'I am. He was a good man.' I hear the gunshot again. See him reaching for mercy from Frank Croaker before the second shot.

'How can you know?'

I fix her gaze with mine. 'I know.'

She is quiet a while. Her fingers play in the water. When she lifts them out, they are red with cold. 'Who do you think killed her?'

My husband, I think. Although I'm not sure if I truly believe it or only wish to think the worst of him.

'I don't know. This place is not like anywhere else. It is lawless and free of the social graces and behaviours we take for granted. All that matters here is gold and power, and the rush of both. Her death plagues me. I have wondered every day since if I could have done something more the day she came here. I could have asked her to stay instead of telling her to leave. But I didn't.'

Her shoulders relax, but only a little. She lifts a hand to place it on mine, then thinks again and returns it to her knee. 'You cannot torture yourself like that. It does no one any good, trust me.'

She speaks from experience, it appears. A regret? A course of action not taken? I wish to know her secrets more than anything else in this world.

'I do not trust you, Miss Kelly. But I believe I am starting to like you.'

She laughs again. She opens her mouth to speak when a sharp yelp cuts her off. In a moment she is on her feet. 'Yukon? Yukon!'

Another yelp and she is running. Back to the meadow. I find her kneeling, cradling her dog.

'Ellen! What has happened to him?'

I skid down beside them. Yukon paws at his muzzle, whining and yelping, throwing his head around. I grab his leg and see. In his muzzle are dozens of white spikes.

My blood runs cold as meltwater. 'A porcupine.'

Kate looks at me with horror. Then back to her poor dog. The quills are stuck in the roof of his mouth, his tongue, his gums, they circle one eye. An eye he will lose if we do not act quickly.

I run to Bluebell and unhitch her. Kate pulls the dog close, holds his front legs. His breathing labours. 'What do we do? We must help him!'

'Get on the horse!'

I hold Yukon as she climbs up, then pass him to her and climb up myself. Kate sits ahead of me, Yukon in her lap. I hold the reins from behind her.

We ride as fast as the trail will let us. Bluebell knows the way. Knows her footing and keeps it. My chin bobs against Kate's shoulder. I feel her lean back against me as Bluebell rides down the steepest part of the trail. When we break from the trees, I snap the reins and Bluebell flies.

At the pen she stops. I slide down first, take Yukon from Kate's arms as she dismounts. His heart is racing, his breathing shallow. A rattle in his chest. His eye is wide and unfocused. He cannot close his mouth. I see inside a mess of white spines, as if he has bitten down on a pile of needles.

'Quickly, into the house.' I run ahead, open the door.

Charlie is dressing. He will expect breakfast on the table. He begins to speak, to reprimand me, but then he sees Kate. Yukon. The distress on our faces. He has the good sense to hold his tongue.

'On the table,' I say, clearing the water jug and a few bowls.

Kate lays the dog down. He is limp, breath nothing but a wheeze. His tongue, studded with quills, lolls from his mouth.

'Get a blanket,' I say, but nobody moves. I grab Kate's arm and her tear-stained face meets mine. 'A blanket.'

She nods and covers Yukon with a brown wool throw.

Charlie pays little mind. He takes bread from the bowl and sniffs it. Takes a bite, speaks with his mouth full. 'He get too close to a porcupine?'

I grab the tongs from the fire.

'That's rotten luck,' he says, chewing. 'Ellen's got a pea-shooter, should you wish to show mercy.'

Kate looks at him. Threat and fire in her eyes.

Charlie shakes his head like it's a damn shame and goes to the door. 'Lunch on the table at noon, and I ain't eating dog.'

He thinks he is funny. He even laughs as he leaves. I wish to show him mercy with my pea-shooter.

Yukon whines. 'Ellen, he's getting worse.'

I want to apologise for my husband, but there is no time. 'Do you have tweezers?'

She thinks a moment then runs.

I take two bowls, fill one with boiling water from the kettle and set the tongs in it. Kate returns with the tweezers – silver, delicate – and I put them in too.

'You must hold him. This will be painful for him, but necessary. Do you understand?'

She nods.

I take out the tongs and begin to pull the biggest quills. They snag and drag his flesh, but come out with a wrench. The poor dog screams. Bucks. Kate lies on him and hushes him. I use the tweezers to take the ones around his eye.

'Hold him tighter. If one of these breaks, it will worm its way through his skin and take his eye.'

Kate pales and leans harder on her dog.

My hand shakes. Yukon's eye stares at me. Terrified. I see my reflection in that brown marble. See how he needs me now to be strong.

I pull them out gently. Check each one is whole. Until they are all out.

Then I must tackle his mouth. I use a stick to hold his jaws open. I see it cut into him, but that is the least of my concerns.

It takes an hour. His tongue is purple and swollen, his palette bleeding. His face puffy.

I look at my hands. Bloody. Shaking. The bowl is full of red-tipped quills.

'Will he be all right?' Kate asks me.

The dog doesn't move. His breathing is shallow, but even. His heart thuds weakly against his chest. 'I don't know. If he makes it through the night . . .'

'If?'

'A porcupine can kill a dog. I've seen it before.'

Kate buries her head in Yukon's side.

'Let's take him to your tent. Keep him warm.'

She carries him as if carrying a child, wrapped in a blanket. Still, as if sleeping. She puts him on her bed, covers him. Pours water from a canteen into a shallow bowl and places it near his head. She strokes him, kisses him.

I realise I have not been in this tent since the cabin was built. Not since she joined us. She has made it her own. It is calm and behind the smell of dirt and old linseed oil is her. A slight perfume made richer in the heat. Her clothes hang against a wall, warming in the sun. Her few possessions are neat, in their place. A large notebook . . . no, a sketchbook, I see a drawing peeking out. Paper for letters. Wax and a seal. A candle. A lantern. I suddenly imagine her here, writing home, holding the red wax stick over the flame. A few seconds of stillness. What does she think then, in those seconds?

Kate stands, faces me. The air is close, she closer. She takes my hand. 'Thank you.'

'He is strong. With a tremendous will to live. He will be all right.'

Kate smiles. 'Because of you. How did you know all that?'

'The Klondike is a fast and fierce teacher. We had a dog when we came here. Charlie hated it, said all it did was get underfoot, but Buck – that was his name – made me feel safe. And he had a fondness for porcupines.'

'What happened to him?'

I look down at poor Yukon. 'Charlie sold him. He told me he would be pulling sleds, but the money he came home with far exceeded any price for a sled dog. Then I saw in Dawson a poster for dog-fighting and I knew he had lied to me.'

'I'm sorry.'

'That is why Charlie must not know about the gold. If he knew, he would take it as his and he would destroy it. Please. Do not tell him.'

Kate takes my hands. Her skin is rough from the work, but her touch is tender in a way Charlie's never is. 'I won't. I promise. But . . . what will you do with it? Surely he will find out?'

'I'll collect enough to leave him. Leave here.'

'That's what you really want?'

I look at this woman, this free woman, who may go and do as she wishes, and I realise she is the only person ever to ask that question of me.

'I don't know. I don't yet see a way to stay, though I think I would like to.'

'There is always a way, if you have the will, and I believe you do.'

I force a smile. Free my hands from hers and go to turn away, when I hear it. Charlie. Shouting.

I duck out of the tent and Kate follows.

Charlie is at the spot where the alders stood. He jumps. Waves his arms.

'What in the world?' Kate says, but I know.

With a sinking dread in my gut, I go to him. Kate a step behind me.

'Gold! Gold!' he shouts and shouts. He runs to me and grabs me by the shoulders, spins me. 'I've done it, Ellen! I told you!'

He pulls my wrist to the pit he has dug. There, in the soil, I see it. A heavy seam of gold. Nuggets and dust. It runs in a curve around a huge boulder.

'The river was here – the bend! It caught the gold. I knew it! I knew it!'

His face is red, sweating, spit flies from his mouth. He runs to Kate. Pulls her into the celebration.

'Good Lord!' she says and kneels. She digs a hand into the pit and it comes out full of gold.

'That boulder! Under there is our fortune,' he carries on.

I see the edges. The boulder is as wide as Charlie is tall and half his height. I kneel beside Kate. She marvels at the gold in her hand, but I see a doubt in her eye. I look and see it too. The edges, again. The gold runs around the boulder as if the stone were a giant riffle, but it stops. I brush away gravel and smooth river pebbles, but it does not extend far.

'Will you say something, Ellen?' Charlie cries. 'I have done it. I have found it! Did I not tell you?'

The heart goes out of me. 'Wonderful. It's wonderful, Charlie.'

His excitement deafens him to my tone.

'A strike of the highest order,' Kate says, standing, brushing dirt from her knees. She holds up a large nugget, perhaps the size of a peach pit. It shines in the sunlight. 'Enough to rival Skookum Jim, that's for sure.'

He takes the nugget from her. 'You're right, Miss Kelly. This will be the biggest find in Klondike history!'

He hugs me then. I let him. I watch Kate, over his shoulder, dust off her hands. She forces a smile. She sees what I see. Charlie breaks the hug and kisses me. It is forced and he pushes his face against mine so hard it hurts.

'What a day!' he cries. 'Kate, help me dig this out.'

And I am discarded. I wipe my mouth of him and turn away.

I feel Kate watching me. A moment, maybe, of her eyes on my back, then she is pulled into the pit with him.

They spend the rest of the day digging, panning, washing, until Charlie deems he has enough. I churn milk for butter, bake a hard loaf and check on Yukon. He sleeps; his legs kick like he chases that porcupine in his dreams. I set some meat scraps out for him and, when I return an hour later, they are half-gone and he is sleeping again. A good sign.

At close to six, Charlie and Kate return to the cabin. In their hands, two pans of gold. Full. Kate struggles to hold hers and sets it on the table with a thud.

Never have I seen so much gold in this place.

Charlie grins from ear to ear and comes to me, throws an arm around my shoulder. Kisses me again on the cheek.

'Look at what your husband has done,' he says.

And I look at Kate. She is red-faced, breathless, muddy. I wish it were her arm around my shoulder. But I push the thought away as I push my husband away.

'Look at that,' I say.

'And it is just the start! Under that boulder is our fortune. We must celebrate!'

Charlie goes to a cupboard and takes out a bottle of whiskey. Three glasses. Three measures. We drink together. A strange trio. Full of secrets and lies.

He goes to the corner floorboard, the loose one, and prises it up. Takes out the three jars. All empty, but for smears of shining dust. He gives us one each and we fill them. One pan fills three. I find a mason jar, empty it of grain, and fill that. Then a bag, until the pans are empty and we feel rich, for a moment.

Charlie picks up two jars. 'I'm going to Dawson tonight. To the assayer.'

To Bill Mathers. To pay his debts.

'I will settle our every account,' he laughs. Another kiss. Another bruise. 'Kate, will you come? This is as much your victory as mine.'

I shrivel within. Her victory? What of mine? My years of toil in this place. Do they mean nothing to him?

'I should like to stay,' she says. 'To keep watch on Yukon. And keep Ellen company. Besides, I'd wager half the men down the valley heard our celebration, so perhaps a second pair of eyes, or a second gun, would deter thieves.'

Charlie nods. 'You know how to use a shotgun?'

'My father believed a woman must know how to defend herself.'

'A wise man. Ellen's father knew only to teach a girl to be a wife.' He leaves the rest unsaid. That my father did a poor job. Charlie has said it before.

I do not believe I could hate him more than I do in that moment. I think of the bloody shirt beneath the boards. I think of how I could engineer his arrest. But the feeling dies. The Mounties have their man. Or at least they have their idea, and that is enough when there are too few men to fill a barracks.

Charlie leaves within the hour. Kate and I watch him mount Goldie. Struggle for a moment to control the beast. Then ride away, waving. Down the valley, the miners watch and he tips his hat. He grins and shakes hands. There are fewer miners than normal. Perhaps half the number. Those remaining are slow. Tired.

Kate leans against the porch post. In the summer sun, her hair lightens. Strands fly loose from her braid and turn to fire in the caught light. The red blush of her skin, the slight glisten of sweat on her brow so disconcerts me I turn away. Watch Charlie's horse grow small in the distance.

Down the valley, the light changes. Clouds rush against the mountainsides. Corralled like a herd of wild deer. In the Klondike the summer storms come fast. Charlie will ride in the rain.

'I'm going to check on Yukon,' Kate says and looks back at me as if willing me to ask her to stay. But fear overtakes my heart and I simply nod.

MARTHA

'Four rooms empty. Two no-shows,' Jerry said.

Jessamine stood with her hands on her hips. 'I got leftovers pilin' up in my kitchen. Not enough mouths to eat it.'

I knew it before they walked in here, worried. I got the money in front of me. The piles smaller than ever.

'You think word got out about Giselle?' I asked them both.

They look at each other. Jessamine crosses her arms. She's all elbows and hips, that woman. 'Not from me.'

Jerry isn't as quick to deny it. 'I heard talk. Miners saying the drink is good here, but the girls are sickly.'

'Shit!' I tapped my nail on the desk. 'Who talked? She's been sick barely three days.'

'I don't know, Ma,' he said and I believed him.

'All right. Make up some hash and beans, use any leftovers for breakfast. I won't have waste.'

Jessamine nodded and left.

'And water down by another fifth,' I said to Jerry as he was getting up to leave.

'You want a riot?' he asked.

'I want to survive past the end of the month. Do it.'

'You got it, Ma,' he said and closed the door behind him.

Empty rooms. Empty tables. Soon-to-be-empty pockets and then what will become of me, my girls? I got a tight chest thinking about it.

The evening was getting going and it was noticeably quieter than usual. I did the rounds, talked to the girls, got them to put on a bit more rouge, a bit more paint on their eyes, undo an extra lace. They all looked at me with sad eyes, except Laura-Lynn. She had a face of stone on her, eyes like pebbles, hard to read, but even a blind man could see she weren't happy with how things were going at the Dawson Hotel. I didn't have time to think on her, or listen to her griping, because if there was one thing Laura-Lynn was good at, it was griping. My room's too cold. My blanket's too rough. My bed's got a spring loose. So when she went to speak, I held up my hand to her.

'Not now, Laura-Lynn, I got to tend to Giselle.'

I left her seething. To hell with her, she could stew for a while. I went to the kitchen for the bone broth and took a bowl upstairs.

I knocked gently on Giselle's door and went in.

She was sitting up. Still pale, but she weren't shaking no more. My heart leapt and I couldn't keep the smile off my face.

'Hey, Ma,' she said. Voice weak as a kitten, but with none of that feverish slur.

'Well, don't you look a picture,' I said.

I sat down on the bed and handed her the bowl. She drank a few sips.

'Doc says I'm strong,' she said. 'He was here this morning.'

'Mmm. He's sweet on you.'

Colour flooded her cheeks. 'Him and every man in Dawson.'

'You're sweet on him, too.'

'You don't miss anything, do you, Ma?'

'Not if I can help it.'

I took her hand, squeezed it, held it, like I should've held Molly.

'I was afraid I'd lose you too,' I said and Giselle took my other hand in hers.

'It weren't your fault what happened to Molly.'

'If I'd been kinder, not thrown her out, she'd be alive, I know it.'

'Why did you – throw her out, I mean? I never understood it, but I thought she must have done something spiteful to make you. Didn't think it wise to ask at the time.'

I looked at Giselle. She had a good head on her shoulders, a better heart in her chest. I trusted her in a way I didn't trust many.

'I thought she went through my private things, read some letters she weren't supposed to, was getting tips from the miners to feed to Bill Mathers, asking all the girls for what they heard. Spying.'

Giselle frowned. 'Molly never done that. That was Laura-Lynn. She asked me what gents were in the gold, tried to get me to tell her their claims. Shit, she was even asking after you and your affairs. I drew the line at that gossip. That girl is a bad sort. Could smell it on her a mile off.'

I felt my edges crumble. 'Molly weren't seeing Bill, was she?'

She scoffed. 'Molly hated Bill. Wouldn't touch him. He was obsessed with her, course. Thought he was in love. But she knew better than to go near him.'

'Then where'd she get those bruises?'

Giselle collapsed back on the pillows, suddenly drained and pale again. 'I don't know. I figured a gent got too rough, but she wouldn't have kept that a secret. She'd have told Harry and he'd have thrown the guy out. It don't make any sense.'

It didn't make a lick of sense, but all of a sudden it made more than it had in months. My mind was racing. It was Laura-Lynn who told me about Molly sneaking into my office. It was her said Molly was seeing Bill. Laura-Lynn said she saw them cosying up in the Tivoli. *She* said Molly was asking the girls after their gents and their gold.

I'd been right, there was a snake in my house, but I'd put out the wrong one. The anger in me. I'd never felt the like. It rose up in me like a storm.

'Ma?' Giselle said, but her voice was muffled over the blood in my ears. The ringing sound of betrayal.

But I had to be sure. I wouldn't make the same mistake.

I patted Giselle's leg. 'You rest.'

'What are you going to do?'

I stood and felt a sharp twinge in my gut that caught my breath. I closed my eyes a second, forced the pain back where it came from. I put on a smile. 'What I have to.'

I left then, to sounds of Giselle calling me back, asking if I was all right. I ignored them and went downstairs. Laura-Lynn was by the poker table, hanging on the knee of a gent too big for the chair. He held her round the waist, the end of a cheroot in his mouth. He had a gold buckle, gold rings, a pouch open beside his hand. The unlucky miners stared at it like a starving dog at a bone.

This kind of gent was dangerous, but Laura-Lynn didn't seem to know it. She giggled and blew on his cards like she was his lucky charm.

The door opened and a group of miners came in and let in

a breeze with them. It carried a smell to me, like sandalwood and soap, incense. I knew the owner. I looked for her and there, in the far corner, on a table I didn't know I had, was the fortune-teller.

Laura-Lynn could wait. I went to the woman. The gaslight was out and she was sat in a shadow. But her eyes. They still gleamed bright white.

'Are you lost?' I said.

She smiled at me. 'Not any more.'

'What are you doing here? I told you you weren't welcome.'

'It's nearly time, Martha. To choose.'

'What are you talking about?'

'Between what you think you want and what you truly want. If you wait too long, the choice will be made for you.'

The gent with the gold buckle must have lost a hand, for I heard a ruckus starting.

'What do you care?' I asked. I put both hands on the table, leaned close to her. 'You ain't welcome here.'

She held a pack of cards in her hand. Big ones. Looked hand-painted. She shuffled them as she spoke. Hand over hand, one over another, like she was casting a spell.

'You need to know this, Martha Malone.'

'You know what I need to know? Who killed Molly? Huh?'

She looked at me then. There was sadness in her eyes. 'I don't know. That's the past. You will find out, I assure you that. But it carries a high price.'

The ruckus grew. Out the corner of my eye I saw Harry move to put a stop to it. Heard a table overturn, poker chips scatter.

'What'll it cost me?'

The fortune-teller grabbed my hand. The one I'd cut, still wrapped in a bandage. The cards dropped. Only one landed face-up.

The Reaper.

She put her mouth to my ear. 'Everything.'

The ruckus became a brawl. Shouts. The roar of fighting men and the hard slap of fists. I pulled free from the woman and turned to face it.

The big man with the gold buckle threw a miner into a table. It smashed beneath him.

'You'd better get ou—' But the fortune-teller was gone. Slipped out like a snake when I weren't looking. On the table, the Death card stared up at me.

Harry shouted for me to get clear. I did just in time. A man flew at the table, crashed right where I'd been standing.

Gold Buckle had two men on him. Laura-Lynn and the girls cowered under the staircase, behind the piano. Jerry reached for the shotgun under the bar as a man, punched by another, flew over the bar and landed right on him.

'Goddamn it! Harry, get this under control,' I shouted, but nobody heard over the din. Except Harry. He made a line for Gold Buckle. Pushed gents out his way, threw punches. If he could get that man out of here, the place would calm down.

Three men jumped on Gold Buckle and drove punch after punch after kick into him. Harry rushed the pile as the big man reared up. Gun in his hand.

The shots rang out clear and cut the noise. Two men fell. Harry ran at him, reached for the gun, but the other man was quicker.

I saw it all as if it was happening to someone else. Time slowed to a crawl. I tried to shout, but my voice was molasses in my throat.

Harry pulled back his fist. The man drew back the hammer. The bullet hit Harry's chest. His fist missed the man's cheek.

Harry hit the floorboards. He didn't get up.

Gold Buckle swung his gun around. 'Anyone else?' he shouted and nobody moved.

I saw the panic hit him. Three dead men at his feet and a room full of witnesses. Even the Mounties couldn't deny that one.

He pushed his way out and ran into the street.

'Harry!' Jerry got there first. He skidded to his knees, dropped the shotgun and pressed his hands over the wound. 'Someone get Doc Pohl. Now!'

But I could see it, from where I stood. The doc wouldn't be able to do nothing. I went to Harry's side. Put my hands over Jerry's. There was no heart pumping. No bleeding to stem. No life to save.

'Everybody out,' I said. 'Party's over.'

The miners scraped up the spilled poker chips and gold, even took scattered coins from the blood on the floor, picked at the pockets of the other dead men. Vultures.

In a few minutes they were gone.

I pressed my forehead to Harry's. Tears didn't sting my eyes. Rage didn't boil my blood. I was numb to it all now. This was the Klondike. This was the rush. Death stood on his hill and laughed.

I stood up, tried to breathe, but it was like sucking in glass. This place. This goddamn place. I went to the bar, found a bottle of whiskey, took a drink, then threw it at the wall. The girls jumped. I saw Laura-Lynn among them, whimpering.

Not tonight. She would keep.

I went to the stairs, stopped at the first step. Giselle leaned over the balcony, arm around her stomach, mouth wide with shock.

'Someone go get Harriet,' I said and Jerry stood and walked

out without a word. 'And cover him up, goddamn it. He deserves his dignity.'

One of the girls rushed by me up the stairs and came back with a sheet. She laid it gently over Harry.

I didn't wait for Harriet. I couldn't face her. Console her. Explain. I went upstairs to my office and locked the door.

I heard her, though, not long after. That wail. That deep animal cry. The true sound of a heart breaking. A sound I knew better than I ever wanted to.

KATE

BOULDER CREEK, KLONDIKE, JULY 1898

Yukon lifted his head, pawing his face and whining like a puppy. I held on to his leg so he could not damage himself, and he did not resist me.

'Hush now, you foolish mutt. You could have died.'

He crept closer, in that inching way dogs do when they know they have done something wrong, and rested his head on my leg. I scratched around his ears, my mind elsewhere, until he yawned and settled.

The wind buffeted the canvas tent, pushed at my back. A breeze at first, but it quickly grew to gusts. The rain joined it, a sharp drumbeat on the walls and roof. Clouds darkened the sky to a degree it felt almost night. I'd always loved storms, the feeling like the world is alive around you, alive and dancing to some cosmic beat. Charlotte hated them. Where I said dancing, she said fighting.

'The world is angry,' she'd said at just nine years old. 'It means to kill us.'

And in Kansas a storm would. The tornadoes in early

summer ripped through the fields, cut up roads and did not care if you put up a fence or claimed land as yours. The storm saw no barriers and county lines. It was a force. I respected that. Then the wind would shout and howl, anything left in the yard would be gone, and the house would need repairing in the morning.

'We're safe,' I'd said, huddled for warmth and comfort in the storm cellar, our father pacing and calculating the damage costs; and we – his children, needing him – only had each other.

The wind gusted now and pushed me off the canvas. All around me the walls flapped and bowed. The canvas snapped against the poles, the sound of the rain eased with a strong wind, then hammered again as it fell. I shrank against Yukon. His ears flattened against his head.

It was easy to be brave in a stone cellar at nine years old. But in a tent on top of the world, hours from even the most basic medical care and among desperate people, I understood why Charlotte saw anger in a storm. This was not a fit of nature's passion, but a force of her rage.

Yukon pressed against me, pawing at my legs. I held him as the water invaded. The rain cut streams through the mud at my feet. The seams on the old tent let in drops, then more. A steady downpour inside to match that outside. I grabbed a cup, caught the drop closest. Then another came, dripping onto the notebook. I lunged for it.

The wind shook the tent and lifted a corner I had not properly staked down. I heard a rip. The loose corner flapped wildly, snapping like a caught animal. The sound of the rain, the wind, the tent taking the brunt of it, drilled into my head.

Another sound cut above it all. A crash from somewhere outside. I didn't dare open the tent, but then I heard a horse cry and whinny.

'Stay!' I shouted to Yukon and the poor beast curled himself up against my bag.

I pulled on my jacket and tied a scarf around my head.

The moment I stepped outside the wind caught me and I was a ragdoll. I stumbled, dropped into the mud, which only an hour ago had been dust. Water ran in sheets over the ground. I got to my feet during a lull in the wind and ran for the horses.

At the pen I saw a figure holding Bluebell's reins. Ellen pulled on them as the horse reared and cried.

'Ellen!' I shouted and she turned. Her hair was untied and whipped around her head.

'Help me!'

I ran to her, skidded on the slick ground. I grabbed the reins and together we pulled the horse.

'We have to get her into the trees,' I shouted over the roar of the wind.

Ellen went to the gate. It blew open the moment she unlatched it. She cried out, clutching her hand. But neither of us had time to worry. She grabbed Bluebell's reins and pulled her out. The horse backed away, whinnying, eyes bulging wild and fearful.

'Come on, you stupid beast,' I shouted and slapped her flank.

She reared again, but half-heartedly.

Lightning flashed downriver. In this treeless valley, it struck a tent on higher ground and the whole thing burst into flames. The miners were like swarming ants, rushing here and there, with buckets and panic.

'Quickly!' I called out.

Ellen pulled on Bluebell as thunder rent the sky. That woke the horse and she would have bolted, if Ellen had not been there to hold her.

I grabbed the reins and we shared a look of understanding. Of fear. We led the horse across the claim. The sluice boxes had fallen, the piles of dirt were washing away. The rich alder pit had filled with rainwater. Great rivers of mud ran down the valley sides, cutting through the loose gravel and topsoil, carrying scrub and debris with them. Loose logs rolled downstream and smashed on boulders. Without trees to hold the land, the mud slaked away in huge swathes.

Under the trees, the respite from the rain was brief. The strong trunks withstood the worst, but the wind ripped the upper branches and leaves flew like confetti. Bluebell calmed under their canopy. We didn't tie her, but took off her bridle and let her go. She dashed off into the trees, tail high, ears up.

Ellen put her hand on my arm. 'Thank you.'

I could only nod, breathless, soaked through.

We fought against the wind back to the cabin. Every step was like walking through deep water, the elements wanted to rip us from the land, hurl us away. Thunder cracked and rain beat down so hard it was like rocks on my head, my shoulders. When the wind swept up the valley, those rocks turned to needles, ice-cold and cutting our faces, hands. It found any inch of exposed skin and attacked.

The cabin had sprung a dozen leaks. Ellen, dripping in her sodden skirts, ran about the place with bowls, jugs, basins, catching them all.

I ran for Yukon. The tent was ripped up and half-blown away. But he was there, still cowered against my bag. I gathered him up in my arms and, with a jolt, saw Charlotte's notebook in the mud, cover open, pages fluttering. I grabbed it, rushed back into the cabin and slammed the door.

The sound of the storm receded. The rain was more distant with walls between us.

I set Yukon down, shivering and yelping, by the stove.

'Is he all right?' Ellen asked.

He looked up at me with those wide eyes. I smiled for him and his tail began to thump. His muzzle was still a puffy mess of pinpricks, but at least he would live.

'A little wet is all.'

Ellen let out a long breath. For some reason, I felt like laughing.

'This cabin has weathered worse,' she said as if it would comfort me and, in truth, it did somewhat. She stood in the kitchen, leaning against the worktop. Every breath she took was a shudder.

'Are you all right?' I asked.

'We must keep the fire high.'

She went to do it herself, but I put my hand on her shoulder to stop her. She eased back, leaned against the table. I took three logs from the large pile beside the burner and fed them into the flames. I watched, for a moment, as the fire took the new wood. The familiar pop and hiss of sap, the clean, bright flame licking off the edges of the logs.

Ellen stared into nothing. Her face had turned pale and she shivered, though she did not seem to notice it. A pool of water grew around her skirts, and her hair was plastered to her head and neck. I was not faring much better.

'We must get out of these wet clothes. Hurry now,' I said, pulling off my jacket and boots.

I went to her and, with numb fingers, undid the buttons of her shirtwaist. She did not protest. I peeled off the garment and dropped it, then she appeared to notice and did the buttons on her skirt herself. The heavy linen fell away and I untied the petticoat beneath it until she stood shivering in just her shift. That was also wet, though I did not think it proper to relieve her of that too. I found two blankets in her bedroom and wrapped her in one, walking her close to the stove.

Outside the wind still howled and shook the windows and door. But the cabin was strong. The walls solid and encompassing.

I worked at my own clothing, climbed out of my pants, took off the shirt and wrapped myself in the other blanket.

My shivering eased and colour returned to Ellen's cheeks. She looked at her hand, as if remembering the injury. Blood pooled in her palm.

I fetched water and a cloth, and brought the chairs close to the fire. I took her hand in mine without a word and began to clean the wound. A gash across her palm from the gate, not deep enough to need sewing, thank God. She did not flinch as I wiped away the blood, nor did she seem to feel it at all.

'Do you think Charlie made it to Dawson?' I asked, if nothing else to break the silence.

Ellen sniffed. 'I think I don't much care.'

'You do not love him?'

She looked up from her hand. 'Show me a Klondike woman who loves the man who brought her here and I'll show you a liar.'

I smiled, wrung out the bloody cloth. 'You intrigue me, Ellen Rhodes.'

'How's that?'

'I see the way you look at this place. At your claim up the valley. You like it here. And yet, forgive me for saying it, you seem so sad.'

I felt her watching me, the weight of her gaze on the top of my head as I tended to her.

'I must stare at the beauty of this place through bars,' she said. 'I can touch it, sometimes, but I am not free to live in it. Not like you.'

I almost laughed. I cleaned the last of the blood from her palm and took a clean strip of linen, wrapped it tight. 'You think I am free?'

'You have no husband.'

'I am a prisoner in other ways,' I said, and my thoughts turned to my sister. Of the rage I still felt, but could now hide well. I would be locked to this land and its people until I found the man responsible. I knotted the bandage and returned her hand to her lap.

'You are kind, Kate Kelly,' she said. Our eyes met, lingered a moment. I felt suddenly uncomfortably hot before the fire. I walked to the window and watched the storm. Rain streaked the glass and, outside, the darkness from the clouds was almost that of a winter's night.

'You should not be close to the window. There is a board, beneath the basin.'

I looked back at Ellen, to where she pointed. I found the board and set it against the glass. Charlotte's notebook lay on the table, wet, and streaked with mud. I took it up.

'What is that?' Ellen asked.

I set it down near the stove to dry. 'It belonged to my sister.'

'Where is she?'

I tried to smile. 'She is dead.'

Her hand found mine and the touch was strangely comforting, as if in that quiet, closed home with a quiet, closed woman, some of the pain I felt was allowed to stay outside.

'I'm sorry,' she said and tears began to well in my eyes.

I prised her touch away and the threat of tears went with it. 'Would you mind if I slept in here? The tent is not quite up to the task.'

'Of course.'

We did not talk much more that evening. The storm continued

into the night, turning the midnight sun black. We ate a small meal together and then Ellen retired to her room, leaving me with the blankets and a pillow from her bed.

Yukon snored. I waited until I heard Ellen settle, until the clock ticked hour after hour. I was tired, but I forced myself awake, for I would not get a better opportunity than this. Charlie Rhodes had been seeing my sister. His face, drawn in her hand, filled that notebook, its pages now crinkled and stiff.

I got up as quietly as I could. The storm had not yet blown itself out, so the sound of the rain covered my movements.

I went to the corner and prised up the board. Inside, the jar and sack of gold we found just that morning. Beside it, a pile of letters addressed to Ellen from an address in Seattle. Two boxes of shotgun cartridges and another of bullets. And nothing more.

I looked around the room. Tried to imagine if I were to hide something from my husband or wife where I would put it. I checked every cupboard, every drawer for a false bottom. I opened jars from high shelves and dug my hands into flour and grain. I opened their tea chest and blanket box. I found nothing. No clue to his guilt. No knife covered in my sister's blood. No easy answer. If Ellen or Charlie hid anything, it was well concealed and would remain that way. At least for now. But the longer I spent with these people, the more I saw the lies writ on their faces. The secrets embedded in their movements, their speech, the way they spoke to one another. I hoped, in a way, that I was wrong about Charlie because, despite his faults, there seemed a kind man beneath the surface, if an incompetent one.

Ellen, on the other hand, I could not get the measure of. I did not think her a killer of course, but I did find myself watching her, wishing to speak with her. A sense of adventure, akin to running the White Horse Rapids, accompanied the thought of her in my mind. I remembered that feeling of exhilaration, the purity of the joy I felt in every inch of my body, despite it being something a woman did not do, should not do. And yet as the river calmed back to normalcy at the end of the canyon, I found myself wanting to do it again, and again.

ELLEN

The morning brings clear skies. I wake from a restless sleep to sounds in the kitchen and I remember Kate. Yukon. I rise and dress. My hand aches and the buttons defeat me. Out the window I see Bluebell has returned to her pen of her own volition. Joy fills me and I go to the kitchen smiling.

Kate cuts bread and puts a side of bacon in a pan. I watch, one hand holding my shirt together. She sees me and jumps.

'Ellen. You're awake.' She has rings beneath her eyes, her hair is wild, as I believe mine is too.

'Did you sleep?' I ask.

'Not well, I'm afraid. The rain kept me up.'

I look down to my shirt. 'Would you mind?' She is confused at first, then I hold up my injured hand and she understands.

She stands before me, so close I can feel her breath. She looks at me and, as if a thought she does not wish for runs through her mind, she shakes her head and looks down at the buttons.

Once dressed, I go to Yukon and stroke his soft head. He lifts it, sees me and his tongue lolls, his tail thumps.

271

'He is a strong animal,' I say.

'And a stupid one.'

He lets out a short bark, as if to rebuke her, and I laugh. Scratch under his chin. 'At least he will not do it again. We must all put our hand in the fire once.'

Yukon stands and pads to Kate, rubs against her leg until she gives him a slice of the bacon. He eats it in one gulp and whines for another. She gives it, smiling, and I see a softness in her. When she sees me looking, however, her face reddens and she turns away.

'Have I offended you?' I ask, for her coldness chills deeper than the rain.

'Why would you think that?' Kate has her back to me, does not turn at my question.

'Just an idle thought, I suppose.'

I reach for her sister's sketchbook and begin idly flipping through the pages. Dry, wrinkled. Some of the drawings have run to nothing but a smudge. Others, the damage is minimal. They are quite extraordinary. There are men, women. Fractions of them both, hands, ears. Studies. The Golden Staircase. The river bend holding Dawson, the view from a boat. A drunk on the steps of a saloon. The Dawson Hotel. Martha Malone.

I feel a sudden chill. A sudden drop in my stomach. There is Charlie, again and again. Drawn in pencil and ink, in poses I have never seen. Shirtless. Lying on a bed. Smiling.

'What is this?' I say.

Kate looks then. Sees what I see. Her expression shifts in a blink. She reaches for the book, but I pull it away, stand.

'You said this was your sister's,' I say.

'Give it back.'

'And that your sister is dead.'

'Please, Ellen.'

272

I flip the pages over and over. The rain has swelled the leather and, in drying, the leather has come away from the board. Tucked inside, hidden away, is a photograph. A wedding photograph. I pull it out, for I know the face. She sat in my house. She bedded my husband.

'What is that?' Kate asks, seeming surprised at my discovery.

I look up from the photograph and I see now. The familiarity.

'Molly was your sister,' I say and it is as if a giant puzzle piece clicks into place. That is why Kate is here.

She reddens, knowing she is caught. 'Show it to me, please.'

The feeling is strange. Not anger at her lies, as I'd expected, but a sadness. And a foolishness on my part that I could have considered any other reason for her lingering. The fortune-teller was wrong. About so much.

I let the sketchbook fall to the floor, but keep hold of the photograph. Kate snatches up the book, kneeling at my feet.

'Tell me the truth,' I say, but before she can speak there is a shout outside. A man's voice. Urgent. Calling for me.

I drop the photograph. It lands near Kate. I do not see if she picks it up, for I am already at the door.

Three men run up to my house. They have their hats off, looks of worry on their faces.

'Mrs Rhodes, are you all right? That storm was a killer,' says the first. I believe his name is Johan, but the recollection is fuzzy.

'Fine, thank you, we weathered it well,' I say.

I look down the valley and see the destruction. Kate is beside me at the door and sees it too.

'Dear Lord,' she says.

The side of the valley is gone. The miners' tents swept into the river and taken in the flood. Twisted stovepipes stick out of the shallow water. Equipment is strewn around the bank.

I look to the men again; they are bloodied about the edges, but unhurt.

'What do you need?' Formalities gone. Never were any in this place. My mind goes to Charlie. Was he caught in the storm?

'To borrow your cart, ma'am,' Johan says.

'My cart?'

He nods. 'For the body.'

Kate steps forward as my world shrinks. 'Body?'

He points down the valley and I am running before I realise. Charlie caught in the storm. Drowned in the flooding. Crushed by debris.

The miners are shadows. Broken men. They pick at the ruins of their claims, uncover dented pans and splintered boxes. They raise their heads as I pass, but none call out. None stop me.

Ahead I see it, the gathering around a sheet. A dozen men. A horse tied, but not Goldie. Was he swept away too?

Under the sheet is a shape, a man's outline. I slow. They see me approach. Behind me I hear footsteps, the clattering of the cart wheels. Kate stands beside me and she thinks what I think, for she takes my hand and I let her.

One of the men, well dressed, breaks away when he sees her.

'Miss Kelly?' he says.

'Doctor Pohl,' she replies and lets go of my hand. I am suddenly unmoored.

'What are you doing here?' he asks her.

'I'm staying with . . .' she looks at me, then back to him, 'a friend. Who is that?'

The doctor goes to the sheet. To my husband beneath. I cannot breathe. I step closer. Kate takes my arm. The miners part as if they already know.

The doctor kneels, lifts the cloth. Reveals the face.

Not Charlie. But familiar still.

'Early?'

'You know him?' Kate says to me, but I cannot answer.

His face is grey and mottled. His whole body is covered in mud as if he was buried, but I see the gunshots.

'What happened?'

'We found him by the river this morning,' says a man. A faceless miner.

The doctor covers Early again, but I will never stop seeing that face.

'By the looks of it, he's been dead a while. Shot twice at least,' Doctor Pohl says. 'He was buried. The storm must have washed him free.'

Kate lets me go and kneels beside him. 'Does he have the scratches?'

I frown. 'What scratches?'

The doctor and Kate glance at me. Then share a look with each other.

'The man who killed Molly is likely to have scratches on him,' the doctor says. 'She fought back. I don't know yet if Mr Early has them. I will need to examine him.'

He has no scratches. I know because I watched him die. Should I speak it? Then I must explain that it was Frank Croaker – that Early was saving me. That Frank tried to violate me in my own home. I can already see the pity in their eyes. The questioning of my character. The notion I should have spoken sooner. That I am at fault, somehow to blame for Early's death. I cannot bear it.

'We have the cart, sir,' says Johan.

'Load him up. Gently,' says the doctor.

The men oblige. They knew Early. Some perhaps were friends.

Kate grabs the doctor's arm. 'What does this mean? For Charlotte.'

The doctor sighs. 'It means nothing yet. Except that Yannick Early did not run away. And he has been in the ground about as long as your sister.'

She lets him go. The men hitch the horse to the cart and the doctor climbs into the seat. Takes up the reins.

'I'll know more soon,' he says. The horses walk. The body rocks in the back of my cart.

Kate turns to me, the anger back in her face. She strides past me back up the hill to my home. I follow.

As we reach the cabin I call out, 'Kate. Stop.'

She slows at the door. I go to her.

'Where are you going?'

'To the Mounties. Early may not have killed her, but the man who did still walks free.'

'You wish to bring him to justice?'

'I wish to kill him.'

I have never seen such conviction in someone's eyes. No doubt. No hesitation.

'The Mounties won't help you.'

'They must.'

I shake my head. 'They will not, and you know it. There is no justice in the Klondike except that which we exact ourselves. They will concoct a story that fits their neat box. Early and your sister died at the same time. That is evidence enough for them that the two deaths are linked. This will do nothing more than keep the case closed.'

'But I have proof now!'

I recoil. Suddenly afraid the bundle beneath the floorboards has been discovered. 'Proof?'

She holds up the photograph of Molly in her wedding dress. A handsome man by her side.

'How is that proof?' I ask.

She points to the man. 'This is Henry Gable. *Her husband.* I had never met him. Never seen this photograph, just a copy in a newspaper so blurred I could never make out his features.'

The mania in her eyes begins to scare me. 'What of it?'

She pulls a letter from her pocket, folded to a nub, and hands it to me. It is from Charlotte. It speaks of her life in the Klondike, of her occupation at the Dawson Hotel and her sorrow at where she has found herself. It speaks of her husband, a man she escaped, but who chased her from city to city until she had no choice but to go to the end of the world. My eyes linger on the final lines:

A letter came from the woman I boarded with in Seattle. Henry threatened her until she told him where I'd gone. She says he means to take the trail this spring. To scare me, of course, and it has worked. I am scared and I have no money to leave here. I am trapped. This may be my last letter. He has finally found me and there is nowhere left to run. I'm sorry. Tell everyone I'm sorry.

Kate nods. 'Gable was in Skaguay. He was ahead of me on the Dead Horse Trail and survived the avalanche. He was stuck at Lake Bennett when I was. We met, but I did not know him. His boat left a day before mine. He arrived in Dawson before Charlotte died. He stood at the fence at her funeral! He is here, Ellen. He is here and he has a rage so fierce—'

She does not speak more. I go to her, wrap my arms around her.

'You believe he killed her?'

'With every inch of me,' she says, pulling away from me. 'I must go to Dawson.'

'And do what? Scour every saloon and gin-hole until you find him? Then what will you do? Shoot him in the street?'

'If I must.'

She goes inside the cabin and I follow. Yukon jumps up, tail going. She gathers what little she has.

'Kate, think this through. There are thousands of men in Dawson and he may already have left.'

She pauses then. The size of her task laid out before her. 'Then I will ask for help. I have friends, I was told.'

'I will come with you.'

It does not take her long to agree. By the afternoon we are ready. Bluebell fed and rested. Yukon strong and eager to run. I take the shotgun and we ride together.

MARTHA

'It was a nice service,' Jerry said. He'd wiped the bar clean three times already, but he started again. Harry was already in the ground, though he was barely cold. I stared at the spot by the door where he'd stood. Seeing it empty broke my heart.

The place was quiet. Too quiet for an evening. The blood stain wouldn't come out of the boards. Nearby was the charred patch Bill Mathers had set on fire. Reminders of all I'd lost, and had left to lose.

'I'm going for a walk,' I said and didn't wait for anyone to stop me.

Dawson City was quieter than usual too. Like all the summer heat had run through the town and left everyone slow. Typhoid had taken another dozen. The Mounties had opened up another patch of land out to the north to bury them all. They dug their holes, salted the earth, dropped them in like sacks of potatoes on a kitchen floor and filled them back in. More than twenty fresh crosses, not all of them with names.

Harry lay near Molly. I insisted on that.

I went to the post office and found it closed, so I went up the steps beside, to the room above. Knocked hard, as I knew she'd be drunk.

Harriet opened the door, eyes swimming in gin. The bad stuff, I could tell from the red around her nose, the stink of turpentine and bile.

'Go away, Ma.'

'I don't think so. I won't have my friend drinking alone.'

She huffed, stepped aside and let me in. I'd never been inside her home. Never needed to. Our friendship was business to business: gossip in hers and drink together in mine. Her place was a mess and I didn't think it was all because of Harry.

'Here,' Harriet said and handed me the bottle.

I sniffed it. Near gagged on it. 'Who sold you this?'

'What's it matter? Fire is fire.'

'This'll kill you quicker than typhoid.'

'Good.' She found another bottle and uncorked it. Drank it like it was water.

I looked at the label. Napoleon. One of the illegal shiners who did business with Bill Mathers.

'Bill gave these to you?' I asked.

She raised the bottle. 'He did.'

'Out of the goodness of his heart?'

She drank and swayed and I had to catch her arm. 'That man don't have a heart.' Harriet slumped down on her bed, bottle hanging between her legs, head hanging off her shoulders.

'I know you're hurting,' I said and she shook her head.

'I ain't hurting. I'm hurt. I'm dead as him. I'm gone already, just my body needs to catch up.'

I hated self-pitying talk like that. Always have. I snatched the bottle off her and threw it out the window.

'Keep going with that poison and it won't be long,' I said and knelt in front of her. 'I loved him too. I miss him. I'm damn sorry for what happened. But this ain't the way.'

She looked up at me and her face was covered in tears. She wiped them with her sleeve. 'I'm sorry, Ma. I'm sorry.'

She swayed, so drunk she could barely sit straight.

'What you got to be sorry for?'

Harriet let out a fresh round of cries. I held on to her, let her sob it out onto my shoulder.

'Hush now, you just need some sleep, some food.'

She pushed me away so hard I fell. 'I don't need food. I need my brother! Every ... minute in this godforsaken place – it's him everywhere ... I can't stand it. And he knew! The bastard knew!'

I got up, put myself at a safe distance. 'Who knew what?'

'Bill! Bill Bill Bill! Fucking Bill!' She pounded her head with her fists and I didn't dare get close enough to stop it. 'He knew I couldn't stand it. He *knew*.'

I felt my gut clench. 'What did you do, Harriet?'

She shook her head side to side, tears and snot and spit all over her, then looked for a bottle.

'It's his now. I'm done.'

'You sold?'

She stood, stumbled, but kept her feet, went to a box.

'You sold up to Bill?' I asked again.

She opened the box and pulled out bars of gold. One after the other. Dozens of them. Thousands of dollars' worth. She held one in her hand, stared at it, swaying and slurring. Then she threw it at the wall so hard it broke a board. Hit the floor with a heavy, dull thud.

'All my brother's worth,' she said.

'Harriet, how could—' But I knew. She'd lost her family. Bill saw an opportunity and he took it, because he's that kind of man. A devil.

'Don't judge me, Ma,' she said. 'You can go. Thanks for the visit.'

I wanted to feel sympathy and I did, but not for that. How could she sell to *Bill*, of all people, after everything? My chest went tight as a drum as I stepped out to the top of the staircase. Dawson spread out around me. My home. And every building it in, but mine and the few scraps I held on Front Street, was owned by that man. He couldn't have it all. It weren't right. My heart beat faster and faster and I felt I might fall, but then I saw him. Walking through his town, his goons flanking him like generals. Miners tipped their hats. Businessmen crossed their arms. He was hated. He was feared. He loved every damn second of it.

I walked down the steps, calm as anything. He stopped when he saw me.

'Martha Malone, as I live and breathe.'

'Bill,' I said and straightened my back.

'Visiting dear Harriet? Such a shame what befell her brother.'

I didn't speak for fear of screaming. I bit my tongue until it bled.

'I've just come to visit my new establishment,' he said and gestured to the post office. 'I've always wanted to be a mail man.'

He laughed and all his men laughed along with him.

'I'm so glad I ran into you, Martha. I have a gift,' he said. He clicked his fingers and a man appeared, carrying something large wrapped in a satin cloth.

I knew that man. Gold buckle and gold rings on his fingers.

Bill's man. Sent to cause trouble. It was like a knife dug into my gut.

'You remember Clancy, don't you?' Bill said and twisted the knife.

He took the package from that murdering bastard and came close to me. Stood right beside me, so I could smell the leather of his waistcoat. He handed me the package and I unwrapped it. In my hands was a silver fox pelt.

'These are rare as hen's teeth,' he said quietly. 'This one came from a trapper up north, name of Sam Bridger.'

The knife stabbed my heart and all the air fled my lungs.

'Sam, it seems, had some grave misfortune after catching this beautiful fox. His leg is in a bad way, I hear. He's easy pickings for wolves.'

'What are you doing, Bill?' My voice weren't mine. It was weak and shaking and he heard my fear and loved it. Lapped it up like cream.

'I'm just looking out for a friend.'

'He ain't a part of this.'

Bill snapped his teeth close to my ear and I flinched. 'You love him? More than you loved me?'

'I never loved you.'

'Oh, now that hurts. If you love this fella so much, wouldn't it do you better to head on up to Sam and let me take care of the hotel while you're gone?'

My men would nearly be with Sam. He'd be all right, I told myself over and over. He'd be all right. 'You are never getting my hotel.'

Bill gave that devil smile and put the pelt over my shoulders. I cringed at his touch, felt my skin crawl away from him.

'I thought you'd like this. Oh, and thank you.'

'For what?'

'Two more men joined my employ. An Irish, by the red hair on him, and another fella. Friend of mine found them struggling up the pass to Beaver Lake. Turns out they was happy to come work for me.'

My world crashed around my head.

'I'll need your answer in three weeks, Martha. Time's a-wasting!'

With that he left me, stiff and shaking. His men leering after me, that gold-buckle bastard grinning. Bill unlocked the door and went into the post office. It took every ounce of strength I had not to run, but I would never give him the satisfaction of seeing me shook. I was, though. To my damn core. Sam was alone, no one coming to help him – all because of Bill. Three weeks to sell up and haul out, and now that bastard had insurance. If I didn't sell, he'd send men for Sam, if he hadn't already. I was the last hold-out in Dawson. I had few friends remaining, snakes in my house and everything still to lose.

KATE

'Ferry's out,' said a man on the shore of the Klondike River. He sat behind a table selling boots for a dollar a foot. The sun was high and already the mud was drying.

'How can the ferry be out?' I asked. 'Didn't a cart come through here this morning?'

'Cart took a boat.' He chewed something and spat black. 'Fancy fella on a horse brought the boat. Fancy fella on a cart took the boat back. Storm broke the ferry line.'

I looked at Ellen. The same look of irritation on her face as I imagined on mine.

'Is there a boat nearby?' Ellen asked.

'Not 'less you got one tucked in your petticoats,' he replied and barked a laugh.

I wanted to wring the man's scrawny neck and perhaps would have, if it would not have infested me with lice. He scratched and spat like a mangy dog and even Yukon didn't go close enough to sniff.

'Is there another crossing?'

The man rocked his head side to side as if it would dislodge a memory. 'A fella set up a ferry at Hunker Creek. Word through is they escaped the worst of the storm up there and it's still running.'

I looked at Ellen.

'Hunker Creek is eight or so miles east, away from Dawson. Our journey more than doubles.'

'Or goes nowhere at all,' I said. I felt the photograph burning in my pocket. That man's face staring, smiling, seeing him in a new light in my memory. The clean man, I had thought. I'd sketched him too, in my notebook. I never had Charlotte's talent, but the likeness was good.

'When will this ferry be running again?' Ellen asked.

'Considerin' Old Man Gerald and his ferry got washed down the river and nobody found him yet, common decency says it'll be a few days till a new one takes the spot.'

Ellen took a coin from her purse and threw it to the man. He grasped at it, but missed and the coin flew into the long grass. He jumped after it and she clicked her tongue for Bluebell to walk on.

There had been a well-beaten trail along the banks of the Klondike River to the head of Hunker Creek, but the storm had washed away long swathes of the riverbank, making it impassable. We stood at the edge, where the trail disappeared. A mudslide from the hill beside had cut away the bank for at least half a mile.

'We must go into the forest, cross over the mountains,' Ellen said. 'Or wait.'

'I cannot wait.'

Ellen heard the fever in my voice and did not try to dissuade me, despite what it would mean for her.

She turned the horse and we entered the wilderness.

*

Ellen had a way about her, a sense of confidence in the trees I had not expected. She was not afraid of the wild, of the absence of path and direction; she was at home here in a way I was not. I could forge through rapids and treacherous trail, but blazing my own had always been a terrifying endeavour. Yet Ellen did so with a confidence I could not yet fathom.

The going was tricky, however, and Bluebell struggled over the uneven, mossy ground. Bracken and vines snagged at her legs and it was not long before we needed to dismount and walk alongside. Yukon bounded here and there, running off to sniff at something, then charging back, pinpricked tongue lolling.

'How long have you been up here?' I asked.

Ellen picked her footing over a rotten log, skirts brushing and collecting dirt. 'It'll be three years this winter. It feels longer.'

'Three years is a lifetime when it is not your choice.' I thought of Charlotte, of her marriage to that cruel man. Those years must have felt endless. It is no wonder she ran, far and fast, to this place. And yet he still found her.

We walked again in silence. Companionable enough. The walk was relatively short, only a handful of miles, but it was not easy. What would have taken a few hours on the trail turned to a marathon in the forest. Yesterday's rain dripped from the canopy, the ground was slick, and had our boots not been good leather, our feet would have soaked to the bone. It did not get truly dark of course, but the light did dip and within the pine canopy, surrounded by dense brush and brown bark, it was dark enough to make us worry for our steps.

'We should stop,' Ellen said.

We reached a flat patch of land so thick with moss it was like stepping on a mattress. The forest was damp and steaming, and small evidences of the storm were everywhere. Fallen branches, a fresh carpet of green pine needles shaken loose by the wind. I itched to continue. To run headlong into the wilderness and hope for the best. But I knew to rein in my worst impulses. Getting lost here, miles from the trails and mines of the creek valleys, would spell an early death for me. I could see myself charge in anger and impatience, slip, snap an ankle, be discovered by a roaming bear.

'Collect some wood,' Ellen said, 'Dry as you can find it. Look for hanging branches broken off by the storm. Pine. Birch. Look for bare trees, long dead.'

I went about my task with fervour. Yukon at my ankles, sniffing the ground, though more cautious now than I had seen him before. The sting of the porcupine still apparent in his mind.

I looked for what Ellen said and found enough branches to sustain us, mostly dry. How did Ellen know so much? But that question was foolish. She was a frontier woman, a Klondike wife; she must have lit a thousand fires, collected a thousand logs for them, endured endless rains. I found myself somewhat in awe. I had always considered myself an adventurer, but my adventures thus far had been tame jaunts. Ellen lived it every day.

She smiled when I dropped the armful of kindling at her side and rooted around for the right piece. A pine branch, ripped from the trunk, with a lumpy end and resinous smell. She used long matches produced from her pocket and held the flame to the branch. The end caught like a candle and continued to burn as she built a careful stack of small pieces atop it. In moments, we had a warm fire and, on feeling it, I began to shiver.

'Come here,' Ellen said. She beckoned to me like an impatient mother and I sat beside her on a log. She put her arm and shawl around my shoulders and rubbed my arm.

We talked little; my thoughts were consumed by finding my sister's husband. The clean man. My mind raced through scenarios: if only I had been quicker on the trail, or he slower and caught in the avalanche. If only I had scuppered his boat. If only Walter and Biddy had rowed faster. If only I had taken up with a younger, swifter crew on the river. If only, if only – a hundred times, a hundred ways. All of them with the same outcome: my sister would be alive and I would not be hunting her killer.

ELLEN

HUNKER CREEK, KLONDIKE, JULY 1898

Kate stares at the fire. I see her mind work. I know what she must be thinking. Could she have stopped him? If only . . . a hundred times. Useless. A waste of good thinking.

Yet I find myself thinking the same, but of my husband. I used to be certain Charlie had been responsible for Molly's death, but now, with this Henry Gable, my certainty wanes. Should I tell her? Should I show her the bloody shirt and speak of what I saw that night?

Not yet.

'You are thinking of your sister?' I say, and Kate looks at me as if to ask how I could know.

'I am rarely not, these days. Maybe once I find who killed her, my mind will be at rest.'

'Will you tell me about her?'

She goes to speak, but in the firelight tears shine in her eyes. 'Charlotte was funny. A real wit. She played tricks on our mother. One time she put a quart of beet juice into the laundry and turned all Mother's linen pink.'

I laugh. 'A terrible trick!'

'My father found it amusing, thankfully, else Charlotte would have been whipped. She always pushed against the rules. "Why must linen be white, Mother?" she'd ask.' Kate pauses, laughs. 'Charlotte wanted to live in the big city, at the tip of the spear, forever driving forward. In a way it was no wonder she ended up here, in her situation.'

'You mean at the Dawson as a—' To speak the word seems too harsh now.

'Yes. And ... well, I do not know if I should tell you this,' Kate says and, despite the fire, a shiver runs over me.

'What is it? I am hard to shock.'

She looks at me and there is a hint of pity in her eye. 'She was with child when she was killed.'

With child ... 'Charlie's?'

'I believe so.'

I think back to when Molly came to the cabin. To the fierce exchange outside. The way he grabbed her arm. The way she pushed him. Had she wrapped an arm around her stomach? Was she telling him her situation?

A sour taste fills my mouth.

'I'm sorry,' Kate says. 'Did I offend you? I thought you should know. Do you think he knew?'

Yes, I think, but do not say. 'I don't know. But how could she be sure it was his – with her profession, I mean?'

'I don't know, maybe it wasn't. But my sister was always careful about such things. Do you know how Charlie would have felt?'

I shake my head. A woman pregnant with my husband's child. I had said I was hard to shock, but this has. I fall to silence. While Kate tries to engage the conversation again, I cannot sustain it. She quietens and we both stare into the fire.

My thoughts turn. To a time in the early days of my courting. I let the memory spill into my head. The sun-dappled streets of Seattle, the smell of heat and horse dung and the steamships in the harbour. The distant sound of saws from the mills.

Charlie and I walked arm-in-arm up James Street, alongside the Hotel Seattle. A chaperone, my father's housekeeper, walked a few steps behind. I barely noticed her, so engrossed was I in Charlie. The first man to show me attention and affection, express a wish to marry. A good family. A strong prospect. Handsome in his way, yet slight, almost effeminate in his build, but kind. My father had wished me to marry an elder son, and Charlie was third in his family, but after my urging, he allowed Charlie to court me.

'A beautiful day to walk with a beautiful woman,' Charlie said and I blushed.

'That is kind. I am happy to walk with you.'

'A warm day. Would you allow me to buy you an ice?'

I nodded and we found a cart. Two lemon ices. Tangy and cold on my tongue and rich with sugar. We walked on to the park, where we took a bench. Behind us, I saw my chaperone huffing, cheeks red, and I felt a pang of guilt that we had not bought an ice for her.

'Should we find some lemonade for Mrs Holt?' I asked.

Charlie looked at the woman and she shot him a narrow-eyed stare back. 'I think she is fine.'

We found a bench and enjoyed our treat. The park was busy with promenading couples and families pushing prams. Further down the path was a commotion. A figure shambling. A bundle in one arm, the other outstretched.

'Look,' I said and Charlie spotted it too.

As it got closer, I saw it was a woman. From the bundle in her arms came a cry and a pink arm waved.

'She has a baby,' I said.

'What of it?' Charlie asked.

The woman shuffled among the park-goers, hand out, head bowed, baby wailing. She was thin, a shawl hung off her shoulders and she looked as if she had not eaten in days, perhaps longer. But she was young too. No older than me for certain.

'That poor woman. She is hungry, it is plain.'

I found my purse and fumbled at the clasp. Charlie placed his hand on mine to stop me.

'You must not.'

'Why? She is in need and I have some to spare.'

He prised my purse from my hand and held it. 'A woman of little means should not have a child if she cannot care for it.'

'Sometimes it is not the woman's choice,' I replied, my pique rising.

'There are ways. A child should only be born in wedlock. A bastard does not belong in the world.'

I concealed my shock at his words. This kind man was not so kind, perhaps?

Charlie noticed me tense and said, 'Do not worry yourself, Ellen, over issues like these. I am here to worry for you, and to protect you from a fate such as theirs. Our children will be born well in the eyes of God, and you will be a strong and doting mother. But I see this woman's plight has affected you.'

'It has.'

'So be it,' he said and stood. He walked to the woman and handed her my purse.

I did not rise to stop him, though I wished to, as that purse was a gift from my mother before she died. The poor woman could sell it at least, get herself a few extra cents. She spotted me behind Charlie, put her hands together as if in prayer and bowed to me.

I felt a swell in my heart so powerful it threatened to bring me to tears. I nodded back and the woman rushed from the park. I hoped towards a place she could buy milk for her child and something hot for herself.

Charlie returned to the bench. 'There. Your future husband is generous, is he not?'

With my money, he is, I thought. 'So kind of you.'

I had no more stomach for the lemon ice, so we walked again. In the days after I thought often of that woman and her baby, and of Charlie's words against them.

Had he said similar to Molly? Had he acted on his disgust? Tried to make her dispose of it? *There are ways* ... Had she fought him back, to protect her baby and herself? Scratched his neck, which he covers now always with a kerchief? If I remove it, will I see the scars?

I do not know how long we sit in that forest, but when the light returns, Kate stands.

'We should go,' she says and I rise.

Yukon nuzzles me as if he senses my unease and whines for food. Kate gives him salted pork. We eat. We damp the fire.

Kate strides intently to the ferry, and her Henry Gable. I stumble behind, more certain than ever that my husband – my kind, weak husband – is a murderer.

MARTHA

'Ma?'

I turned round. Giselle stood at the doorway to the outside balcony. 'Up and about, I see,' I said with a smile.

She pulled a blanket around her shoulders and stepped out to join me. It weren't cold, but any fat that girl had on her a week ago was gone now. She was bone and, now she could eat again without vomiting, Jessamine was intent on feeding her back up.

'What are you doing out here?' she asked.

'Looking at the town.'

The balcony was a narrow stretch along the front of the hotel, behind the big sign. We used it to get air without having to get our boots on, and the girls loved to hang about, smoking and calling out to gents to come visit. I didn't encourage it, made us look like a common whorehouse, but I'll be damned if it didn't bring in the crowds.

Giselle stood beside me, leaning on the railing. 'I think this might be my last summer up here.'

I smiled. 'Good. Take that doctor down south and marry him.'

I didn't say it might be mine too. Didn't want to admit it or scare her. I felt the mass in my stomach every now and then. Could press on my gut and there it was.

'Speaking of . . .' Giselle said and straightened up.

There he was, driving a cart up Front Street, single horse pulling it. There was something long and covered in the back of the cart. The blanket was near falling off and it didn't take a genius to see it was a body.

Giselle whistled and waved and the doc looked up. He had a grim look about him, but put on a smile for her.

People had stopped to watch the cart. They knew its cargo. Some took off their hats, others turned away. Others still craned their necks to see who it was under the cloth. Some kid, on a dare, ran up behind the cart and grabbed the end of blanket, yanked it away and the dead man was revealed.

It weren't what I expected. A body covered in mud from head to boot, looked buried already. Maybe a poor miner caught in a mudslide. The cart went on and past Bill's assayer. Frank Croaker stood outside, drinking from a brown bottle. I fixed my eye on him and saw his face change when he saw that body.

He stood straight, lowered his bottle from his lips and looked about him, like he thought every eye in Dawson was on him. He stepped out from under the awning and got a better look. His face paled, he capped his bottle and hurried off.

'What interest you think Frank Croaker's got in that body?' I asked Giselle. 'He saw it and near pissed himself.'

Giselle shrugged. 'Maybe he killed the fella.'

Or Bill did.

I kissed Giselle on the cheek and told her to keep warm, then went downstairs and out the hotel. By the time I got to the doc's office, the body was on his table.

'Who is it?' I asked, barging in without an invite or welcome. The smell hit me hard. The stink of the dying out the back and the dead in here. That body weren't fresh, that's for sure.

Doc gave a sigh like he was sick of seeing me, but I didn't care.

'Yannick Early,' he said and rolled up his sleeves.

'Early? The man they say killed Molly?'

He nodded. 'But I don't think he did. He's been dead a while. Gunshots to the chest. By the look of it, he was buried and that storm washed him loose.'

The wind went out of me. 'Does he . . . the scratches?'

'Hard to tell under the mud. If you're going to be here, you might as well help me.'

He held out a cloth and bowl.

'You're getting saltier, the longer you're up here, Doc,' I said and took both. 'I'm glad to see it.'

He took a small tub of something from a shelf, opened it and dabbed his finger in. Then he swiped whatever it was under his nose.

'It'll help with the smell,' he said and handed it to me.

It was a pale salve, smelling of mint and herbs, a sight better than the stink of the body. I applied it same as him and we got to work.

Doc cut off his clothes, pulled off his boots. I washed his arms, chest, face. Every stroke of the cloth I was expecting to see them scratches. Doc started on his other side and I figure he was thinking the same. When Early was cleaner than he'd ever been in life, the doc went over every inch of his skin. It was grey and looked like it'd been eaten by maggots in places, but for the most – and except for two great gun holes in his chest – intact.

There weren't a scratch on him.

'It weren't him,' I said.

'No. It wasn't,' Doc agreed and started washing his hands.

No wonder Frank Croaker had turned white, seeing Early. The man the law, and Bill Mathers, blamed for Molly's death. So convenient that Early had disappeared around the time she was killed. But he hadn't disappeared. He'd been dead and buried someplace. And Frank Croaker must've known it. Must've known it because he put him there. Made that poor man a scapegoat, so all eyes would be off him. Off those scratches on his neck.

'That son of a bitch,' I said to myself.

'Who?'

But I was out the door.

KATE

The ferry at Hunker Creek was smaller than the one at Bonanza and had twice the traffic. We waited in a line, but I couldn't sit still. Ellen, Yukon and Bluebell kept our place and I went from man to man with the photograph and my sketch of Henry Gable.

'You seen this man?' I asked, shoving both papers in their faces.

Most of the miners shook their heads, mumbled no and I moved on. Some tried to swindle me. Others were worse.

'I seen him. I seen him,' one chirped. Small man, no broader or well built than a shovel pole.

'Where?'

He put out his hand. 'Gram of gold will loosen my lips.'

'You've either seen him or you haven't. I'm not paying you for what your eyes got free.'

'Nothin's free in the Klondike, lady.'

I went to walk away, but he grabbed me by the hand. 'If you don't have gold, you can pay another way.' He winked, licked his lips and bobbed his eyebrows up and down as if I hadn't got the hint already.

'No thanks,' I said and tried to pull free of him, but he held tight.

'I'll be nice,' he said.

Nobody was helping me. No man was standing up to him as he tried to pull me off the trail. Ellen was too far to call for, and she had the shotgun.

'Let me go!'

I pulled and felt his grip loosen. Then I yanked him closer and kicked. My shin hit the spot between his legs and he let go of me, doubled over.

'Bitch!' he huffed and I kicked him in the side for good measure.

He cried out and rolled over into the mud. The miners around us laughed and whistled. Some patted me on the back as I passed them.

One grabbed me by the shoulder and I was ready for another fight. I spun round, knife in hand, but he had his hands up in surrender.

'What?' I snapped.

'That man. In your picture.' He spoke with a thick southern accent. I'd shown him the picture already as I'd gone down the line. He'd looked, but not said anything. I'd figured he didn't know, so I'd moved on.

'What about him?'

'Well, Miss, I saw him just a few days ago.'

I sighed. 'Don't waste my time. Unless you want to end up in the mud too.' Though this man was clearly newer to the mines and still had his muscle and his teeth. I doubted I could land a kick.

'No, Miss, I surely don't.'

'Where did you see him?'

'I've only been here a week, though it feels longer, and I got myself a fine position now, but when I arrived I'd lost everything on the trail. Our boat went over on the rapids, you see, and my brother went down with it.'

I felt a sting of guilt for being so harsh. 'I'm sorry to hear it. Those rapids are treacherous.'

My hand went to my head, to the red line near my scalp. He noticed and gave me a sombre nod. Every man around had craned in to listen. A southern gent can spin a story like no other.

'When I washed up in Dawson I barely had two pennies to my name and I found myself at the dog-fights. A dirty sport if ever there was one. But they gave credit and that's what I needed.'

The line shuffled on as he spoke, and I knew it would not be long before it would be our turn to board. I was growing weary. 'And the man in the photo?'

'He was there. Betting on the dogs. I saw him every night for three nights straight.'

'Where are these dog-fights?'

'In a storehouse at the dock. I can't recall which one.'

That was enough to find Gable. I rushed away, calling my thanks. The man waved his hat and I hoped he'd been truthful. I would find out soon, at least.

At the head of the line, I heard my name. Ellen called, Yukon barked. They were aboard the ferry and were holding up the crossing. I ran to catch them. The ferryman began to push off, despite Ellen's protestations. When I reached the bank I didn't stop. I jumped and landed heavily on the deck. My ankle went from under me and a jolt of pain surged up my leg. The miners cheered, though I suspect more than one of them would have cheered louder had I gone in the water.

Yukon fussed over me, licking my face and pawing at me until I scratched his head and gently pushed him away. Ellen helped me up. I held her by both shoulders and could not contain my fervour.

'I know where to begin our search,' I said, breathless, and told her what the man had said.

Ellen gave a clipped smile. 'That's good.'

She was distracted. Had been since we'd left the forest and our small camp. As if she'd discovered something in the trees that had changed her mind. The truth of my sister's predicament perhaps; or maybe she was suddenly regretting her decision to accompany me. I could not dwell on her mood. I had a lead on the man who had killed my sister and, in the face of that, everything else fell away.

ELLEN

The ferry crossing is short but not uneventful. The river is swollen, full of logs. The ferry goes over one such and the bump sends a young man into the water. He is caught, thankfully, but shivers the rest of the way.

So many young men. New faces. Fresh and plump. Unravaged by scurvy and poor feeding. Nothing in their heads but teeth and dreams. The Yukon will take them both in time.

On the other side of the Klondike River the trail is clear and Bluebell moves well.

'What will you do?' I ask Kate, who walks beside. She cannot sit still on a horse, she says, and must move. Yukon trots faithfully by her side.

'Hmm?'

'When you have found Gable. When justice is served. What will you do?'

She is quiet for a moment. 'In truth I had not thought so far ahead. My entire purpose coming here was to find Charlotte, help her. And since I arrived it has been to find her killer. I

303

have thought nothing of what comes after.'

'You'd best decide. Winter is cruel here. The cold locks the river in early November and then the only way out is by dog-sled.'

'Will you leave before winter?'

There is a curious note in her tone, as if my answer may influence hers.

I think of what awaits in Dawson. Of Charlie and his secrets. 'I suppose it depends on what my husband does.'

Kate nods. 'Of course. Forgive me. Not having a husband means I rarely think of other people's.'

I laugh. 'Have you never been tempted to find one?'

She screws up her face and shakes her head as if she has just swallowed a rotten grape. 'They are a nuisance more than a help, as far as I can tell. Dangerous too, it appears. Little more than boys grown up, but twice the headache.'

We laugh, then fall to silence. The question between us left unanswered.

'I suppose we will both have a decision to make when all is said and done,' I say.

Kate only nods.

We reach Dawson City in the afternoon. The sun is hot on our backs and the sky clear, the wooden buildings already sending up steam as the rain dries. Bluebell shakes flies from her mane and the air carries a chill edge, a remnant of the storm.

'I must find Charlie,' I say as we enter the city. I cannot take another step with Kate while she believes one truth and I another. I feel as if I am lying with my presence.

'Are you sure?'

'Yes. I must speak with him about the baby,' I say, but that is only part of it. Kate, however, takes me at my word. I give her the shotgun. 'Be careful. And keep Yukon close to you among those people.'

She slings the shotgun over her shoulder. 'If I'm not at the Dawson Hotel in a few hours, come find me.'

I smile, nod. She walks away with Yukon and I cling to the hope that I will see her again.

I begin my own search at the Arcadia Hotel. Goldie is not outside, though that means little as she could be stabled elsewhere. Inside, Barnum the manager stands behind the desk.

'Mrs Rhodes. What a surprise. How may I help?'

'My husband was to collect a package that should have been sent here. Has he been for it yet?' A wife must never admit when she has lost her husband.

He looks perplexed, as he should. 'I'm sorry, but nothing has been dropped off and Mr Rhodes has not been by. I haven't seen him since the last time you two stayed together.'

I nod. Unsurprised. 'Perhaps I have mixed up my days.'

I leave before Barnum can say another word. Charlie has been in Dawson for two nights and if he is not staying at the Arcadia, there are only a handful of other places he could be. I lead Bluebell to a nearby stable and give the hand, a boy of little more than ten, a few small nuggets of gold to keep her safe and fed. He looks so delighted I am sure I have overpaid. He will treat my girl well, at least.

I go. Tread the muddy boards of Dawson in search of a murderer.

MARTHA

DAWSON CITY, KLONDIKE, JULY 1898

'Bill!'

I burst through the door of the Nug. The place was full of lounging drunks who jumped at the noise. Frank weren't there. He'd scurried into some hole someplace. One of Bill's men tried to stand in my way, but I gave him a look of fury so fierce he moved. I went round back, up the stairs and all but kicked down the door of Bill's office.

He weren't alone, of course, had a girl on his lap, hand in her bodice while he wrote in a ledger. She jumped when the door opened.

First time I ever saw Bill Mathers surprised. 'Martha?' But he quick recovered himself. 'Here to sign the paperwork?'

'Get rid of her.'

The girl scowled at me and leaned back into Bill, but he pushed her off, clicked his fingers like you would a dog and she left, casting a look of disgust over her shoulder at me.

'Here for something else?' he said and hooked his eyebrow.

The rage in me was burning and I didn't have the stomach

for his games. 'You loved Molly, right?'

The mention of her name wiped the smug off his face. 'What of it?'

'You'd kill the man who hurt her, wouldn't you?'

'I'd rip his head clean off his shoulders. What you getting at? The fella who did it is long gone. I got men out looking for him.'

'Frank Croaker one of them?'

He sensed my tone then and stood up, came round the desk to me.

'You'd better explain yourself,' he said, but it weren't a threat.

'Mounties think they got their man, but they don't. You and me got a common enemy till this is done.'

Bill crossed his arms, sat on the edge of his desk. 'I'm listening.'

'I want a trade,' I said.

'I'm taking your hotel, Martha. One way or another.'

'I'd give my land and my hotel to a drunk for a dollar before I'd sell to you.'

His lip curled. 'What, then?'

'The man who killed Harry. Shoot him or put him on the next boat out of here. I don't want to see his face in this town.'

His face twitched as he considered it. The anger building and burning inside him. 'Fine.'

We shook on it and his grip was hot iron.

'When Doc examined Molly's body, he found skin and blood under her nails.'

'What's that mean?'

'Means she fought back. Means she scratched whoever killed her and drew blood.'

'And the coward hightailed it out of here.'

I shook my head. 'They found Yannick Early's body this

morning. He's been dead an age, gunshots to the chest. And he don't have no scratches. Frank does. Right on his cheek.'

I saw it dawn on him. The weight of betrayal settling on his shoulders. 'He said he got them in a bar fight.'

'He lied, Bill. They were fresh the morning after she died.'

Then the rage came. Hot and storming inside him. I'd seen it before. Frank Croaker was as good as dead. I'd set the fuse and all I had to do now was sit back and watch the show.

Bill strode out the office and roared from the balcony. 'Bring me Frank Croaker!'

KATE

I found the storehouse easily on the south side of Dawson. Yukon barked beside me as we got close, could smell the dogs and their blood. Men filed in through wide doors and as I went in with them, I was assaulted in every sense. The sight, dozens of men crammed inside a ring of crates, hidden from the rest of the building, crates topped with oil lamps giving off a greasy orange light. The smell of sawdust and animals, of sweat and spilled bourbon, raw meat to rile the dogs, half-rotten. The sounds! Shouting, growling, jaws ripping dog flesh, men calling bets and roaring on their dog, a few voices above them all shouting odds.

I was jostled to a corner by the surging weight of the crowd. Yukon clung beside me, his tail tight between his legs, eyes white with fear. I should never have brought him. I went down to my knees and held his face, rubbed his ears and chin and raked my hands over his fur.

'Don't worry, Yuke, they won't hurt you.'

A vicious bark went up from the dog in the ring and Yukon's

ears flattened. He whined and pawed at me. I found a short length of rope and tied it loosely around his neck, made him a leash so he would not get lost. I wrapped the rope around my hand and gave him a piece of dried meat from my pocket.

This place was as I imagined hell. A roaring, stinking pit of violence and sin, of disregard for life in the name of sport and money. Gold dust littered the floor, sparkling when the crowds moved and light shone through the door. A few small boys darted about, fingers black with muck, picking up flakes.

I moved through the crowd, watching the men and dogs. The ring was bounded by waist-high boards; two men, one on either side, stood inside with heavy sticks and goaded and shouted at their dogs. The animals themselves were distortions of the kind creature beside me. Both were covered in blood from scratches and bites. One had no ears, either clipped off by his owner or torn off by a past opponent. The other, no tail.

The fight reached its climax as the tail-less dog, a large black canine similar to a husky or a wolf, bit down on the smaller dog's neck and did not let go. The smaller, a skinny pitbull, thrashed around and wailed, but could not break free.

The men in the ring went wild. One cheering on his victory, the other admonishing the fallen.

The crowd erupted, waving betting slips at a few men handing out winnings. The victorious dog's jaws were prised apart with a stick and he was dragged away, out of the ring and behind yet more crates. The loser, however, was still and, despite his owner's kicks, would not rise again. My heart broke and I pulled Yukon closer to me, felt his warm body against my leg. As the poor creature was carried away, I saw on the far side of the ring a large chalkboard and a man standing upon a crate, calling the odds for the next fight.

I knew him immediately. The clean man. The one who had

shouted at me for sitting beside Lake Bennett. My sister's husband and her killer.

Henry Gable.

He was a changed man from the one who had walked the Dead Horse Trail and could not control his horses. His hair was longer, his face carried stubble and he seemed thinner beneath his clothes. He had rings around his eyes, dark and deep, and I wondered if he assuaged himself of his guilt in one of Dawson's many opium dens. The man at Hunker Creek had said Henry was betting, but now he seemed to be running the place. In only a few days. Things changed fast up here; the whole city had appeared almost overnight and it was men like Gable who profited from it. Some men knew how to charm their way to the top, others how to use their fists. I wasn't sure yet which Gable was.

I felt my knife in my pocket, made sure it was in the right place, should I need to grab it quickly. Around me the men had quietened somewhat, waiting for a new fight to begin.

Someone grabbed Yukon's leash. 'I'll give you twenty dollars for him.'

He could have been anyone, another faceless miner. I whipped the knife from my pocket and cut his hand. He snatched it back with a yelp.

'No.'

The man spat at my feet and turned away, disappeared into the crowd. Another tried the same, but just a look at the knife and the set of my features was enough to say my dog was not for sale.

I found space at the wall, as far from the action in the ring as I could get. I watched Gable, but as more and more men squeezed into the space, it became more difficult to keep my footing. Dogs began to bark and a low, rhythmic thump from hundreds of stamping boots made the floor shake.

'Gentlemen! Last bets!' Gable shouted and a rush began. Men in suits and brown bowlers came through the crowd with bags, handing out betting slips and taking gold and money.

A pair of stocky pitbulls were brought into the ring, snapping and snarling at each other, straining on their chains, taught only to bite and kill the animal before them. It made my insides boil. No dog deserved to be treated that way. These men, and a few women among them, blood-hungry at the end of the world, could find nothing more gentle to occupy themselves. When there was no word of law beyond the turned, blind eyes of those meant to uphold it, men devolved into beasts. Without consequence, my species had no morals and no thought to the suffering of others. It made me sick.

I tried to block out the sounds of the dogs, their pained barks, the smell of their musk and blood, the animalistic roaring of the crowd. I set my sights on Gable, tightened my grip on Yukon's leash and moved through the masses.

As I approached, Gable stepped down from the crate, oblivious to me, and tried to push by, wiping sweat from his neck with a dirty cloth.

I grabbed his arm. I felt him tense and he spun to face me. A flicker of confusion passed over his face. He had taken me for a man no doubt, then he saw Yukon.

'Bruce handles dogs. Go round back,' he said and tried to free his arm, but I held on.

'Henry Gable?' I asked.

'The fuck you want?'

His voice was different too from the sharp, clean sounds of the city. Now he spoke with a fuzzy slur, as if he was permanently sucking in one cheek. I had imagined this moment from the second I saw the photograph. I had thought of how I would confront him and what he would say, but now I was here, the words deserted me.

He yanked his arm from my grip and sneered. 'Fuck off then.'

He barged past me and my anger flared. This man had hurt my sister. Beat her in their marriage. Chased her across the country and threatened his way here. I found myself imagining Charlotte's last night, her fear upon seeing him. The terror when she realised his intent.

The rage overtook me, the knife was in my hand. I rushed at him, put it to his throat and pushed him back against the wall in one quick movement. The few men close by moved aside, unwilling to get in the middle of it, focused on the dogs.

Gable didn't seem concerned about me, or the knife, just looked at us both like we were children playing and he was fast running out of patience.

'I owe you money or something?'

Yukon growled at his tone and he almost laughed.

'No. You owe me far more than money,' I said and he frowned.

'What are you talking about?'

'I'm Kate Kelly. I believe you knew my sister.'

His smile vanished.

ELLEN

Again I search for my husband in this mud-caked city. Again I walk the boards, invisible. I make up stories to ask, without asking, after his whereabouts. Most have not seen him. Some have news. Sutter saw him yesterday, looking proud as a peacock.

'I've struck,' so Charlie said to the grocer. And Sutter patted him on the back and settled the account.

In Sweet's Café the woman who serves the plates said he was there that morning for his breakfast. He was crowing over his gold.

I stand on the boardwalk outside Sweet's. The smell of bread and bacon floats on the air and I do not remember the last time I ate a full meal. Music plays from somewhere close by. The sunshine after the storm brings out the best of this town. The wind blows strong from the south, bringing mountain freshness with it. I wish I could enjoy it, without worrying always over what Charlie is doing. Where he is. How he is growing our debt. Who he may be hurting.

Every moment I am on those streets I see him again. Running from the alley, black bloodstains on his shirt and face. I see her again. Still. I brush her hair from her face and in my memory she stares up at me and speaks: *He has finally found me.*

In the letter she'd spoken of her husband, but in my mind she speaks of mine.

I can think now of only one place Charlie could be. In line at the assayer's.

I go to the corner of Dawson I have rarely visited. There stands a building stronger and more ably built than those around it. Outside stand two men with clubs and guns. Along the muddy street runs a queue of miners, gripping their pouches and jars and canvas bags.

I stand away and watch. Take in the features of every man waiting. Those free of mud and those caked in it. There are those with plenty and those with little. The latter hold small pouches, where the former hold jars and canvas sacks. I see the weight of them. The poor are alone, but the rich are in groups, for protection.

Charlie is not among them. He must have been and gone. I must know for sure.

I go to the door of the assayer's. One of the large men bars my way. 'I have no gold to weigh,' I say, 'but a question to ask.'

The guard leans into the open door. The men around me tut and shuffle. 'Got a lady here with a question for you, Ham.'

A bark comes back. 'Let her in.'

The guard steps aside with a nod.

I've never been in here before; the business of gold and its stages was Charlie's alone. The room is not large. A door at the far side is open and I can smell a coal fire in a tall, square stove with an open top. A wiry boy tends it with a poker.

Inside, a long countertop runs the length of the room, upon it the tools of the assayer's trade. A scale with brass weights and a wide trough. Smelting moulds. Bottles of acid for testing the purity. A tall safe. The floor is gritty with dropped gold. A trick the assayers used, so Charlie said, to spill a little dust here and there to fill a dustpan by the end of the day.

The man behind the counter is stocky, though short, and wears a shirt and an open black waistcoat. His moustache is curled with oil and he wears thick glasses to protect his eyes from the heat of the smelting and the spit of the acid.

A miner stands at the counter, awaiting his pay.

'What do you need, love?' the assayer asks. His accent is strange, not one often encountered up here.

'You are from England?'

He smiles. A jovial man clearly, for why would he not be? He takes ten per cent of every smelting. 'Manchester.'

A whistle comes from the boy outside.

'Hang on there,' the assayer says and comes round the counter. Pulls on a pair of canvas gloves, takes hold of heavy iron tongs.

The boy shuffles aside. The assayer lifts a white-hot crucible from the coals and pours the contents into iron moulds waiting outside. Molten gold flows like syrup. It glows, unearthly, like the inside of the sun.

The mould does not take long to cool and, in a few minutes, he taps out the bars and drops them into a bucket of water. They hiss and spit. He pulls the four bars from the water and brings them to the desk.

They are black. The miner who pulled this gold from the ground steps between me and his bounty.

The assayer takes a thick-bristled brush and begins to clean the gold.

'You had a question, love.'

I am brought back to myself and my purpose with a jolt. 'Yes. I am looking for someone. Charlie Rhodes.'

The black crust begins to crumble away. 'He was in here this morning. First in line.'

'How much gold did he bring?' He had taken three jars with him.

'A mason jar, almost full. He was telling everyone about his strike, really laying it on. But when I burned it, I had some bad news for him.'

'What news?'

'Purity was for shit. Ten or twelve carats at most. Barely worth the cost of mining it. Some pockets are like that. Can have rotten gold ten foot from the good stuff.'

My heart sinks. All the toil and bluster, and finally the relief, at finding it and it was worth half what it should be.

'Bad luck, eh,' says the miner, shaking his head, not taking his eyes from his gold.

The assayer finishes his clean, and the yellow brick gleams with that impossible warm light. The miner's smile grows. The assayer scratches the edge along a black stone so hard it almost hurts to watch. Then he takes a bottle.

'Here's the magic,' he winks.

He pours a few drops of the liquid onto the line of gold left on the black stone. We all crane to look. He takes another two bottles and does the same. The gold remains beneath the first two, but is gone under the third drop.

'Congratulations, fella,' says the assayer, 'this is good gold. Eighteen-carat.'

The miner claps his hands and takes the bars, handing over some money to him. He leaves and the assayer wipes the stone clean.

'What does it mean?' I say. 'Those liquids.'

'The acid dissolves what ain't gold,' he says. 'Pure gold don't disappear. Your man, Rhodes, his went on the first drop.'

'Do you know where he went?'

'Sorry, love.'

I go to leave, but stop. From my pocket I take one of the bigger nuggets I found at the high claim.

'Can you test this? You may keep it as payment.'

He takes it and turns it in his fingers. Looks at me. 'You sure?'

A call comes from outside. 'Line's getting longer, boss.'

'I'm sure.'

He takes a clean black stone and scratches it deeply with the nugget. It leaves a long line of gold. He repeats his process with the three acids. The gold remains beneath all.

He raises his eyebrows. 'Pure as pure. Twenty-four-carat.'

Heat rises within me. Pure gold. In abundance. And all mine.

'Thank you,' I say.

The assayer tucks the nugget in his pocket. 'Thank *you*. Congratulations, love. You got yourself a gold mine.'

I leave the assayer's with a light step and a lighter heart. How much gold can I pull from that river before winter? Enough to leave here rich, I suppose. Yet I will need help. I will need Kate.

MARTHA

'We found him!' came a hoarse cry from the door of the Nugget. It had been a few tense and uncomfortable hours stuck in Bill's office, watching him watch me. I wouldn't leave. Wouldn't miss the show for all the gold in the water.

At the call, Bill shot up and put his Smith & Wesson in his belt. 'Stay put.'

'Like hell I will.' I ignored a sharp pain in my gut and followed him down to the bar.

Frank Croaker stood between two men, one bigger, one thinner. He looked shaken, shifting his weight from one foot to the other, looking man to man, woman to woman – what few of us there were.

'Bill, what's going on?' he asked, but he weren't angry. He was scared pale.

Bill walked right up to him and grabbed his face. Turned it to the side. There were the scratches. Scabbed up now, after a week, and half-hidden under his beard.

'Where'd you get those?' he asked.

Frank tried to pull his head out of Bill's grip, but couldn't. 'A fight.'

Bill sneered and brought his face right close to Frank's. 'I ain't never known a man to scratch that like in a brawl. Means you must've been fighting a woman.'

Frank's eyes widened just enough for Bill to know he was right.

'It ain't like that,' Frank tried, but Bill shook his head, tutted for his man to stop talking.

He turned away from Frank and slowly pulled out his gun. Made sure Frank and every other person in that place saw.

'Molly scratched who killed her. Doc said so,' Bill said.

Frank figured it out then. I saw the panic rise in him, from my spot by the bar. His eyes went to every face, looking for sympathy, but no one there would dare go against Bill, and that bastard knew it.

'You think . . . ?' Frank's mouth opened and closed and he huffed out his disbelief, but it was all false. In my line of work you can read men easy as a bill of fare, and Frank was hiding something.

Before Frank could speak, Bill whipped him with the gun. Punched him down to the ground with vicious jabs, striking gun metal to soft cheek until one of them gave. Bill stopped quick as he began. Frank moaned and spat blood and teeth, holding up his hands to stay his old friend.

'I didn't touch Molly,' he said in a weak voice I knew would just make Bill angrier.

Bill pointed the gun in his face. Blood dripped from the barrel.

'You lie to me again. I dare you!'

He grabbed Frank, yanked him to his feet. Frank could barely stand, his legs kept going from under him, but Bill had him by the collar. He dragged Frank across the room, threw him against the door. The wood cracked and burst open, and Frank rolled out into the street. Bill followed. We all followed.

Dawson held its breath. The town stopped moving, it seemed. Soon as anyone saw Bill, they paused to look. Then they saw his gun and who he was pointing at, and they froze.

Frank held one hand to his broken cheek, right where those scratches had been, now torn up by Bill's rage. He was bent double, blood pouring from his mouth, own hand held up to stop Bill; but nothing would stop Bill.

'I didn't hurt her, I swear it,' he spat and tried to straighten up. 'You're right. It was a woman, not a fight, but it weren't Molly.'

'Then who, Frank?' Bill said.

Frank didn't answer right away and that was enough fuel on Bill's fire. Honest men don't take an age to speak the truth. Frank was finding a lie and Bill knew it.

I stood at the door of the Nugget, heart in my mouth. I chewed down on it, hoping to God I was right. But I had to be. Frank was a devil. He knew Molly. Maybe he tried to bed her, or take her by force to Bill. She fought back. She died for it.

'What about Yannick Early?' I shouted and Frank saw me over Bill's shoulder.

His eyes went white.

'I didn't . . . he was . . . interfering,' Frank stammered out.

I couldn't see Bill's face, but I could imagine it. His sneer. His breath heaving in his chest. Eyes like silver dollars.

'You killed a man who tried to stop you killing a woman?' Bill's voice was quiet, deadly.

Frank's jaw dropped. He was done. He had nothing left. He went to his knees.

'Please, Bill, I swear I didn't hurt Molly. Please, I didn't.'

Bill thumbed the hammer on his gun. 'Get on your feet.'

Frank scrambled up, mud clinging to him. 'Come on, Bill. Let's talk about this. I didn't do it. I swear on my life.'

'I'll give you to the count of five,' Bill said.

Frank knew what that meant and he started to panic. 'Goddamn it! Someone! I didn't kill Molly!'

'One.'

'Bill, for God's sake! I didn't do nothing.'

'Two.'

'You all just gonna watch this? You fuckin' pieces of shit!' Blood sprayed from his mouth with the words.

'Three.'

Frank backed away. Everyone on the street moved, pressed their backs to buildings, took cover behind barrels and crates.

'Four.'

Frank turned. Ran. People parted. He stumbled.

I never heard Bill get to 'five'. The shot rang out and Frank fell.

Bill's arm fell to his side. The gun looked suddenly heavy. On the other side of the street, the Mountie, William Deever, stepped toward Frank. He nudged the body with his foot. Then he turned to Bill.

Bill spread his arms wide as if to say, go on then, but Deever didn't move. He looked at the crowd, at Bill, down at Frank. He'd heard it all, of course. His man for the murder had been Yannick Early. Frank killed Early. Frank killed Molly. End of story. Again. I held on to the door frame. If I didn't, I would've collapsed then and there. My heart didn't dare beat, watching that Mountie make up his mind. Could've heard a pin drop on mud in that street.

Deever spotted me and we shared a look that I thought meant relief this was done and the right man was dead. Then, without saying a word, he walked away.

That broke the spell. Every person let out their breath and went back to their lives. They stepped over Frank's body. A few young'uns and scabs rushed up and picked his pockets clean.

Bill passed me as he went back into the Nugget. He stopped. 'I'll see to our deal.'

I nodded, believed him. Bill was a lot of things, almost none of them good, but he did have a streak of honour in him. A deal's a deal, after all.

KATE

I was so focused on Gable I didn't see the other man, or his fist, until it hit my cheek. I staggered. Bright spots sparked across my vision. Yukon barked, but barely made a sound above the din of the fighting dogs.

It was one of the men in suits and brown bowler hats who had hit me. Gable put his hand to his neck where my knife had been pressed. The force of the man's punch had knocked me away, but my knife had sliced deeper, I'd felt it. Gable pushed the man and growled.

'You fuckin' idiot!' He took his hand away and blood seeped down his neck in a smeared sheet.

I raised my knife, cheek and head throbbing, and shouted, 'You killed Charlotte!'

Gable turned on me, shock in his eyes. The other man looked at us both.

'I didn't touch her.'

'Liar!'

I ran at him. He grabbed my wrist and punched me in the

stomach. My legs went from under me and I lost my grip on Yukon's rope. He went wild, snarling, teeth out. He bit down on Gable's leg and the man roared, started kicking, trying to shake him loose.

Bowler grabbed Yukon's scruff and pulled, but Yuke didn't let go.

Gable cracked my wrist against a wooden beam, the knife fell and pain shot up and down my arm.

Over his shoulder, I saw Bowler. He'd found a club. He raised it. One hit and Yukon's skull would crack.

'Yukon. Drop him!' I shouted and he did. 'Run. Go, Yukon!'

He looked up at me, confused, as Bowler rushed for us both, club high. Gable, finally free, wound up to kick him.

'Go!'

Yukon saw the danger and dashed to the side as the club came down. Gable's kick caught his back leg and he sprawled, rolled, but quickly got up and bolted for the door.

Gable still held my wrist, but my other hand found my knife in the straw.

Yukon was out the door, ears back, running. Safe. Bowler tried to chase him, but he was gone.

Gable turned his attention back to me. I was on my knees, knife hidden behind my back.

I looked up at him. 'Admit what you did.'

'I didn't do anything.'

'You killed Charlotte.'

'The hell I did. I got to this shithole and went door to door asking after her. Every place I could think of. Nobody knew Charlotte Gable. Or Charlotte Kelly. I figured she was gone already.'

'You're a liar,' I spat the words. 'You hated that she got away from you. I'm glad she did. She's better off in the ground than with a man like you.'

His lip curled in anger, teeth bared like one of those dogs. His fist crashed down on my other cheek. Black pain blazed across my face and I hit the ground. But I wasn't done. I lifted myself up on shaking arms.

'This what you did to her? This how you showed how much you loved her?'

'You want to find out?'

Bowler had returned and stood behind Gable. 'What you going to do with her?'

'None of your fuckin' business,' he barked and Bowler took a step back.

Gable grabbed me by the hair and started to drag me. I screamed. A few people turned, looked, but none helped. None stopped him.

He dragged me behind some crates, where nobody could see us. New dogs were brought to fight and the crowd raged. Nobody would hear him. Or me. Nobody was coming to help. I'd learned on the trail, at the ferry, that a woman has to save herself in this place. I gripped my knife.

He pulled me to my feet and pushed me against the wall, hand to my throat.

'You were at Bennett,' he said, so close I could smell his breath.

'You got here just before Charlotte was killed. You were at her funeral, weren't you? I saw you.'

'Ain't a husband allowed at his wife's funeral?'

'Not if he was the one who put her in the ground. You should hang.'

'I didn't kill her.'

I pushed my face closer to him, despite his bruising grip on my neck. 'I don't believe you.'

'That bitch left me. Took the money out of my wallet and left in the night. What kind of woman does that?'

I tasted blood in my mouth, wanted to spit, but couldn't turn my head. 'And you came here to teach her a lesson, right?'

He tightened his grip. 'I told Charlotte I'd always find her. She was mine. I tracked her down to a boarding house in Seattle. Only took a few dollars and that old woman sang like a canary.'

I wanted to kill him. Take my knife and drive it into his throat.

'And now you're running dog-fights? What about all the supplies you bought?'

He scoffed. 'I only did that to hit the weight limit. The Mounties wouldn't have let me up here otherwise. This is where the real money is, and I'm a businessman.'

I remembered the weighing station along the trail, a memory from a different life.

'What business is that? Beating women?'

His lip turned in a lurid smile. 'If they need to be kept in line.'

'Did Charlotte need to be kept in line?'

He didn't answer, just squeezed my neck harder.

'Admit what you did.' My voice was weak, cracked, and my vision began to swim.

'I didn't kill her, but I wish I had.'

I met his eyes. My last ounce of energy poured into my defiance. 'Prove it.'

'How am I meant to do that?'

I coughed and blood filled my mouth. I swallowed it down and my gut clenched. He loosened his grip enough for the air to rush in and give him an answer.

'Take off your shirt.'

He laughed. 'You're serious?'

'You want to prove it – this is how.'

He finally took his hand from my neck and stepped back. I doubled over, coughing, retching blood. He'd decided I wasn't a danger to him. My knife was in my hand, hidden behind my back. I'd wait until I knew for sure. Until I saw those scratch marks. Until I confronted him with the proof writ in his own skin.

Gable took off his waistcoat and pulled the shirt over his head. He spread his arms wide and turned around slowly.

'Seen enough?'

I pushed off from the wall and grabbed an oil lamp to get a better look.

Beyond the wall of crates, the dogs gnashed at each other and something, a body perhaps, thudded against the wooden ring. The crowd cheered.

He was covered in scratches, old and new. A crescent of livid red welts on his forearm, a criss-cross of scratches on his chest. When he turned, they were on his back too.

'No ...' I breathed. There were so many. Some still bled. Others scabbed over. Others red and raised. There was no way to know if these were from Charlotte.

'Dogs don't train themselves,' he said and picked up his shirt. 'You get what you needed?'

He had to have killed her. Any one of these marks could be from her nails. From her fighting for her life as he drove a knife into her body. Her blood had spilled over his hands. He had watched her die. I knew it. I knew it in the bone-deep part of me. He was guilty and nobody but me could do anything about it. How long before he hurt someone else? Found another wife to beat? Another life to take?

'Now, what am I going to do with you?' he said in a low voice.

I snapped out of my spiralling thoughts and Gable was but a breath away from me.

'Stay away,' I said, but he stepped closer.

'You look like her, you know. Prettier even.'

I raised the lantern, meaning to smash it against his head, but he was quicker. He grabbed my wrist and twisted. I cried out, dropped the lantern. He slapped me across the cheek.

I still had the knife in my other hand, hidden behind my back. His hand was in my hair, yanking it, driving me back against the wall.

'Let's see if you taste like her,' he murmured into my ear.

Bile rose in my stomach. I did it without realising, without choosing. My blade slid through his skin, under his rib, right up to the hilt. The air went out of him. I pulled the knife free.

This is what he'd done to Charlotte, despite his talk of innocence, of not even knowing; he was a liar, a charming snake in a man's skin. Charlotte had fallen for those lies and married him. I would not make her mistake. I thrust the blade again.

Gable's grip went slack and he staggered. He clutched his side, saw the blood, confused at first and then the pain came. The anger. His face changed, his eyes turned to mirrors, lifeless. He ran at me, kicking the lantern. I heard glass break.

I couldn't move fast enough. He was on top of me, fists raining down on my face and head.

I stabbed wildly with my knife. He grabbed my wrist again and smashed it on the ground until I couldn't hold on any more. The knife flew away. He had his hands on my throat. Squeezed.

Brightness filled my eyes, but it wasn't spots or sparks or the great light. It was fire.

Fire all around us. Growing and shifting. He didn't see. I couldn't speak. My vision darkened at the edges.

Then his hands were gone. I heard him shouting, screaming. Saw the flames. Fire licked up his legs. He tried to pat it
away, but the fire clung and climbed and spread. The floor was
ablaze with tiny infernos. The crates around us caught. The
walls turned black.

Then the cries went up.

'Fire! Fire!'

The ground shook with panic. Gable spun in frantic circles, blood covering one side of his body, fire the other. He
screamed, ran and was caught in the crowds.

I struggled to my feet. Fire caught the side of my hand,
but I barely felt it. My head was a mess of blood. I felt like
my skull had been crushed. I tasted only blood. Smelled only
smoke. The fire caught my pant leg. Pain seared my skin and
brought me to my senses.

The whole storehouse was ablaze. The dry straw, the sawdust, more oil lamps tipped over in the panic, a tinderbox. The
dogs barked, frenzied and abandoned in their cages.

I breathed smoke and coughed. Blood and tar hissed in
the flames. The storehouse was empty – everyone gone, me
abandoned.

A woman must save herself.

I crawled beneath the smoke as drops of fire fell from the
rafters like rain. The door seemed to move further away. The
light seemed to shrink.

Then a shadow, a silhouette at the door. A woman.

'Help . . .' I tried, but my voice was gone with the smoke.

ELLEN

DAWSON CITY, KLONDIKE, JULY 1898

A gunshot rings out in the next street. I wonder if it is Charlie. Fallen foul of Bill Mathers and Frank Croaker, his debt finally called in. My husband, parading his gold amid a town of sharks he's promised his blood to.

I hope it is him.

I hope it is not.

I cross between the buildings. No matter the weather, the summer heat, in these shaded alleys the mud remains and my boots are soon thick with it.

I come out of the dark and into a thin crowd. They are still and waiting. A body lies in the middle of the street. A few yards beyond it stands Bill Mathers, gun in hand. From this distance I cannot tell who the dead man is, but I know it is not Charlie.

I am not sure if I am relieved that I get to hear his story from his own mouth, or fearful of the same.

A Mountie, the same one who questioned me over Molly's death, stands rigid and silent. Dawson holds its breath. The Mountie nods to Bill and walks away.

The crowd breathes. Skinny youths rush upon the body and strip it of value. I step into the street and the youths scatter, their job complete. Blood pools beneath the dead man and I know him now. Up close.

Frank Croaker.

Shot by his own boss. But why?

I look around as if the answers are writ in the air. Then I see Martha walking towards me.

'I didn't think I'd be seeing you again,' she says with half a smile.

'What happened here?'

'Frank killed Molly.'

It is a jolt to the chest. 'He did?'

I look at him again. No longer a danger to me, and yet still I fear him. It is the first time I've seen Frank since he came to the cabin. I remember his touch, his force, his breath. I feel the ache still in my back where he pushed me against the fence. I am glad he is dead.

'He saw Doc bringing Early's body through here and turned white as a sheet,' Martha said. 'Frank shot Early, let him take the blame for Molly, said Early was interfering, can you believe that? He had three scratches on his cheek from her nails. I saw them the day after she died.'

I nod slowly. Martha is wrong. I gave Frank those scratches. I recall the feeling of my nails dragging across his skin so vividly it makes my fingers itch. I still hear the way he roared, a hurt beast turned all the more dangerous.

Martha smiles down at the body. She holds an arm across her midriff and is hunched slightly. The straight-backed madam has been reduced somewhat.

'Are you sure?' I ask and she frowns.

'As the snow falls and the wolves piss in it.'

I wish to tell her. Unburden myself. But she looks relieved. Happy almost to have the matter closed in her mind. She takes my arm and squeezes it.

'Finally Molly can rest easy,' she says and I cannot let the lie stand. Molly is not at rest, she is writhing in her grave as we stumble towards justice. Kate on her path, Martha on hers, and me on mine. I do not know if Charlie killed her, or if Henry Gable did, but Frank Croaker did not. He was not an innocent man and his crimes are long, not least the murder of Yannick Early, for which justice has been served. But of this, of Molly – of this he is innocent. It makes me sick to defend him, but for Molly, for Kate, I must.

'Martha, you must know—' But I am cut off by the sound of a bell.

'Fire!' the shout goes up from down the street. 'Fire! Fire!'

We turn. A column of smoke rises in thick plumes from the south side of town.

'Dear Lord,' Martha says. 'The storehouses.'

'Storehouses?' My heart races. I grab Martha's arm. 'Kate is there.'

Martha looks at me in shock. 'Kate? You know her? What could she be doing?'

'No time to explain,' I say, already moving away. 'I must go, see if she is all right.'

'I'm coming with you.'

The town is alive with panic. The fire bell is relentless. Men rush to the flames, volunteers all. By the smoke, I can see it is spreading already. One plume is now three. More buildings have caught.

We run to the riverbank in time to see the steam-pump. A large metal tank pulled by four horses, a roll of hose and a pump on wooden wheels. One man pilots it, another five run alongside. Brand-new, they say, shipped from Seattle this spring. It's a fantastical piece of equipment, all valves and pipes. We follow it.

Black smoke fills the sky, the blaze lights it orange.

Finally we reach the storehouse. We are kept back while men form a line from the river, hauling buckets. Throwing them. The ice-cold Yukon water turns to steam and the fire remains. The storehouse is covered in flame. Two buildings on either side have caught and the firemen direct the buckets at those.

They work quickly, a fireman running a hose to the river. He slides down the bank and stumbles on the shingle. He throws the hose end and it lands well.

He shouts. I do not hear what he says, but the message passes to those manning the steamer. But they are talking among themselves. They are pointing to the pump and waving their arms. One tries a valve; the machine sputters. Another pushes him away and tries another lever. Another jumps up to the giant steel tank at the back.

'What is going on?' I ask. Martha clutches my arm, her breathing heavy. The effort of running has taken its toll.

'I don't know,' she says, squinting against the blaze. 'What was Kate doing here?'

I scour the crowd for her, but see nothing. 'Looking for Molly's husband.'

Martha turns to me. 'Her *husband*?'

'He is in Dawson, so Kate says. Molly wrote to her, said he'd found her. Kate believes he killed her.' I say it without thinking of what had happened to Croaker. Of Martha's conviction of his guilt. There is no time to dwell. We must find Kate before—

An almighty crack splits the sky, and the roof of the storehouse collapses.

A great ball of fire explodes from the ruin. Sparks and flaming debris rain on the firemen, the crowd, the surrounding buildings. I can barely breathe through the heat of it. Kate could be in there. Could be gone already. Am I too late? I must try. I must know.

I move through them. I see men with fighting dogs. I see men burned. But I do not see her.

'Kate!' I shout. 'Yukon!'

Martha calls too. 'Kate Kelly!'

The firemen pile wood into their steamer, their fire clearly gone. Time wastes and the flames spread. The wind carries north to the rest of the city. Hundreds of wooden buildings built too close. Hundreds of stovepipes coated in creosote – tiny bombs in every home. This fire will take them all.

I put it from my mind. All I can think of is Kate. How she got out of that building before the fire. How she is looking for me at the Dawson Hotel. How she must be anywhere but here.

I grab a burnt man. 'Have you seen a woman in pants, a dog with her?'

Stunned, he shakes his head.

The doctor, Pohl, is here, rushing between the wounded.

The firemen shout, 'Move back! Get clear!'

The people shuffle. Other men take charge and begin to push us. The sound! The fire roars so loud I must shout to be heard. The cries of pain, of fear; of order, order, move, quick, light the fire, prime the pump, move-move-move.

I feel Martha's hand on mine. She pulls me.

'This way!' We circle around the other side. Men work frantically here too; more and more come from the camps with buckets, cups, pans, anything that holds water. They form lines to the river. They spit on the inferno.

Here at least the wind blows the heat and noise in the opposite direction and we are spared it for a moment.

'Kate! Yukon!' I call at every step, but no answer comes. I whistle. I shout. Martha echoes me.

Then I hear barking.

Martha grabs me, points. 'There!'

The dog bounds through the teeming streets. Dodging feet, legs, kicks. He leaps at me and I catch him. He licks my face, his fur singed and stinking, blood at his mouth. He is frantic, scratching up my body, clawing to be close and safe.

'Where is Kate?' I ask, as if he can answer. 'Where is she?'

I grab his face, spots from the porcupine quills still livid on his muzzle. I hold him, look him in the eyes.

'Find Kate. Find her, Yuke.'

He blinks. Cocks his head. Licks my face again.

I stand, frustrated and fearful. I look from where he came, hoping to see Kate rushing after him, but the streets are a mess. She is not there. I look again at the storehouse, now a black skeleton belching smoke. I cough at the smell, the heavy feeling of burning in my lungs.

I am lost in the chaos. Another building collapses and the rush of heat and noise and running bodies nearly knocks us over.

'What do we do?' I say, to Martha, to the dog, to the desperate city.

'To the river, it'll be safe there,' Martha says and takes my hand again.

MARTHA

DAWSON CITY, KLONDIKE, JULY 1898

'Get more buckets!' a fireman shouted. 'Form a line!'

We came out the crush of streets, where buildings were catching easy as straw in a furnace, and skidded down the riverbank to the shore. It was swarming, the beach was alive with running, rushing men and women, some tending the wounded, others screaming out their pain. Ellen and the dog followed me like I knew where the hell I was going. I held on to her like she was the only thing solid in the world.

Up the bank, the steamer pump finally got to working. It chugged out a gush of water, sputtered and died for a minute, then went hell for leather, but it was too late. The storehouse was gone and every building around it was blazing. The wind was picking up, blowing the fire north-east, right up Front Street and into the heart of the city. The flames jumped roof to roof, tents and canvas turned to ash and sticks.

I thought of my hotel, sitting proud at the top of Queen, right in the path of the wind. I hoped the girls were out and up the hill, I hoped Jerry had the good sense to take the ledgers and leave the safe. I hoped Harriet weren't sleeping off her gin, unknowing there was death on the way. But right now, it was Kate who was front of my mind.

She was here someplace, searching out a killer who'd already been found. At least I'd thought so, before Ellen put the doubt in me. It made sense. Molly's husband come looking, didn't like what he found. But Frank had them scratches, and this husband could be anywhere.

So could Kate.

'Do you see her?' Ellen asked. The girl was frantic, panic took hold of her and gripped tight. I put my hands on her shoulders.

'You need to stay calm,' I said. 'If she's here, we'll find her. If she's not, she'll be safe someplace else. But you got to keep your head.'

She blinked, like I'd slapped sense back into her.

Then the dog went wild. Barking and running off down the beach.

'Yukon!' Ellen cried and chased him.

I followed best and quick as I could. My insides were heavy, the ache in my gut growing sharper with every step.

I passed by a man with burns up the side of his head, hair gone, ear gone, staring at nothing, swaying in the breeze. Another fella had a broken arm, bone twisted and sticking out, screaming that a beam fell on him. Two fighting dogs were whimpering in a wooden cage, fur burned off, couldn't tell what injuries were caused by fire and what by each other.

I hurried on past it, away from the worst of the walking dead, past the lines of buckets draining the Yukon River. Caught up with Ellen and the dog, tail thumping so hard he must have found his mistress.

The tent they stood outside was white, with red and yellow painted swirls. A board outside read:

Madam Renio
Past, present and future readings
Mining readings a speciality

I could smell the incense from out here and hear the twinkling of wind chimes and bells outside.

Ellen looked at me and I saw in her eyes what I felt in mine. She didn't hesitate, just pushed open the tent and went inside, Yukon nipping at her heels.

Inside, the roar of the fire, the panic of the people, all fell away. Muffled by carpets and velvet drapes. No amount of fabric could quiet the hell that raged outside, yet it did. The tent seemed bigger on the inside, and at the same time felt like the walls were closing in. There was a table, a great glass ball on top of it and, in a shadowed corner, a couch. Yukon made right for the couch, sniffing and whining, and I soon saw why.

There was a body lying on it.

Ellen and I were at Kate's side in an instant. She was bloodied up, eye swollen, face black with bruises. The fire got her in places too. She had smoke stains up her face, scorch marks up her arms. She was breathing, thank Christ, but she was barely there. Her arm hung out over the couch. Yukon licked her fingers, so gentle, and rested his head beside her. Her hand, her palm, was red with a black mark in the centre, like she'd put out a candle with her hand.

'She will live,' came a voice from the back of the tent.

Ellen and I turned to see the fortune-teller walking toward us with a tea service on a silver tray. The smell of sugar and mint took over the incense, made my mouth water. First and last time Sutter's had had peppermint was the summer of '97.

'It's you,' Ellen said and the woman smiled.

'You know her?' I asked.

Ellen nodded, then looked to her hands like she was embarrassed. 'I had a reading, the cards there,' she pointed, and I saw a deck beside the crystal ball that I was sure weren't there when we walked in.

'She just spouted some horseshit to me,' I said.

The fortune-teller laughed, a warm intimate sound that felt all wrong for the situation raging outside. She put the tea set on the table and poured three cups. I weren't sure if the third was for her or for Kate.

'What's your name? I figure "Renio" is just for show,' I said.

She paused, teapot in hand, and after a moment of thought said, 'Cora.'

'That your real name?'

She set down the pot and handed Ellen the first cup. 'It is as real as any.'

'Do you know what happened to Kate?' Ellen asked, and I suddenly felt like a cat for trying to scratch the woman instead of caring for a friend.

Cora handed me a cup. 'I found her in the storehouse, where they make the dogs fight. She spoke of a man. Of scratches. It was incoherent.'

'I ain't surprised,' I said, looking at how beat up the poor girl was.

'Scratches?' Ellen asked. 'She said the man had scratches?'

'I believe so.'

Ellen looked at me like her world had cracked open with them few words. 'Where is he?'

'I do not know.'

Ellen turned, panicked. 'Can't you look in that crystal ball or read the cards again?'

Cora gave a sad smile. 'It does not work like that. Do not fear – the truth will reveal itself. It always does.'

340

Kate gave a groan, like she was dreaming, but didn't wake. It was enough for us all to quiet down. Cora went to her side and knelt, took the girl's hand.

'I told you all you needed to hear at the time I spoke it. A love, a death, a future.'

The memory of her reading came back to me in light of all the horrors outside the tent. 'You told me fire was coming. You knew this would happen?'

Cora didn't even seem to hear me, just looked down at Kate like a mother at a sick child.

'Women have within them an innate magic. We are all bound together across time and distance, by centuries of shared pain and responsibility. You feel it when you see a child by itself. You will watch it until you know it is safe with its mother. Our connection to each other is what makes us strong. You three are bound by the threads of a life cut short. You must draw your strength from that. We are each other's bellwethers and watchmen; we all toil under the same invisible yoke, that of a world made by us, but not for us. So it is that I told you not what you needed to hear, but what you already knew. Here, at the end of all things, a woman may be anything. A miner. An explorer. A tycoon. Even a wife, should she wish.'

At the last she looked right at me and I felt a squirming in my gut. I only ever wanted to be wife to one man, should the right time come and the yoke not feel too heavy. But that man may already be dead. I couldn't think on it for a moment or I'd find myself curled up on this carpet, weeping into the pile.

'Before she came to the Klondike, Kate's future was mapped for her – as was all of yours – though she did not know it. Her sister's letter changed it all and now, you see,' the fortune-teller turned over Kate's hand to show the burn on

341

her palm, 'her lifeline is obscured, broken by her choices, and her future unwritten. Same as the rest of you.' She laid Kate's hand on the couch and looked up at Ellen and me.

'What does that mean?' Ellen asked, looking at her own hand, at a cut across her palm, as if an answer lay there. And at my own – the cut from the broken glass.

'It means you are each free to make the choice you truly wish for yourself. To live the life your heart desires, rather than the one other people, or your head or your pride, convinces you is right.'

It'd been so long since I'd listened to my heart that I weren't at all sure it still spoke to me. Ellen looked down at Kate and I knew similar thoughts were running through her. This woman had been right about a lot of things, maybe she was right about this too. This fire would eat up Dawson and pick its teeth with the sticks. What would be left for me? For my girls?

'Please,' said Cora, that constant smile still on her face, 'drink. All comes clear with a cup of tea.'

She swiped a curtain aside and ducked through into a private space at the back, and Ellen, Kate and I were by ourselves.

I sat on the edge of the couch by Kate's feet, Yukon huffed near her shoulder and Ellen took her hand.

We sat like that, staring at Kate's parts to save staring at the horrors that man and the flames had done to her. There weren't no outside, no fire, no burnt men on the beach, no half-burnt city. There was just us. Ellen reached for me and I saw she was crying. I held on to her hand and didn't need to ask what she spent her tears on.

Her hand tightened around mine. 'Ma,' she said in a quick breath.

I looked up, saw her staring at Kate – and Kate staring at both of us.

KATE

'I don't remember anything after that,' I said, speaking of the sight of a woman coming into the storehouse and all that came before it.

My voice was raw, my throat burned by the smoke. It had taken me so long to get out each word, but the women before me were patient, fed me warm tea and held me as I coughed black tar from my lungs. My dear Yukon would not go more than an inch from me, his head always touching my shoulder or arm. He had a patch of burnt fur on his side and, seeing it, the raw red skin beneath brought tears to my eyes.

'The fire started because of me.'

Ma shook her head. 'Fires start in Dawson if someone drops a hot shit in the wrong place.'

She told me of Frank Croaker and what had befallen him.

'It was him then,' I said, my voice a gritty whisper. 'Croaker. What he did to Early. The scratches.'

'It looks like it,' Ma said. 'But I don't get why.'

'It wasn't,' Ellen said, her eyes fixed firmly on her lap.

343

'Ellen?' Ma asked.

She glanced up at us, barely a flicker before she looked back at her hands. A heavy sigh lifted her shoulders.

'It wasn't Frank. The scratches on his face, they weren't from Molly . . . Charlotte.'

'How can you know that?' Ma asked.

'Because I gave them to him. I scratched him when he tried to violate me.'

Despite the pain in every inch of my body, I sat up and took her hand. I met her eyes and held them and didn't know what to say. Yukon put his head on her foot, as he did that first day in the cabin. She stroked his ears.

'I'm sorry, sweetheart,' Ma said, like she'd heard such a tale a thousand times of a thousand women.

'Yannick Early was a good man. He tried to stop Frank. He pulled Frank off me. Told me to run. Frank shot him. Twice.' Ellen was a tight coil of a person and, as she spoke, she began to slowly unwind. 'I should have helped. Stayed and tried to fight Frank off.'

Ma shook her head. 'Frank was a grizzly of a man. It would have done no good.'

Ellen suddenly looked so young, so vulnerable, where I'd always seen her as a woman cast in silver. She kept herself hidden behind a mirror, but there was softness there, within the metal of her.

'Why didn't you say anything?' I asked.

'I didn't want pity. Or gossip. Frank did what he did – what he tried to do – and that was terrible, but worse would be to have people know. I wanted to tell, when the Mounties put Charlotte's death on Early's shoulders, but I knew him to be dead and out of reach, while I still had to live in this place.'

My head and heart throbbed. My dear sister was no closer

to justice and her rest. Frank had not killed her, nor had Early. The town, the law, had moved past her, had closed the chapter on her life and death, yet I could not. Dawson, stricken now with a fire that would consume everything, had no time for the murder of one woman when ruin was on the horizon.

'Who killed her?' I asked, so tired of not knowing. 'I do not know if it was Gable. He had a good story. He said he wished he had been the one to kill her and, seeing the hate in his eyes, I believed him.'

Ellen tightened again, but just for a moment. She turned to me, held my hand in hers and seemed suddenly full of sorrow. 'Try not hate me after you hear this.'

Ma straightened her back as if preparing for the worst, and the worst it was.

'I didn't tell you this, Kate, but I was the one who found Charlotte, that night.'

A piece of ice lodged in my chest at her words. I looked at Martha, who did not seem surprised. 'You?'

'I was looking for Charlie, after Frank attacked me. I had no one else. I searched for him all over Dawson until I finally saw him,' she stopped and tears welled in her eyes. 'He was running from an alley, covered in dark stains. I went into the alley and . . . well . . . you know the rest.'

I felt as if I had been shot through the heart. I pulled my hand from hers. But Ellen was not finished.

Ma put her hand over her mouth. 'Oh, child,' she said, but could say no more. 'You didn't mention your husband was there.'

'I did not believe it at the time,' Ellen said, 'for how could I? My gentle, weak-willed husband a murderer? He said he had found her like that; he was in such a state, crying, incoherent, I believe he loved her.'

'Does he have scratches on his body?' Ma asked, for I could not speak.

'I don't know. We are not what you would call an . . . intimate couple.'

'He wears a kerchief around his neck,' I said slowly. 'He would not take it off, even as the sun burned us.'

Ellen's face was a mask of shame and sadness. 'I could not say anything, you must know. If Charlie was taken away, I would have nothing here. We have two claims, but one is worthless and so far in debt to Bill Mathers that he would take the land, and my cabin, and nobody would stop him. The other is rich, but difficult to mine at any large scale. I had not enough hidden away to hire men to mine with me, to room while I did so, nor even enough to secure passage home. My father had forsaken me entirely. I would have no protection from men like Bill Mathers who would take my land, or from Frank Croaker who would claim my body. I could not speak the truth then.'

'Why now?' I said, with more vitriol than I truly felt.

Ellen flinched at it. 'Everything is different now. I have gold of my own. I can pay Charlie's debts and take the claim for myself. I have a choice. A way to freedom.'

The anger built up inside me like a coming storm. In moments it would break from me. 'But I don't. I came here for my sister and, until she is at peace, I cannot be.' I tried to swing my legs from the couch. Searing pain shot up my side.

Ma put a hand on my chest. 'You are in no state.'

'You will not stop me.'

Ellen stood. Yukon, rudely awoken by her movement, shuffled away with a snort. I struggled to my feet. She went to help, to steady my arm, but I pulled away from her. I could not look at her, for all I saw was lies where once I had seen so

346

much more. I hurt everywhere, but most in my heart, for the betrayal of a friend burns hotter than any flame.

'Kate, don't,' Ma said, but I was up.

'I must know,' I replied.

A cough came again, fiercer this time than any other, and both women were at my side, each holding me up, Ma with her arm around my waist. The cough passed and I breathed carefully to ease the burning ache in my chest.

'Sit down, rest,' Ma said and tried to guide me, but I resisted.

'If you care for me at all, you will let me go.'

I met Ellen's eyes then and a thread of understanding passed between us. She released my arm. 'I'm going with you.'

'No. You have lied to me from the moment I met you, and I—' The cough returned and shook my body.

'It was not all lies,' she said, struck from silver once again. 'If my husband is guilty, then I must know, and you will not make it to the end of this beach without help.'

Ma let go of my other hand and stepped away. 'You both go. I need to see to my girls.'

Ellen held out her hand, waiting for me to take it.

I looked between the women – these people who had known my sister in their way and who now I saw, despite my current anger, as friends. More than friends in fact, but rather as something more like family. That was why Ellen's betrayal stung so deeply, and yet I found I could not hold on to the hate, for I couldn't say I wouldn't have done the same in her place.

I took her hand. Her shoulders dropped, as if in relief, and she smiled.

'Be careful, the both of you,' Ma said. 'Come see me soon, understand?'

I nodded.

We held on to each other for just a moment more, before Ma broke away, opened the door to the tent and let the burning world back in.

ELLEN

DAWSON CITY, KLONDIKE, JULY 1898

Outside the tent, the world is chaos. Kate and I watch Ma pick her way across the beach, if one could call it that. More a gravelled mudflat.

I dare not look at the city.

Kate holds my arm; I feel her weight and it is a comfort. Yukon presses his body against us both.

'Lord,' she breathes.

I look then.

Dawson burns. The blue summer sky is black with smoke. The buildings along the beach are charcoal. Ash floats on the breeze like snow. The flames have cut a swathe of ruin through the city and, further north, the blaze rages on. Fire licks the heavens. The shouts are distant now, the panic elsewhere.

I think of Bluebell, stabled on the north side of town. My heart aches for her, but I can do nothing.

'We need a boat,' I say.

Kate points. A few hundred feet up the bank, away from

the commotion, a skiff bumps against the shore with the lap of the river. Two oars. No owner in sight.

We are on the river and away in minutes. No one comes running down the beach, shouting our theft, and I wonder if the owner of this skiff now lies beneath a canvas.

'It is two miles upriver to the end of Bonanza Creek, then another eight or so on foot up to the claim,' I say, taking the oars.

Kate does not respond, just stares out into the wilderness on the opposite bank.

I row, for Kate cannot, and I see how it irks her.

On the river, the picture of Dawson's destruction is clearer. Dozens of buildings on the south side destroyed already, dozens more soon to follow. The fire sweeps through the timber in moments, then leaps to the next. There is no stopping it. The smoke blows away from us, but the smell is overwhelming. I fear I will stink of it for the rest of my life.

I row hard against the current, put distance between us and the fire, and turn into the mouth of the Klondike River. I do not even know if Charlie will be at the claim. He could be drinking that rotten gold in the Horseshoe Saloon or gambling it away at the Monte Carlo, perhaps even throwing those useless nuggets at the dance-hall girls. He could be hauling water to quench the fire. He could be burned.

My husband is a stranger to me in his actions, yet not in his character. I believe he ran from the truth he discovered at the assayer's. It is his one constant. To run. To hide. To lie to me. To dig more dirt. To cling to his dream of being a Klondike King.

I look at Kate, but she does not look at me. A friend lost, when barely made.

'I am sorry,' I say as I row. 'Kate, you must understand. I am not like you.'

She glances at me, then away. Yukon, curled in the bow of the skiff, yawns.

'You have a freedom to move about the world as you may,' I continue. 'I am locked here, with one man. Without him, I am nothing.'

'You believe that?' she asks. Her voice is a shadow of itself. A creaking shade.

'I do. I did. Before I married, I was under the shackle of my father. He only passed the key to Charlie. I had to follow him, obey him, no matter what he did. I followed him up here on the promise of a quick few months of toil, then a lifetime of wealth.'

I remember the talk we'd had, the excitement in his eyes and how it ignited my own. Adventure. Travel. Hardship, yes, but only for a while. What a fool I was.

'I knew of Charlie's activities in town,' I carry on. 'The women he bedded with money my father gave him. When one such woman came to my own house, I still had to smile and entertain. Can you imagine how that feels?'

The boat catches in a swirl. I strain against the oars, my chest begins to ache.

Kate grabs the oar and pushes with me. We break free of the eddy. She sits back, wincing, holding her burnt arm.

Along the banks, men rush to the city with buckets.

'You could have left him,' Kate says, watching them instead of me.

'And go where? When I saw the blood on him, when I made the decision to hide it, I had no money of my own to secure passage south; my father had disowned me, because of Charlie's lies and borrowing, and we sat on worthless land. There are few paths for women alone here and I could not bear to lower myself to them. I protected him to protect myself, even when I thought he had done something unfor-givable.' I thought of the gold sitting in my claim, and of the woman sitting in my boat. 'But things are different now.'

Kate's gaze falters and I believe she begins to forgive.

'The fortune-teller,' I say, 'she told me months ago I would meet a stranger. One who ignored the rules of the world. She said they would change my perspective, and perhaps my heart.' I look at her and she finally meets my eyes. 'I believe that person is you.'

I do not talk of the rest. A desire we cannot speak, a pas-sion that goes against what the world says is right. For I believe that figure, that devil, that desire, belong to Kate too, yet I still don't understand the feeling enough to put words around it.

So I row and remain silent.

We reach the head of Bonanza Creek and I loop a rope around a tree stump. Not far up the bank, a new ferry is being built, with a new face overseeing it. So it goes here; there is always another to step in when the previous one falls.

Miners and their overseers gather at the river, watching the smoke, their work forgotten. Some rush to us, help us out of our boat and pepper us with questions.

'Another fire?'

'Was it a saloon girl again?'

'How bad?'

And so on. I say only that I do not know. Kate says nothing.

We are up the trail and away. The road is quiet, but for the stragglers running to the river to see Dawson burn. The mine camps are empty.

It is a two-hour walk to the claim and we walk it in silence. Kate struggles through the last few miles, her breathing becomes a wheeze and she limps on a burnt leg. I put her arm around my shoulder and she does not shy away. Yukon trots behind us.

We come upon the cabin and my steps falter.

'What is it?' Kate asks.

'Goldie is in her pen. Charlie is here.'

'Good. He must answer for himself.'

Kate walks on, but I grab her arm. 'He has a temper.'

'So do I.'

She tries to break free, but I hold her. 'What are you hoping for? For him to admit it? And if he does, what will you do then?'

Kate looks at the dirt. At the sky. Finally at me. 'Nothing. The Mounties will not listen. The town is burning. Nobody else cares. But I must know. That is all.'

'And if it wasn't Charlie?'

She takes my hand and prises it off her arm. She does not answer, for what answer is there? If Charlie did not kill Molly, then any man of the thousands in Dawson could have. It would be madness to accuse them all.

'Yuke,' she says and the dog's tail flaps back and forth. She limps to the horse pen and ties him up, ruffles his flank. 'Stay here. Good boy.'

Kate passes me slowly, I see pain in her every step. She climbs the three steps to the cabin door. It is ajar and, inside, the sound of movement. The smash of something fragile. Kate does not hesitate. She pushes open the door and, over her shoulder, I see him.

My husband. A look of rage on his face so foreign I almost believe a stranger has broken in. In one hand, the bloody shirt he wore and told me to burn. In the other, the silk pouch full of my gold.

MARTHA

DAWSON CITY, KLONDIKE, JULY 1898

'Doc!' I found him on the beach. He'd made a makeshift hospital, canvas tarp strung over poles. People with scrapes and burns, and one man with a spike of wood sticking out of his leg from a collapsed roof.

Pohl had his sleeves pushed up to his elbows, his nice white shirt smeared with blood and black soot, a look of horror on him.

'Doc,' I said again and he saw me. Blinked a few times.

'Martha. Are you hurt?'

'No, but you are.' I took his hand, bloody from a cut above his wrist.

'There are so many . . .' he said. 'I can't . . .'

'You can't. You keep yourself safe. I'm going to look for the girls. Goddamn, I hope my hotel ain't caught.'

'Giselle. She'll be safe, won't she?'

I put my hand on his cheek. 'That girl senses trouble and she's a rat down a pipe. She'll be halfway up the mountain by now, with everyone in tow – even half-dead after that bout of typhoid.'

His eyes widened and he grabbed my hand. 'The clinic. The typhoid patients. Oh God. I need to get them out.'

He began to fuss and pace, and breathe in and out like he'd run a mile in sand. I slapped him hard as I could. 'You get a grip, Doc. This ain't your time to panic. This is their time to panic.' I pointed to the burnt people all around us. 'You can have your moment later, but right now you fix them up.'

I stepped out the tent and called to some of the gawkers. A few women were huddled up, watching like it was a damn show.

'Hey!' I said. 'Make yourselves useful and tear bandages, haul water for cleaning. Help the doc.'

They looked past me to the tent and then to each other. Women see a need and they fill it. They were in that tent in a moment, making order out of chaos.

I went up the beach as far as I could, then climbed up the bank onto Front Street. The fire was blazing, backed by a Yukon summer breeze. People were rushing or staring or trying to help. Some were already looting the burnt buildings. Fights broke out on the streets between shopkeeps trying to save their wares and unscrupulous folks trying to steal them. Mounties – what few of them there were – tried to keep some order, but there wasn't none to be had.

I went fast as I could down Princess Street. Smoke stung my eyes and made me cough out tar. I cut through an alley and came to the post office.

I pounded on the door. 'Harriet! Harriet! You in there, girl?'

No one answered and I couldn't hear anything inside, not even snoring, though over the roar of the town she could be singing in there and I'd never know.

From the top of the steps, I got a clearer view. I could see the fire coming. One or two more blocks, a strong westerly would be all it took to get here. It had burned a nor'-east cut right through the city, from the south-west storehouses. It chilled me, though I could feel the heat of it. It didn't look real. Black smoke billowed up into the sky and, beneath it, red-orange flames ate away at my town. Wooden walls. Wooden roofs. All built so close you couldn't slide a sheet of paper between them. One spark and the whole tinder pile went up.

I could see my hotel. The fire was only four or five blocks away. I had time. Just.

I ran. Ignored the stabbing pain in my gut until I couldn't no more. I stopped to breathe. People rushed about me, hauling supplies from stores and saloons onto wagons. Horses smelled the smoke and strained against their handlers, wanting to get the hell away.

I came up Fifth Avenue. Far ahead, on the corner of Fifth and Queen, Frank Croaker's body still lay in the dirt, trampled and ignored. Further down the street, the fire had reached the east end.

'Get buckets!' came the shouts and I knew the voice.

I crossed to see better. The corner of the Nugget had caught and Bill Mathers was standing out front, barking orders, gun in hand. His men, mostly drunk and stumbling, were worse than useless. His girls, bleary-eyed from opium and whiskey, stood in a huddle outside.

The Nug would be ash in minutes – and Bill's crown jewel with it.

I didn't have no time to pull up a chair and watch, though I wished to.

My hotel was on the corner of Queen and Front, on the western side, though the fire was spreading in all directions now.

I pushed open the door and was met with a shotgun to my face.

Jerry dropped it quick. 'Shit, Ma!'

He had blood on his temple and, behind him, the hotel was a mess. Every table overturned. Every glass smashed. The wall behind the bar was cleared of booze, and Jessamine stood at the foot of the stairs, a cleaver in each hand.

'Looters. Animals, the lot of them,' Jerry said and spat out blood.

'You both all right?' I asked and they nodded.

'They didn't get in the storeroom,' said Jerry.

I went to the stairs and hugged Jessamine. 'Where are the girls?'

'Cleared out,' she said. 'No one here but us.'

'Good. You should get someplace safe too.'

They looked at each other and weren't in no position to argue, nor did they want to.

Upstairs, a floorboard creaked in my office. If the place was empty . . .

'Jerry, leave the gun, will you?'

He handed it to me. 'You sure, Ma?'

'I'll be right behind you, just need to get some things.'

The pair left and I heard another creak. Then the scrape of my chair on the boards. I hooked the shotgun under my arm and climbed the stairs to my office.

'Figured it be you,' I said.

Laura-Lynn jumped up from my safe. 'Ma! I thought you was—'

'Dead? Run away? Sorry to disappoint, sweetheart. What the hell you think you're doing in my office?' I raised the shotgun. 'And don't lie.'

Laura-Lynn looked from me to the gun. Her mask dropped then. Those innocent eyes turned hard and her voice dropped a note or two.

'You're done here, Ma. Sell up and go rot someplace else.'

'It was you told Bill about my letters?' She didn't answer, what gave me all the answer I needed. 'And you gave Molly those bruises?'

The only person Molly would protect would be another one of my girls. I realised that now. She'd have told me if it was Bill, if it was one of her gents, but not if it'd mean getting someone here in trouble. Cast out. My heart broke a little more. Hurt a little more.

'She weren't cooperating,' Laura-Lynn said. She folded her arms.

Tears stung my eyes, but I forced them back. 'Cooperating how?'

'Bill wanted her, and Bill always gets what he wants. You, of all people, should know that.'

The way she looked at me, like I was no better than her, made me want to pull the trigger and wipe the damn smile off her face.

'You kill her?' I asked, though it stung to even say the words.

She shook her head. 'Wish I had. That bitch would've taken Bill from me. I owe the man who did it a free ride.'

A girl she shared a home with was dead, and all Laura-Lynn could do was sneer. It made me sick to look at her.

'You better leave before I lose my temper,' I said. My voice was all strain and smoke and it was all I could do to get the words out. 'Your precious Bill needs you to haul water. The Nug is burning. So is his bank. Your Klondike King will be king of ash by the morning.'

Her smile faltered then and she looked out the open window. The smoke and flames filled the view. I could hear the crackle and roar of timbers breaking, falling, see sparks jump and dance against the darkness.

'You're lying,' she said.

'Go see for yourself.'

Her eyes twitched, from the window to me to the gun. She had a look about her, one I knew well from miners with empty pockets and big debts.

'Bill wants this place,' she said, wringing her hands.

'He can't have it.'

'He always gets what he wants. If I give it to him ...' She trailed off, her gaze settled on a letter-opener. She snatched it up and pointed it at me.

I took a step back. I had a gun, but I truly didn't know if I'd be able to pull the trigger.

'Don't, Laura-Lynn,' I said.

'I love him, Ma,' she replied, her hand shaking. She stepped around the desk, so there was nothing between us. 'If I give him this place, he'll love me too.'

'Men like Bill can't love no one but themselves.'

'That's a lie!' she screamed and ran at me.

Laura-Lynn was a whippet of a girl and I couldn't move quick enough. She brought down the letter-opener, meaning to stab me through.

I couldn't shoot. Finger wouldn't pull the damn trigger.

I lifted the gun, blocked her hand. The force of her bearing down on me set off every ache I had.

She pushed me and my back hit the wall, knocking the air out of me.

'Stop,' I tried to say, but my voice didn't have nothing behind it.

She came at me again, screaming like a banshee. I whipped the gun round and smacked her wrist, sent the blade spinning away.

Laura-Lynn wailed, grabbed her arm and went at me with

her claws. She was stronger than she looked. She raked at me, scratched down my arms and hands. I used the shotgun like a barrier, pushing against her. Her eyes were wild, and not hers. What poison had Bill fed her? What lies to make her into this?

She grabbed the gun and, in one swift movement that almost broke my wrists, yanked it away. Then her hands were round my throat. She squeezed and dug those nails in. All the energy drained out of me. It hurt to stand. I dropped to a knee, as she stood above me. Squeezing. Killing. For a moment I figured I could just let her. I was so damn tired, after all. But then I saw Sam. Those big, bright eyes of his staring at me from a bed we shared for a spell. I saw him kissing me goodbye the last time he visited Dawson. Saw him in his cabin in the trapping lands, leg messed up, fever taking hold, dying without me.

I drove my fist into Laura-Lynn's gut. Once. Twice. Again. She huffed and her grip went slack. I pushed her off me and swung a punch right to her face. Sure I felt something crack. The rings on my fingers cut her up and she screeched.

'You old bitch!'

I scrambled away, on hands and knees, and got hold of the gun. She rushed at me and I turned, lay on my back, raised the barrel, finger on the trigger.

'Stop!' Something in my voice told her I weren't messing this time. One more step and she'd find out. She froze.

'Ma.' She held up trembling, blood-smeared hands. A cut on her cheek was streaming. 'You wouldn't.'

I aimed the gun at her head, barely caught a breath. 'Test me, girl.'

Laura-Lynn backed away toward the door. 'He'll have this place, one way or another.'

I got to my feet without breaking my aim. 'Get out. I see you here again, I'll kill you; I swear on Molly's grave, I'll shoot you where you stand.'

Something clicked in Laura-Lynn's head. She looked past me, out the window at the burning city. She backed out the door, onto the landing, then she ran.

I waited until I heard the doors close downstairs. Felt how empty the place was suddenly and knew she was gone. Then I dropped the gun. It clattered, so loud in the quiet, despite all hell breaking loose outside.

I went to my desk, unlocked the bottom drawer and took out Sam's letters. A neat bundle I'd tied with a ribbon. They were the only things worth saving in this place.

The wind shifted then and smoke billowed through my open window. I needed to get out, and quick. Every inch of me screamed, the black pain in my gut turned angry and bone-deep. I held the letters close and went for the door, but the world turned dark and I don't remember hitting the floor.

KATE

'What is this, Ellen?' Charlie said, holding up a pouch. I couldn't take my eyes from the shirt covered in my sister's blood. His shirt.

'It's . . .'

Around his neck was the kerchief. It was too hot to wear one and yet he did. All day. All night. I could not take my eyes from it, for I knew what lay beneath. It had to be. I wanted to rip it from his throat.

'And this?' He held up the shirt. 'I told you to burn it.'

He was coiled. Ellen was struck dumb by his tone.

'You kept it,' he carried on, getting more and more impatient with her silence. 'Why? Answer me, damn it!'

Ellen glanced at me, and it was only then that Charlie seemed to notice I was there. He looked me up and down, saw the extent of my injuries and, I'm sure, went to ask, but I spoke first.

'Proof,' I said for her, 'that you killed Molly.' I hated to use that name, but he did not know I was her sister and I wished to keep it that way a while longer.

362

He stared at me for a moment, and something passed over his features that I couldn't discern, then he laughed. 'This again? I didn't kill her! How many times must I say so?'

'Then how did her blood get on your shirt?' I asked.

Charlie looked from me to Ellen. I could see he was more concerned with the gold than the death of my sister, and my questions were irritating him further, but I did not care. I would know the truth.

'I found her,' he said, in a stilted tone as if the memory was too painful to recall, or the lie too big to conceal. 'I held her as she died.'

I stood straighter, felt the tight, burnt skin on my leg pull and tear. The pain was a lance, but I kept myself.

'Take off your kerchief,' I said slowly, for if I spoke fast I believed I would scream.

Charlie's hand went to his neck, as if he'd forgotten he wore it. A flicker of something in his eye – was that fear?

'I won't.'

'Why?' I asked, taking an uneasy step forward. Everything hurt, the burns, the bruises; even my blood felt scorched, and every beat of my heart sent it scalding through my body.

'How dare you come here and question me in my own house,' he said with a false bluster. I could see through him now; pain brings clarity and it was all I felt, from my body to my soul. 'Ellen, tell her she is speaking madness.'

Ellen looked to the floor, would not see either of us. In that second I was not at all sure what she would say. What, or who, she would choose.

'Ellen?' I said and she met my eyes. Held them.

Then turned to her husband.

'Take off the kerchief, Charlie,' she said, and my heart beat again.

His indignation flared to rage. 'I am the man of this house,' he shouted. 'You will mind me and my word, or I will take a belt to you both and teach you obedience.'

His voice shook, like a puppy trying to bark. I looked for a weapon, but the shotgun was behind Charlie. The kitchen knives put neatly away. The axe outside. My own knife lost in the fire.

Charlie dropped the bloody shirt and opened the pouch. He dug into it and pulled out nuggets. Then more. Then he poured the rest onto the floor. They hit with a heavy thud. Ellen flinched at the sound and I knew she wanted to scoop them up. They were hers, after all.

'Where did you find this?' he asked with such venom, it was clear where his anger lay. Not with the death of a person he supposedly loved, but with the gold. It was always about the gold here.

Ellen stood straighter. 'I won't tell you.'

He stepped closer to her. 'Did you work for it? On your back, like those other whores?'

'How dare you,' I said and he whipped towards me.

'You shut the hell up. You come in here, with your questions. I see through you, Kate Kelly. You poisoned my wife's mind.'

'She did not,' Ellen said, strength growing in her voice. 'You did. With your lies, your debts, your whoring all over town, your failure. You are a failure, Charles Rhodes, and I won't stand for it any longer.'

'You . . .' He moved towards her, violence in every inch of him.

I rushed between them, felt the burnt skin on my leg tear.

'Move,' he growled. 'This is none of your business.'

'You will not touch her,' I said. 'I won't let you.'

He grabbed my arm and dug his fingers deep. His grip was a vice, after years of manual work. He pushed me aside and I tripped on a rug. My body hit the floor, my head hit the table, and every cut and burn and bruise screamed as one. Spots filled my vision and bile rose in my mouth.

'Where did the gold come from, Ellen?' he said in a low, dangerous tone.

I looked up, my eyes swimming, head dizzy. He had Ellen by the arm, lifting her, so she looked like a child in his grasp. His face was close to hers and I saw her terror. Her strength gone, her defiance gone.

He had a fistful of gold and pushed it into her cheek. 'Where?' he said.

She didn't answer. He pressed his fist harder and she cried out. I tried to rise, but my arms were lead.

'Where?' he screamed in her face, so loud my ears hurt.

She finally pointed.

'No!' I shouted and his ire turned, momentarily, to me. Without letting her go, he drove his boot into my stomach.

The air blasted out of me and I couldn't take any more in. Couldn't breathe. Couldn't see straight. I coughed out blood and collapsed, my face pressed against the boards. I felt their footsteps shake the wood. The cabin door opened and Charlie dragged Ellen out.

'Kate!' she shouted. 'Kate!'

She reached back for me. I tried to crawl, but my body was broken. I reached out a hand, but he pulled her down the steps and they were gone.

ELLEN

'Kate!' I scream. I shout. I wrench at him, but he does not let go.

We are out of the cabin. Yukon barks, strains at his rope. Charlie drags me across the claim. My foot catches on a board and I fall. His grip does not loosen and my arm is near pulled from its socket.

'Charlie, stop!' I cry. 'I will take you there, just let me walk.'

I look up into his face that does not look like his. That damn kerchief still around his neck. He pulls me to my feet and finally relaxes his grip.

'Show me, now,' he says.

We walk. Me a step ahead. I feel his eyes burning into my back. His hand on the back of my arm, in the place he held so tight I feel the bruise coming already. He grabbed Molly like this when she came to the cabin. Was she telling him, then, about the baby? Asking for his help?

'Hurry up,' he snaps and pushes me.

We go to the trees in silence. I have a terrible feeling that I

366

will not return from here. I believe now, more than ever, that Charlie is capable of killing.

I glance over my shoulder as we rise on the hill. The mining camps are stripped of men. They are gawking at, or helping with, the fire. They will not hear my screams.

And Kate . . . half-dead on the floor. She stepped between us. She put herself in danger for me. The feeling that surges within me is too strong to put into words. It takes my breath and my step falters. My hand goes to my chest. It aches as if I have been shot there. I feel my husband behind me, his ire and strength, but he is nothing. Nothing compared to that feeling.

A new resolve turns to rock inside me. I will climb back down this mountain. I will see her again.

We reach the meadow.

'What is this place?' Charlie says. 'This isn't meant to be here.'

'You never looked up here,' I reply, weary of him. 'You just put this land in my name because you thought it worthless. I kept trying to tell you, but you know best, don't you?'

He looks at me, wide eyes turn narrow. 'Where is the gold?'

I lead him to the river. He sees it immediately. The gold glinting beneath the shallow water. He drops to his knees on the rocky bank. His face lights up, gold fever takes him.

He reaches in, collects a handful of gravel, lets the rocks and silt fall away until his palm is full of gold.

'Look at this, Ellen,' he says, voice full of awe. 'We are rich. Rich, I say! Finally!'

He jumps up and takes me by the shoulders. He is Charlie again, bounding, smiling, full of big promises.

'We can spend the rest of the summer mining up here, and live like king and queen in Seattle for the rest of our lives. No, not Seattle. San Francisco or New York or Paris! Of course I understand now why you didn't tell me. You didn't see what we had here. Thought, as I said, the gold was not worth mining. This is why this business is for men, Ellen.'

'I see,' I say, for I do see now – the truth of him. Clearer than I ever have.

He kneels again and digs at the water. He churns up silt and turns my river brown. He is wet through, but gold piles bit by bit beside him.

'I'm rich,' he says, over and over. Every nugget he holds to the light and laughs.

A rage burns in me. I am rich. It is my claim and, by law, every flake on it is mine. And he is a liar. A fraud. A cheat. A man full of hate for women. He hides it, but not well. Not any more. And not from me.

'Did you know?' I ask.

But he does not listen. Does not hear. 'Hmm? Will you run back and fetch a bucket, a shovel?'

'Did you know?' I ask again and Charlie turns.

'About this fortune? Of course not. You should have told me sooner, Ellen. We would not be living in that hovel.' He goes back to the water. Rakes his hands through the pebbles.

'Did you know Molly was with child?'

He stops.

His hands linger in the water. 'What?'

'Did you know Molly was pregnant when she was killed?'

His back is to me. I cannot see his expression. He lifts his hands, they drip.

'How do you know that?' he asks.

'It doesn't matter,' I say. 'You knew. Is that why she is dead?'

I see a battle in him between love and hate, gold and fury. He wants to keep digging in the water. He wants to ruin this place as he has ruined so much.

'Don't speak of things you know nothing about, Ellen.'

'I know enough to know I do not wish to be married to you any longer.'

He turns then. 'You don't mean that.'

'I do.'

He knows what it means. Unmarried, my gold is untouchable. That is where his heart lies. In the dirt.

'Ellen,' he tries, his tone soft. 'You are upset, I understand. I have made mistakes. I have been weak and let the vice of this godless place into our marriage.'

He steps to me, and my muscles turn rigid. I look only at the kerchief around his neck.

'You deserve better than me,' he says, 'but there is no other man who will love you as I do.'

'If this is what a man's love is, then I do not want it.'

He moves closer. Within an arm of me. 'You do not mean that. We can make a real go of this now. We have the gold, we can make a home. We can make a family. Is that not what you want? A house full of children?'

I'd thought it was, once. When my aunt was preparing me for my wedding, she asked the same. I'd said yes, of course, because I was meant to. Because I was reading from a script of a life, not living a true one.

'We can have it all, Ellen, just you and I.' He smiles. He is handsome still, despite the grime and grit. Despite the lies.

'You believe that?' I ask.

His hands gently cup my shoulders. 'I do.'

'Then you must do something for me first.'

'Anything.' He kisses my cheek. My neck. I cannot bear it.

'Take off the kerchief.'

He stalls, lips brushing my collar. Hot breath makes my skin itch. He pulls back, hands drop from my arms. 'Why?'

'I must know the truth. If we are to begin this marriage

369

afresh, I must know.'

Charlie's lip twitches, curls. He looks behind him to the gold. The pile of it on the bank. The fortune waiting in the water.

His hands go to the kerchief and he works the knot.

As it falls away, I see them. The four lines I knew were there, but did not want to believe. Four scratches from four finger-nails, more than a week old, but unmistakable on his pale skin.

My hand goes to my mouth. 'You did kill Molly.'

He reaches for me, but I step back. 'Ellen, you don't under-stand, it isn't what you think.'

'You *killed her.*'

'It was an accident.' He rushes at me, grabs me, gentleness gone. 'She meant to tell you about the child. She meant to ruin us.'

I push against him, but he holds me. 'You ruined us! With your lies and cowardice. You took money from others to hide your mistakes.'

'No, no, it wasn't like that.'

I pound my fists on his chest. 'Let go of me!'

Charlie digs his hands in. His nails cut my skin. 'Not until you listen, damn it.'

'I'll never listen to another word you say. You're a murderer. You're a *failure*, Charles Rhodes. My father knew it, and so do I.'

His pleading tone turns savage in an instant. 'Your father was happy to be rid of you. A plain girl. No prospects. I did him a favour.'

'You're disgusting.'

'And you're *nothing*. Not worth a penny to a desperate sailor.'

His cruelty stings. My breath catches. 'I have gold.'

'You believe that is yours?' He laughs, sour and unfamil-iar. 'You're as stupid as your father said. You have nothing. I own everything you have, including your worthless body. You could not even give me a child. What kind of woman are you?'

I cannot believe I am hearing such bile from my husband. The man I'd once thought sweet. He is a sugar-coated boil.

'What kind of man are you, to speak so?'

He laughs again. A huff. A sneer. 'I will speak as I like. You are my property, and that gold is mine by right.'

'You're wrong, Charlie,' I say, finding my courage once again. 'About so much. I bet Molly saw right through you. Knew you'd be no better a father than a miner, and you are certainly no miner.'

The slap catches me off-guard. An open palm to my cheek. The force shocks me and I stumble away. My eye feels as if it may burst. Then the pain comes, hot and relentless.

I look up at him. At this man I was to spend my life with. I see a stranger. I see hate in him, violence I'd never thought him capable of. I do not know what he will do in this place, where laws don't reach.

I run.

He grabs my dress and I fall. Half-buried rocks dig into my back, my legs, a sharp stone pierces my shoulder, I hear my dress rip. Feel blood. He is at once on top of me, scrambling. I twist and strike with my fists. One glances his head and he drives his knee onto my forearm. Then the other. Still I struggle.

'Stop, Ellen!'

'Let me go!'

I free a hand and twist, scratch, punch. I grab his ear and pull. He roars. Grabs me by the hair and wrenches my head up, then sharply down.

My head hits a rock and the world spins.

Bright spots. Bursting. Pain.

'I'm sorry, Ellen, but I must have the gold.' His voice is distant, breathy. 'It's mine. You see? Mine. I earned it. I did things . . . I earned it. If you're gone, it's mine.'

My eyes clear and I see him atop me. A large rock in his hands.

'Charlie . . . please.'

'You won't take it from me.'

He raises the rock above his head.

A gunshot explodes the silence. Charlie startles. The rock falls beside me. He looks beyond, to the shooter.

'Get off her.' A woman's voice.

My heart aches in relief. Kate. She lives. She came.

'I won't ask again,' she says.

He climbs off me and the blood rushes down my arms. I roll over, try to push myself up. I see my blood on the rocks. Touch the back of my head. My hair is matted, sticky. My fingers come away red.

'Ellen?' Kate says.

'I'm all right.' But I'm not sure.

Charlie backs away to the river, to his meagre gold pile. Kate limps closer. Sees the kerchief on the ground. Sees his neck, finally exposed.

'Did he . . . ?' she asks.

'He did,' I say.

Her jaw clenches. She trains the gun at his chest. 'You killed my sister.'

For a moment he is confused. Then I see it clear from his eyes. 'Molly was . . . That's why you came here.'

'I could kill you,' Kate says. 'Nobody would know. Nor care, I suspect. Why do you get to live when she does not?'

The gun shakes. Her eyes blaze with hate. Charlie sees her intent, her anger. She would do it, pull the trigger and have her justice. His eyes widen in fear and I cannot say I don't enjoy the sight.

'Kate, please,' he begs and drops to his knees. 'Please, don't. I loved her.'

'*I* loved her. You *killed* her.'

He buries his face in his hands and cries. 'I'm sorry! There is nothing I can do. Nothing I can say. I am a weak man. A fool! Have mercy!'

'What happened? In the alley that night. Tell me.' Her swollen eye tears blood. It cuts red rivers down the dirt on her face.

'Molly . . . she had a knife,' he begins, his voice a trembling shadow. 'She carried one. Always. I went to meet her the night after she came to the cabin. She was upset. I . . .' He stalls and Kate levels the gun to his face. He raises his hands higher and trips over his words. 'She told me about the baby. Asked for money. I – to my shame – I asked her if she was sure it was mine. She said she was always careful, washing and the like, except with me. Because she loved me, she said. But I didn't believe her. She became angry. I became angry. I said terrible things. We fought. She held the knife and . . . it slipped.'

'It slipped. Just an accident? But then you strangled her. You wanted her dead. Her and her child.'

He sobs and has no answer.

'I should kill you,' Kate says, her tone sharp as pine needles. 'No. Please!'

'Wait,' I say. I can't bear to hear Charlie's begging a moment longer. I get to my feet. The world finally stops spinning. I see a war within Kate. To kill and avenge and be no better than him, or to allow justice to take its course, whatever shape that may take.

I put my hand on the barrel of the gun and press it down gently. She meets my eyes. Tears fill hers.

'He is not worth hanging for,' I say, and Kate lets her anger and grief out in tight sobs. She hands me the gun.

For a moment, I see Charlie relax. Believe he is saved. Then I turn the gun on him. I breathe and realise my hand is steady.

My voice does not shake.

'You are stealing my gold, and it's within my rights as claim owner to shoot you,' I tell him.

Charlie's eyes widen. He begs again, but I have stopped listening.

'But I won't. I'm not going to kill you, Charlie. Though there isn't a court in the land that would blame me for it.'

He cries. Blubbery tears like a scolded child. 'Please, please, please,' he says; talk of love, of promises he will keep this time, of plans we can make together, children, growing old. I think of the fortune-teller's reading. A choice to be made.

Here is my choice, on his knees before me.

'You will face justice. Whatever shape that takes in this place. You will come with us to Dawson and you will tell the Mounties what you have done.'

Shock slackens his jaw. 'But ... I'm your husband. We are married.'

'We shall divorce. If they do not hang you.'

He tries to stand, as if talk of divorce is the most abhorrent subject of the day. I aim the gun and rest my finger on the trigger. He sinks back to his knees.

'You tried to kill me, Charlie, for gold,' I say and the weight of that hits my chest.

A moment longer and Kate would have found me, head dashed upon the rocks. Charlie bloody once again. Kate stands beside me, her hand on my shoulder and her presence calms. Strengthens.

Charlie weeps.

The shotgun grows heavy in my hands, but I do not let it waver from what is left of my husband.

'It is time to go.'

MARTHA

DAWSON CITY, KLONDIKE, JULY 1898

'Well, hey there, sleepyhead,' Giselle said as I opened my eyes.

I was in my bedroom, not on the floor of the office where I fell. The room weren't burned. The hotel weren't burned. Sunlight streamed through the window and only a few strands of smoke marred the blue sky. My bundle of letters lay on the nightstand. The relief hit my heart.

'It's over?' I asked and my throat felt stripped raw and salted. I coughed and black came out.

'Burned itself out sometime in the night,' she said.

I pushed myself up.

Giselle put her hand on my shoulder. 'Careful now, Ma. You were in the smoke for a good while.'

'Is everyone all right?'

Giselle nodded. 'Safe as houses,' she said with that grin of hers.

'Help me up.'

She held my arm to the window and when I saw what was left of my town, I clung to her.

Almost everything was a black wreck. Like the Devil

himself had taken his pitchfork and swiped the place off the map. Dozens of buildings were gone. Roofs collapsed, charred timbers sticking up like bones out a carcass. Broken things. Broken people.

'Goddamn,' I said.

Giselle squeezed my arm.

The north end of Front Street and the west side of Queen had escaped the flames, but the east side of the town was gone. I could see the stage at the Marcello Theatre, black and holding up, but the rest of the place was no more. The post office was smouldering, and I prayed to anyone who was listening that Harriet weren't in there when it caught. The North American Bank's roof had collapsed, the cashier cages twisted metal, the vault hanging open.

Destitute men and women picked over the ruins, swarming like rats. They were black with soot, digging through the wreckage, holding up specks of gold, searching for hidden corners now exposed where miners hid their jars.

But Dawson could never be beat so easy. From the timber yards north of town, wagons already hauled new planks. Someone had set up a tent for nails and hammers, marked up a thousandfold, and I couldn't blame them. Up here, you could make and lose a fortune in the same afternoon and everyone in Dawson had felt the hard truth of that yesterday.

'Triple the rates,' I said to Giselle. 'There's going to be a lot of folk wanting a bed tonight.'

On the streets the mood was a mix of opposites. Most folk stared disbelieving at the ruins; some picked through their lives to find anything worth keeping; others tried to find any way to profit from it. Keen-tongued men in suits harried the poor business owners, saying they'd buy their lease, take care of everything, build again, sell them a wagon of lumber for a price what'd make you think the trees themselves were made of gold. The most desperate hunted in the wrecks, before being chased on.

Dawson weren't a stranger to fire. There'd been four or five in my time here, but this was something else. A third of the city was gone. The banks were gone. The warehouses to the south of the town, where most kept their stocks, were gone. I passed Sutter. His store was ash and he sat out on the step with a bottle of brown while a couple of looters picked through the remains. He was smiling, having just sold up to Bill.

The town would change, but I felt, with a sinking in my stomach, it would stay exactly the same. Repeat old mistakes. Build higher and closer. Wait for the next spark.

I dodged charred and twisted junk. The boardwalks were burned up and the mud dried to cracks. It was quiet – a fire is like a snowfall, takes the sound from a place and leaves people staring, open-mouthed at what your home has become.

I went to the post office first. What was left. I grabbed someone nearby and asked, 'Harriet. You know if she got out?'

The woman shook her head. 'People been gathering in the church. She might be there.'

I thanked her and let her go.

I walked with aching steps; my gut and my back weren't happy and let me know. I sought out Doc Pohl. His clinic, his tent of typhoid victims, were on the east side of town. I knew what I'd find.

The doc's office was a skeleton. Walls and roof collapsed, only the timber struts left. Inside, Doc was kicking charred wood out the way, looking for anything he could use.

'Doc?' I said and he saw me through what used to be his wall.

'Thank heavens,' he replied. 'I'm glad you're all right. Is the hotel . . . ?'

'She's standing. You all right?'

He came out and he weren't the man he used to be. Behind the soot, he was a decade older and half a man lighter. He weren't jittering and panicked no more. His soul had been beat out of him by this place.

'Three dead, Martha. One man found by the storehouse where it began and two dead out there,' he pointed to the yard, full of broken, burnt-up things. 'Dozens with injuries, but to lose only three is a blessing.'

'What you planning on doing?'

He threw down a glass vial he'd been holding. 'I'm going to leave. Start a practice somewhere else. *Any*where else. Giselle wants to accompany me.'

I smiled. 'Good.'

'What about you?'

I looked back through the wreckage and saw my hotel, proud and tall at the far end of town. A view I never thought I'd see. 'I still got the Dawson, so I guess I'm staying.'

Felt his eyes on me. Them knowing eyes. 'If that's what you want.'

Was it what I wanted?

He smiled. 'Giselle said you'd never leave this place. Pine box would be the only way.'

'She's a smart one,' I said, distracted by my own thoughts. 'Take care of her.'

I left him then with a wave. Doc turned back to the ruins of the life he'd built, then looked to the mountains, to the dock, to the river that could carry him and his love someplace new. He didn't look so broken then.

I walked for a spell. Around the ruins and what had escaped.

I heard snatches of conversation. The cost of the damage would be in the millions. More than a hundred buildings burned. Folks lost everything.

I hadn't lost anything, but still, I felt like I'd been hollowed out.

I stood on Front Street. Half-paved now. Work stopped, but only for today, I reckoned. Tragedy passes quick here. The rush goes on, and more and more come.

Outside the city that I'd made mine, I saw the beauty of the land again. The low mountains to the north where mist would settle in bands. The pine- and spruce-covered hills across the river.

I thought of Sam. My Sam. The only man I ever loved. I still felt him in the world. Knew he breathed up in that cabin of his, in a part of the country still wild. But I didn't know for how long. After all that happened this summer could I really walk back into the Dawson and do it all over again?

The answer came swift and easy. Like I'd known it all along, from the moment the fortune-teller said I'd have to choose the life I truly wanted, not the one I thought I did. I finally knew what she meant.

I walked then, without a hint of pain, right to his front door. What was left of it.

He stood at the bar like nothing had happened. First time I'd seen the Nugget empty of his men. The wall to his left weren't there no more, but the rest of the place stank of wet wood and smoke. The floorboards were soaked.

Bill Mathers, my curse for years, didn't have no quick wit about him today. He looked smaller. Thinner. An emperor in bare feet.

'You can have it,' I said and he looked up.

'I ain't in the mood today, Ma,' he replied.

'Me neither. I'm done, Bill. You can have the Dawson.'

He stepped around the bar, frown deep on his brow. 'What's the catch?'

'Fifty thousand.'

He let out a short laugh, but knew I weren't joking. 'I look like I got fifty on me?'

'It's the only hotel still standing. Only storeroom not looted. You need it.'

He sucked on his teeth. 'Twenty-five. That's generous.'

'Forty-five. And you can have it in two days.'

'Thirty.'

'Forty-five, Bill. Or I go to one of the well-heeled rich folk stepping off the boats every day.'

He considered it. I could see his mind whirring around. 'Forty.'

I made a show of thinking it over. 'Fine, but my girls, and Jerry, Jessamine, they get a choice. They can leave if they want.'

'What changed, Martha?'

I felt the weight of the mass in my gut. 'I did. After Molly, after Harry, after this fire. Life is too short. Do we have a deal?'

The way Bill looked at me, like we were old friends jousting and I'd bowed out early. He held out his hand. 'Deal.'

I shook it and a weight came off me so quick I felt I'd lift off the ground.

He went to his safe and measured out gold, in bars and loose nuggets. He put it in a case for me and pulled out paperwork he'd had drawn up months ago. I laughed to see it and he made some quip about knowing I'd fold.

I signed away the life I'd made in the Yukon and, soon as I had, I knew I'd done right. It was time now for me and Sam. Whatever years we both had left, I'd be damned if either one of us would spend a moment more of it alone.

I left Bill, carrying more gold than I'd be able to spend in the north.

Over the next two days I packed what I cared for. The hotel weren't mine no more and it didn't feel it, either. I realised then it hadn't for a long time.

Jessamine cried when I told her, but I gave her a bar of gold to start up her own café. 'People will come from Whitehorse just for your brisket,' I said.

Jerry said he'd stay on with Bill, make sure he didn't wreck the place.

The girls made their decisions by themselves and I didn't know which way they went. Their lives were theirs alone, but I was glad Giselle had her heart set. She hugged me and said her goodbyes.

'Look after the doc,' I said.

She laughed and kissed my cheek.

I walked through my hotel once more. The same but changed. There was the black patch on the boards where Bill had lit his whiskey. There was the scrubbed-raw bloodstain where Harry died. There was Molly's drawing, hanging on the wall. A world of memories, dark and light, and I was finally ready to leave them behind.

I didn't linger. Didn't see the point of it. I weren't a sentimental woman and when I make my mind up, there's little can change it. I'd come to the Klondike to make my name and my fortune and I'd done both. Now it was my time.

Winter was coming, the first snowflakes were dusting the mountains and it wouldn't be long before the trails and the rivers were iced up. I paid a mail carrier and his dogs to take me north. Up into the wild place, where there was no gold and no fire, where I wasn't Martha Malone, where nobody was trying to take from me, or swindle me or lie to me.

Where I could rest and breathe.

Where I could just be his, and he mine.

KATE

DAWSON CITY, KLONDIKE, SEPTEMBER 1898

Dear Mr Everett,
I enclose a full report of the hardships and realities of mining
in the Klondike, along with a series of articles for publication
wheresoever you see fit, reporting on my adventures on the
Dead Horse Trail, the White Horse Rapids and a first-hand
account of gold mining on a placer claim. I trust your readers
will find them diverting.
*   One word of advice, if I may: do not come to the Klondike.*
The rush is done. The claims staked and the gold found. I have
heard rumours of a gold discovery in Nome, Alaska. Given
that Nome is a coastal town and easily accessible, I suggest you
invest your resources there.
Yours,
Kate Kelly

I mailed the letter in the new post office. The wooden
boards were still rough, and the smell of sap and saw filled the
room. A jaunty man in a blue cap took my penny and when

I asked after any post for me, he handed over a letter. I knew the writing right away and smiled. Thanked him. He didn't stare too long at my face; the bruises and scars were healing. It had been a long time since I could smile without pain.

I lived with a terrible guilt in my heart at my part in the fire, but Dawson was rebuilding. Yellow-white wooden frames grew like new saplings from the ruins of the last. A café went upon a café. A store upon a store. A new theatre upon the stage of the old. There was an industrious mood to the town. Men who could not fit on mines were employed to build. The Mounties patrolled and the fire department bought in a new pump. Dawson City grew from its own ash and would grow stronger, so said the politicians on the corners, so wrote the *Klondike Nugget* newspaper. One would almost believe it.

I walked past the Dawson Hotel on my way to meet Ellen and Yukon. I thought about going inside, seeing the place where my sister had lived once again, but the urge passed. Without Martha, it was not what it was. I went to the graveyard and paused at two graves. Henry Gable, victim of the fire, found outside the storehouse. The guilt came again; he was not a good man, but I had caused his death and I would have to live with that. In the row behind him, near the fence where the grass barely grew and spiked devil's club snarled around the crosses, lay Charles Rhodes, hanged for murder. I didn't linger on this one, nor did I feel guilt.

On the other side of the graveyard, where the sun hit and bright-purple fireweed bloomed, I found my sister's grave.

Flowers, old and new, lay on her cross. I set down my own posy.

'I'm sorry it has taken me so long to visit. I felt I could not until I had found the person responsible.' I sat, cross-legged, beside her. 'I know him now. I did not kill him, I know you wouldn't wish that of me, but he was brought to justice. You'll be happy to know Martha is well. She sent a letter. It arrived just today.'

I took the new letter from my pocket.

Dear Kate and Ellen,
By the time you get this, more than a month will be past and the weather turning. Sam is well, his leg healing fine. Now he has a woman about the place, it smells a darn sight better. I got my aches and pains, but I'm feeling better than I have in years. Plenty to do here. Sam and I will be travelling down to Whitehorse at the turn of the year for trading. We'll stop in at Dawson, say hi to the old place.

I put the paper in my pocket and sat for a moment. Wished my sister was with me, here, so I could speak with her, hear her sass and spark, knowing the two men who had hurt her were in the ground. I hated that they were laid near her, but the dead don't mind. Again the wash of regret came over me. Again the words 'what if' threatened to spill out of my mouth. What if I'd got here sooner? What if I'd found her first?

I looked at my sister's name carved in the cross. 'Ellen says I must stop blaming myself. Do you think she is right?'

I felt a stirring in the wind, the smell of Charlotte's perfume on the breeze. I smiled.

'I came here for you. I thought of little beyond helping you. What do I do now? I don't believe I can stay, but I don't know where to go.'

A light snow began to fall, but gave me no answer. I stood, a chill already settling in my bones, and kissed my hand to her cross.

'I love you, Charlotte.'

I did not say goodbye, because there was no goodbye between us. She was beside me, silent and invisible, with every step, wherever those steps would take me.

I went to the north end of Front Street, where Ellen waited. Yukon bounded to me and I saw immediately a happy sight.

Ellen, grinning as wide as I'd ever seen, held the reins of her horse, Bluebell; she'd been found in the forest a week after the fire. The stablehand had let the horses out when the fire took and Bluebell had found her way back.

I gave Ellen the letter. 'From Martha. She is well.'

Ellen took it, read it, her face broke into a smile. But faded soon after.

'Are you all right?'

She handed me back the letter. 'I am happy for her, at the start of her life with Sam, but I can't help feeling a little envious too. To be here alone is better than being here with Charlie, but still, I wish for companionship. I've been so grateful for yours these last two months.'

'I've never worked so hard in my life as I have on your claim, but the gold is worth it.'

'And there is so much more there. I will leave here a rich woman one day.'

I smiled. 'I hope so.'

We walked a little in silence until Ellen asked, 'Are you well? You seem thoughtful.'

I could not answer right away, for I hadn't found the words. They came slowly, as a winter freeze. 'I think I have to leave.'

From the corner of my eye, I saw Ellen smile. 'I was wondering when you would say so. I have seen your passion for this place wane.'

'And yours has grown.'

'I always loved it here, I just never loved who I had to share it with.'

'You'll stay?' I asked.

She thought for a moment, then nodded. 'Dawson City is new again. I have a home, a rich claim, and I will hire women to work it. I believe I can make something more of myself here. I am free, finally, to choose this life.'

My heart burst and broke, for this meek, quiet woman had turned to steel. I took my own strength from that. I was free too. I had money, thanks to Mr Everett's over-compensation and Ellen's generosity.

'I believe I will go west, as I suggested to Mr Everett. To Nome. A Swedish man spoke of gold lying on the beach there. People in the south will want to hear of it.'

'That is a thousand miles. Near double the trip from Skaguay to Dawson. The journey will not be easy.'

'The river and mountains do not scare me any more. Maybe I shall buy a bicycle to take me.'

Ellen laughed. 'I believe you would, Kate Kelly.'

I thought of all I had endured to get here – the trail, the avalanche, the death and exhilaration, the sorrow and rage and pain and the overwhelming mania, the rush of gold and hate and love – all in one summer, one place, one corner of the world. I had been stripped of myself and rebuilt, same as Dawson. My life was changed now and I could never go back to what it was. To Topeka. To my family and their wish of marriage and settling. I could not sit still any longer. Could not live a life on a path laid for me by someone else. I had to decide myself, live my own way. I would, as Ellen said, choose my life, as the fortune-teller always said I must.

I ruffled Yukon's head. 'Ready for another trip, Yuke?'

He licked my hand and wagged his tail. Tongue lolling, not

a hint of what he'd endured, save a patch of singed fur that was gradually growing out.

Ellen took my hand. She saw it all in my eyes in that one moment, smiled at me and looked at the new city rising from the ash of the old. She shook her head, almost laughed.

'The rush begins again.'

Another foray into the wild land, following fortune and those brave and foolish enough to seek it. My heart leapt at the thought of it. A new journey. A thousand miles. A thousand dangers and trials and elations. The excitement and terror and awe of it all. Of this country. Of the land untamed. I would see it all, for now I was untamed and untethered. But wherever I went, I knew I'd have a friend here and another in a cabin in the north. I knew I could call on them, should I need to, and I would see them both again over the years of our lives. We three were tied together by the threads of a life cut short. Our fates entwined, as all women are.

HISTORICAL NOTE

Stories of the Klondike Gold Rush, sometimes erroneously called the Alaskan Gold Rush (the Klondike is in Canada), are dominated by the voices and experiences of men. There is a romance to the grizzled adventurer, climbing the Golden Staircase along the Chilkoot Trail like the famous E.A. Hegg photograph from 1898. Tales of the Gold Rush start with Jack London, with his stories of the man or boy against the wild. It's a masculine place, a testing ground for 'real men', and as such, the stories of the women of the Gold Rush are often overlooked. Thankfully there are some books redressing that imbalance, notably a contemporary account by Mary Evelyn Hitchcock, *Two Women in the Klondike: The Story of a Journey to the Gold Field of Alaska* (1899) and more recently, a detailed collection of the experiences and histories of multiple women who journeyed north, *Women of the Klondike* by Frances Backhouse (1995). A few other books exist, mostly from small presses and hard to get hold of, but nonetheless act as excellent sources for stories of these women: *Gold Rush Women* by Claire Rudolf Murphy and Jane G Haigh (1997); *Good Time Girls of the Alaska-*

Yukon Gold Rush by Lael Morgan; and *Rebel Women of the Gold Rush* by Rich Mole (2009).

When I talk about the town of Skagway in the novel, I have used the contemporaneous spelling of 'Skaguay' as used in historical accounts but in this note I have used the modern spelling for clarity. My characters are fictional but all are inspired by real people or combinations thereof.

Kate Kelly is based on Emma Kelly, a journalist from Topeka, Kansas, born in 1873, who travelled to the gold fields to report on the conditions and realities of the Gold Rush. Emma was an adventurer at heart, the daughter of an ex-senator, and while working for a Chicago newspaper, met financiers who were interested in mining. They sent her to the gold fields in 1897, at just twenty-four years of age, with over $2,000, a fortune by today's standards. She wrote beautifully about her experiences, particularly her trip on the rapids. It is said she was the first woman to work an oar on the White Horse Rapids and was certainly the first woman to ride it twice, just for fun. She wrote up the experience in *Lippincott's Monthly Magazine* in 1901 which formed the basis for the similar scene in this novel. She owned gold claims, returned to the Klondike several times, gave lectures on her experiences, wrote for many magazines and newspapers, and was the subject of salacious rumours about her marital status. She became famous for her travels and experiences but her name isn't spoken of with the same status as male writers like Jack London. Emma lived on her own terms, had her own adventures, and broke the rigid mould of Victorian society's expectation of women. She also had a dog by the name of Klondike, who of course is the inspiration for Kate's dog, Yukon.

Martha Malone is based on a combination of Belinda Mulrooney and Harriet 'Ma' Pullen. Harriet Pullen was a remarkable woman. She left her four children to travel to Skagway in an attempt to make enough money to support them. She arrived on the dock with $7 in her pocket and quickly found work as a cook. She became famous for her apple pies and soon realised the real money wasn't to be had from gold but from the miners. Harriet used her pie money to start a freighting business, then used those profits to open a hotel. She opened the hotel a year after she arrived in Skagway. Her children soon joined her, along with her husband who left to seek his own fortune in gold. She lived her whole life in Skagway and was buried near her hotel.

Belinda Mulrooney was known as the 'richest woman in the Klondike'. A canny businesswoman, she also mined the miners, reasoning it was the finer things in life they'd crave and she was right. She opened the Fairview Hotel, on the corner of Princess Street and First Avenue, where Martha's Dawson Hotel stands. She owned five gold claims and even ran the sweepings from the floor of her hotel through a sluice box, collecting over $100 a day in dropped gold dust.

Ellen Rhodes is loosely based on Ethel Berry and similar 'mining wives' at the time. Ethel Berry was known as the 'bride of the Klondike'. She and her husband Clarence went looking for gold early on in the Gold Rush and fortuitously, Clarence tended bar to make ends meet. It was in a bar that he met George Carmack, one of three people along with Kate Carmack and Skookum Jim who struck the first major gold which sparked the Gold Rush. Clarence Berry staked a claim on El Dorado creek and the pair lived there, working the mines together. They left the Klondike as millionaires.

Molly/Charlotte is loosely inspired by Molly Walsh and Ella Wilson. Molly Walsh ran a grub tent on the trail, feeding gold-crazed miners. She had many suitors and ended up marrying a man named Mike Bartlett, whom she later left. However Bartlett was an abusive man who tracked her down, chased her into an alley and killed her. One of Molly's suitors, however, was still in love with her and when he found out she was dead, commissioned a statue of her, which still stands in Skagway. Ella Wilson was an African-American sex worker living in Skagway. Being a sex worker during the Gold Rush was one of the most dangerous professions a woman could take. Ella was tragically murdered in what appeared to be a robbery. The prime suspect was a man named Jeff 'Soapy' Smith (who inspired Bill Mathers), but he was never convicted and to date, her murder remains unsolved. Sadly, just as Charlotte in this novel, she is said to be buried in the same cemetery as her murderer.

The fortune-teller, Madam Renio, is based loosely on a real fortune-teller of the same name. Otherwise known as Cora Madole, she was a palmist, psychic reader and fortune-teller operating out of Dawson City from around 1898 to 1903. Fortune-telling was illegal at the time, being considered an occult act, and the NWMP (North–West Mounted Police, the 'Mounties') cracked down on Dawson's few practising fortune-tellers. Madame Renio was the only one who did not shut up shop. She was arrested and became the only person in the Yukon to ever be charged with witchcraft, though she was never convicted.

Bill Mathers is loosely based on Jeff 'Soapy' Smith, a notorious criminal and conman who operated out of Skagway. He owned property and land, ran scams across Alaska and Canada, fleeced miners and was no stranger to violence to achieve his means. He died in a shoot-out in 1898.

Officer William Deever of the North–West Mounted Police is fictional but the leader of the Mounties stationed in the Klondike at the time was a man named Sam Steele. He was, by all accounts, an honourable man in a dishonourable place and took a zero-tolerance approach to the disorderly and unruly stampeders. He was the one who made it a rule that any stampeder must carry a year's worth of provisions to avoid the risk of starvation, making an already long and dangerous journey even more so. His policies and approach reduced crime in Dawson City significantly and his success in the area made the NWMP famous and ensured its survival.

In regard to three of the major events of the novel, the typhoid epidemic, the avalanche on the White Pass and the fire in Dawson City, these are all real events that occurred during the Gold Rush, but I have taken some creative liberties with their timings and locations to better serve the story.

Typhoid was a constant threat to miners along the trail, in the mining camps and in the cities. There were regular outbreaks caused by contaminated water and unsanitary conditions and several people died. It would have been far worse had miners not heeded warnings to boil water. To escape possible infection, miners drank liquor but that was so watered down in Dawson that it made them sick as well. For the purposes of this story, I focused on typhoid but miners also suffered from scurvy, meningitis, tuberculosis and malnutrition. It was a dangerous place to be from all sides.

Avalanches were common at the time on both the major trails from the coast to the gold fields, the most famous of which was the Palm Sunday Avalanche. This happened on 2nd April 1898 on the Chilkoot Trail. Heavy snowfall in the preceding few months coupled with warm spring winds made the tragedy almost inevitable. There were several snow slides over two days, which resulted in the deaths of around sixty-five people. The deadliest single event in Gold Rush history